Christmas at Rosie Hopkins' Sweetshop

Also by Jenny Colgan

By Jenny T. Colgan

Christmas at Rosie Hopkins' Sweetshop

A Novel

JENNY COLGAN

WM
WILLIAM MORROW
An Imprint of HarperCollinsPublishers

HarperCollins books may be purchased for educational, business, or sales promotional use. For information, please email the Special Markets Department at SPsales@harpercollins.com.

Originally published as *Christmas at Rosie Hopkins' Sweetshop* in Great Britain in 2013 by Sphere.

FIRST WILLIAM MORROW PAPERBACK EDITION PUBLISHED 2019.

Designed by Diahann Sturge

Title page and chapter opener art © Yanok / Shutterstock, Inc.

Library of Congress Cataloging-in-Publication Data has been applied for.

ISBN 978-0-06-237119-5

19 20 21 22 23   LSC   10 9 8 7 6 5 4 3 2 1

To J. Delphine-Waverley-James-Bond-Spiderman-Buzz-Lightyear-Come-in-Peace Beaton, who grows older and smarter and lovelier every day but whose little Spider feet I hope will always caper through the pages of this book.

Sweet bells! Sweet chiming silver bells!
Sweet bells! Sweet chiming Christmas bells!
They cheer us on our heavenly way,
Sweet chiming bells.
(Traditional)

A Word from Jenny

Hello!

Now it is a rule of life that parents should never ever ever have a favorite child. And neither do I (although the one who just drew all the way up the rug with an orange felt tip "because it is SOME CARS RACING and the baddies were winning and the goodies had to get away!" may do well to stay out of my way while I type this bit).

A similar thing applies to books: writers are supposed to feel the same way about their books, really, and call them your children and say that you love them all the same, and I am sure some authors truly do. I personally just enjoy the idea that my children would all come and sit quietly lined up next to each other on a shelf all day.

Anyway, *Sweetshop*, or *Welcome to Rosie Hopkins' Sweetshop of Dreams* to give it its full title, was not just another book to me. It was quite a rare experience; it came out, more or less, exactly as I had seen it in my head. And for those of you that also felt very strongly about it, and got in touch with me to let me know, thank you so much. I just grew very fond of Rosie, and Lilian, and thought about them from time to time and my lovely editor took me out to lunch and said, "Well, this is what *I* think would probably have happened next" and my agent said, "Well, I would have liked THIS to happen . . . ," and even my copy editor, whose job isn't really to read the book at all, but to check it for spelling mistakes and fill it with funny little typesetting marks that I don't really understand, put a big handwritten note on the bottom saying, "Well, I just hope that man is good enough for Rosie," and then it even won a lovely prize, which was very exciting. So, without being too big-headed about it, I knew it wasn't just me who wanted to know a bit more about the story.

And I will be honest, I really wanted an excuse to go back to Lipton again, to eat chocolate caramels and think about old English sheepdogs. I grew up a massive fan of James Herriot books (in the beginning because we were skint and they were really cheap at jumble sales), and *Sweetshop* and Lipton are a little in homage to those books; if you were a fan too, see if you spot any references.

So here is a new book about Rosie and her friends, all in time for Christmas. It is kind of a sequel, but you TOTALLY don't have to have read the first one to know what's going on, because I am going to tell you everything you need to know right now:

Rosie Hopkins is an auxiliary nurse, a London-dweller all her life, who was all ready to settle down in the city with her boyfriend Gerard, who was, between you and me, a bit of a mummy's boy.

Her mother, Angie, lives in Australia taking care of her brother Pip's kids. When Angie's aunt Lilian fell ill in a small Derbyshire village, Rosie was the only person available to look after her, which involved taking over the running of Lilian's old-fashioned sweetshop. While there, she made friends with Moray, the nice village GP, ran afoul of Lady Lipton, the local lady of the manor, and met—and eventually fell for—Stephen Lakeman, who was blown up working for Médecins Sans Frontières in Africa and returned to Lipton traumatized and determined to shut himself off from the world. Rosie managed to help him pull it back together partly because she tries to be a good person and partly because he is an utter fox, even when he turned out to be Lady Lipton's estranged son.

Anyway, although Rosie meant to sell the sweetshop, she decided instead to stay in Lipton and run it, and I will tell you now that Gerard, who does not appear in this story, was very, very good about it.

Meanwhile, Lilian, who has spent a lifetime mourning a young man named Henry, who died in the Second World War, has moved into a home with Ida Delia Fontayne, Henry's widow. Lilian had three brothers; Terence Jr., Ned, who also died in the war—Henry comforted her through this, which made her fall madly in love with him—and Gordon, who was Rosie's grandfather.

So here we are! Stephen is just about to take up his new job as a teacher in Lipton's local school. . . .

I really hope you enjoy it.

Oh, and another note: you may not have heard of the carol "Sweet Bells," which appears in this book. It's an old variation on "While Shepherds Watched," and I think it's absolutely beautiful (and huge fun for children). I discovered it via the ever-magnificent and talented Kate Rusby, and you can find it on her splendid Christmas album *Sweet Bells* www.katerusby .com.

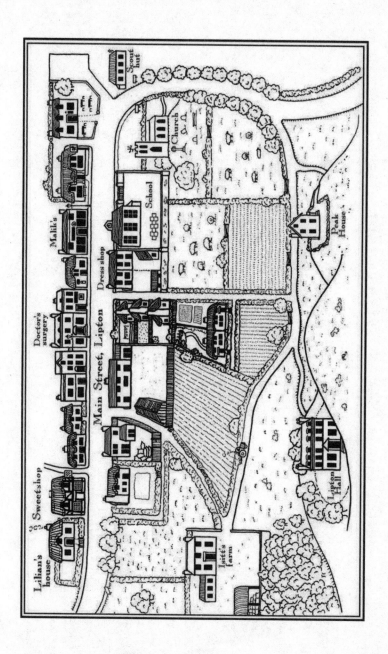

Spout hut

Church

School

Dress shop

Peak House

Doctor's surgery

Main Street, Lipton

Lipton Hall

Sweetshop

Lilian's house

Maliks

Isitt's Farm

The Hopkins Family

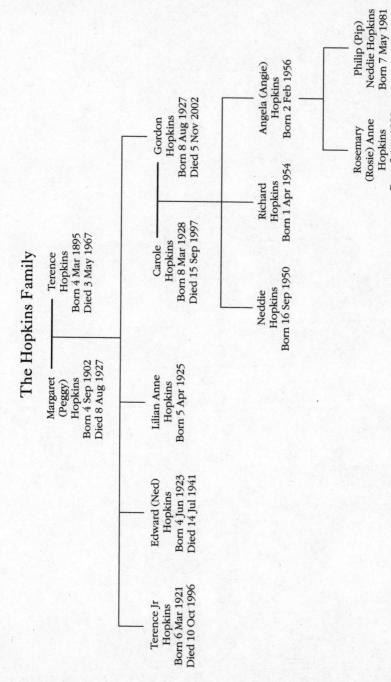

Margaret (Peggy) Hopkins
Born 4 Sep 1902
Died 8 Aug 1927

Terence Hopkins
Born 4 Mar 1895
Died 3 May 1967

Terence Jr Hopkins
Born 6 Mar 1921
Died 10 Oct 1996

Edward (Ned) Hopkins
Born 4 Jun 1923
Died 14 Jul 1941

Lilian Anne Hopkins
Born 5 Apr 1925

Gordon Hopkins
Born 8 Aug 1927
Died 5 Nov 2002

Carole Hopkins
Born 8 Mar 1928
Died 15 Sep 1997

Neddie Hopkins
Born 16 Sep 1950

Richard Hopkins
Born 1 Apr 1954

Angela (Angie) Hopkins
Born 2 Feb 1956

Rosemary (Rosie) Anne Hopkins
Born 5 Apr 1980

Philip (Pip) Neddie Hopkins
Born 7 May 1981

Christmas at Rosie Hopkins' Sweetshop

Chapter 1

Lipton was quiet underneath the stars. It was quiet as the snow fell through the night; as it settled on the roof of the Isitts' barn and on the bell house of the school; as it came in through the cracked upper windows that needed mending in Lipton Hall; as it cast a hush across the cobbled main street of the high street, muting the few cars that passed it by; lying on the roofs of the dentist's and the doctor's offices; it fell on Manly's, the dated ladieswear boutique, and on the Red Lion, its outdoor tables buried under mounds, its mullioned windows piled high with the stuff.

It fell on the ancient church with the kissing gate, and the graveyard with its repeated local names: Lipton, Isitt, Carr, Cooper, Bell.

It fell on the sleeping sheep, camouflaging them completely (Rosie had made Stephen laugh once, asking where the sheep slept when it got cold. He had looked at her strangely and said "In the Wooldorf, of course, where else?" and she had taken a moment or two before she kicked him crossly in the shins). It fell on birds cozy in their nests, their heads under their wings, and nested like a sigh, piled soft and deep in the gullies and crevasses of the great towering Derbyshire hills that fringed the little town.

Even now, after a year of living there, Rosie Hopkins couldn't get over how quiet it was in the countryside; there were birds, of course, always, singing their hearts out in the morning. One could usually hear a cock crow, and every now and then from the deeper sections of the woods would come a distant gunshot, as someone headed out to hunt rabbits. (You weren't meant to; the woods belonged to the estate, so no one ever owned up, although if you passed Jake the farmhand's little tied cottage on a Saturday night, the smell of a very rich stew might just greet your nostrils.)

But tonight, as Rosie went to mount the little narrow stairs to bed, it felt even quieter than ever. There was something different about it. Her foot creaked on the step.

"Are you coming up or what?" came the voice from overhead.

Even though they had lived there together now for nearly a year, Rosie still wasn't out of the habit of calling it Lilian's cottage. Her great-aunt, whom she'd come up to look after when Lilian had broken her hip, had moved into a lovely local home, but Rosie and Stephen still had her over most Sundays, so Rosie felt that, even though legally she had bought the cottage, she rather had to keep it exactly as Lilian liked it. Well, it was slightly that and slightly that Lilian would sniff and raise her eyebrows when they so much as tried to introduce a new picture, so it was easier all around just to keep it as it was. Anyway, Rosie liked it too. The polished wooden floor covered in warm rugs; the fireplace with its horse brasses, the chintz-covered sofa piled with cushions, and floral curtains; the old Aga, and the old-fashioned butler's sink. It was dated, but in a very soft, worn-in, comfortable way, and as she lit the wood burner (she was terrible with fires; people from miles around would come to scoff and point at her efforts, as if growing up in a house with central heating was something to be ashamed of), she never failed to feel happy and cozy there.

Stephen had the use of Peak House, which was part of his family estate, a bankrupt and crumbling seat that gave Lipton its name. Peak House was a great big scary-looking thing up on the crags. It had a lot more space, but somehow they'd just come down more and more to be at Lilian's cottage. Also, as Rosie was just about eking out a living from the sweetshop and Stephen was in teacher training, they were both completely skint, and Lilian's cottage was substantially easier to heat.

Stephen may have scoffed a bit at the décor, but he seemed more than happy to lie on the sofa, his sore leg, damaged in a land mine accident in Africa, propped up on Rosie's lap as they watched box sets on Lilian's ancient television. Other nights, when the picture was just too grainy, Stephen would read to her, and Rosie would knit, and Stephen would tease her for making the world's longest scarf, and she would tell him to hush, that he would be pleased when it turned cold and if he wasn't quiet she would knit him a pair of long johns and make him wear them, which shut him up pretty fast.

"In a minute!" shouted Rosie up the stairs, glancing around to make sure the door was shut on the wood burner—she was always nearly causing conflagrations. The heaviness of the air struck her again. They hadn't moved into Lilian's downstairs bedroom; all of them were keeping up the pretense that one day Lilian might want to use it again, so they kept it pristine, the bed made up, her clothes still hanging in the wardrobe. Rosie kept a shrewd nurse's eye on her eighty-seven-year-old great-aunt. Lilian liked to complain about the home but Rosie could see, in the rosiness of her cheeks (Lilian took great pride in her excellent complexion) and her slight weight gain (this, by contrast, made her utterly furious), that actually, living somewhere with help on hand all the time, and company, was just what Lilian needed. She had lasted a long time by herself in her own home, trying to pretend to the world at large that everything was absolutely fine, when clearly it wasn't. She might complain, but it was obvious that it was a weight off her shoulders.

So they kept their bedroom in the attic, adapted years before as a spare bedroom for Lilian's brothers. It was clean and bare, with a view on one side of the great craggy Derbyshire fells, and on the other of Lilian's garden, the herb and vegetable patches tended with surprising care by Stephen, the rose bower trimmed from time to time by Mr. Isitt, their local dairy farmer.

It was utterly freezing up in the unheated attic. Rosie saw with a smile that Stephen was already in bed, tucked in tightly under the sheets, blankets and thick eiderdown (Lilian thought duvets were a modern intrusion for lazy people. Rosie couldn't deny there was a certain comfort in being tucked in tight with hospital corners, plus it was much harder for your other half to steal the covers).

"Hurry up," he said.

"Oh good," said Rosie. "You've warmed up one side. Now can you move to the other side, please?"

The shape under the covers was unmoved.

"Not a chance," it said. "It's brass monkey bollocks up here."

"Thank goodness I share my bed with a gentleman," said Rosie. "Move! And anyway, that's my side."

"That is NOT your side. This is the window side, which

you insisted, when we were stifling up here in the summertime, was making you too hot so you needed the other side."

"I don't know what you mean," said Rosie, coming around the far end of the large sleigh bed.

"Now, budge."

"No!"

"Budge!"

"NO!"

Rosie wrestled with him quickly, avoiding, as ever, his weaker left leg, until eventually Stephen suggested that if she really needed warming up, he had a plan, and she found that she liked that plan.

Afterward, now cozy as long as her feet didn't stray to the far regions of the mattress (if she didn't think it would turn Stephen off forever, she would have worn bed socks), she felt herself drifting off to sleep, or would have done if Stephen hadn't felt so rigid next to her. He was pretending to be asleep, but she wasn't fooled for a second.

Still distracted by the heavy weather, she turned around to face him in the moonlight. Rosie liked to see the moon, and the countryside was so dark they rarely closed the curtains, a novelty she was so keen on it made Stephen laugh, as if it were a house feature. Stephen looked back at her. Rosie had curly black hair that she was always trying to wrestle into straight submission, but he loved when it curled, as it did now, wild and cloudy around her face. Her eyes were direct and green, her face freckled. Her skin glowed pale, her curvy body lit by the moonlight. He couldn't resist running his hand around the curve of her waist to her generous hips. He could never understand for a minute why Rosie worried about her weight when her body was so voluptuous and lovely.

"Mm," he said.

"What's up with you?" asked Rosie.

"I'm fine," said Stephen. "And don't look at me. That wasn't an 'I'm fine' I'm fine. That was an 'actually, I am TOTALLY fine.'"

"That one's even worse."

"Ssh."

Rosie looked out the window.

"It's weird out there."

"That's what you said the night you heard the owl."

"Come on, owls are really scary."

"As opposed to drive-by shootings in London?"

"Shut it." Rosie did her proper cockney voice that rarely failed to make him laugh, but she could see in the light, as her fingers traced his strong brow, his thick dark hair flopping on his forehead, his long eyelashes, that he wasn't even smiling.

"It's just kids."

"I know."

Stephen had been waiting for a job to come free at the local school for a while. He had only ever taught overseas, so had been considered underqualified and was sent off to do his time in various schools, including one in central Derby that had taught him a bit. Nonetheless, he was still nervous about tomorrow.

"So what are you worried about?"

"Because I'm not just their new teacher, am I? They all know who I am."

Stephen was from the local family of landed gentry. Even though he'd rejected everything they stood for and broken from his parents—he had now made up with his mother, after his father had died of a heart attack—his every doing was subject to constant speculation in the village. Rosie also got her fair share of snotty gossip for going out with him as several local worthies had had him in mind for their own daughters, but she kept this from him as much as possible.

"Well, that's good," argued Rosie. "All the young mums fancy you and all the kids think you're Bruce Wayne."

"Or they all still think I'm a sulky, pretentious teen," said Stephen sorrowfully.

"Well, that's okay too," said Rosie. "You'll work well with the kids."

She could tell he was still wearing the brooding expression.

"We should definitely have had this conversation before we had sex," she said. "Then the relaxing bit could have come later."

The moonlight caught a glint in his eye.

"Well, maybe . . ."

She grinned at him.

"You know, for a wounded war dog, the Right Hon. Lipton, you still have some moves . . ."

Just as she moved toward him, however, she leapt up out of bed.

"Snow!" she shouted. "Look at the snow!"

Stephen turned his head and groaned.

"Oh no," he said.

"Look at it!" said Rosie, heedless of the cold. "Just look at it!"

The previous winter in Lipton, after an early flurry, it had simply rained all winter; they had had hardly any snow at all. Now here it was, great big fat flakes falling softly all down the road, quickly covering it with a blanket of white.

"It's settling!" shouted Rosie.

"Of course it's settling," said Stephen. "This is the Peak District, not Dubai."

Nonetheless, with a sigh of resignation, he got up and pulled the eiderdown off the bed and padded over the cold wooden floor to Rosie, wrapping them both up in it. The snow flurried and danced in the air, the stars peeking out between the flakes, the mountains great dark looming silhouettes in the distance.

"I've never seen snow like this" said Rosie. "Well, not that's lasted."

"It's bad," said Stephen soberly. "It's very early. There was late lambing this year, so they'll need looking out for. And no one can get around; it's treacherous for the old folks. They don't clear the roads up here, you know. People get trapped for weeks. We're barely stocked up, and we're in town."

Rosie blinked. She'd never thought of snow as a serious matter before. In Hackney it was five minutes of prettiness that bunged up all the trains then degenerated quickly into mucky, splashy roads, dog poo smeared into sleet and big slushy gray puddles. This silent remaking of the world filled her with awe.

"If it blocks the pass road . . . well, that's when we all have to resort to cannibalism," said Stephen, baring his teeth in the moonlight.

"Well, I love it," she whispered. "Jake's going to drop us off some wood, he said."

"Ahem," said Stephen, coughing.

"What?"

"Well," he said, "he'll be probably nicking it from somewhere that belongs to my family in the first place."

"Well, it's just ridiculous that a family owns a whole wood," said Rosie.

"Ridiculous or not, I can get Laird to deliver it for nothing," said Stephen. "Seeing as it's, you know. Ours."

"Yeah yeah yeah. Because your great-granddad times a jillion shagged a princess by accident," said Rosie, whose interest in Stephen's ancestry was hazy. "Whatever."

"Whatever," said Stephen, kissing her soft, scented shoulder, "means a warm cozy house. Unlike this icebox. Come, come, my love. Back to bed."

Chapter 2

Five miles away, Lilian slept in a single bed in a neat little room filled with her pictures and knickknacks, snoring gently under a duvet she professed to despise. And she dreamed, as she often did, of the past: of a boy with nut-brown eyes and curly hair and a ready smile and a farmer's tan who made her laugh when she was happy and comforted her when she was sad, and all the while the silent snow fell and wrapped itself around the house like a blanket, like soft cotton wool covering the well-heated building.

She was walking down the road at the end of a day in the sweetshop, a busy Friday when the men got paid and the ration books were out. The Red Lion would be packed tonight. The harvest sun was hanging heavy in the sky, bathing everything in soft gold, and she was going to post a letter to Neddy, not yet dead. . . . In the distance, his curly hair springing up, his face wiped clean after a day in the fields with the sheep. He was waving to her excitedly, and all she could feel was the joy bubbling up in her as she prepared to skip down to meet him, to let him walk her home, even though "home" was the cottage next to the sweetshop. They liked to take a circuitous route. The older folk of the village used to smile to see the two of them, their heads together. That was what they would do, just as soon as . . .

Lilian had this dream often. It was real, she knew; Henry did used to meet her from work, trying his best to wash up in the stream so he wasn't too filthy. And they had had happy times before she'd lost Ned, her brother. She treasured them all, because in their short time together, there hadn't been enough of them. She remembered how he used to pull her pigtails at school, and she had thought he was being annoying. How he used to hang around the sweetshops; buying caramels for her because they were her favorites. How the back of his neck turned brown in the sun, and how much she wanted to caress it; the warm sweet hay smell of him when he was near her; his long fingers. The way he held her close when her brother died and made her feel that everything would be all right; the plans they had made. And then he had been caught out; a girl he had slept with before, her erstwhile best friend Ida Delia, had turned up pregnant, and that was the end of everything. And then his call-up papers . . . and the following year, the dreaded telegram. That Lilian had had to hear about secondhand.

But she didn't like to focus on that. She liked to keep her memories deeply hidden, like pearls, taking them out to polish them. His easy gangling stride, the way he used to put her on the front of his bike and cycle her down to the fields to help him feed the lambs, her dark hair whipping in the wind. The taste of a shared bottle of brown ale, and some butter humbugs, eaten in the sunny churchyard.

But her dreams were never like that. In her dream—the same one, repeated so often—she could never reach him, never make herself walk forward to hold his hand. He would be waving, and she could not get to him and she would wake up frustrated and alone.

Ninety miles away, a man called Edward Boyd checked that all the lights were off in the house, double-locked the door and made a final check in the spare room—he liked to be careful about everything, he couldn't sleep otherwise, plus the old man was always wandering off. Upstairs, his wife, Doreen, was already fast asleep and snoring. The whole house, in fact, was asleep. Well, young Ian wasn't home yet, but he did keep these funny hours. It was odd, Edward had spent so long comforting Doreen when Ian had left home—and the girls of course, but it was Ian whom Doreen had mourned the most—and now, here he was, couldn't find a job in Manchester, so he was back living at home.

Edward didn't begrudge it—and Dor was delighted—but he found it odd. In his day he'd left as soon as he could and never gone back. He'd been so proud to buy the big house—as manager of the local building society, he'd explained to Dor, they should live smartly in the community, and the Grange was as smart as it got (it wasn't called the Grange then; it was plain old 39 Cormlett Drive, but Edward liked a name on a house, so the Grange it was).

Of course he hadn't foreseen (though Doreen clearly had) that with its high ceilings and its granny flat it would be a perfect place for the children to come back to, and for his elderly father to move into, so now he felt rather like the manager of a hotel, but that was the problem with being responsible—everyone just assumed you would do it. He checked the heavy bolt of the back door again. Yup, sorted. The house was still. He could risk going to bed.

Edward was not a man who liked risk.

"Good morning!"

Rosie had made poached eggs. It is not easy to poach an egg. Poached eggs, as far as she was concerned, meant love. As far as Stephen was concerned, they meant a shocking waste of an egg. He looked at them in perturbation.

"Ugh, these eggs have skin."

"You're not at boarding school now," warned Rosie. "They're lovely! Eat them. You need a good breakfast."

Stephen grumbled, still cross at the weather. But Rosie had woken with the lark, lying on her back in the big attic room, wondering at the lovely pattern of white light that danced frostily across the ceiling. She felt excited, as if it were Christmas, even though it had never once snowed at Christmas during her childhood. She had always felt cheated by those adverts that insisted that it would, that a Christmas without snow was somehow lacking.

But now, here it was: November, and snow was here already! She wondered if it was too early to go and get a tree. Probably. She wondered if Stephen would get a tree from his land, like last year. What a lovely thing that had been. They had gone mad and gotten one that was far too big for the little cottage, so they had had to leave the staircase to the attic door down all the time which meant they had to slide past the stairs to get to the kitchen and basically climb a tree to get to bed at night. The intense scent of the wild pine invaded everything until Rosie had felt that she was sleeping in a forest. It had been wonderful.

She had already stoked the fire—they didn't really have enough money for the fire to be on all day, but Rosie figured they could make an exception for the first day of snow—and had peeked her head out into the garden.

"Close the door!" barked Stephen, trying to fill up on toast and wondering if he could slip the eggs into his pajama pockets and dispose of them later.

"Just a sec," said Rosie. She couldn't resist it; she hopped into her special Wellington boots with the little sweets printed on the lining—a peace offering from Stephen's mother—and leapt out into the virgin snow.

Stephen watched her through the window. Even though Rosie had told him a million times that she'd had a happy childhood—that she and Angie (her mother, very young when she'd had her) and her younger brother Pip (who now lived in Australia; Angie had joined him and was looking after Pip's three children, who according to Rosie were wholly terrifying) had had a good time, growing up in a council flat without a garden, eating fish fingers in front of the television, catching the bus to a school that had one high-fenced concrete play area and not a blade of grass; even though she, on balance, had probably had a better childhood than he himself had had, isolated, and butting heads with his father, his mother always busy with her dogs and the crumbling, creaking house, and money troubles at every turn—Stephen still enjoyed seeing her take pleasure in her new life.

He knew Rosie had grown up poor, but she had never seemed to feel it; she had related to him without embarrassment how one year Angie had had absolutely no money and had resorted to wrapping everything in the house in cheap paper—toothbrushes, hair combs, ashtrays, forks, individual Quality Street chocolates—and leaving it all under the tree, which had led to much joy and jubilation as Pip and Rosie had exuberantly torn off all the packaging, breathless at the sheer mound of gifts and display of plenty, and caring nothing for what lay within. Perhaps it was because no one she knew had much, whereas the schools he had been sent to had made him always aware of the gulf.

Anyway, he relished the sheer joy she got from things he had always taken for granted—a garden, for one. He liked working in there too, growing things, providing the odd stunted lettuce or minuscule carrot.

However happy Rosie's childhood, though, she was certainly adding to her enjoyment of life now as she played hopscotch in her pajamas, the daft Wellingtons flying. Stephen finished the last of his coffee with a gulp, then used the last of his freedom to hurl the poached eggs into the bin before the cold drove Rosie in again. Although, he reflected on seeing her delighted face, obviously she was now just going to think he adored poached eggs and make them three times a week.

"Do you want me to make you a packed lunch?" asked Rosie as she prepared to open up early—catching passing school traffic was always lucrative.

Stephen made a face.

"I'm not GOING to school, I am a teacher," he said grumpily. Rosie knew better than to try and talk him out of a mood like this. His handsome face looked a little taut and nervous.

For a man who had walked into war zones unprotected, who had worked in some of the most dangerous regions on earth, it was quite amazing that he was so anxious about a clutch of eight-year-olds. But, wisely, she said nothing, instead kissing him lightly on the nose.

Stephen opened their front door—which opened directly onto the cobbled main street, still thick with snow, but showing a couple of Land Rover tracks and some hoofprints—and sniffed. The snow was still falling.

"Half the kids won't be in," he said. "They'll be needed on the farm, or their parents won't send them in case it doesn't let up and they can't get them home."

"Excellent!" said Rosie. "Well, you inspire the hell out of the ones who do make it."

Stephen smiled, shrugged on his heavy waxed jacket and stepped out into the snow.

"AHEM," said Rosie, and he came back into the doorway and kissed her firmly on her plump pink lips.

"That's better," said Rosie. "I always fancied my teachers anyway."

"Your PRIMARY teachers?" said Stephen, horrified.

"Oh, God. No," said Rosie.

"Oh, well, that's a relief," said Stephen. "One CRB check was quite enough, thank you."

Suddenly he grabbed her face and gave her another kiss.

"I love it when you make me breakfast," he said. Rosie smiled up at him.

"Well, don't expect poached eggs every day."

"A tiny piece of toast to me," said Stephen, pushing a strand of hair behind her ears, "is like a feast. Sorry I'm a bit cranky and nervous."

"I like you cranky and nervous," said Rosie, kissing him again. "Anything else would make me suspicious."

Stephen laughed, extricated himself from the kiss before it threatened to turn more serious, tightened up his heavy boots, then tramped out down the road, which was slowly beginning to fill up with people—the baker's, down by the war memorial, was already open and doing a brisk business; Malik's Spar, of course, would have been getting the daily papers in since six A.M. Rosie looked at the falling flakes and the pale blue dawn light. She would need to get moving herself. She watched his tall figure, limping only slightly down the cobbled street, lifted the tea towel she was still holding and waved it at him.

At 8:30, she unlocked the door of the Hopkins' Sweetshop and Confectionery, the sign to which had been standing outside the door now for nearly ninety years, give or take something of an interregnum when Lilian hadn't been able to manage on her own.

Rosie, sent up from London to close down the shop and arrange care for Lilian, had instead completely fallen in love with the old place and had ended up restoring it to its former glory. She still used the old pre-decimal till (with a card reader on the side), and had kept the great glass apothecary jars, filled to the brim with favorites old and new: flying saucers, barley sugar, lemon sherbets, lime sherbets, melon sherbets, chocolate peanuts (all the peanut candies Rosie now kept on a side shelf, like dynamite, to avoid the possibility of their mixing with another sweet and affecting an allergic child, something Lilian thought was modern nonsense simply, Rosie knew as a nurse, because she hadn't ever seen it happen).

The old wooden shelves with the library ladder that swung along them held the less popular and out-of-fashion items: travel sweets, humbugs, jujubes, jawbreakers; rhubarb and custards; rosy apples and fairy satins; farther down were the sharp, sour flavors, the branded jellies and soft flumpish marshmallow items popular with their younger clientele.

There were tightly packed rows of mints and gums, and of course a traditional selection of chocolate bars, excepting Topics, which Lilian had taken against in a fit the previous summer; despite Rosie's insisting that it was the most innocuous of chocolate bars, she had never been able to stock them again.

The old advertisements—cleaned up and polished if they were tin—still lined the walls; for Cadbury's Cocoa and Dairy Milk, all with healthy apple-cheeked children wearing purple, or skipping, with large blue eyes and extravagant hats.

The bell above the door, taken apart, degunked and cleaned, now made a healthy ting when rung, which it did now. Rosie, distracted with counting change from the till, hardly glanced up until she saw who it was.

"Good morning, Edison!"

Edison was the son of Hester and Arthur Felling-Jackson. His mother was terribly up on all the latest fads in child care, which meant she had been utterly horrified when he had befriended Rosie with her refined sugary ways (although not too horrified to let Rosie take care of him all the time when she was out at yoga classes). This morning he was wearing a coat with an ethnic scarf tightly wrapped around the bottom half of his face and coming nearly up to his glasses, and the kind of ridiculous hat people bought when experimenting with substances at music festivals. Rosie wished Hester would just let him wear clothes like the other kids; it might help him make a friend. Plus, it made him a little difficult to understand.

"How's your mum doing?"

Edison's mother was pregnant again. She had announced this by sending a round-robin email announcing she was "with Mother Gaia," so no one had known what she meant until she started appearing with a noticeable bump. It was, however, difficult to tell how pregnant she was as she had started pushing out her stomach and huffing and groaning from about two months on, so it seemed to Rosie she had now been pregnant for about two and a half years.

Edison sighed. He was a very literal child.

"I don't want to watch."

"You don't want to watch what?"

"I don't want to watch the baby coming out."

Rosie raised an eyebrow.

"Well, that's okay," she said, her hand going out instinctively to the strawberry bootlaces she knew he loved. "I'm sure Hester won't make you if you don't want to."

Edison looked at the floor.

"She says I need to understand patacky."

"Patacky?"

"Why men are naughty to women ALL THE TIME."

Rosie thought for a bit. It was still early. She sipped the coffee she'd brought in in her special Scrabble mug.

"Do you mean 'patriarchy'?"

"Yes!" said Edison. "That's what I said."

"So she's going to make you watch . . . hmm."

Rosie decided, under the circumstances, to just get back to organizing her new line of chocolate animals.

"Did you know babies come out of baginas?" asked Edison.

"I did know that," said Rosie, although she knew her elder niece Kelly referred to it as a foofoo. She supposed Hester's way made more sense. Edison sighed sadly.

"Are you going to have a baby?" he asked. "Out of your bagina?"

Rosie nearly dropped some of the chocolate animals.

"Well, if I ever do," she said, "I promise you don't have to watch."

"Good," said Edison. He glanced at the chocolate animals.

"No," said Rosie. "It's too early. Edison, can I ask you a favor?"

Edison frowned. "Do I have to go on a march?"

"No."

"Okay."

Rosie bent down. He was getting taller, she noticed, and needed a haircut. His glasses were smeared. She didn't quite understand why not cleaning Edison's glasses was against Hester's principles, but she took them off him and set about with a wipe.

"Now, did you know what's happening at school today?"

Edison shrugged.

"Some kids will be mean to me because of my superior intlechew?"

"Um, possibly," said Rosie. "Learn to clean your own glasses, please."

She handed them back to him, and he blinked, looking surprised at how clear the world seemed.

"No," said Rosie. "You have a new teacher starting."

"Oh yes!" said Edison. "Mr. Lakeman. He hops. Does he hit people with his stick?"

"Is that what you think?" said Rosie, appalled. "No. He has to use the stick to walk sometimes."

"It's not a hitting stick?"

"Edison, you have never been hit in your life. You have to stop worrying about things."

Edison's brow furrowed.

"It's a very big stick."

"Can we forget about the stick, please? All I was going to say is, it's his first day. Do you remember your first day at school?"

"Every day is like my first day," said Edison sadly.

"Okay," said Rosie. "Well, it's Ste . . . Mr. Lakeman's first day. So can you be very nice and kind to him, please?"

"I'm always nice to teachers," said Edison in surprise. "Even when they say, 'PLEASE put your hand down, Edison, I think we've all heard enough now.'"

He did a surprisingly accurate imitation of Mrs. Archer, Stephen's predecessor. Rosie smiled.

"Okay, good," said Rosie. "He's lucky to have you in his class."

There were only two classes at the little village school, under and over sevens, with around fifteen children in each class. The local council talked from time to time about busing them out to Carningford, the nearest town, but the village was dead set against it. The schoolhouse, next to the church, dated back to Victorian times and had a pitched roof with a bell, and two entrances with BOYS and GIRLS carved in stone, although they were never used. There was a hopscotch outline painted on the playground concrete and a Portakabin for music and art, i.e., for making gigantic amounts of noise and mess. Playtime could be heard all the way up the main street.

Rosie compared it, sometimes wistfully, to the school she

had gone to in London, which had had a high wire fence every-where and a locking door and a tiny playground and hundreds of huge kids everywhere kicking out at other kids. Here the great hills cast shadows in the winter sunlight, and the children tore out at the end of the day in their blue sweatshirts, satch-els flying, charging home to run about with the friends they'd known all their lives, on farms or big meadows. Rosie wished Edison realized what a lovely place it was to grow up.

The phone rang in the shop. They had kept the original with the heavy old rotary dial. Lilian didn't want to get rid of it, which meant, annoyingly, that whenever Rosie wanted to call someone, she always did it on her mobile phone for the speaker, and that was annoying because Lipton's signal was erratic to say the least. In fact, she thought, it was probably Lilian now. Rosie had gotten her a mobile phone with enormous buttons that didn't do anything except make phone calls. The shop was speed dial 1, and the price plan she was on allowed free local calls. This meant, in practice, that quite often Lilian would just call and leave her phone plugged in on speaker, occasionally chipping in with remarks on the business of the shop. Newcom-ers to the village found the disembodied voice rather alarm-ing, particularly when it was recommending which licorice to buy or telling Rosie off for over-ordering watermelon-flavored candy that nobody liked. But everyone else was used to it; it was just Lilian, and most people had a friendly word for her as they came in and out.

"Hey," said Rosie, casually. There was static on the line

and somebody was yelling. Somebody yelling down the phone was not at all uncommon; it meant that her mother, Angie, was phoning from Australia, where she lived and looked after Rosie's brother Pip's three unruly children, who, as far as Rosie could ascertain, used any instance of Angie's being distracted to attempt to slaughter each other with kitchen knives.

"G'day," said Angie, who had adopted an unaccountable Australian accent despite only having lived there for two years.

"Hi, Mum," said Rosie, glancing at her watch. "Isn't it, like, ten P.M. there?"

"Yup."

"Why are the children still up? You never let me and Pip stay up."

"Oh, you know . . ."

"Have they been locking you in the linen cupboard again? Mum, you HAVE to get tough with them."

"It's three against one," said her mother. "And Desleigh thinks they're just fine."

Rosie didn't know her sister-in-law very well, just that she worked long hours and when she wasn't working, she liked a lot of what she called "me-time," which seemed to involve Angie's being left with the children on weekends while Desleigh had spa treatments.

"So," said her mother. "I was thinking. About Christmas?"

"We can't, Mum," said Rosie sadly. She would love to go to Sydney to see her family, but they were limited to Stephen's holidays, and the shop couldn't run itself and they couldn't really afford the tickets and . . .

"We're coming!"

Rosie swallowed hard.

"You're what?"

"We're coming. We're all coming to have Christmas in Lipton. And to see you and Lilian!"

"ALL of you?"

"Yes!!"

Rosie paused a mere millisecond as the huge and complex implications of doing this suddenly raced across her brain. Not a single sensible response presented itself, but all the myriad problems were completely overshadowed by her desperate desire to see her family.

"That is a BRILLIANT idea," she said.

Rosie spent the rest of the morning serving customers in a daze and got the red and black kola cubes mixed up twice. She was desperate to see her mother; she had felt so abandoned when Angie had left the country. On the other hand, what were they going to do with Shane, Kelly and Meridian in Lipton? They were used to swimming pools and beach parties and amazing fish caught fresh from the sea . . . It was entirely possible that it would rain for three weeks solid like it had last Christmas and, when she thought about it, unless you liked wet-weather hiking, or going to see the new Waitrose in Derby, there really wasn't a massive amount going on. By which, she realized, she meant nothing going on. This was the country, it was quiet; her mother was always going on about all the amazing things Sydney had to offer, and the fabulous weather and . . .

Rosie realized she was working herself up into a bit of a state when the door tinged and Lady Lipton walked in. She and Rosie had always had something of a tricky relationship, although Henrietta was a dear friend of Lilian's and was, of course, Stephen's mother, so Rosie always felt she should make more of an effort. Before Stephen had gone off to work in Africa, he had had a terrible row with his father. His mother had taken his father's side. When Stephen was in a military hospital in Africa, his father had had a heart attack and died. Stephen's relationship with his mother had been very up and down ever since.

Today, Lady Lipton was looking even more imperious than normal.

"Cough drops?" said Rosie promptly, even though she knew that Lady Lipton fed them to her dogs, which she shouldn't really do. A flash of panic grabbed at her heart. What if Lady Lipton didn't like Angie? Because Angie had absolutely no problem telling people exactly what she thought of them, and if she thought this woman wasn't being nice to her, there was no telling what she would do. And, she thought with a sinking heart, how would Stephen behave? She loved him with every fiber of her being, but he wasn't like her ex, Gerard, who liked to please and get along with everyone. Stephen's family had always been a bit wobbly, and joining in family games and meals with everyone would not be the kind of thing he would want to do at all. . . . Oh Lord.

"What's the matter with you?" said Lady Lipton. "You look like someone's just thrown up on your slippers. Are you pregnant?"

Sometimes, thought Rosie, living in a small village where everybody knew everybody's business was not at all what it was cracked up to be, especially when that knowledge was wrong.

"No," said Rosie.

"Oh, good," said Lady Lipton, without indicating whether

this was because she didn't approve of her being with her darling boy. "Now, listen. Wonderful news! Bran's had a litter!"

"I thought he was a boy dog."

Lady Lipton looked at her scornfully.

"He's SIRED a litter."

"So, more cough drops then?"

"And," went on Lady Lipton, "I'm giving one to you and Stephen. As a Christmas present."

"I thought you couldn't give dogs as Christmas presents," said Rosie, shocked.

"Yes, it's political correctness gone mad," said Lady Lipton, which was her stock response to literally anything on earth that wasn't exactly how it had been when she was eleven years old. "Anyway, would you prefer a dog or a bitch?"

"But we don't have space for a dog!" said Rosie. "Or time to look after it . . . or . . ."

Lady Lipton looked at her as if she were completely incapable of understanding how a person could not want a dog—which was, indeed, exactly her state of mind. Her face clouded over. Rosie felt she'd said something akin to "I eat babies."

"Well, perhaps I'll mention it to Stephen," said Lady Lipton stiffly.

Rosie ran out of steam.

"Of course," she said meekly, bagging up the cough drops.

It wasn't, she thought, as the door banged heavily behind her, that she didn't like dogs; of course she did. But she'd grown up without any pets at all, not even a fish, as they didn't really have anywhere to keep it, and the dogs she was familiar with were one or two really dangerous-looking pit bulls on the estate, dogs whose owners swaggered up and down with them, letting them shit in the middle of the street, then eyeing passersby as if daring them to suggest they clean it up. And the idea of having their little house filled with a big dog—Bran was undeniably a big dog—who would make Lilian's nice things dirty and put muddy paw prints everywhere and need endless walks and those cans of stinky food and . . . Rosie sighed. Oh, and three strange Australian children in the house. She had suddenly stopped looking forward to Christmas quite so much.

She was slightly cheered by her friend and colleague Tina, who arrived with six boxes of candy canes.

"I thought we could hang them all around the doorframe," said Tina. "Start to make the place look Christmassy."

"Yes," said Rosie. Then she frowned. "Wouldn't that be basically inciting children to nick them?"

"It's Christmas," said Tina. "I think we can probably lose a few to sticky fingers. Oh, and let's get the super-duper expensive chocs, the really crazy Belgian ones. In boxes."

"Why? Do people like those for Christmas?"

"It's not a question of like," said Tina. "The nearest supermarket is an hour away and shuts early on Christmas Eve. If we stay open late right up to the very last minute, we'll be able to sell every single piece of stock in the shop, no matter what we charge, to lazy people, or farmers who don't get the chance to leave their farms before then. You see it every year. It's what keeps the boutique afloat too."

"You're an evil business genius," said Rosie, leafing through the catalogue. "I don't know why you stay with me instead of going on *The Apprentice*."

Tina smiled shyly and blushed a little bit.

"Are you staying here for Christmas?" asked Rosie. Actually, it was a bit of a daft question around here; of course they were. It was different in London, where everyone was from their own different places and went home to their extended families. London emptied out at Christmastime, leaving the few stray locals born and bred, plus lots of people who didn't celebrate it anyway. When Rosie told people shops and cafés in London were open on Christmas Day, they looked at her as if she were a heathen Martian.

"Yes," said Tina. "Jake's coming over."

Jake was the handsome local farmhand Tina had fallen for last year. He was something of a well-known rake about town who'd always liked the girls—and they'd liked him back—and no one was more surprised than Jake himself by how hard he'd fallen for Tina, a single mother of twins, in return.

"So it'll be us and my mum, you know, and Kent and Emily, and Jake's mum and dad. It'll be lovely and we'll have a big lunch down at my mum and dad's—my mum does everything, she loves cooking for Christmas. All I have to do is watch the kids open their presents, get drunk and watch telly."

"That sounds BRILLIANT," said Rosie, enviously. Then she explained what she was doing. "It is wonderful they're coming," she said. "I'm just a bit worried about what we'll all do, where we'll all fit . . ."

"No, it'll be great!" said Tina, who lived two streets away from her mother and wished they were closer.

"I don't know what Stephen wants though," she added. "Plus, we'll have to see his mother, and—"

"It'll be fantastic!" said Tina. "It's nice to have children at Christmas! Can't you have it up at the big house?"

"Hmm," said Rosie. "I don't think so. Shane and Meridian will have broken the lot by first kick."

"Don't worry so much," said Tina. "It'll be fine."

"You think?"

Rosie meant to tell Stephen straightaway that night, but he looked so happy and full of himself that she made him tea in front of the fire instead.

"How was it?"

"Amazing!" he said. "They were great. So keen and nice and of course I know half of them. They all wanted to know what happened to my leg."

"Did you tell them?"

"Of course I told them. What did you think?"

"I don't know," said Rosie. "I might have been tempted to tell them I hurt it in an intergalactic space raid to make them impressed with me."

Stephen lifted his cup of tea.

"That didn't occur to me. Anyway, I told them so they won't worry about it. And also, I wanted them to see the lengths some kids in this world have to go to to get an education. How lucky they are."

"No kid ever thinks they're lucky," mused Rosie.

"Some adults do," said Stephen, looking at her for a second until she smiled, her worries forgotten. She'd tell him later, she thought.

"Oh, and I almost forgot!" said Stephen, his face lighting up. "Mother says we can have one of Bran's pups when they come!"

"I know," said Rosie. "She told me."

Stephen looked at her face.

"This is amazing!" he said. "They're worth a fortune, Bran's pups. He's a wonderful working dog."

"Where are we going to put a gigantic dog?" said Rosie, glancing around the cozy little room, the logs crackling in the fireplace, the light dancing in the old brasses.

Stephen shrugged. "Well, it'll just go where we go, won't it? And it's not like we'll be here forever."

Rosie looked up in surprise.

"Why, do you have a plan?"

"No," he said. "But, you know, it's not ideal, is it?"

"It's lovely, and five seconds from our jobs," said Rosie. "Seems pretty ideal to me."

"Yes, but that's because you grew up in a box."

"You are SUCH a disgusting snob!" said Rosie.

"I know," said Stephen. "That's why you love me and the dog so much."

Chapter 3

Rosie was good friends with the village GP, Moray. On Friday she persuaded him to come with her to see Lilian. Stephen had already started planning the school concert.

"He's so into it," said Rosie in wonder. "I've never seen him like this."

"That's Stephen," said Moray, who'd grown up with him. "Intense."

They both smiled. The snow had stayed on the ground, with more threatened, but for now, the Land Rover was managing over the undulating single-lane roads through the hills. With the sun sparkling across the mountaintops, it was like being at the top of the Alps.

"Well, it's good," said Rosie. "I like him happy."

"I would hope so," said Moray, giving her a sideways look. "How are you? Not missing the smoke?"

"Have you ever been to London at Christmas?"

"Yes," said Moray promptly. "Full of people wearing suits getting off with other people wearing suits at four o'clock in the afternoon completely pissed. Awful."

"No, it's lovely!" said Rosie, surprised. "All the shops decorated, and the taxi lights and the Oxford Street displays . . . okay, it's freezing, and the Oxford Street displays are all sponsored, and you can never get a taxi . . ."

"And everybody's pissed . . ."

"And everybody's pissed . . . No. Shut up, it's brilliant."

"Feel free to hurtle about pissed in the day," said Moray. "I'm sure no one will notice or comment. Or be remotely surprised, actually."

"I think you're off my Christmas list."

"Oh, boo-hoo," said Moray. "I shall have to wave goodbye to seventy-nine pence worth of cost-price, slightly damaged licorice allsorts."

"It was going to be lemon sherbets actually."

"How will I overcome the pain?"

Lilian's care home wasn't decorated for Christmas yet, but it looked pretty nestled in its lovely gardens, tucked in cozily under a hill. It had, in its time, been a grand house built by a newly rich cotton trader from Derby. Then it was a First World War hospital, then a school, and over the years it had been scraped out so often that it was amazing they had managed to make it as homely as they did. The matron, Cathryn Thompson, greeted Rosie warmly. Regular visiting was practically an order here; you had to sign something promising that you would.

"Nothing kills as fast as loneliness," Miss Thompson had said, to which Moray would add sotto voce, "Just typhus, pneumonia, cardiac arrest, septicemia and being shot," at which she had given him a look and said, "Do you remember your first visit here, straight out of medical school?" which had shut Moray up faster than anything Rosie could have possibly imagined.

"She's in the games room, playing canasta with Mrs. Carr. I'm glad you're here, actually, they're on the verge of actual violence."

Sure enough, an icy silence had descended in the games room. A ring of gray hair surrounded the table where two people were facing each other, locked in mortal combat, like a scene from *Casino Royale*.

"May I go out?" Ida Delia was grimacing.

"Yes!" said Lilian decisively.

Ida Delia laid down seven cards, and there was an intake of breath at the table. Everyone's face turned to Lilian expectantly. She didn't lose her cool for an instant.

"Well, I suppose so," she said, laying out a trail of kings and sevens on the table. It didn't make any sense to Rosie at all, but the rest of the table gasped and burst into applause.

"Thank you," said Lilian calmly as Ida Delia swore loudly and appeared on the brink of angry tears. Lilian carefully scooped up the large pile of chocolate caramels that had been accumulating in the center of the table. She peeled off a large corner and donated them to an old chap who'd been dealing, as a tip. He thanked her.

"Aunt Lil," said Rosie softly. Lilian's face lit up as she saw her favorite relative. She got up slowly and, although normally not in the least bit demonstrative, put her arms around her. All of this was done very much for Ida Delia's benefit, Rosie could see. Ida had had one child, the sullen offspring of her short-lived marriage to Henry Carr, the love of Lilian's life, and they had had no further children. Although it was not at all an appealing habit, Rosie knew Lilian took great pride in rubbing her closeness to her grandniece in Ida Delia's face.

"Rosie!" said Lilian loudly. "Now you must tell me all about your gorgeous young bloke, Stephen Lakeman, son of LADY LIPTON UP AT LIPTON HALL."

Rosie gave her the look, but Lilian returned it with one of complete innocence.

"Let's go talk by the coffee bar," said Rosie. The reception rooms downstairs—without television; residents had those in their rooms if they wished to watch, but the communal areas were for reading, playing cards and making conversation—were divided into themed areas, to make people feel they had more places to go than they actually did. It worked rather well.

Lilian looked a little disappointed. She would have liked to carry on a discussion of her grandniece's virtues and triumphs at high volume in front of everyone, but she acquiesced—not, however, before saying, "Oh, and it's Moray, our HANDSOME LOCAL GP. Here to see JUST ME, SOCIALLY, and there's NOT EVEN ANYTHING WRONG WITH ME."

Medical diagnoses were a hot game of one-upmanship in the home. Moray already saw more of the place than he would generally have chosen to without his hefty salary, so this was a prize indeed. Lilian tilted up her cheek to be kissed, which Moray did with a twinkle. He was fond of the old stick.

"So," said Lilian, as they all sat down with very acceptable cappuccinos. This was not that surprising; Rosie had led the whip-round the previous year to buy the place a Nespresso machine. Matron had confided in her later that its installation had raised the number of visitors significantly. "What news?"

"How's life here?" said Rosie. "Because it looks to me like you're rather enjoying yourself."

Lilian did her best to disguise a smirk.

"No, no, not at all, abandoned in the depths of despair, as

you well know. Sad, alone, unwanted, without visitors, nothing to live for . . ."

Rosie rolled her eyes.

"Well, actually. About that. Angie's coming over."

Lilian's face lit up. She had always been particularly fond of her niece, a pretty, headstrong type. If Angie wanted to do something, she just did it. Which sometimes worked out well—Australia—and sometimes badly—Rosie barely knew her father. But on balance, Lilian thought, it was always easier to regret the things you had tried in life that had gone wrong rather than the things you hadn't. She knew that better than anyone.

"Oh, MARVELOUS!" she said. "I must tell Ida Delia."

"Leave off that poor woman," said Moray. "Hasn't she suffered enough?"

"No," said Lilian shortly.

"That's not all," said Rosie quickly. "Pip's coming too. And Desleigh, his wife—"

"What kind of a name is Desleigh?" said Lilian.

"Well, her father was called Des and her mum was called Leigh," explained Rosie. "You could think that was rather sweet."

"It's repulsive," said Lilian.

It was going to be a long five weeks, thought Rosie. And she hadn't even told Stephen yet.

". . . and their children," she said.

Lilian perked up. She liked children, which was to say, she liked well-behaved, interesting children. Rosie privately wondered if Shane, Kelly and Meridian were going to fit those parameters.

"Where are they going to stay?" asked Lilian with a frown.

"I'm not sure," said Rosie. She wasn't even close to figuring this one out. Peak House, Stephen's old home, was empty. It was also right on the top of a very bleak mountain, and absolutely freezing cold, and impossible to get to without a car.

"If this snow keeps up, in the village hall, probably."

If worst came to worst, she had thought Pip and Desleigh could sleep in the living room, she and Angie could share her room, the children could take Lilian's, and Stephen could go back to his mother's. This would have the added bonus of pleasing absolutely nobody.

"It's going to be a long time cramped up in the cottage," prophesied Lilian. "Well, if it's easier on everyone, I can stay here."

"You can't stay here!" said Rosie. "It's Christmas!"

Lilian's eyes sidled toward a menu placed on the top of the coffee bar. CHRISTMAS MENU it said. Rosie picked it up.

"Champagne sorbet? Oysters? Goose or roast topside of beef?"

Lilian looked slightly wistful.

"What IS this?"

"Well, the local cookery school has a lot of kids from bad homes and so on. One of those Jamie Oliver charity projects. So they come here on Christmas Day and cook for us."

"Give me that," said Moray, running his eye down it.

"Goose fat roast potatoes? Ginger pig chipolatas? Chocolate and raspberry bavarois? That's it, I'M coming. Okay, Lilian, at about eleven forty-five on Christmas Day, I want you to feign stomach pains, okay? NOT chest pains—that's an ambulance job, they'll bypass me completely. Just stomach pains. Pretend you don't want me called out on Christmas Day. That will make it more realistic."

Lilian nodded and looked around for somewhere to jot this down.

"Pack it in, you two!" howled Rosie. "It's already tricky enough. They're coming about eighty thousand miles to see you and have a lovely Christmas, which means we all have to be there and have a lovely time."

"Eating in a circle on the floor," said Moray.

"YOU are not invited!" said Rosie. "What do you do at Christmas anyway?"

"Go to Carningford and spend ten hours telling my parents why I haven't met the right woman yet," said Moray with a last longing look at the menu.

"I cannot understand why a sensible medical man like you, not exactly in his first flush of youth, still can't come out to his parents," said Rosie.

"And that," said Moray, "is the one thing I envy you about growing up in London."

Lilian had calmed down.

"It will be lovely to see Angie," she said.

"It will," said Rosie firmly.

"And I need to thank her," said Lilian.

"I know, it's such a long way to come."

"Oh no, no no, not about that," said Lilian. "That's going to be a nightmare, clearly."

Rosie rolled her eyes again.

"Why then?"

"For bringing you to me, of course."

Outside it had started to snow again, gently. Moray looked up at the sky and groaned.

"Oh, but it's lovely," said Rosie.

"It's deadly," said Moray. "It means our district nurse has to check in on all the old folks, make sure they've turned on their heating and that they have someone to get to the shops for them."

Rosie looked at him.

"Was that a hint?"

She helped out from time to time. She had hoped it would help her fit in and become more a part of the community. But it didn't really seem to work at all; people still saw her as the London interloper, so she still got a bit of the cold shoulder. Moray had told her this would probably start getting better in about three generations' time.

"Well, you're snowed under with this family visit . . ."

"Not quite yet," said Rosie. "Just say the word. I'll fit it in."

She relieved Tina to go and pick up the twins, then set about dealing with the after-school rush—plus, with the snow, a huge pick-up on lozenges and cough drops—making sure she asked after her older regulars. Then, at five, she tinkled the bell and set about cashing up. Often she let Tina do it, but she liked to keep an eye on it, though Tina was so accurate that it made her job much easier anyway. She ran her eyes over the figures. They were good—the shop was busy and flourishing, but even so, by the time she'd bought stock and paid Tina and the book-keeper and the tax man, there wasn't a lot left over. What there wasn't, she thought, looking at it, was enough to pay for a week at the Red Lion for Pip, Desleigh and the kids. (They would be in Lipton for a week and would spend the rest of the time sightseeing and visiting other cousins.) Which meant she was no closer to fixing the problem. She glanced at her calendar. Five weeks till Christmas.

When Rosie arrived home, the smell of the stew making a warming greeting—she slow-cooked as many of their meals as possible with the reasonable assumption that as she worked next door, she would smell it if the house caught fire. It meant she could buy the cheapest cuts of meat from the local butcher, and they would still taste ambrosial if slow-cooked long enough.

But there was another smell in the air, she thought. Something she couldn't quite put her finger on. And then, in the next moment, a strange noise, like the tiny pattering clip-clop of nails on a polished wooden floor.

"Hello?" she shouted.

She heard Stephen's careful tread come through from the tiny doll's-house kitchen. He had a bottle of red wine in one hand, which usually boded well, and a grim expression, which did not. But she barely registered this. Instead, her eyes swung down to his feet. Cowering there like a shy child was a tiny bundle of fur with a little pink tongue hanging out.

"Oh, my God," she breathed.

"My mother's been," said Stephen, neutrally.

"I told her we didn't want a dog," said Rosie, feeling she had to get her defense in first. But she couldn't help it, her curiosity was piqued. She knelt down and stared at the little creature. It had misty blue eyes and was basically a gigantic ball of gray fluff.

"Well, of course we want a DOG," said Stephen. "This isn't a DOG. It's a MOP."

Rosie held out her hand. The tiny thing crept out to sniff at it, and she smiled at it encouragingly. Stephen braced himself against the doorframe and opened the wine bottle with a loud popping noise.

"She said it was one of Bran's. She didn't say she hadn't studded him. He's obviously got some tarty mongrel bitch up the duff. This dog can't work, it's completely useless. My mother is such a witch."

But alas, it was too late. Rosie had scooped the ball of fluff into her arms and buried her nose in it. The puppy was wriggling and squirming with pleasure.

"Who's a big beautiful boy, then? Hm? Who's a lovely boy?"

"Just as well you don't want a dog," said Stephen, pouring two large glasses. "Mother said you were dead against it."

"But it didn't stop her," muttered Rosie, completely entranced by the little creature.

"It would be nice to have had one of Bran's offspring," said Stephen. "Not this one though. He's useless."

Rosie clutched him.

"What on earth are you talking about? He's gorgeous."

The puppy obligingly licked her hand.

"I'll get Mother to take him back."

"You will not," said Rosie crossly.

Stephen looked at her with a mixture of fondness and exasperation.

"But you don't even want a dog, and this is a rubbish dog!"

"Ssh," said Rosie, putting her hands over his tiny silken ears. "He can hear you."

"You said you didn't know what a dog would do all day."

"Guard the shop?"

"Please!"

"Stay out in the garden?"

"I don't think so. I'll take it back."

"NO!" Rosie felt the little rough pink tongue licking her hand. "No. We'll think of something."

She realized this was one of the many, many things she was adding to her list of things to sort out in her head later, but she didn't care.

They sat down. Rosie ate one-handed while stroking the dog on her lap.

"We'll need a name for him."

"You know you can't eat with a dog on your lap. It's unhygienic and will give him bad habits."

"He's not a dog! He's a tiny little baby."

The dog whined obligingly, and Rosie gave him a little bit of stew.

"Rosie Hopkins, put that dog down immediately! You're both filthy animals!"

"Shan't!" said Rosie.

"In that case I'm going to have to do things to you that aren't appropriate in front of minors."

Rosie squealed and jumped up as Stephen attempted to smack her bum from the other side of the table, hopping nimbly out of his way.

"I can't believe our entire life together is predicated on your trying to hit me with that stick," she said as she went through to put the tea on. "It's like *Fifty Shades of Earl Grey*."

Later, she made up a little bed for the dog, still unnamed— Rosie was finding it hard to resist the urge to call him Fluffy or Rainbow, and Stephen would narrow his eyes at her and say that if they absolutely had to keep the common mongrel mutt, there was nothing wrong with Monty or Archibald, and they hadn't managed to agree yet, so Rosie was calling him Mr. Dog in the interim. He whined a little, but as she wrapped around him the old red blanket that she'd stolen off a holiday flight a long time ago in the distant past when she used to take actual holidays, he quieted down and was off to sleep in his little doggy way.

"I want to congratulate you on putting up with the awful, terrible concept of having a dog," said Stephen as they went up to bed.

"I still can't believe you were just going to go ahead and get a dog when you knew I didn't want one," grumbled Rosie sleepily.

"Because I don't actually know you at all and thus took you completely at your word when you were so adamant that you didn't want one." He gently slung his arm around her neck, which was his way of pretending it wasn't useful to him to have a little help going up the narrow pull-down stair to their room.

"Oh," said Rosie, feeling his chest against hers, and wondered if this moment, as he nuzzled her neck, when they were so very close, would be the right time to drop the bomb that six of her very, very noisy relatives were descending on their little idyll for Christmas. Oh, it was weeks away, she thought. Plenty of time.

Chapter 4

But there was not, as it turned out, plenty of time at all. Two things happened in Lipton—one small, one big—that were to change things faster than any of them had ever thought possible.

First, two weeks later, the snow still hadn't stopped falling. All the online shopping places stopped delivering, which was agitating, Rosie realized, because her winter wardrobe, even in her second winter in Lipton, was still inadequate. In London, after all, you were never really more than two minutes from a boiling hot tube journey or a bus. Last year she'd eventually been forced to shell out for a parka that had made Moray laugh, hard, for longer than was strictly necessary and tell her she looked like a small child playing at being a Dalek. This year she really needed gloves and a scarf and a hat that actually matched, given that she was going to be wearing them for a reasonable proportion of the day, every day. And suddenly Malik's principle of stocking the Spar with as much tinned food as possible made a lot of sense. Stephen made them buy a great supply of tins, as well as bottled water in case the pipes froze up, which Rosie thought was very over the top and quite exciting even though Stephen warned her that it absolutely wasn't, at all.

Rosie shook her head.

"No," she said. "Me and Mr. Dog take it very seriously indeed, don't we, Mr. Dog?"

And she made his little head shake.

"Put that dog down," said Stephen. "You'll turn him into a lapdog and he'll get too big. And give him a proper name, like Ludo."

"Ludo is not a proper name!" said Rosie. "It's the name of some ghastly little dweeb whose father shoots grouse and wants to bring back hanging."

Stephen sighed as he stomped out, the road clearers had just been, but in their gritted path, new flakes were already beginning to fall. There were fewer children at school every day; it was simply too risky to bring the children down in the morning from the more remote farms and outposts if they couldn't be absolutely sure they could get picked up again at night. Tina already had a spare room made up, and Rosie likewise made sure Lilian's bed was ready in case they were faced with any stranded waifs and strays.

Cough sweets and comfits—anything long lasting—had gone through the roof in the shop. Nobody wanted fondants or pastel colors; that felt like sunshine. Even the chewy ice creams had fallen completely out of favor. And, Rosie noticed, the boxed chocolates had started to sell. That was a slightly worrying sign because it meant Christmas was approaching. Her email was full of jolly messages from her mother, telling her how much the kids were looking forward to seeing snow and playing out in the garden, and Rosie didn't know what to say, apart from telling her she should make sure they were properly dressed. But if you'd grown up in a hot climate as the children had, how would they even believe her? It was impossible to imagine one climate when you were in another, and how on earth did you tell a small child there could be such a thing as too much snow?

Rosie was worrying about exactly this when Edison came in. Just once, she thought, just once she'd like to see him march downtown like the other children did, the girls in pairs with linked arms, admiring each other's snow boots, and the boys in great groups, hurling snowballs and making a huge cacophony.

"Hello, Edison," she said. Edison eyed Mr. Dog warily.

"Oh, don't be silly," she said. "He's only a puppy."

There was, at the back, a connecting run between the shop and the cottage. Stephen had decreed that that was where the dog was going to go; he had brought home a smart new kennel (Rosie had noticed that even though they didn't have a lot of money to spare, it was absolutely top of the line. Nothing more had been said about giving their supposedly below-par dog back to Stephen's mother) and lined it with straw and a blanket. The puppy was meant to run about there until he was old enough to get taken outside on a lead and taught how to behave, but he didn't spend much time there. Rosie washed her hands frantically and used plastic gloves when serving, but nobody seemed to mind at all. Dogs were, Rosie now realized, everywhere in Lipton. The lawyer had his in his office; the barber's dog strolled around the place making friendly inquiries of clients; and the Red Lion of course was full of them, partaking liberally of the water provided for them outside, snoozing gently under their owners' stools at the bar and occasionally guiding them as they meandered home slightly wobbly. So nobody batted an eyelid about Rosie's puppy, and the children, on the whole, adored him.

"Strange dogs are dangerous," said Edison.

"Yes, but he's not a strange dog," said Rosie patiently. "Is he? He's my dog. And he's not the least bit strange."

"He could bite off my nose," said Edison.

"He could lick off your nose, possibly," said Rosie, laughing. "I promise, he doesn't bite. Look at his tiny teeth. You can barely see them."

Edison sidled closer.

"When I am a pinering scientist, I will need to get used to things like this," he said glumly to himself, straightening his glasses. "I'm not sure I want to be a pinering scientist."

"What *do* you want to be, Edison?"

"A pinering scientist who will break new barriers in astrophicks for the good of mankind," repeated Edison, clearly by rote.

"Not a vet, then?"

Edison shook his head fiercely.

"Animals are our friends," he said. "I couldn't fix a pig to get eaten."

Rosie tried to untangle this in her head.

"Well, what would you REALLY like to do?"

Edison looked around.

"I'd like to have a sweetshop just like you. Except without the black bombers."

"Well, some people like black bombers."

Edison shook his head. "Strange people."

Rosie filled a bag with his beloved Edinburgh rock and sent him on his way.

The day had hardly gotten light with the heavy clouds and the flakes still coming down fiercely. Once the school and work rush had passed, Rosie set about refilling stock and cleaning seriously. Mr. Dog sat in the corner looking at a newspaper.

All of a sudden the bell tinged with some urgency, and a rather portly balding middle-aged man rushed in, all in a panic. Rosie straightened up.

"Can I help you?"

"Could I . . . could I possibly have a glass of water?" said the man, out of breath. His voice was educated, and from Yorkshire, the next county along. Rosie had only just begun to be able to make the distinction. Up until very recently, the way Derbyshire people discussed Yorkshire people as a completely different species had been a total mystery to her.

"Of course," she said. "What's up?"

The flustered man swallowed, glancing around nervously behind him, trying to see into his car, a gray Vauxhall Astra that he had parked outside.

"It's my dad," he said. "He's having some kind of . . . a bit of a turn."

"Bring him in," said Rosie immediately. "It's okay, I'm a nurse. Auxiliary nurse. Bring him in. Let me take a look at him now."

She pulled out the chair that Lilian sat in when she came to visit. The man darted out, and after a lot of cajoling, brought into the shop a tall, stooped figure, very thin, with white hair.

"Come on, Dad, sit down. Sit down," he said.

Rosie brought a glass of water. The old man was muttering incomprehensibly. She helped him sip it and checked his heart rate.

"I'm just going to call our local doctor," she said. "He's only down the road."

"Are you sure that's necessary?" said the man. "He seems to be quieting down."

The man was gesticulating and talking feverishly. Rosie couldn't understand a word he was saying.

"It's dementia," said the son. "Sorry. He's not well."

"I can see that," said Rosie, speed-dialing Moray. "Has this happened before?"

"All the time," said the man, and as Rosie looked at him more closely, she saw the marks of strain around his eyes and mouth. "All the time, and getting worse. And this one came out of the blue. There is . . . there is no getting better."

"I know," said Rosie softly, hanging up the phone after talking to Moray's receptionist, Maeve. "He's on his way. Would you like a cup of tea?"

The man nodded, then glanced apprehensively out the window at the weather.

"Although maybe we should get on."

The old man was moaning now, rocking himself back and forth. Rosie found the new blanket they'd bought for Mr. Dog and put it around his shoulders and gradually, with the man's arm around him, the old chap's breathing slowed, and he stopped jabbering, although not before a great tear had rolled down his cheek.

"It's a horrible disease," said Rosie sympathetically. "A total pig."

The man winced in agreement.

"Yes. Yes, it is rather." He held out his hand. "Edward Boyd. And my father's James."

"Nice to meet you," said Rosie. "Rosie Hopkins."

By the time Moray arrived, the kettle was whistling, and he gave the old man a thorough check over.

"He's stopped . . . he's stopped recognizing me at all," said Edward, sadly. "He keeps shouting things that don't make sense."

"That's very common," said Moray, assessing his vital signs. "His pulse is a bit thready, but that might just be the shock. What caused him to react like that?"

"I've no idea," said Edward, gratefully accepting the tea.

"I'll cool it down for your dad," said Rosie quietly, adding cold water.

"I had to take a detour through this town because we normally take the Hiftown road, but it's shut . . . I don't even know where we are."

"Lipton," said Moray

Edward looked worriedly out the window. It was so overcast that it felt like night. "I'll need to get on."

Rosie gave the old man his tea, holding the cup while he sipped it.

"Thank you," said Edward again. "Okay, well, we drove into town and he got very, very agitated and took off his seatbelt and was all over the place."

"Could he have been here before?" asked Rosie.

"I don't think so," said Edward. "He was born and raised the other side of Halifax."

They regarded James quietly. He now seemed perfectly happy and at home in the chair and was looking around approvingly.

"Does he live with you?" asked Moray. Edward turned to face him and, just for a second, Rosie caught sight of the tiredness and anguish behind the polite mask.

"Yes," he said, his face stricken. Then he straightened up again. "I mean, yes, he does. It's fine, we have some home care, and of course my wife helps a lot, of course . . ."

"There's no shame," said Moray quietly and kindly, "in getting someone the help they need. You know, after a certain point, many of the nicer homes won't take dementia patients."

"He's my dad," said Edward stoically and swallowed. Rosie decided that she liked this Edward Boyd. Lilian had had to go into a home after several falls and a minor stroke; Rosie couldn't look after her and work at the same time. She admired this man who had clearly tried to do both. And Lilian had kept her marbles, which made everyone's lives so much easier.

"Come on, Dad," said Edward, looking at his watch. "It's time to go."

James looked around confusedly, his hands gripping the sides of his chair.

"No!" he spat hoarsely. "No!"

His face was full of confusion and panic.

"Come on, Dad. We're going to go home. You can see Doreen, okay? We'll have vegetable soup for lunch. I know you like that."

"NO!" said the old man, looking surprisingly strong. "I'm staying here!"

Moray and Rosie exchanged looks, but Edward just looked downtrodden and resigned.

"We have to go, Dad."

James looked mutinous.

Finally, Moray stepped forward and took out his card.

"If you need someone to talk to," he said, "give me a call and I'll talk to your GP about making a referral, okay? It doesn't have to be like this."

Edward looked down at the card as if he might cry.

"Thank you so much for your kindness. Oh, let me take some sweets, that might help tempt him out."

"Of course! What does he like?" said Rosie.

"Mixed boiled usually," said Edward.

"NO!" came the quavering but determined voice again. "Caramel!"

"You don't like caramel," said Edward. "It sticks to your teeth!"

"Caramel."

"You can have caramels if you get in the car."

"Don't want to," said the old man.

"Caramels in the car?"

Rosie made up a bag, and Edward paid for them and once again thanked them profusely for their kindness. Then he led the old man, the caramels clutched in his hand, out of the shop and back to the car. As they left, Rosie noticed another tear rolling down the old man's cheek.

"That's it," she said as she came back to pick up the tea cups. "I never want that to happen to me. Never. Honestly, I think I'd rather . . . I think I'd rather be *dead*."

"Stephen will do it," said Moray, waving his hand. "Doctors get into trouble for that kind of thing."

Rosie shook her head. "How awful. It's just such a horrible thing. I wonder what set him off."

"Probably nothing," said Moray. "Stumbling across an old memory in the brain that just happened to coincide with passing by. It's a filthy disease, dementia. I see the guilty grown-up children in my office all the time. They should really do what's for the best and get him somewhere nice. No point in everybody's life being ruined."

"Poor chaps," muttered Rosie again, and she put the old man and his son out of her head.

Rosie went right on decorating. She had found a box containing some old Christmas decorations in the attic and was considering dragging them out. Among them were a couple of lovely old wood carvings that were clearly handmade—seeing their varying degrees of proficiency, she wondered if they'd been done at school by Lilian's brothers. Lilian confirmed this, so Rosie saved them while letting the disintegrating tinsel and tarnished baubles head for the bin.

She made up the vast Christmas order for the shop, and while she was doing so, Tina, who was an online shopper extraordinaire, came in and showed her a picture of the most amazing half-price Santa she'd found.

"But online merchants aren't delivering," said Rosie. "Because of the weather."

"Yes, they aren't delivering to normal people. That's why it's half price before Christmas," said Tina, who'd nearly gone bankrupt from her bad habit. "But they'll always deliver to me."

Rosie smiled and looked at it again. It really was lovely: a miniature Santa train with empty carriages they could fill with sweets, tootling around a little model village with its roofs all covered in snow and little candles in all the windows.

"It looks like Lipton," she said.

Tina nodded. "I know," she said. "We must get it. We'll cause a scrum."

Rosie thought briefly of the amazing bright lights and astonishing designer displays on Oxford Street in London. It was hard to imagine a small tootling train being the center of attention. But then, Malik's was currently displaying a pyramid of discounted tinned macaroni and cheese, so she supposed things could be worse.

"You're on," she said.

"It whistles!"

"I said you're on!"

"Yay!" said Tina, who wasn't really allowed to shop anymore. "I ordered it last week."

Rosie rolled her eyes.

"So what are you getting Jake for Christmas?"

"Oh, nothing interesting," said Tina sadly. "I wish I were a millionaire. No offense."

"None taken," said Rosie promptly. "I do too."

"But I saw this beautiful Burberry shirt he'd look amazing in, and this really gorgeous cashmere scarf."

"Jake wouldn't like any of that stuff."

"No," said Tina. "But fantasy Jake I go out with in my head does."

"I thought Jake was your fantasy Jake."

Tina's face softened.

"Oh, he is. He is. But, you know."

Rosie did know. Jake was gorgeous and charming and worked as a farm laborer. His usual outfit was a rubber waistcoat to avoid stains and a hacking jacket that Rosie strongly suspected was older than he was.

"What do you think he's going to get you?"

Tina shrugged. "I don't know. Last year he got me a pair of socks."

"But you'd only been going out five minutes last year."

"Still."

"And it was a very nice pair of socks."

Tina rolled her eyes.

"Okay, okay."

Rosie sold two pounds of Parma violets and said hi to Anton, the fattest man in town. Formerly, he'd been going for the fattest man in the country. The fact that he was now only the fattest man in their village was, Rosie felt, a credit to him. And slightly to her, given that she controlled his sweet intake in a way that frankly counted as an act of charitable giving.

Anton looked around.

"Christmas decorations!" he said cheerfully.

Mr. Dog came padding up to lick his hand, as he always did. He was growing bigger and hairier by the week but was no less lazy and affectionate. Rosie was madly in love with him, to Stephen's alternate amusement and slight annoyance. He kept banging on about how their dogs were bred to work. But every time Rosie turned her back, if she whipped around quickly enough, she would catch Stephen skritching the puppy behind his ears or secretly telling him he was the best fellow in the world, yes, he was, yes, he was.

"He likes you," said Rosie to Anton.

"He likes fish and chips," said Anton.

"Anton!"

"A small! I had a small!"

"What'll it be? I feel like a drug dealer."

Anton smiled dreamily, his face slack as he perused the shelves.

"We're pushers," said Tina. "I think we just need to deal with that fact."

"Never," said Rosie.

"How's that young boy of yours?" said Anton without taking his eyes off the shelves he must have known by heart.

"Not so young," said Rosie, still going pink even now, nearly a year after they'd started dating. "Actually, he's really well."

"I still can't believe he loves teaching school," said Tina. "Who'd have thought?"

"I know," said Rosie, thinking back to the bitter, empty shell of the man she'd met when she first arrived. "It's healed him, I think. Inside, really. You should have seen him this morning, off with their Christmas song. It's about bells. Edison keeps reciting it to me to show me how fast he can do it. I'm quite fed up with it, and the concert isn't for another three weeks."

"Raspberry creams!" shouted Anton, his lips practically smacking in satisfaction.

"You may have four," said Rosie.

"Eleven," said Anton.

"Four plus one for good behavior," said Rosie.

"I make that nine," said Anton.

Outside, the village was quiet. The snow was falling, still falling, the sky a gray blanket that made it feel as if day had barely come at all. Jake was laboring down at Isitt's farm, trying to work out what he could buy that would be special enough for a girl as special as Tina. Stephen was leading his children in another rousing chorus of "Carol of the Bells" in the open-play Portakabin by the side door of the school. Anton and Rosie were bickering in their familiar way. Lilian was dozing by the window, remembering a curly-haired lad who threw snowballs at her way past the age when lads throw snowballs at girls.

Edward Boyd had hit the outskirts of town and glanced anxiously at his father who, thank goodness, appeared to have fallen asleep. He felt his wallet for the card that nice young doctor had given him. Maybe, after all, it was time. Maybe it was. But his dad . . . he was his dad. Years of summer holidays down at Scarborough, and practicing his spin bowl and . . . he wasn't sure quite when he'd noticed his dad wasn't well. He'd always been a quiet man, injured in the war, a good father—there had been holidays and pocket money and fixing up a motorbike and rugby league matches, but sometimes James was so introverted it had been hard to notice at first that something was wrong.

Lost in thought, he didn't realize that his father had abruptly awoken and was eyeing the bag of chocolate caramels that was sitting on the dashboard. Suddenly, as Edward took a tricky bend in the gloom, a massive flare of headlights half-blinded him. At exactly the same moment, his father made a grab for the sweets, startling Edward into a half jump. The car jack-knifed on the road, and the truck was suddenly on them, honking with all its might as it skidded and slid for purchase across the white ground.

"JESUS CHRIST," screeched Edward as the enormous headlights hit him straight in the face, dazzling him. He pulled the wheel sharply to the left with what he presumed to be his last wish, just that his father should feel nothing, that it would be only a flash and a bang and then silence.

"'To you in David's town this day is born of David's line,'" trilled Stephen's class as he nodded them on furiously while trying to accompany them (badly) on the old slightly out-of-tune piano.

"A saviour who is Christ the Lord and this shall be the sign."

Then the handbells came in. The challenge was to make them not too enthusiastic with the bells, as they forgot to sing. Except the very little ones. Pandora Esten was only four and a half, and it seemed unfair to get in her way.

"SWEET BELLS!" (Chime, clamor.) "SWEET CHIM-ING CHRISTMAS BELLS!" (Chime, clatter as one of the bells dropped to the floor.)

"SWEET BELLS!" (Chime.) "SWEET chiming Christmas bells . . ." (Slight fading off as the class collectively attempted to remember the forthcoming slightly tricky line.)

Kent and Emily, Tina's twins, always got it right, however.

"They CHEER us ON our HEAVEN-lee WAY, sweet CHIM-ing BELLS!!!"

The left-hand side of the Astra sluiced down into the ditch and bounced along the hedge. They shook and bounced up and down as Edward tried to force the wheel to the right and not close his eyes, his breath choking in a shriek in his mouth. Amazingly, the car kept on going, eventually found its footing again and righted itself.

Edward found himself dripping with sweat, panting hard,

unable to stop or remove his hands from the wheel. He caught a glimpse of red taillights in the mirror behind him, but he couldn't think about that; couldn't think about anything other than the pounding of his heart and his need to get back to the motorway and on home as fast as he possibly could. Beside him his father was making puzzled noises, and he forced himself to say, "There, there, Dad. It's all right. It's all right." He would never, he vowed grimly to himself, ever leave the house again.

The truck, however, was not all right. The cab was knocked off its axle, and the driver suddenly found the steering listing terribly. His own nerves—he was normally a calm sort, fond of a cooked breakfast and his wife—suddenly started to fray at the edges. He couldn't see in his rearview mirror to figure out if anything had happened to the car. He'd had the radio playing loudly, and he hadn't heard a bang or seen any lights, but that didn't mean they weren't upside down in a ditch somewhere. But he couldn't stop here, it was a deadly single-track hairpin. He wasn't even meant to be out on deliveries in this weather, but his boss had insisted it was a special customer, so he'd volunteered. And now this. He cursed. He'd stop at the next town, get them to send someone out to have a look at his steering. Bugger it. Bugger bugger bugger. He pulled the great lorry up the hill, praying that he'd make it, cursing the local councils, who had all cut down on their street lighting so much they didn't light any roads at all if they could help it, even in these conditions. He was nearly there . . . nearly there . . .

It was cresting the hill that did it. There was a slight bump on the road at the entrance to Lipton, just past the churchyard, and as he felt the cab head up over it and heard the ominous crack, he knew that this was bad news. But the upward acceleration he'd had to use to get the truck over the top of the hill was still with it, powering it forward far too fast, the vehicle suddenly transformed into a huge weapon beyond his control. Slowly, incredibly slowly, he tried to steer it away from the building on his right, but the steering wheel was nowhere close to obeying his instructions and he watched in horror as the great stern of the truck pulled closer and closer. Then, at the last minute, he grabbed hold of his seatbelt, ducked, covered his eyes, and prayed.

"They CHEER us ON our . . ."

The throaty, roaring, crashing noise was slow and undercut the tremendous tumult of twenty-one little hands clanging bells all at once. The back of the jackknifed lorry pulled down the wall and ripped through the side of the Portakabin that held the art and music classes. Its headlights were suddenly beaming through the open air, the storm whipping into the hot little room, flurries of snowflakes dancing in the lighted air. An openmouthed scream went up, and the children automatically shrank back, mindlessly obeying the loud voice that immediately shouted, "GET DOWN! GET DOWN! GET DOWN!" then a figure hurled itself forward, a cane clattering to the ground, throwing itself on top of the boy singing the solo, standing apart from the others, his dirty glasses already slipping down his face from the force of the inrushing wind, the air pushed ahead of the great machine.

The noise shook the village. Then everything went dark.

Chapter 5

What was that?" said Rosie. The lights had all flickered out, then on again. "Was it an earthquake?"

Tina and Anton looked confused. Rosie let Anton sit down in Lilian's special chair (normally he wasn't allowed to; Rosie was trying to keep him mobile for the sake of his veins).

The great glass jars had wobbled on their shelves, but apart from a row of mints and a couple of the chocolate boxes propped up for display, nothing had fallen. Rosie dashed out into the street. She could see other people emerging from their homes, looking confused. The day was still so overcast and gloomy that it felt like the middle of the night. Rosie ran down to Malik's shop. The fruit and veg he kept outside had tumbled to the ground, but he wasn't paying any attention to that. Instead, he was gazing down the hill, eyes wide open, pointing. Rosie followed his finger, and her hand flew to her mouth.

"Oh my God," she said. "Oh my God."

He was pointing at the school.

She didn't have to knock up Moray, he was already running, trying to pull on his jacket at the same time, which made Rosie curse as she ran back to her own home for blankets. They would need them. Please God, they would need them. All the time her heart was panicking. She ran back past parents, mothers, all of them fleeing down the hill, all of them thinking one thought, she knew: "Please let it not be mine. Please let it not be mine."

The scene of devastation, the fuel in the lorry already smoking, had clenched her heart, and she couldn't let herself think about Stephen, or the children in the school, every single one of whom bought lollies and chocolate and ice cream and bonbons, every single one of whom she knew well—the guzzlers, the expectant choosers, the value-for-money buyers and the indecisive agonizers. She knew all of those children.

Tina was walking down the road in a trance, like a zombie. Her eyes were looking at the school, but she wasn't seeing it. Rosie threw herself into the house and snatched all the blankets from the linen cupboard. She was going to need more than this for shock. They'd have some down there . . . and tea, they'd need tea. She ordered her brain to behave itself. She'd worked in accident and emergency for years. She needed to go into that mode now, not think about who was there, just about what she needed to do. She knew Moray could do it; she could do it too. She had to.

The sirens filled the air—there was a fire station at Carningford. Mrs. Baptiste, the head teacher, was filing children from the main building and into the street. Some looked dazed, the littler ones were crying, and some of the boys were rather excited. One by one they were fallen on by desperate, weeping parents, filled with guilty, overwhelming relief.

Moray was by the door of the cab, desperately trying to open it. Rosie ran and screamed at him to stop being an idiot and leave it for the firemen, it could go up any second, and he looked at her confused, then realized the sense in what she was saying and jumped down.

They could hear the sirens in the far distance, but they weren't here yet. And Mrs. Baptiste was doing a wonderful job, but Rosie was now scanning the lines of children, who were being shepherded farther and farther away up the hill, and she didn't see them.

She couldn't see Stephen, and she couldn't see Edison.

She glanced at Moray, both of them looking at the smoking, ruined wreck of the Portakabin.

"We have to go in," she said. Mrs. Baptiste was already running down the hill.

"No, you're right," said Moray. "We should wait for the fire brigade, it's not safe. Mrs. Baptiste, get away from there! Get away at once!"

The usually brusque gray-haired teacher looked up at him.

"But they're not all out," she said, her voice quavering.

"You've done what you can," said Moray. "Get away, please."

Mrs. Baptiste shook her head and glanced toward the awful sight of the Portakabin. No more figures were emerging.

"Now," said Moray, in a voice that brooked no argument.

He turned around.

"EVERYONE GET BACK!" he shouted. "BACK as far as Malik's! We don't know whether the truck is going to explode! Get back!!"

As he said these words, a helicopter appeared over the side

of the hill. A man with a loudspeaker leaned out. He too was shouting, "GET BACK! GET BACK! GET BACK!" He clearly meant Moray and Rosie too, but they ignored him, glanced at each other, and quickly dived into the cabin.

Inside, it was like a vision of hell. Light came through the great rip in the wall, but it only showed a great big cloud of gray dust and shredded paper that made it nearly impossible to see. Rosie heard a whimper, but she couldn't make out where it was coming from. She tore off her apron and tied it around her mouth so she could breathe; she saw Moray do the same with his handkerchief.

"Who's there?" she said. Kneeling down she saw Kent, Tina's boy, cowering behind the piano, one eye shut and colored black and purple, blood and scratches all over his hands.

"Oh darling," she said. "Can you move?"

Kent looked up at her with his one open eye.

"It hurts," he said, terrified. "It hurts."

"I know, my love," said Rosie. "I'm coming for you."

She clambered over fallen chairs. Sheet music floated through the air.

"Come on," she said. He was a big boy, but she could still lift him. He winced in pain as she touched his arm and she nodded.

"I know it's sore," she said. "And the ambulance is going to be here soon and sort this out. But just for now I really, really have to get you out of here."

Kent swallowed and nodded bravely.

"I'll try not to touch it, okay?"

"Okay."

She took him in a fireman's hold around the waist, and as she did so, she started in surprise, for underneath, crouching and rolled up in a ball like a tiny hedgehog, was his twin sister, Emily, with barely a scratch on her.

"Did you cover up your sister?" she asked Kent in shock.

Kent didn't say anything, his bottom lip quivering with the pain.

"Okay, okay, let's get you out of here," she said. "Emily, darling, can you walk?"

Emily's eyes were huge and white.

"Mummy!" she said, in a wobbly voice.

"Mummy's outside," said Rosie, taking a quick glance through the rip in the wall, where the tanker was still smoking. "Mummy's outside, darling, but we really have to go and get to her quickly, okay? Quickly. Like, now. We're going to Mummy, okay?"

The magic word "Mummy" had its effect on the little girl, who was paralyzed with fear. Emily nodded carefully, and Rosie hoisted Kent over her shoulders—he cried out, then tried to stifle himself, but she could hear him weeping on her back—and they moved slowly toward the open door. Outside, Mrs. Baptiste had point-blank refused to leave her post and helped them back toward a makeshift barrier that had been set up.

When Tina saw them, she simply sank to her knees in the middle of the wet snowy lane. Jake had come hurtling up the road from Isitt's farm as fast as his legs could carry him and was there now, red-faced and puffing. He pushed past the barrier and lifted Kent up in his arms as if he weighed nothing, looking into his face with a tenderness that could not have given two figs for whose son this boy was. Emily had run to her mother and buried her face in her shoulder; Tina had taken her in her arms, but her eyes were still wide open, staring straight ahead, as if still fixed on the possible alternative, gazing in horror on another life.

Finally the fire brigade was here; a man in full breathing apparatus stood in front of Rosie.

"Stand aside now please, ma'am. Let us do our job."

Rosie stared at him. She knew he was right, that he was the man to go into that awful dark space again, that it was unprofessional and downright dangerous of her to stand in his way. She had had to do the same thing herself, many times: persuade panicking and desperate relatives to leave the professionals alone to get on with their jobs, that that would be the best for everyone, the victims included.

She couldn't help it. She turned around and shot back through the hole.

"Moray!" she shouted. Now the fire brigade were setting up big arc lights that could cut through the dust, and it was even harder to see in the gloom. "Where . . . where . . ."

Her voice choked, her lungs filled with dust. She tried to collect herself for a moment in the swirling dark.

"Here," came the voice, quick and clipped.

She could see what had happened right away. The clothes were ripped from Stephen's back in a line. He had obviously dived right on top of the boy who even now Moray was crouched over, trying to save. She knelt down, but straightaway she could tell that, thank God, he was breathing; his back was a mess, but it was not bleeding extensively, it was just going to hurt like absolute buggery when he woke up. But he would—even as she looked at him, broken and twisted on the ground—wake up. If they got him out in time. The air was filled with the smell of spilled petrol.

"Here," she shouted desperately to the rescuers behind them. "Here!" And she grabbed Stephen's hand tightly.

Lying there on the ground beside them, Edison was a different matter. Moray had cleared his airways and checked his breathing; he was in the recovery position but completely unconscious. His face was a mess, his little body horribly contorted where it lay. Moray was gently trying to protect his spine. Rosie looked at the GP's filthy face, but it was absolutely unreadable.

"He's a doctor," she said to the paramedics now fighting their way through.

"Who are you?" one of them barked back at her.

"It doesn't matter," said Rosie, and she knelt down between Stephen and Edison, and refused to move until the stretcher was lifted and she felt Stephen grimace and painfully and briefly come to as he was lifted.

"You do go," she managed to say chokily as she felt his eyes rest upon her and saw the relief in them as they did so, "to quite ridiculous lengths to try and get the attention of a nurse."

Outside, to her intense relief, the fire brigade was training its foam hoses on the big lorry, which no longer had smoke coming from it. The driver had been brought out, a little concussed, but otherwise perfectly well. He was standing by his cab, crying. A policeman was talking to him in a serious, low tone of voice. The street looked like a film set of a war zone, lit up with huge arc lights, surrounded by people in uniform. Many of the children had been spirited away home, but some of the adults remained, gripped, chatting and comforting each other. Mrs. Baptiste stood to the side, stiff and covered in dust, and Rosie led her to a St. John's ambulance to get her some tea. Then she looked around for the heavily pregnant form of Edison's mother and saw with a terrible pang of horror that she was not there.

They lived in a tiny cottage set in the forest at the far end of the village. Hester didn't like to mix much; she had very strong views on almost everything and had moved to Lipton to try to raise her son in a pure way. She disliked the efforts of everyone else to live a normal life with cable television and ready meals. Someone was going to have to go.

Rosie raised Stephen's hands to her lips and kissed them, fiercely wiping a tear from her eye. Over by the ambulance they were still working on Edison. She swore furiously to herself, kissed Stephen one more time, then ran to fetch her bicycle.

It was the hardest trip she had ever made, through the pummeling snow, visibility almost nothing. She realized only subsequently that she didn't even have a coat on because she'd run out of the shop so fast. She'd remembered to bring blankets for everyone else in case of shock; she hadn't realized that she would suffer it too.

Hester's house was set in a little glade at the end of the lane. It was beautiful, like a tiny fairy-tale cottage, planted with neat rows of organic vegetables. Say what you like about Hester, Rosie had often thought, but she walked the walk. Wood smoke was rising from the chimney pot, so at least she was home. Someone must have called though, surely. Somebody must have.

Hester, her bump fully formed now and pendulous, answered the door calmly. Rosie saw at a glance that she didn't know. She didn't seem to notice Rosie's disheveled state, which on some level reminded Rosie that she had to sort out her wardrobe.

"Hello," she said. "I was just performing my sun saluta-tions."

Edison's father, Arthur, did something important at a uni-versity in Derby and was often away during the week.

"Didn't . . . has nobody phoned you?" asked Rosie, the words tumbling out.

Hester looked confused.

"I keep my phone off when I'm doing my meditations, of course," she said. "Why . . . why?" A tone of steel entered her voice as she finally noticed that Rosie was covered in ash and filth, her hands scraped and bloody.

"What's happened?"

"Oh, Hester," said Rosie. She heard the noise of a car be-hind her and realized it must be the police. She needed to be there with her.

"Can you . . . can we go inside and sit down?"

"What's happened?" repeated Hester. All the earth-mother calm had drained from her face. Rosie had dealt with people like this before. Sometimes people wanted to sit down, to be held, to have small decisions taken away to give them scope to deal with the new landscapes of their lives. And sometimes they were defi-ant, determined to meet it head-on, to conquer it through will alone, as Hester was now.

"Is it Edison?"

And Rosie had to say the words she hadn't said in so long, words that took her back to her very hardest days of A and E nursing—the pastel room, the crumpled faces, the shattered lives. But this time, the words were about somebody she knew.

"I'm afraid there's been an accident."

Hester was astonishing, Rosie thought, as she sat, upright and dignified, completely silent, in the back of the police car as they prepared to take her to the hospital over at Carningford. The helicopter was transporting Edison; apparently there wasn't a second to lose. She fetched a bag for Hester from inside, adding her phone, her handbag, a sweater, and a toothbrush and pajamas; she didn't think Hester would be back for a while.

"When's the baby due?" she had asked gently, but Hester had shaken her head. One awful experience at a time. So instead, Rosie gently took her hand in the police car, checking her phone every two seconds. Still no signal. Moray needed to phone her about Stephen . . . and Edison. Oh, Edison.

A choking noise escaped Hester's mouth suddenly, and her hand flew to her mouth.

"He's so . . . he's just so . . . *special,*" said Hester suddenly. And Rosie, who had long thought that Edison was terribly mollycoddled, that his parents were trying to turn him into something he wasn't, with awful consequences for his popularity at school and his social standing, saw with real clarity that of course he was. That they all were, but Edison . . .

It was slow going on the whited-out roads. With the mobile signal so patchy, it was the longest ride of Rosie's life. She kept flashing in and out of those moments in the dark and terrible ripped-apart cabin, searching; the sight of Stephen blown across the room, the boy's contorted body . . . she realized she was shaking and tried to force herself to calm down.

The kindly WPC in the front seat turned around to them with a large flask.

"I'm sorry, it's all I have," she said, pouring them a large cupful of hot tea to share. "We hope it won't be long."

Rosie took it gratefully and forced Hester to drink some.

There were few cars on the road on such a dreadful day and only the odd tractor. Every time she saw a lorry, Rosie winced. They were so dangerous on these little roads. So dangerous. She grasped Hester's hand and held on to it tightly, as much, she realized, for herself as for Hester.

Finally they made it to the bypass, and the roundabouts began on the entrance to Carningford, a large town on the other side of the dales from Lipton. Liptonites called it the big town, but to Rosie it was embarrassingly small; it didn't even have a Topshop. But it did have a hospital.

The driver put the siren on, and they sped through the heavier traffic. The snow not quite as thick here in town, but it was still driving along on the heavy wind.

Rosie closed her eyes for a few moments and tried to take a few deep breaths. The last thing she needed to do was go into shock; it was already quite hard enough for everyone else. She was fine. She was fine. She was going to have to be.

Chapter 6

They both ran through the emergency doors. The waiting room, full of bored people who had slipped on icy walks or over-indulged at their firm's Christmas lunch, looked up, interested in the distraction. The nurse on duty bustled them through, and Rosie and Hester were separated. Rosie gulped. Did this mean Stephen was worse than she thought?

"He's heavily sedated," said the nurse.

"Is he going to be all right?" asked Rosie desperately. "He seemed . . . he seemed like he would be okay."

The nurse put her hand gently on her shoulder.

"He will," she said. "He'll be okay."

"Edison Felling-Jackson," said Rosie immediately. "What about the little boy?"

The nurse's face darkened.

"I can't . . ."

"I'm his . . ." Rosie couldn't work it out. "Oh."

Fortunately, Moray came dashing up to her from the waiting room. They hugged briefly.

"How's Edison?" she barked quickly.

Moray bit his lip.

"It's . . . well, he's in theater. They're having a look. He's pretty knocked up, Rosie."

Rosie stared at the ground.

"His neck?"

"They're checking. He's in good hands."

They stood apart.

"Fuck," said Rosie, staring at the floor.

"It's early days," said Moray.

Rosie looked at him.

"I know. Fuck," said Moray.

"Did you want to see Mr. Lakeman?" said the nurse to Rosie.

"Of course," said Rosie. Moray hung back.

"He's all right?"

"Going to be. Thank God." Rosie's face relaxed slightly. "But oh, Moray."

Moray shook his head.

"Come over later and we'll get drunk," he said.

Rosie nodded. "Okay," she said. "I'll need to talk to Lilian."

"I'm sure she doesn't mind you getting drunk once in a while."

"No, I'll need to tell her everything."

Moray rolled his eyes. "You're joking, aren't you?. That place is like a telephone exchange. She'll know. But yes, check in and call by later."

Rosie nodded.

"How do I look?" she said.

Even in the midst of everything that was going on, Moray still felt a smile.

"Apart from the dust covering your hair and the black smudges and the scrape on your cheek?" he said.

"Oh, bloody hell!" said Rosie.

"Rose, he'll be off his tits on morphine. He'll think you're Cameron Diaz. Don't worry about it."

Rosie rubbed her face quickly but decided to take him at his word.

"Okay. Later. Text me as soon as you know anything about Edison."

"No mobiles in hospital," said the nurse automatically. Rosie and Moray exchanged glances. Rosie took one last deep breath and marched confidently into the side bay.

Stephen was propped up on his side, which made him look oddly nonchalant. He looked sleepy and a little strained, and Rosie's heart skipped out of her chest in relief and love.

"Darling," she said softly. Stephen, even drugged up, seemed to relax at the sound of her voice.

"R?" he said.

She ran across the room to him.

"Careful!" he said. "They gave me some nice stuff . . . very nice stuff actually. It was very nice. I can't remember what I was saying. Oh yes. My back. It's still very—"

"Ssh," said Rosie, burying her nose in his thick, curly dark hair. It too still held traces of dust and a faint smell of burning. Her eyes were dry, but she felt a huge sense of relief.

"They're going to do a skin graft," said the nurse. "When there's a theater free."

"Really? That bad?" said Rosie, lifting her head. She looked at Stephen. "Did you just get your arse blown off?"

Stephen found this quite funny but the nurse shook her head.

"Just a little. On his side and shoulder. He jumped on top of the child and took the brunt of it."

"Hear that?" said Rosie. "You're a hero." She kissed him tenderly. Stephen shook his head.

"Too late," he said, suddenly looking stricken. "Too late."

"Hush," said the nurse, glancing at her watch. "Don't get agitated."

A doctor came in, followed by two porters.

"All right, Mr. Lakeman. We're going to prep you."

For a moment Stephen's drug haze seemed to lift, and he looked Rosie right in the eye.

"I can't believe I'm here again," he said, his face clouded with pain. Rosie took his hand.

"Because you're brave," she whispered. "And you can be brave again."

He half-smiled.

"Now, go get your bum transplant. Tell them not to change the shape. I like it as it is."

She squeezed his hand once more, and they took him away.

At five o'clock, hours and hours later—she had neither eaten nor drunk a thing all day and didn't even notice—Rosie was sitting next to Hester in a private waiting room when Arthur came running in. He was a tall, very thin man with glasses and pale hair; Edison was his absolute double. She tried to give them privacy, but they could barely talk to one another. Every so often Arthur would get up and try to harass any passing medical staff into giving them information, but they couldn't or wouldn't. Eventually, Rosie got some coffee for everyone from the vending machine. It was utterly foul, but it gave their hands something to do as the clock ticked on.

It was strange, Rosie thought, and had often thought when she'd worked in A and E: the hands of time in the hospital always moved far too fast, or far too slowly, and everyone watching the clock was locked in their own private universe of pain, or misery, or the joy of recovery. The idea that outside somewhere not very far away there was life going on—jobs and shopping and marriages and holidays and nights out and lunch breaks—when you were waiting in hospital for news, the idea that the world just went on its merry way seemed incomprehensible; unlikely and thoughtless. Rosie had been wondering about buying a Christmas tree. The idea that she had had that mild, useless, amiable thought in her head now seemed stupid and pointless.

She envied the people she had often seen in hospitals who were able to pray. Rosie had seen too many young lives cut short, too much potential lost to accident and disease, to be very good at praying. But not Edison. Surely not.

At long last, a silhouette appeared at the venetian blinds. A surgeon. He was taking off his hat. Rosie eyed him fiercely, feeling her heart pound. Hester and Arthur clutched hands, the strain evident on their white faces.

He entered the room, a heavyset man.

"Mr. and Mrs. Felling-Jackson?" he said gravely. He looked at Rosie.

"I'll leave," she said straightaway.

"No," said Hester. "No. You stay."

Rosie felt she was going to be sick.

The surgeon sat down.

"We think . . . we're not sure, but we think . . . that Edison has broken his neck . . ."

Hester immediately burst into enormous, choking sobs. She grasped Rosie's hand painfully tight. Rosie squeezed back. The doctor gave her a few moments, then carried on.

"But there are several ways to do this. At the moment, the indications seem to be that Edison has a C7 break, here."

He indicated high up on the right-hand side of his neck.

"What does that mean?" asked Arthur. But Rosie let out a gasp. She knew.

"Oh my God," she said. "Oh my God."

The doctor nodded at her.

"I know."

Hester gazed at them both, her eyes dry and wide.

"WHAT? Tell us!"

"It means," said the doctor, "that we think Edison might have been very, very lucky."

It was only then that Rosie was able to cry, she explained to Moray later in the Red Lion. They were on their second bottle of white—on a weeknight, but needs must. They were also the focus of attention as everyone was whispering and speculating on the awful thing that had happened to their little school. It was, everyone said, a miracle that nobody had been killed. Edison would have a long, slow recovery, much of it in a full-body cast, but there was every reason to suppose that he would get completely well again. The bricks from the wall had struck his vertebrae and thoracic cord, but Stephen had protected him from the rest of the blast. Stephen was out of surgery, but they wouldn't say much more to Rosie on the phone, except that he was fast asleep and she was welcome to visit in the morning.

Little Kent had fractured his wrist and was sporting a massive cast. People around him were talking about how brave he had been and how he deserved a medal, so on balance was feeling pretty pleased with himself, although he slightly wished his mother would stop collapsing in tears every five minutes. Rosie had finally gotten back to find the sweetshop door still unlocked, but of course not a thing had been taken. She locked up carefully and wondered if it would be mawkish to put up a picture of Edison.

"What's happened to the bloke driving the lorry?" asked Moray. Valiant work by the fire brigade—some of whom were now reliving their day in the corner of the bar—had removed the lorry, goodness knows where. News teams had descended to report on the incident, but many had retreated as the weather got nasty.

"He's in custody in Carningford," said someone. "He'll have to go to prison. He could have killed all those kids!"

Rosie shook her head.

"Oh my goodness, that poor man."

Moray looked at her.

"Don't give me that. It's not like the school ran into the road. If they find out he was texting on his phone or something, I'll pull the lever myself."

"I know, I know," said Rosie. "It's just, I can't help thinking of everyone waking up this morning, thinking it was going to be just another normal day . . ."

"Ssh," said Moray. "I know. I know. It's awful. But it's going to be okay."

Inside, Rosie wasn't so sure.

"You know what Stephen went through last year," she said quietly.

Moray eyed her.

"Rosie, if you'd wanted an easy life, you'd have stuck with that fat bloke you used to go out with."

Rosie smiled.

"True," she said. "But . . . you know . . ."

When Stephen had returned, injured, from Africa, he had shut himself away from the world, brooding. It had, the town agreed, taken Rosie to bring him out of himself. This might set him back again.

"Look at it this way," said Moray. "This time, he did save the child. He did it right. So he's going to have to deal with that. And it's only a bit of skin off his arse. So."

Rosie nodded.

"Yes," she said. "Yes, he's going to be fine."

She had to believe it.

"And if he isn't," said Moray, "we'll do what I wanted to do last time and get a posse go and kick him up the arse."

They clinked glasses.

"You look like hell," observed Lilian usefully the next morning when Rosie popped in to see her en route to the hospital (she had woken ridiculously early and knew that people got up early at the nursing home too).

"That's because I've just been through the most traumatic day of my life," said Rosie indignantly.

"Oh. Because it looks like a hangover."

Rosie didn't answer.

"They should never let lorries through the town," said Lilian. "Bloody awful big things."

"I know."

"I wonder what they'll do about the school now," said Lilian, musingly. She was cozy in a chic woolen top and a little beret, even though they were inside.

"What do you mean?" said Rosie. "They'll patch it up and fix it."

Lilian raised her eyebrows.

"They've been trying to shut that school for years. Bus all the children to Carningford."

Rosie looked horrified.

"But they can't! It'll kill the village!"

Lilian nodded.

"I know. It'll be the end of us, to be sure."

Rosie felt a hand of fear clutch at her heart.

"They wouldn't close the school?"

"Well, it's obviously dangerous . . . and enrollment has been falling."

"But parents move here for the little class sizes!"

"Then they move right away again when their children get to secondary. It's not really sustainable. And Manly's too."

"What about Manly's?"

Manly's was the defiantly unfashionable boutique in town.

"Well, she does all the uniforms, doesn't she? She stops supplying those, she's really in trouble. It's not like anyone wants her fuchsia size 18 cocktail dresses, and once you've bought one waxed jacket, that's pretty much all you need for the rest of your life . . . You need a waxed jacket, by the way."

"Thank you, Lilian," said Rosie, but her brain was whirring.

They wouldn't shut the school, would they? Lipton was so proud it had managed to hang on to its post office, its Spar, its pub, its chippy—it even had a bus service, of sorts. But losing the school would rip the heart from them.

"It'll be fine," she said. "There's no way the council could be that evil."

"No," said Lilian. "Elected officials never work in a disgusting way."

"Are you talking about democracies, Lilian?" came an imperious voice. "Awful things, never bloody work."

Rosie bit her lip as Lady Lipton bustled into the room, looking as usual a combination of ridiculous—she was wearing far too many slightly holed clothes—and rather magnificent—her cheekbones and gait rendered her dignified whatever the circumstances. It was, Rosie had ascertained, slightly arrogant and slightly habitual, the way Lady Lipton dressed, as if she simply didn't care (she obviously didn't), but also as if the reason she didn't care was that she felt so socially superior to everybody else. It was almost a way of showing off—"My house has so many rooms I can't possibly heat it so I need to wear four cardigans that have been in the family for several generations."

"Lilian, I swear you are too young to be in here."

"I know," said Lilian complacently. "It's nice for the others."

Rosie stood up.

"Hello," she said.

"What have you done to my boy now?" said Lady Lipton, without smiling. Rosie was so surprised by this that she forgot to close her mouth.

"What on earth do you mean?" she said. She hadn't, to be fair, slept as much as she would have liked.

"Well, you persuaded him into that school."

"I did not! He was desperate to do it."

Lady Lipton gave Lilian a sideways look. She thought Stephen's job should be with her, running the crumbling estate. Having a son who was a primary school teacher seemed to her to be some kind of admission of failure, particularly after all the money they'd spent on his schooling, as she announced from time to time.

"And he's a wonderful teacher," Rosie went on crossly.

"Oh, don't get wound up," said Lady Lipton. "A teacher and a shop girl, perfect combination really. Now, Lilian, have you heard how awful it all was? Shall we go through it again?"

"It *was* awful," said Rosie honestly. "It's a miracle no one was hurt worse. It's going to take Edison a long time to get back on his feet as it is."

"Well, you've got Stephen back where you want him," said Lady Lipton, which was such a vicious thing to say that Rosie was on the point of walking out.

Instead, and fired up by the last twenty-four hours—which included a sleepless night—Rosie drew herself up and said, "As you well know, Stephen only goes where he wants to go. Amazing it's never with you, isn't it?"

Then she left, feeling wildly guilty and a bit pleased. And then guilty again. And then happy. And then she remembered that whatever she thought, this was still Stephen's mother so she had a duty of politeness, and making Lady Lipton think the worst of her didn't help anything. So by the time she got back to the shop she was cursing.

She hated driving Stephen's old Land Rover. It was a temperamental beast he'd inherited from his father, so it was about forty years old. It had no proper heating, no power steering and was a vehicle of last resort, but at the moment she had no choice. She packed Mr. Dog into the front seat, wrapped up in a blanket, then remembered that hospitals weren't too hot on the whole dog thing, and if she left him outside in the car, he'd probably freeze to death, so she decided to drop him off at Tina's house, with a huge bag of jellies for Kent and Emily.

"Hello!" said Tina. The children were romping around, still in their pajamas, playing bears with Jake, Kent keeping his cast well up in the air.

"Oh, look at you guys," said Rosie, genuinely pleased. "You're like a Christmas advert in here."

Tina took her to one side.

"It's all fake," she said quickly to Rosie. "I keep wanting to throw up. I've never felt so terrified in my whole life."

"I know," said Rosie, giving her a quick hug. "I know."

"When I stood outside that school and every other kid came out except mine . . ."

"You can't think like that," said Rosie. "I know. You just have to think that it didn't happen. It didn't."

"I can't sleep a wink," said Tina.

"Me neither."

Rosie nodded into the sitting room. "It looks like someone's being helpful."

Tina lost her anxious look for just a second.

"Yes," she said, "he's been amazing. And the children, they've kind of forgotten all about it, except for Kent being this massive hero. He's happy as Larry. Jake's just carrying on being sweet. I'm the only one who's become a complete basket case."

"I know I don't have firsthand experience apart from Mr. Dog," said Rosie. "But I think that might just be motherhood."

She thought briefly of Lady Lipton.

"Well, most motherhood."

Tina nodded.

"You're medical and know this stuff. Will it stop?"

Rosie heard the squeals of delight as Mr. Dog plucked up the courage to leave her side and join the revels next door.

"If it doesn't, you go see Moray and he'll recommend someone for you to talk to," she said. "But between you and me, yes, it will. It might take a while, but for most people, they pick up again. Okay? You're being totally normal."

Tina smiled.

"Totally normal."

"Yes."

"Crying in the bath?"

"Check."

"Not letting them out of my sight."

"Check."

Tina shook her head.

"Fine."

Rosie peered back into the happy scene.

"It seems to me someone is very happy to help you with everything you're going through."

Tina colored prettily.

"I know," she said. "I'm very lucky. I'm so . . . so . . . Oh, I'm going again."

The tears started down her face.

"Let it out," said Rosie, giving her a cuddle. "I'll pick up Mr. Dog later, okay? Thanks."

"Not at all," said Tina. "Look at them. They've forgotten all about it."

"Children are very resilient," said Rosie. "And so are you. I promise."

Rosie drove as slowly as she dared along the snowy winding roads. Would it ever stop? She was nervous now too; nervous of a huge lorry, out of control, looming out of nowhere, smashing everything in its path with a terrible devastation. She inched her way to Carningford, and to the hospital.

She'd made a special effort tonight, after yesterday. Her hair was washed, she'd reapplied lipstick in the car and she was carrying an enormous bag of mixed bonbons, and some grapes for vitamin C.

Stephen had been moved to a side room and she had to scrub up to avoid giving him an infection. The hospital was quiet, so he had the room to himself. She knocked, feeling suddenly nervous, then feeling that was utterly ridiculous. They'd lived together for nearly a year; it was absurd to be worried.

But she knew him; she knew how his earlier experiences had affected him. Being proud and sensitive was such a tough combination. Please, please let him not be too upset. She thought about what had happened in Africa. He'd been working out there as a teacher and had accompanied his class on a field trip. One of his children had strayed off the track and stepped on a land mine. Two boys, brothers, had died, and Stephen had suffered severe wounds—both physical and mental. It had taken meeting Rosie for him truly to come back to himself, something his high-handed mother, who found communicating with her wayward son extremely difficult had never forgiven her for.

But could something like this set him back?

She didn't hear a reply, so she pushed open the heavy door. She paused for a second, then stepped into the room.

Stephen was lying on his front, which at first gave him the aspect of a sullen teenager, but Rosie realized immediately that it was of course to avoid pressure on his scar. He could barely lift his head.

"Hello," he said glumly.

"Hello," she said. "You look like you're going surfing."

He didn't raise a smile.

"Please," he said. "Cresta Run."

Rosie went over and kissed his head.

"Hey," she said.

"Hey," he said. "I look stupid."

Rosie glanced at his back; his side was swathed in bandages, but the muscles, bare in the overheated hospital room, still stood out.

"Actually," she said, "you look surprisingly hot for someone who's just had a bum transplant."

Stephen tried to force a smile.

"I think I preferred things a lot more yesterday when I was monged off my face on all the drugs."

"Did you not get any drugs today?"

She flipped through his chart.

"I did," said Stephen. "But not the really good ones like yesterday."

Rosie raised her eyebrows. "They gave you diamorphine?"

"Mmmm," said Stephen.

"Yes, well, no wonder, that's basically heroin."

"Oh," said Stephen suddenly.

"What?"

"Nothing. Only I thought I wrote a song and it was brilliant. But that was probably the heroin, wasn't it?"

"I must hear your song," said Rosie instantly.

"Um, no."

"Was it about me?"

Stephen winced and smiled again.

"Seriously, I thought it was going to change the shape of music forever."

"Was it to the tune of 'Agadoo'?"

"Now you come to mention it . . ." He winced again.

"Is it awfully painful?"

"Skin is REALLY SORE," said Stephen. "It's all right when it's your insides. Peoples' appendices don't feel a thing, do they? It's that skin thing that will really do for you. I wish I hadn't seen *Prometheus.*"

"Everyone wishes that," said Rosie reassuringly.

"Have you seen Edison?"

"I'm going to see him when I get bored with hanging out with you."

"Is he going to . . ."

Stephen tried to twist his neck around. It looked painful.

"I think so," said Rosie. "It's going to be a long road, a really long road, but it looks like . . . he should walk again. Moray thinks so."

There was a long silence.

"Oh, dear Jesus," said Stephen finally. "Thank God." A single tear ran down his cheek.

"Can you get that?"

Rosie leapt up with a tissue; he really couldn't move.

"Didn't anyone tell you?"

"Yes," said Stephen. "But I only believed it coming from you."

Rosie put her arms around his neck.

"Are you going to be okay about this?" she demanded.

He knew immediately what she meant. Stephen's brusqueness could sometimes mask a real fragility, and Rosie was worried about this more than anything else.

She moved her hands to his face.

"My love," she said.

He cast his eyes down.

"I . . . I . . . You know, at the moment, they're giving me things to make me sleep, so I don't really have to think about it . . ."

"There's nothing to think about," said Rosie fiercely. "There was a terrible accident. You saved a child. You got the rest out. It would have been much, much worse without you. What happened before wasn't an accident, it was evil. They are not the same."

"I know," said Stephen.

There was a pause.

"But the smell. And the dust, and the noise and the darkness. That was all exactly the same."

Rosie spent an hour with him reading him stories about celebrities out of the newspaper until he begged for mercy. Then they came to change his bandages, and she went upstairs.

Intensive Care was very quiet. There was no bustle, no patients making demands, just the squeak of rubber-soled white shoes on highly polished floors, and the steady beep of monitors and the decompression of breathing apparatus. It felt disconnected from the rest of the hospital, a bustling ship.

She found Hester and Arthur by the farthest bed, closest to the window.

"Hello," she whispered. There was no real need to whisper, nobody was napping, but it felt right somehow. Hester was standing up, despite her pregnancy; her face held none of the full-moon glow of women preparing to give birth, but was pale and drawn and sleepless.

They acknowledged her but didn't respond. Rosie decided not to take out the Edinburgh rock she'd brought, Edison's favorite.

"What are they saying?" she asked. Hester gazed at her as if she wasn't there, but Arthur looked grateful.

"They've put him in this coma," he said.

Edison's body on the bed looked absolutely tiny; he seemed younger without his dirty glasses on, and very pale. He was breathing peacefully, tubes everywhere, like an aberration; something foreign in the little body.

"It's to stop him moving his head. They need to keep him absolutely still for as long as possible. Give him the best possible chance."

Rosie nodded.

"That makes sense."

"Then they're going to put a cast on him. . . . He's going to be on his back here, then they'll keep turning him . . ."

He swallowed, deeply upset at having to talk about his only son in this way.

"It's for the best."

Hester sniffed loudly. Arthur motioned Rosie away.

"She's taking it very hard," he said.

"Of course she is," said Rosie. "Of course she is. Can't you get her to sit down?"

"She won't. She hates modern medicine and all it stands for."

"Even now?" said Rosie.

"She hates giving up," said Arthur, looking slightly sheepish.

"Well, she wouldn't be able to treat this with herbs, would she?" said Rosie, then felt ashamed of her harsh tongue.

"No," said Arthur. "But it makes it very difficult, having to interact with doctors and so on."

"She doesn't have to interact," said Rosie. "She just needs to say thank you."

Arthur smiled nervously, and Rosie instantly felt awful and harsh. To change the subject, she indicated the large pile of paper next to the bed.

"What's this?"

Hester looked at it dully.

"Oh, Mrs. Baptiste dropped it off," said Arthur. Rosie went over and looked. It was a huge pile of cards and letters, drawn by all the children in the class.

"We miss you, Edison," said one. Another had a very clear drawing of a stick man with a massive head and dirty glasses.

"I think they've caught him," said Rosie, smiling.

"We MISS YOU DOING ALL THE TAKING IN CLAS," said another. They were all colorful and beautifully drawn, many with a Christmas theme.

"Oh, these are wonderful!" said Rosie. "We have to get these strung up so they're the first thing he sees. How fond people are of him and how much they miss him."

Hester glanced up briefly.

"Would you like me to put them up?" asked Rosie, desperate to be useful. "I'll bring some tape tomorrow. I'm in every day anyway, to see Stephen, you know."

Hester nodded blankly. Rosie wondered if she even knew

that it was Stephen who'd saved her son. If she did, she didn't seem very interested. But then, she obviously had a lot more on her mind than that.

Rosie kissed Edison gently on the cheek. It was as cold as a marble statue.

"Oh, little man," she said. "I miss your prattle."

And then it was back on the long lonely journey to an empty house with accounts to be done and stock to be counted, where the fire was unlit, and dinner was unmade, and it was so cold and empty without Lilian or Stephen there, and Rosie was so anxious and exhausted that, after she finished her work, she had a single glass of water and took herself unhappily to bed.

Chapter 7

Rosie had expected the school to reopen the next day—there were still another three weeks before the Christmas break—but it didn't. She opened the shop as usual, as much to let the gossip come to her as to sell sweets. Although she sold plenty of those; lots of children were getting terribly spoiled after their big fright, and she was completely sold out of Edinburgh rock for Edison; he could probably build his own full-sized rock out of it by now. Which would, she mused, have been just the kind of project that would have appealed to him.

Everyone gathered at the sweetshop for news, then headed down to Malik's and the bakery and Manly's for more news, then sometimes popped back in again on their way home just to update everybody.

Mrs. Baptiste came in for cough drops and was forced to admit that yes, the local council had suggested that the children be bused to Carningford Primary "until a solution could be found."

"That sounds ominous," said Rosie.

Mrs. Baptiste nodded her head.

"I agree," she said. "As soon as they start, there'll be no go-ing back. And it's an hour there and an hour back; they're too little for that long a day. So what will happen?"

"They'll move away," said Rosie glumly.

"Yes," said Mrs. Baptiste sadly.

"But the parents will get anxious, won't they?" said Rosie. "About the children missing school."

Mrs. Baptiste sighed. "Yes, I know."

Just then the bell tinged, and Lady Lipton swept in. "I'm going to see Stephen," she announced crossly. "Can you give me his toothbrush and a change of clothes."

"Of course," said Rosie, still feeling guilty about being so aggressive the other day.

"I'm sorry if I was rude before."

Lady Lipton looked completely surprised.

"You?" she said, as if Rosie were a bug who'd passed her on the street. "Oh, I didn't notice."

Rosie internally rolled her eyes.

"Okay, good," she said. "You can take him his post too."

A huge mound of cards had arrived that morning, illustrated similarly to Edison's.

'What is this rubbish?" said Lady Lipton.

"I'll take it," said Rosie, conscious that it might end up as kindling otherwise. "I think he'll be out by the end of the week."

"Good," said Lady Lipton. "I've no truck with hospitals."

Rosie popped out and came back with a change of clothes and the new Tom Holland book.

"Tell him I'll be up later," she said. "In fact, if you want to wait, we could go together."

Lady Lipton looked astonished.

"Why would we—"

"Never mind!" said Rosie quickly. "Just tell him I'll be up later."

As Henrietta clanged out of the shop, Mrs. Baptiste and Rosie exchanged a glance.

"Oh, she is DIFFICULT," said Rosie.

"She's all right," said Mrs. Baptiste with the instinctive village loyalty. "And you know . . ."

She paused, as if something had just struck her.

Rosie saw it straightaway from her face.

"She does have the space," said Mrs. Baptiste.

"Oh my God!" said Rosie. "I didn't think about that. Move the school! Do you think she would? Yes. I mean, she'd have to, for Stephen's sake."

"Doesn't she hate him being a teacher?"

"Yes, but if it was under her roof . . . she could keep an eye on him."

"And there'd be a million and one health and safety hoops to jump through," mused Mrs. Baptiste.

"Well, it's only a temporary emergency measure," said Rosie. "Just till the council fixes the school."

"Decides on a solution," corrected Mrs. Baptiste. "Well, it would save them the cost of a bus."

"I think it's a great idea," said Rosie. "Well, no, it's a terrible idea given that Lipton Hall is unheated and slightly falling down. But it's about a million times better than sending them all away. If Lipton loses its children, it'll lose everything."

"I completely agree," said Mrs. Baptiste. "So would you be a darling and ask her?"

"WHAT?" said Rosie, spying a well-laid trap. "Me? Why do *I* have to ask her?"

"Because she'll do what Stephen wants. Anything from us, it'll just go straight over her head."

"She hates me."

"Don't be daft," said Mrs. Baptiste. "She talks to you. If she really hated you, she'd never notice you at all."

"I think I'm going to join the Socialist Workers Party," said Rosie crossly.

"Could you get Stephen to do it?"

"He's a bit off his box at the moment," said Rosie. "Also, anything that involves him setting foot in that place for longer than is strictly necessary makes him extremely uncomfortable."

"There you go then," said Mrs. Baptiste. "You know, in the old days, Lilian would have done it."

"Now you're just trying to make me feel guilty on purpose," moaned Rosie.

"Is it working?"

"Yes."

The phone rang.

"SO, I've booked the tickets," came a loud and lively voice. "We can't wait!"

Rosie's heart stopped. She had completely and utterly forgotten about Angie. Or, to be strictly accurate, Angie, Pip, Desleigh, Shane, Kelly and Meridian. All of them. Descending.

"Oh my God," said Rosie.

"What is it now?" said Angie. "It's not like you ever get up to anything in that sleepy little place you live in."

"No," said Rosie. "Hardly anything at all. When are you arriving?"

"Next Tuesday! We'll be there for two weeks! Isn't it bonzer!"

"You don't say bonzer," said Rosie. "Surely. Do you? Do you say that now?"

"Oh yeah! Good on yer!" said Angie. "Listen, it's twenty-six degrees today. The kids aren't going to know what's hit them."

"They sure aren't," said Rosie, glancing outside at the deep drifts. There had been no more snow today, but the top had crusted over with ice. The attic room, without Stephen's comforting presence, had become unspeakably cold; there was frost on the inside of the windows. The previous evening Rosie had had to pile every article of clothing from her wardrobe on top of the bed just to keep the heat in. Fortunately, the combination of a sleepless night the night before and the knowledge that nobody was actually going to die had combined to make her drop off almost immediately, whereupon she had dreamed repeatedly that she was being buried alive.

"Okay," said Rosie. "Great! We can't wait . . . either . . . Did you say you've booked the flights?"

"Booked, paid for, non-refundable!" said Angie. "We had to use up basically all of our savings, but it's totally going to be worth it, I can tell."

Rosie gently let her head slip to the countertop. Mr. Dog, who was having a quick snooze underneath, reached up and licked her hand. Rosie nuzzled him.

"You," she said after she'd hung up the phone, "are the only uncomplicated person I can relate to around here."

"Aooow," said Mr. Dog in a comforting fashion.

"We have never been busier," said Rosie to Lilian.

"Don't show off," said Lilian fussily. "They feel sorry for the children."

"Yes, I know that," said Rosie. "I was just looking for, you know, the bright side."

They were doing up the home for Christmas in nice traditional wreaths, no cheap tinsel. Every resident had been invited to contribute something from their own past Christmases, and Rosie had brought up the carved wooden manger, which fit beautifully on top of the drawing room mantel.

Lilian sniffed.

"Well, when you have to sell the house and the shop, try and sell it to some City banker who'll pay far too much money for it, so I can stay here. I don't want to come and live in your London squat."

Rosie was horrified.

"What do you mean, London squat? I live here."

"Yes, but what would you do with no school, no sweetshop? Live off Stephen's teaching earnings?" Lilian chuckled, a hollow sound.

"I can't believe you're being so defeatist about everything."

"I'm an old lady," said Lilian. "The world is in the business of letting me down. It's not for the fainthearted, getting old, you know."

"Well, that's fortunate," said Rosie. All the trepidation she'd felt about approaching Lady Lipton about the school situation suddenly drained away in the face of Lilian's lack of confidence. She'd show her!

"Actually, I have a plan to save the school."

"Do you?" said Lilian sniffily.

"Yes! We're going to move it into Lipton Hall."

Lilian blinked twice and her lips twitched.

"You've mentioned this to Hetty?"

"Not exactly."

"Okay. Well I can't imagine anything she'd like more than fifty snotty-nosed brats charging around the Constables. And who'll pay to heat it?"

"The council," said Rosie stubbornly. She had only the very vaguest idea of who the council was and what it did.

"Oh, Roy Blaine?" said Lilian. "He's agreed to help you, has he?"

"He's not—?" said Rosie.

"Head of the council," confirmed Lilian.

Roy Blaine was the local dentist who'd been waging war against the sweetshop for years; he'd wanted to buy the property and turn it into a car park last year, but Rosie had managed to fend him off. This had made him more disagreeable than ever.

"Well, he doesn't want Lipton to shut down!"

"He's talking about moving to Carningford, taking on a bigger place," said Lilian. "He reckons he's gotten too big for Lipton. So if the council sells the schoolhouse to developers and gets a load of second-home incomers in here, it'll be all to the good as far as he's concerned. I heard him talk to his grandfather about it. He shouts. He pretends it's because Jim is deaf, but he isn't in the slightest bit deaf. Roy just likes everyone to know how well he's doing. He is such an insipid worm of a man. And those teeth scare me."

Roy's teeth had been veneered and whitened to within an inch of their life. The rest of his face was sunken and a little gray. The effect was horrific.

"Oh BUGGERATION," said Rosie, exasperated. "Do you think *you* could talk Hetty around?"

Lilian looked at her.

"I'm not in the business of upsetting my few visitors by irritating them," said Lilian.

"Really? You don't seem to mind with me."

Lilian ignored this.

"Where's tea? It's scones today."

"I'm going to move into this care home," said Rosie, not for the first time.

"So tell me about Angie and Pip and everyone," said Lilian. "Do you think Angie will remember me?"

"Of course she will!" said Rosie. "Pip remembers you too. You used to send us sweets at Christmas, and he used to guzzle the lot and throw up all over the place. Every single year."

Lilian smiled. "I have a soft spot for a greedy boy," she said. "It's the hoarders and the misers I can't abide."

"Everyone likes Pip," said Rosie. "He's the most laid-back guy on the planet. That's why Australia suits him so well."

Lilian nodded. "And the children?" She had a crotchety look for children, but it was all for show. Lilian had never forgotten a child she'd served—she knew half the assistants in the care home by their first names—and always had a generous hand on the scales for the poorer mites.

"Not sure," said Rosie tactfully. "I hear a lot of yelling. But that might be, you know, just 'kids' as a concept."

"Speaking of which," said Lilian, fixing her with her sharp eyes. "I don't believe I see you getting any younger."

"As always, my dear great-aunt, that's my cue to go," said Rosie, kissing the old lady gently on the cheek and nodding to Dorothy Isitt, Ida Delia's daughter, on the way out.

That left Stephen. He was lying on his side today, facing the window.

"Ha, you look like you're ignoring me," said Rosie. "Or posing for a life model class. Can I sketch you like this?"

"I have never been so fucking bored in my entire life," came the voice, slightly drawling. "I haven't slept a fucking wink and I want to go home."

"You're better," she observed and came around the other side.

"Ooh, you're growing a beard," she said. "Do you want me to shave you? Or no, maybe leave it, it's sexy. A bit painful. But quite sexy. Hmm."

"Ha, can you shush, please, so I can kiss you?" said Stephen. "Do notice I'm kissing you, even through my terrible pain."

"What would you rather have, a kiss from me through terrible pain or more drugs?"

"Don't make me answer that."

"When can I take you home?" said Rosie with feeling.

"Today if you like," said a passing nurse. "He's been nothing but a pain in the arse." But she had a smile on her face.

"Why do you get to be a pain in the arse but people still like you?" said Rosie once the nurse had gone. "It's really, really annoying that you're good looking."

"You still like me," said Stephen. "Don't you?"

"I do," said Rosie. "Do you still like me?"

"Yes."

"Good. Because you're not going to in about a minute."

She explained the plan to move the school to his mother's house.

"Oh Lord," said Stephen. "Really?"

"She'd do it for you."

"She'd do it for me and then lock me in the cellar."

"Just be clear. Say you're not going to move back in, you're not going to take on the estate, you're just going to borrow it for a bit."

Stephen bit his lip.

"Come on, what's the alternative?"

Stephen shrugged.

"Maybe they would be better off in Carningford, without some maniac trying to run them over. Be a bit safer."

He was facing the window, looking out over Rosie's shoulder.

"No," said Rosie. "Don't be stupid, okay? It was a freak accident. It's not even in the papers anymore."

Stephen shrugged.

"It happened. Maybe Lipton isn't the best place for them to be."

"You can't believe that," said Rosie, horrified. "You can't. You wouldn't leave Lipton to die."

"That's being a bit overdramatic, don't you think?"

"A lorry crashed into the building," she said. "There's a kid upstairs hovering between life and death. How dramatic do you want me to be? We need to fix it. And I want you . . . I want you to be where you belong. What are you going to do if they shut the school? You've always been a teacher."

"You're the one who wants me to move back to Mummy's house. I guess that's where I belong."

"Now you're being spoiled," said Rosie crossly.

Stephen shrugged. "You asked me what I thought and I told you."

"I didn't ask you what you thought," said Rosie. "I asked you to help me."

There was a pause.

"Look at me," said Stephen. "I can't even help myself."

Rosie slammed the huge pile of cards and letters down on his bed.

"Fine," she said. "I'll do it by myself."

"Are you being Saint Rosie again? You do just love those lost causes."

Rosie stared at him and decided to leave before she said something she'd regret.

"Yeah, anyway, so that went well," said Rosie to a comatose Edison.

Hester and Arthur weren't upstairs—perhaps they'd finally cracked and gone to get something to eat—and the ward was quiet. Rosie sat down by Edison's bed and held his hand, and sniveled a bit. But she didn't change her mind.

Downstairs, Stephen glanced again at his watch, wondering how long he would have to wait for his painkillers, trying not to focus on the pain. He shouldn't have snapped at Rosie, but really, couldn't he catch his breath, just for a moment? He . . . couldn't let her see how shaken up he was. Not by the operation, that had been nothing . . . but the whole thing had brought Africa right back to him, and he couldn't . . . he couldn't bear to feel that way again.

Chapter 8

The next day, Saturday, was torture. Rosie was hard-pressed at the shop, run off her feet. The Santa train had arrived, finally, and just as Tina had predicted, every family in town brought their children out to look at it tootle around the snowy little hillside on its merry way. Rosie liked seeing the happy faces of the children, such a contrast with their confused, pained looks of the week before. The adults, though, still bore traces of the fright they had all had.

"All right, all right," she said, knowing how very strongly Lilian would disapprove, and coming out with a bucket of little wrapped bonbons. "One each for all being very brave and doing exactly what Mrs. Baptiste told you."

The children converged on the bucket, chattering excitedly.

"Can I have one?" said Hye Evans, the other local doctor.

Rosie looked at him severely. "I don't know. Do you sit on the local council?"

"Of course," said Hye. "I'm an alderman."

"Are you going to close the school?"

"I'm afraid that's not something I can discuss with you," said Hye, his pink face turning red.

"Well, no sweetie," said Rosie. "Unless it would help?"

She watched as Hye stomped off. "I'm rubbish at corruption," she noted gloomily.

She hadn't been able to get the fight with Stephen out of her head. He hadn't texted her or anything, which meant he was obviously still adamant that he was right. She could barely serve the flow of customers without checking her phone every two minutes, even though she couldn't get a signal, and her face was so glum that Moray actually laughed when he swung by for some sweet golf balls to take to his new doctor boyfriend in the next village over. He was being very secretive about him for some reason.

"Look at you, exactly the right kind of person to be in charge of a sweetshop. What happened, eat too many of the lime sours?"

Rosie explained while frantically rearranging fudge.

"I'm not sure what you're saying here," said Moray, absent-mindedly helping himself to one of the golf balls. "Are you trying to tell me that Stephen is a stubborn old git?"

"YES," moaned Rosie.

"Oh my God, let me phone CNN," said Moray. "Well, you knew this. Hang on—ha! Did you think you'd be able to soften him up and change his mind?"

Rosie shrugged.

"No!"

"And make him do what you want? Ha! This isn't just about the school, is it? It's about your personal reputation as the only woman who can get Stephen to do something he doesn't want to do."

"It is not," said Rosie. "Except a bit."

"Ahh," said Moray. "Oh, you're so cute when you're cross. So, what are you going to do?"

"Wait for him to come around."

"Got two years, have you?"

"Bollocks," said Rosie. "He's not going to come around, is he? He just won't talk to his bloody mother."

"I would say," said Moray, "that anything he can do for anyone, he would always do for you."

Rosie half-smiled.

"You're going to need more of those golf balls."

"Oh, yes. So . . . ," said Moray.

"So you're saying . . ."

"If you want to save the school . . ."

"Into the lion's den," said Rosie unhappily. "Lady Lipton."

"The council is taking the vote on Monday. They can have the buses out by Wednesday."

"Dammit!" said Rosie. "Damn damn damn. Will you support me?"

"Hmm, what do you want me to do?" said Moray. "I'm not on the council. I could make several subtle poisons with which to dispose of Hye and no one would ever suspect a thing, but I think I would probably have done that already."

"Just talk me up," said Rosie. "Tell people."

"I've been talking you up since you got here," said Moray. "Then you go and let me down by wearing ridiculous clothes and pulling unlikely people. What's that?"

He spied a parcel by the till and grabbed at it. It was a tiny ruffled red coat with a tartan trim.

"You're not?" he said.

"Ssh," said Rosie. "It's freezing outside."

Moray continued staring at it in disbelief.

"If you seriously start dressing up your dog, you'll be dead in this town."

Early the next morning, after a long evening with still no word from Stephen apart from a depressing exchange of formal text messages in which they'd both ascertained that the other person was "all right" but with no further discussion of the matter in hand, Rosie woke up and decided enough was enough. And she was going to cycle. No snow was actually falling right at this moment, so it was as good a day as any: she was going stir-crazy without any exercise.

She left her bike by the gates at Lipton Hall and started trudging up the snowy driveway. Mr. Dog had had his final injections, so she'd decided to take him out on a long run, albeit wearing the very snazzy new red dog jacket, in the full and angry knowledge that Stephen would find it absolutely appalling.

The big house looked ominous and dark ahead, its chimney stacks cold and empty, its windows blank. Rosie had only been here once before, the previous year, for the hunt ball. Then it had been all lit up and glittering, cleaned up for the occasion, a glamorous outpost of light and dressed-up people getting drunk and dancing. Now, in the bleak snowy light it looked slightly sad; unloved and deserted.

Rosie had been in the country long enough to know that nobody opened their front door, you had to go round the back, but it didn't matter; as soon as he got close enough, Mr. Dog set up a delighted howling as three other dogs, clearly related to him in some way—but much smarter—came tearing out from the courtyard around the back and gave him a hero's welcome. All four of them rolled about together in the snow in delight. Rosie wasn't sure, but it looked as if Mr. Dog was trying to pull off his coat. None of the other dogs had coats.

"View halloo!" shouted Hetty, stalking around to the side gate. She was wearing, as usual, a bizarre collection of gardening clothes and ridiculously expensive cashmere that was full of holes.

"Um, hello," said Rosie. She'd wanted to practice a speech, but she'd ended up so cross at Stephen that she hadn't had time, spending half the evening mentally continuing her argument with him instead. She took a deep icy breath to gather her thoughts.

"Have you got time for tea?"

Hetty scratched Mr. Dog's neck.

"Hello, you lovely chap. What is this awful travesty you've been wrapped in then? Is she trying to make you gay? Are you trying to make your dog GAY?"

Rosie screwed up her eyes and reminded herself to keep calm.

"I thought he might be cold," she said.

"Nonsense!" said Hetty. "He's part lurcher, part . . ." She looked a bit doubtful. "Well, anyway. That's ridiculous. Next you'll be letting him sleep inside."

Rosie didn't explain that she had to let him sleep inside, on her bed, otherwise she'd freeze to death.

"And have you got a name for him yet, huh? What about Monty? Monty's a fine name for a dog. Or Ludo."

"Not yet," said Rosie. "Mostly we just call him Mr. Dog."

Hetty looked at her.

"Does Stephen call him that?"

"No," admitted Rosie. Stephen called him the most lovely gorgeous boy in the whole wide world, but she didn't want to explain that to Hetty.

"Well, quite. The dog needs a name, it's undignified."

Rosie noticed, however, that she was giving him a massive cuddle.

"Sorry, what did you want, *tea*?" She made it sound as if this were the most ridiculous demand she'd ever heard. Maybe it was, reflected Rosie.

"Hmph. Well we'll see if Mrs. Laird has anything."

Rosie was led through the back way for the first time. She was surprised by how cozy it was. A little kitchen, dated but immaculate, led on to what had obviously once been the big kitchen—it was a massive room with a huge table down the middle—but that now functioned as the kitchen diner. There was ample room down at the other end for a faded little three-piece floral suite and a small old-fashioned television; a massive, terrifying-looking Aga bathed the entire room in friendly warmth.

"Oh, it's lovely in here," said Rosie spontaneously.

"Hello, Rosie," said Mrs. Laird, who bought a pound of orange creams every Saturday night to watch her shows with and wouldn't have confessed in a million years that, contrary to all the town gossip about the London upstart, she thought Rosie was the best thing ever to happen to Stephen. She'd been the one who'd tried to look after him when he got back from Africa in such a state, and like everyone else, she'd failed until this girl had come along.

"I've just made some mince pies, would you like one?"

"Yes!" said Rosie. "It has been so long since someone offered me anything to eat, I can't tell you. I'm ravenous. Do you have lots?"

Mrs. Laird set out the tea things. On the rough-hewn old kitchen table, the sight of an incongruously perfect, utterly beautiful gold-rimmed fine china tea service, complete with milkmaid jar, a plate of lemon slices, and sterling sugar silver tongs seemed very strange, but neither Hetty nor Mrs. Laird seemed to notice a thing.

"It is lovely here," said Rosie, looking through the massive sash windows at the lazily falling snow. The dogs had followed them in and sniffed their way around the mince pies before being shoved out again to frolic in the snow.

"You should try upstairs," said Lady Lipton. "That'll put hair on your chest."

She set down her tea cup.

"So. Is this a social call?"

"Um." Rosie was halfway through a magnificent mince pie. She tried to swallow it as quickly as possible without coughing up too many crumbs.

"Um, kind of."

Hetty sighed.

"Spit it out then."

"The school," said Rosie.

"Never used it."

"Didn't you go there?"

Hetty looked at her incredulously.

"Of course not. I had a governess. Gerda Skitcherd. Do you remember her, Mrs. Laird?"

Mrs. Laird nodded. "First woman in town to get a divorce."

"That's right! Poor little Maeve."

"The receptionist at the doctor's?" asked Rosie in amazement.

"Oh yes," said Hetty. "That's right. Well, it turned out for the best then."

"She's lovely."

"She is, but SUCH a scandal."

They enjoyed their mince pies in a slightly more leisurely way after that, trying to bond over gossip, even if it was forty years old.

"So, the school," prodded Rosie gently.

"Yes. When are they going to fix it?"

"Well. That's the thing. They don't want to fix it."

"What do you mean, they don't want to fix it?"

"They want to bus all the children out of the village. Take them all to Carningford."

"Oh, that's dreadful," said Mrs. Laird, who had two grand-children at the school. "Poor mites. They need their school."

"And if the school goes . . ." said Rosie.

"Well, the town will go," said Lady Lipton. "It's a dreadful shame."

"Yes," said Rosie. "Yes, it is. Which is why I was thinking . . ."

Lady Lipton made an inquiring face. Suddenly it seemed to Rosie that she was suggesting the most ridiculous idea ever.

"Um, I was thinking . . ."

"Yes? Spit it out, dear."

"Um, maybe we could have the school here." The last bit came out in a bit of a mumbled rush.

"The what?"

"The school. Just until they get it fixed, have it here."

"In this kitchen?"

"No, but in this building."

Lady Lipton looked around in horror.

"I mean, you've got the space, and . . . it wouldn't be for long. We could make the council fix it . . . tell them we don't need their buses . . ."

"But you can't just turn a house into a school," said Lady Lipton. "This place is protected."

"Yes, but for special measures . . . or they could be your guests. Just as a temporary measure. We'd only need two rooms."

"But what about the cleaning? And the toilets? Children throw up almost constantly in my experience. And the heating?"

"Well, the funds that aren't being used to heat the school right now would have to come to you," said Rosie. "We'd just need to talk to the council."

"And you think Blaine will go for that, do you?"

"You're on the council though," said Rosie quietly. "And I think if anyone could talk other people into things, it would be you."

"Would it?" said Hetty, a small smile playing around her mouth. "Looks like it's also something you like trying your hand at. But honestly, Rosemary, it's just not practical."

"Of course it's not practical," said Rosie. "Practical would be sending in some builders to fix the school. THAT would be practical. If the bloody council would actually do it."

"You know we're responsible for more than just Lipton," said Hetty.

"Yes," said Rosie stubbornly. "But this is the place you really care about."

"Ofsted won't allow it," said Lady Lipton.

"Ofsted wouldn't deny you anything, not after all the press. It's for two weeks." Rosie played her trump card. "And Stephen gets out tomorrow. . . . He'll be here. Every day."

Her voice faltered a little as she said it.

Lady Lipton paused, then started in again.

"It would be torturous," said Lady Lipton. "The noise. It would upset the dogs. And it would be too much work."

Mrs. Laird was cleaning up the cups and saucers.

"No, it wouldn't," she said, her voice slightly trembly. She wasn't at all used to contradicting her employer. "No, it wouldn't. I'd get my church rota up here."

Hetty stared at her.

"Are you telling me you clean the church in your *spare time*?" she asked in amazement.

"I like things nice," said Mrs. Laird. "I think . . . I think everyone in Lipton would like things to be nice for the children, after the shock they've had. Those schools in Carningford . . . they're pretty tough. It's too long a day for our little ones. I think . . . I think we owe them."

Both Hetty and Rosie were silent after this little speech. Rosie mouthed "thank you" behind Lady Lipton's back. Lady Lipton shook her head.

"I'm sure I won't be able to get it through," she said slowly.

"But you'll try?" said Rosie eagerly.

"There's an emergency meeting tomorrow. To talk about the buses."

"We don't need the buses!"

"All right, all right, hold your horses. A week, okay? I'll take them in for a week, for heating money. After that, it'll be off my hands." Rosie felt like kissing her but wisely did not.

"And now I'm going to church. You should come to church. Everyone thinks you're a heathen."

"I am a total and utter heathen," said Rosie. "But I'd pray quite a lot if it would help the school."

Rosie left after repeating her thanks so often that she realized she was in danger of becoming very annoying. Lady Lipton kept also saying that it probably wouldn't happen, that it was a terrible idea and that it would leave the house even more of a wreck than it was already. After Rosie had retrieved Mr. Dog from his pile of brothers and cousins—he wouldn't come when called; Hetty had stood there and sniffed and suggested she get him trained immediately—she picked him up, took him out of his ridiculous jacket, for which he licked her face massively in gratitude, and said goodbye one final time.

"Honestly," said Hetty. "Between you, Mrs. Laird, Stephen and bloody Lilian bugging me to let the school thing happen, I haven't had a second to myself. Bloody phone hasn't stopped ringing."

Rosie stopped in her tracks.

"What?" she said, sure she'd misheard. "Stephen called you?"

Hetty rolled her eyes.

"I might have known you two would cook up something like this between you."

"Really? Ha! HA!" she said. The ridiculous lightness in her shoulders suddenly made her realize how much her disagreement with Stephen had been weighing her down. "Really? That's amazing. Amazing."

And before the older woman could object, she darted forward and kissed her quickly on the cheek.

Chapter 9

Thank you."

"It's still a ridiculous idea."

"I know. Thank you, though."

"I have to turn my phone off."

"Stop being annoyed with yourself that you did a nice thing."

"I didn't do anything. I reflected on the logic of the position."

"You did a good thing, Stephen Lakeman."

"Could you stop bothering me on this number, please, whoever you are?"

"I'll pick you up tomorrow after the council meeting."

"If you're still dressing that dog up in ballgowns, please don't bother."

"I cannot believe how much gossip gets around this town."

"You've made him a laughingstock."

"He likes it."

"Right."

"Good night, you."

"Are you in bed?"

"Maybe."

"Is that dog there?"

"Awroa," said Mr. Dog.

"Okay, could you remove the dog, then tell me what you're wearing?"

Rosie looked down at her tartan flannel pajama bottoms and thermal top.

"He's gone," she lied, putting her hand over his muzzle.

"Go on then."

"Um, I'm wearing a push-up Agent Provacateur bra, with my breasts kind of spilling out the top of it . . ."

"Go on."

"I hope you're not doing something naughty in the hospital."

"I'm not, actually," said Stephen. "It's still too bloody painful. I feel like my skin is going to rip every time I move my arms. But I find it soothing to hear you talk to me."

"Wouldn't you rather hear a story?"

"Yes," said Stephen. "A story about the imaginary underwear you're wearing while you pretend you don't have the dog in the bed."

"Okay," said Rosie, smiling. "Well, I'm just unwrapping the long silken ties at the side of my navy satin French knickers trimmed with red lace . . ."

"Awroa," said Mr. Dog, settling himself down comfortably on his duvet, and Rosie continued to talk on the phone, and outside the snow fell again until she could tell by the breathing at the other end of the line that Stephen was finally asleep.

Ironically, the council meeting was usually held in the school-house, which was still surrounded by police tape. They had adjourned instead to the Red Lion, the pub's convivial atmosphere slightly marred by the tension evident in the room. Rosie had to sit outside until the matter of the school came up on the agenda. She was surprised when she was called in to see no sign of Hye. Roy, on the other hand, was looking at her with an unpleasant sneer on his face.

"Ah, MISS Hopkins."

He emphasized the "miss." Rosie had heard Roy was married, but she steadfastly refused to believe it. She also didn't believe he could go out in direct sunlight, eat garlic or touch a cross.

"Here for the good of the town's children as usual, I suppose?"

"Always," said Rosie. She looked around. Lady Lipton was chairing. An empty seat where she guessed Hye was meant to be. Roy, and his lawyer brother, looking ponderous in a gray suit. The nice woman from the bakery. The fat Reverend, looking cheery as ever at the prospect of a free cup of tea, and both Dorothy and Peter Isitt, who ran the farm across the way. Dorothy had never liked Rosie ever since she accidentally ruined her vegetable patch. She eyed Rosie balefully.

Rosie was tempted to make a speech, but it wasn't really the right time to do it, so she decided to just focus on the most important thing.

"This is best for the children," she said. "It's clearly the best. They've had a fright. Sending them away is a terrible idea."

Roy showed off his ghastly teeth.

"I believe what's best for the children is the best educational environment. Not a draughty, unsuitable room, but a state-of-the-art primary facility with a running track and a new play-ground, as well as professional teachers in the best of health."

"Yes, but it's an hour away," said Rosie.

"Added to this, the money the town would save busing the children would allow much-needed repairs and work required in the village for the benefit of everyone."

"There won't be a village if you shut the school," begged Rosie. "It'll just turn into some chocolate-box second-homers' place, full of retired people and just pointless."

"I didn't realize you thought Lipton was pointless," said Roy. "No doubt you'll be wishing to shoot right back to London then, your 'first' home."

Rosie bit her lip. This wasn't going well at all. She looked at Lady Lipton imploringly, but Hetty was having none of it.

"The money we save," said Roy, "could do so much. And the buildings here were old anyway. They needed any number of improvements we simply can't fund. For so few children it simply doesn't make economic sense."

"But it makes our kind of sense," said Rosie, hot-faced and tongue-tied. "It makes emotional sense. It's just right to have our own school for our own children."

"It's not about keeping our children here," said Roy. "It's about what's best for them, remember? And I don't think what's best for them is letting a lorry plow through the middle of them."

Rosie bit her lip at the harshness of his words. He then pulled out a long list of figures. There was absolutely no deny-ing they made terrible reading. It would save a huge proportion of the budget to shut down the school. Rosie thought of Tina having to give up her job because she'd have to drive hours ev-ery day just to get Kent and Emily to school. How long before she jacked it in and moved? She thought of Stephen, and what he would do without a job—or would he commute, too? She hated this idea. Stephen wasn't made for sitting in a car. He was made for striding happily with his stick in a town where everyone knew him, teaching his own way—Mrs. Baptiste let him get on with things—instead of stuck in endless meetings and marking sessions. He would be miserable in Carningford, with its chain stores and fast-food outlets and 2-for-1 drinks nights, lit up by neon signs. Saturday night in town was an absolute no-go area unless you wanted to get into a fight. She sighed. But the figures . . .

After everyone had had a chance to properly digest them, and a few more people had pontificated one way or the other, it came time for the vote. Roy was looking smug, confident that his economic talk would prevail. And then the hands went up.

"All those in favor of moving the children to Carningford, active immediately?"

Roy, his brother and Dorothy Isitt raised their hands.

Roy looked annoyed.

"And against?"

The woman from the bakery, Lady Lipton and, to Rosie's surprised delight, Peter Isitt raised their hands. He'd be in trouble with Dorothy tonight. She was already shooting him rude looks across the table.

"Well, Hye agrees with me," said Roy immediately and fussily. "He told me already, we can't afford it."

"But Hye's not here," said Lady Lipton.

"But he would vote against! He told me already."

"Unfortunately, Hye's not here," repeated Lady Lipton. "And as chairman of the council, I'm afraid I have the casting vote. Which means I have to welcome an enormous bunch of the little brats into my own home. I can't believe what I was thinking of."

Rosie had leapt up excitedly.

"Yay!"

Roy looked absolutely furious.

"But Hye—"

"It's too late!" said Rosie, resisting the temptation to add, "in your face." "The vote's binding, isn't it?"

The woman from the bakery was already excitedly typing up the minutes.

"And Stephen gets home tonight!" said Rosie excitedly. "He can start back practically straightaway!"

Roy was still staring at his page of figures, stabbing it with a pen.

"Can you leave us while we get on with other business?" said Lady Lipton to Rosie, who bounced up before anyone tried to change their mind. She winked at Peter Isitt, who blushed and looked down at his hands.

Rosie swung by the doctor's office.

"Can't stop," said Moray, dashing into the waiting room. "I'm rushed off my feet today. Shorthanded."

"Because Hye . . ."

"Food poisoning," said Moray, his handsome face totally smooth and unreadable. "Poor chap. Something he ate disagreed with him."

Rosie stared at him.

"Of course you would never—"

"What on earth are you implying?" said Moray. "I hope you wouldn't be making dreadful medical and legal slurs against me."

"No," said Rosie quickly. "Not at all."

"If a man guzzles his body weight in oysters and foie gras at the golf club every night, statistics say it's bound to catch up with him sooner or later."

"Okay, okay."

And she waltzed up the high street to tell Tina the wonderful news.

Rosie was terrified of driving home in the dark on the snow-covered road. Having an irritable passenger behind her wasn't particularly helping.

"Watch out for that," Stephen was saying. He was, ridiculously, lying along one of the sideways seats in the back of the Land Rover, piled high with blankets. Rosie felt as if she were driving a mission in the Second World War. But sitting up was still a little too painful even though the doctors had said his wounds were healing faster than anyone they'd ever known. He could stand and move around perfectly well, but sitting was more difficult.

"They should have fitted you with a robot bum," Rosie had said, and Stephen had ignored her in front of the consultant. He had made a couple of remarks about missing the painkillers, but seemed quite chipper on the whole. Only Rosie could tell from the clench of his jaw that he was still in a lot of pain.

"Watch out for deer on the road."

"Deer?" said Rosie. "Oh for goodness' sake. I slightly have

my hands full watching out for snow, ice, darkness, great big horrible lorries, hedges and schools. And I can't see any of those things. And someone is distracting me from the back."

Stephen flopped back on the bench seat. Rosie checked out his strong profile in the rearview mirror. He was biting his lip distractedly. She had to force herself to keep her eyes on the road, he looked so handsome. They hadn't seen another car in miles; it felt as if they were alone in the universe. The moon shone full in a cloudless sky and lit up the frosted countryside all around, so it was barely dark at all, despite Rosie's complaining. One by one, the bright yellow stars popped out, and the moon gave off a cold light so that the outline of the distant hills was visible. The cold and stillness gave them the feeling of being on an alien planet.

Stephen gazed out the window, steeling himself. This time he was not going to fall into his old trap of getting caught up in his head. He would not close his eyes and see, again and again and again, the shape of the huge lorry pushing a hole through the classroom; he would not hear the roar of the engine and the sharply rushing wind. He blinked and focused on the distant stars.

Rosie put on the radio. A young choirboy was singing "Do You See What I See?" very slowly and sweetly. It was incredibly beautiful. They both listened to it in silence. When it had finished, Rosie noticed Stephen surreptitiously wiping his eye.

"Are you CRYING, Lakeman?" she said, reaching back and squeezing his hand.

"NO," said Stephen, forcing himself to buck up. "It's so flipping cold in here my eyes are watering."

"That's right. You're not at all crying."

"No."

"'A star, a star . . . dancing in the night . . . with a tail as big as a kite,'" sang Rosie tunelessly.

"'And is it true?'" quoted Stephen, looking out at the night sky. "'And is it true?' For if it is . . .'"

"Are you going pious on me in my old age?" said Rosie.

"No," said Stephen. "But on a night like this . . . so silent . . ."

"Yes!" said Rosie. "Almost like, you know, some kind of SILENT NIGHT."

Stephen laughed, finally.

"Do you ever feel that things are meant to happen in a certain way, Rosebud?"

Rosie didn't take her eyes off the road.

"Of course not," she said.

"You don't think you and I were meant to meet? I mean, we wouldn't normally."

"What, because you're posh and I'm common as muck?"

"Yes," said Stephen.

"Oh," said Rosie. "Well, anyway, no, of course I don't."

"Nobody's up there guiding us?"

"Nobody was guiding those rebels in Africa, no," said Rosie softly. "It's rubbish. The idea that somehow some benevolent deity sends an angel to watch over whether American football players will win a match but wants every third baby in Liberia to die. It's disgusting. That God would bother about whether we fell in love but wouldn't bother that there are kids in India whose eyes get eaten by worms while they're still alive. Okay, you know, I don't THINK so.

"It's just us, my love. Making the best of the here and now."

Stephen was silent for a bit.

"Okay," he said. "Gosh, I didn't realize you felt so strongly about it."

"Try working in A and E," she said. "Anyway, you of all
people know life isn't fair."

"I know," said Stephen with a sigh. "Just, on a night like tonight . . . so beautiful . . . and I'm on my way home, and Edison
is getting better . . . No, you're right, of course."

He was still gazing out the window.

"Well, whatever gets you through the night," said Rosie. "If
it makes you happy."

"I think I'm just so relieved," said Stephen. "I'm coming
home, all fine, nice and cozy, and we're going to have a lovely
quiet Christmas and not go out at all, apart from to my bloody
mother's every day, but at least I'll be working . . . and Mrs.
Laird can bake us things, and we'll have Christmas just the two
of us in front of the fire, all to ourselves, and not get dressed all
day and it's going to be amazing. . . . It's not been easy, Rosie.
But it makes me happy now."

Rosie glanced at him one last time.

OH GOD, she thought in despair. I HAVE to tell him Angie's coming. I MUST.

But looking at his beautiful face, no longer screwed up in
pain, or irritable or cross, just tired and homesick, she found
she was too drained—or, to be strictly honest with herself, too
much of a coward—to tell him QUITE yet. She would, she
would, she would.

"All I Want for Christmas Is You" came on the radio.

"Now THIS is my religion," said Rosie quickly, whacking
up the volume, and they bopped home along the bumpy road
to Lipton.

Earlier the man had walked around the care home on his own. Matron had been welcoming but a little puzzled.

"So he's outside?"

"Yes, he's in the car," said Edward Boyd. "We're looking at homes . . . you're quite far away, but we heard really good things about you."

Cathryn Thompson raised her eyebrows.

"Well, that's nice."

Edward, whose car had barely a scratch on it, and who had not a clue about what had happened with the lorry, had emailed Moray after the incident in Rosie's shop, and Moray had obligingly sent back a list of decent homes that could cope with dementia. He'd made it entirely clear that Cathryn's was quite the best he'd seen, and Moray had seen them all.

"It's a bit of a drive, but nothing we don't mind making."

Cathryn looked at him. "Does he still know it's you?"

Edward shrugged.

"Sometimes. He spends a lot of time talking about his boyhood. . . . It's odd because when I was little, he never mentioned growing up at all. He was badly injured in the war, and we knew better than to ask him. But now he talks about it a lot."

"That's very common," she said. "People lose their recent memories but retain their old ones—especially youth. For some reason, adolescence writes itself ridiculously strongly on the brain, which, given what an awkward time it is in most people's lives, is a bit annoying. But it means that those memories stay, even when people can't recognize their nearest relatives. Your mother?"

"Breast cancer," said Edward. "It was . . . it was a long time ago now."

"And your father was fine?"

"No, he was heartbroken. But then he got over it, and he seemed all right."

"Did he meet anyone else?"

"He never did," said Edward. "We were really surprised, to be honest, he was only sixty, and a really handsome man."

He grimaced. "I take after my mother's bald chunky side of the family, I'm afraid. My father had a wonderful head of hair."

Cathryn nodded politely.

"But no, he was just a one-woman man, I think. He always kept to himself rather. I don't even know what happened to him in the war, not properly. Then in the last five years . . ."

Cathryn nodded.

"It's difficult to watch."

Edward looked out the window. He'd had to leave the engine running to ensure that his father didn't freeze.

"Money isn't a problem," he said. "It's just . . . oh, it's hard to say goodbye."

Lilian and Ida Delia were earwigging furiously through a partially open door.

"Is it a man?" came Lilian's voice finally.

Cathryn turned around. "Get back inside, you two," she said.

"Don't listen to them," she added to Edward. "They're boy-crazy."

"We just need a man to make up the . . . men contingent," said Ida Delia. "It's really not fair."

"Also apparently he's handsome," added Lilian.

"Have you been listening at the door all this time?"

Edward couldn't help smiling. The other homes he'd seen—the one his mother-in-law had ended up in—had been places of sadness and despair, simply waiting rooms for death. This seemed rather more like a nice country house hotel.

Of course that was reflected in the price, but they'd sold his father's house when he'd moved in and kept the money safe for exactly this, and, well, they were doing all right, had a bit put by. Of course they wouldn't inherit anything, and his dad probably wouldn't notice if they stuck him in the Ritz or a jail cell, but that didn't matter. It was about doing the right thing.

Edward believed very strongly in doing the right thing. He sometimes saw himself as being part of a thin line preventing the world from being overrun by texting hordes of terrifying hoodies. This meant he occasionally found the modern world a rude and uncertain place. But it also meant that when it came down to the wire, doing the right thing meant a lot to him, and he was bloody well going to do it now.

He eyed the two women.

"Are you the troublemakers around here?" he asked with a smile.

"They most certainly are," said Cathryn.

"We most certainly aren't," said the slender one in the dainty peach day dress, which was beautifully ironed. "We're just sick of dancing with each other."

"She leads," explained the one with the long blond hair, incongruous against the old face, the blue eyes milky and nearly buried, but still valiantly lined with violet eyeliner.

"I have to lead, I'm tallest."

"Not anymore, you've shrunk. When we were ELEVEN, you were tallest. And looked like a boy."

"Compared to you looking like a tart."

"Jealousy will get you nowhere."

"Jealous? Of you?"

"Ladies!" Cathryn stepped in.

"You know, we probably could do with a few more men here, now you come to mention it," she said to Edward. "Let me see what we can do."

"Well, that would be wonderful."

"But you're sure you wouldn't want to bring him in to have a look?"

"I'll try," said Edward, sighing.

The old man, after some cajoling and some sweets, agreed to come up the steps. Lilian and Ida Delia watched excitedly through the window.

"Ooh," said Lilian. "He's tall. I like a tall man."

"You know who he reminds me of . . . ?" said Ida Delia, but a sharp glance from Lilian reminded her that, although it was many, many decades ago, the tall man they had once both loved, and lost, was not up for discussion.

"His hair still curls," said Ida Delia quickly. Indeed, the patrician figure with the stick, his back still straight despite his great age, did make a good impression.

"How much dementia?" said Lilian. "Like, out of ten."

"You two," said Cathryn with a warning note in her voice. Then she stepped forward.

"Mr. Boyd," she said kindly, holding out her hand. The old man took it.

"Nice . . . nice to meet you," he said in a voice that, though quavering, was still surprisingly deep. "Call me James."

"Welcome to our home."

"Delighted."

Edward beamed, happy that his father was having one of his more lucid moments.

"Now, would you like me to show you around?"

"It's nice and warm in here . . . I think I can take off my coat."

Edward took it and hung it neatly on a hook by the door.

"Come through and I'll show you some of the facilities," said Cathryn. "Could you wipe your feet, please?"

James did so.

"I think he's fine," said Ida Delia.

"I saw him first," said Lilian, an out-and-out lie.

The man looked up and saw them both. It was as if he froze for a second. And without warning, a tear began to fall from his eye.

"Dad?" said Edward, desperate that this wouldn't go wrong. "I'm sorry," he said to Cathryn. "He's been much better recently."

"New surroundings can be upsetting."

"You," said James, but it wasn't at all clear who he meant or who he was pointing at.

"Come and sit down and have a cup of tea," said Cathryn. "And you two, SHOO. I mean it."

Lilian and Ida Delia headed off to watch television together. They had a shared loathing for everyone who took part in scripted reality shows, and thus absolutely had to watch all of them together in order to better anatomize and discuss the faults of the young people taking part in them and therefore of today's society in general. They felt this was important work that often required tea and Smarties.

James recovered quite a lot once he'd sat down and had a cup of tea. He was almost voluble.

"I am finding things difficult," he said haltingly. "My brain . . . it just won't . . . the words won't appear in my hands. No, not my hands. My mouth."

Cathryn nodded.

"I understand. It's upsetting."

"And I know, I know I was born in Halifax, and I grew up there, but I don't remember it, not at all. I just remember strange things all the time, like nothing makes any sense."

"I won't lie to you," said Cathryn, taking in Edward too. "This is a horrible illness. We will do everything we can here to make things comfortable and easy for you. When it's not snowing, a lot of people like to work in our garden."

"I used to shear sheep," said James suddenly. "Do you have sheep?"

"He didn't have anything to do with sheep," said Edward sotto voce. "He managed a printing company. He gets confused."

"No, we don't have sheep at the moment," she said. Then turning to Edward, "We find it is often easier to agree with clients about what they think is happening. When it's unimportant, it avoids unnecessary stress."

Edward nodded.

"Okay."

"We might get sheep later and you can help us, okay?"

"Yes, yes, I could still do that," said James. "You never forget. Well, I forget. Ha. I forget. Can I have some tea?"

"There's your tea," said Edward, pointing to the cup already poured. James turned around and immediately knocked it to the ground, then stared at it as if he had no idea what he'd just done. Cathryn leapt forward to take care of it immediately and summoned one of the care assistants to mop up while she comforted both of the men. James was very upset.

Suddenly Edward's eyes, too, filled with tears.

"I can't . . ." he choked. "I don't . . . I mean, to leave him here."

"He'll be in safe hands," said Cathryn reassuringly. She had taken to Edward. He would pay his bills, visit his father, and appreciate the kindnesses done rather than complain about the occasionally mismatched furniture or worn wall coverings.

"He was . . . I mean he was a good dad," said Edward, holding his father's grip tightly. "He wasn't demonstrative, we knew that—he was distracted, and busy a lot of the time. But we knew he loved us. And when he got upset about the war . . . well we knew he liked us to be near."

His voice choked again.

"And now we're dumping him."

"Ssh," said Cathryn. "Ssh. You are lucky, both of you. Edward, to have a father who you love and who loves you, and James, to have a son who is willing to take the very best care of you, right to the end. But it's not the end, I promise. Many of our residents—well, you have met a couple. But many of them flourish here. When Miss Hopkins came to us, she was so weak she could barely walk; and now she has found a completely new lease on life tormenting Mrs. Carr. And you will get your nights back, and sleep again, and stop worrying constantly about what James is doing and how he's being looked after, so you'll be happier too, and you can visit him and sit with him whenever and for as long as you like. I could tell you how much money I've been offered to go run large health-care home groups, and big chains of institutions, Mr. Boyd, but I won't. I think it's wrong. I think we do better on a small, local level where people know each other. And I give you my solemn word that we will all do the very best we can for your father."

It was as if a weight had been lifted from Edward's shoulders. Suddenly, he looked like a younger man.

"Thank you," he said. "Thank you. I'll have to talk it over with Doreen, but . . ."

Cathryn Thompson smiled at that. She knew, in the end, it was always the women who were the least sentimental. And who did the most laundry. She didn't think Edward would have the slightest difficulty convincing Doreen.

Chapter 10

For the first two seconds after she awoke, Rosie felt almost completely happy. She was buried under the blankets up to her neck, like a rabbit in a hole, warm as toast. She could feel Stephen next to her, finally sleeping soundly, breathing quietly—he had found it hard to settle and get comfortable. The familiarity of him back in her bed filled her with a great sense of security and happiness and peace, of the world being as it should be, and the snow on the window ledge felt as if it had always been there. She stretched out her toes luxuriantly, putting off as long as possible the second when she'd have to roll out of bed onto the icy floor. She kissed Stephen's head gently so as not to wake him . . .

Then she remembered. And groaned. It was Wednesday, two days after the council meeting. Mrs. Laird and all her ladies had been working around the clock to get two rooms ready for the children and install the infamous luxury Portaloos Lady Lipton hired in for her hunt ball. Rosie had even heard that a chimney sweep had come in and cleared the great fireplace in the hallway, but that couldn't be true, could it? Health and safety would have a fit. A fire officer had checked the place out, everything was moving for once at super-fast speed. Rosie tried to imagine this happening in London. She couldn't. Everything would have to go through ninety-five levels of complicated management meetings and take about nine months. Here, however, they had called it an emergency protocol and everything was fine. She supposed, when she thought about it, that Carningford probably hadn't been too keen on taking fifty new, slightly traumatized children either and had been only too happy to hand back the problem.

She hopped up and started to fill up the tub. The water steamed in the chilly bathroom. Water was much cheaper up here, and the pressure was fantastic, flowing down from the mountains. Rosie did not miss her spindly little shower in the old London flat, and she luxuriated in the bath every time she had a moment, which wasn't that often. She nipped downstairs and turned on the coffee machine, stoked up the stove, and glanced at the time. She had twenty-five minutes, plenty. It was pretty cool not to have a commute.

But. But. She wasn't as relaxed as she normally was sinking into the tub because she knew. Somewhere on the other side of the world, right now, six people were getting on a plane. Ready for the holiday of their lives. And she had done nothing to sort it out. This was awful. No more excuses. Nothing. It had to be done.

"What are you looking so thoughtful about?" asked Stephen, groaning and holding his back a little as he came in the bathroom door.

"Sorry, sweetie," said Rosie. "I didn't mean to wake you."

"Well, you probably shouldn't have charged up and down the steps like a baby elephant then."

He wiped the mirror, then glanced at Rosie behind him. The bath had made her skin turn all pink.

"You look nice," he observed.

"I can probably make space," said Rosie.

"Oh no, can you imagine? Can't get it wet."

"You are really going to honk very shortly," grumbled Rosie.

"You can give me a bed bath, Matron," said Stephen.

"I will do that," said Rosie. "You won't enjoy it as much as you think you will. Are you going back to bed?"

"No," said Stephen. "If I do that, I just lie there thinking about how itchy I am. I'm going to limp up to the school actually. You know, just have a look."

"Are you sure? You're on sick leave," said Rosie. "You're not well."

"I'm mending," said Stephen. "Out and about is apparently the best way to mend. As I remember a certain someone telling me last year."

"They'll be pleased to see you."

"I doubt that, back to school."

"They need stability right now. Even though you've just started, they need to see you. I'm glad you're going."

"Me too," said Stephen grudgingly.

Tell him, Rosie said to herself. TELL HIM.

But instead she heard herself say, "Would you like some poached eggs?"

"Christ no," said Stephen. "I mean, my doctor said they're not advisable at this point."

"Oh," said Rosie. "Okay, one, two, three." And she leapt up, forcing herself out of the lovely bath into the frigid room. Stephen picked up one of the rough old towels they'd somehow inherited from Peak House and dried her, tickling her breathless.

"Stop that!" she squealed.

"Why, what will we do, wake the neighbors?" teased Stephen. "We *are* the neighbors."

"Stop it or . . . or I'll touch your back," said Rosie, a threat that worked sufficiently well for him to release her. She shimmied into a burgundy woolen dress and cardigan, thick tights and boots, ran a comb through her hair, put on a little lipstick and mascara and charged out the door. Then she stuck her head back in, still furious with herself.

"We have to talk about something tonight," she said.

Stephen's brow furrowed.

"Can't we talk about it now?"

"No," said Rosie. "It's longer than now."

"Am I going to like it?"

"Um. Not sure. But it's not that bad."

"Okay," said Stephen. "No, tell me now."

"Later."

His deep blue eyes caught hers.

"Are you pregnant?"

Rosie jumped back, almost as if she'd had an electric shock.

"Oh, oh God. No. NO. Definitely not. Cripes. Is that what you thought?"

She watched his face closely. She couldn't tell if he was happy or unhappy.

"No," said Stephen quickly. "I saw you with the red wine bottle last night."

"Oh, yes, ha." Rosie tried to laugh, but neither of them could quite manage it. Rosie's mind started racing; they'd hardly been together that long or anything . . . on the other hand, she wasn't as young as she used to be . . . but she'd just started the business . . . and she couldn't tell if he thought it was a good idea or a terrible idea, the way he just sat there . . .

Her head spinning, Rosie forgot all about her family.

"I have to go," she said.

"Yes," said Stephen, looking embarrassed. "Yes. Okay. See you later."

"Later. Yes."

Still in a daze, Rosie opened up the shop in the dark. Lights were already moving up and down the main street, and many people stopped outside to get the little ones an extra something for their first day at the big house.

"How are you, Crystal?" Rosie said to one of her regular customers. Lilian had known the name of every single child she ever served, and Rosie saw that as good business too, but she wasn't as practiced at it as Lilian was.

Crystal shrugged and pointed to the alphabet letters. This wasn't like her. Rosie glanced at her mother.

"She thinks Lady Lipton is a witch who's going to eat them," whispered her mother.

"No way," said Rosie. "Do they all think that?"

"They're petrified."

Rosie clapped her head in her hands. "Oh my Lord, this is what's called the Law of Unintended Consequences. Crystal, you know that Lady Lipton isn't a witch?"

Crystal shrugged, eyes fixed on the floor. Finally, a very quiet voice:

"Have you seen how she dresses, though?"

Rosie laughed.

"Oh, that's just how posh people dress! Honestly. She's not a witch."

"She lives in a haunted house."

"It's just a big house."

Crystal stuck out her hand and took her sweets without saying thank you until her mum prompted her. This wasn't like her at all.

"Don't worry," said Rosie. "I've put some witch repellent in with your sweets, okay? If you share them out, you'll all be safe."

Crystal perked up.

"And, also, she's not a witch!" Rosie added hurriedly as they left the shop with a ding. It was the same with every family that came in: nervous children somehow convinced that they were being driven to a terrible doom.

"I can't believe we thought we were doing them a favor," Rosie said to Oliver, the baker's husband, who'd brought in little Fraser-James to buy him a chocolate Santa to stop him crying.

"I know, I know."

"I'm going to phone Mrs. Baptiste. Tell her not to read them any Roald Dahl today."

At 9:30, as the morning rush slowed and Rosie started dusting and polishing the shelves, there was a ding at the door.

"You've missed a bit," came the unmistakable cranky voice.

Rosie turned around.

"Lilian!" she said. "I wasn't expecting you today!"

In truth, she was glad of the distraction. She was finding her own thoughts a bit overwhelming at the moment.

"Let me get your chair. Tea?"

"Moray ran me in. He was up seeing some old duffer up-stairs."

"You really shouldn't talk about the other residents that way."

"But they're so *old*. Oh, we have someone new coming."

"Really? What's she like?"

"No! It's a man! And he's a dish."

Rosie filled the two cups from the newly boiled kettle.

"Excellent," she said.

"That Ida Delia Fontayne has set her cap on him, but I saw him first."

"Ida Delia would never get picked over you," said Rosie scornfully, bringing in the tea from the tiny galley through the back.

"Hmph," said Lilian. "Well, not twice."

Rosie smiled. It amazed her how much Lilian still thought about Henry Carr. She put the tea down on the counter.

"Okay, what will you have?"

Lilian's eyes sparkled and flew among the shelves, even after all these years.

"Two flumps, two flying saucers and three soft vanilla fudge," she said, quick as you like.

"Coming up," said Rosie cheerfully. "Oh, Lilian, I need your advice."

Little was more likely to make Lilian happy. Even if her advice normally involved people getting on with things and not making a fuss and going back to pre-decimal currency and out of the European Union, which was apparently where everything bad had started.

"Oh yes?" said Lilian, stirring two sugars into her tea. She stayed dainty as a mouse, Rosie often thought, because she ate nothing else at all. "You couldn't possibly need advice from a useless old lady like me."

Rosie rolled her eyes.

"Okay, okay."

She explained about Angie arriving the next day.

"I was going to tell Stephen before," she said. "But there was the awful business with the school, and I was so worried he was going to . . . react badly. And now, he just seems so happy that I hate to give him all this hassle and . . . well, it's kind of gotten away from me."

Lilian sipped contemplatively.

"Have you ever," she said, "had a problem that got better by your ignoring it?"

"Yes!" said Rosie. "All the time! Loads of problems go away by themselves. Look at that weird lump I had on my leg."

"Well, all right. But this one won't," said Lilian. "Short of a plane crash."

"Let's not wish for a plane crash, okay?"

"That's the problem with falling in love with those Mr. Darcy types," said Lilian.

"Hmm," said Rosie. She sold some chewing gum to a gas man in a hurry.

"But Rosie, you know you can't expect someone just to love you when nice things are happening and everything's cozy. If you dedicate yourself to making someone else's life happy at the expense of your own . . . well, obviously, I'm only a silly old idiot, but I don't believe either of you can be happy like that."

Rosie was silent for a while.

"No," she said.

"What do you think he's going to do?"

"Go all grumpy and weird."

"Well, he's a grown-up. People have families, yours is nice, he has to understand that. Maybe he wants to meet your mum."

"She can't be worse than his," said Rosie.

"Exactly."

"But where am I going to put them all?"

"What about that house of Stephen's?"

"Peak House?" Rosie made a face. "It's kind of closed up. He's never there."

"Well, you're going to have to unclose it then, aren't you?"

"Oh God, I don't think I can ask Lady Lipton for more of her property."

"Why does she need to know? It's technically where Stephen lives."

Rosie giggled slightly hysterically.

"Maybe I won't tell Stephen either. Maybe I can just leave them up there for two weeks, and no one will even notice."

Lilian gave her a look.

"I'm kidding, I'm kidding."

"At least they're hiring a car," said Rosie. "I'm not sure I could get Angie on a bicycle."

"So you'll have a job getting Peak House ready," said Lilian.

"Oh crap, I know. Mrs. Laird is too busy with Lipton Hall," said Rosie. "Great. I'll be working all night."

"Whereas if you'd dealt with this problem head-on, you'd have been organized weeks ago."

"All right, all right, I know."

"You can go now if you like. I can stay in charge of the shop."

Rosie looked at Lilian curiously. She'd given it up when she could no longer manage, but . . .

"How will you get up to the high shelves?" she asked. "If

you fall down a ladder and break your hip, we're all doomed."

"I'm not going up a ladder!" said Lilian. "I'm old, for good- ness' sake, not an idiot. If anyone asks for something that's up the ladder, I shall simply tell them no, and direct them to a more reasonable piece of confectionary."

Rosie smiled and glanced at her watch. "Well, Tina's in in about an hour . . ." she said, wavering. "Give me your big phone."

Lilian handed it over from a dainty knitted pocket cover she'd made for it.

"Very nice," said Rosie. "I'm going to make it call me and leave it on, okay? So it's like a walkie-talkie. Are you sure . . ."

Lilian tutted.

"I have actually run this place before, you know? Just for seventy years?"

Rosie nodded. "I know, I know. Is it warm enough?"

"Stop fussing!"

Anton, the fattest man in town, came in.

"Anton!" said Lilian, her face wreathed in smiles. "What can I get you?"

Anton's mobility had improved so much in the last six months that he hardly needed his stick anymore, though he was a little out of breath. He beamed wildly when he saw Lilian.

"Hello! I missed you!"

"I am still here," said Rosie, scooping up Mr. Dog, who was snoring blissfully by the heater in the back room instead of manfully protecting their property.

"What can I get you?" said Lilian. Anton sent a sideways glance at Rosie, who stared at him crossly.

"Ignore her," said Lilian. "I'm in charge today."

"In that case . . ." said Anton. "Can I have . . . a pound of mixed creams, please. And another pound of mixed creams. And that chocolate orange there. And another one, actually. And from the top shelf . . ."

"Anton!" said Rosie in exasperation. "Calm down. Come on. Don't be daft."

Anton shuffled his feet.

"Lilian, no more than one of each thing he wants. And no more than five things."

"You'd better get on before your Australian family all arrives tomorrow!" trilled Lilian.

Anton's eyes went wide. "Ooh, you've got family arriving."

"Great," said Rosie. "That'll be all round the village in about five seconds."

"What?" said Maeve Skitcherd, who'd just come in for a slab of mint cake.

"All Rosie's Australian relatives are turning up tomorrow," explained Anton helpfully.

"Ooh," said Maeve. "Where are they all going to stay?"

"I don't know. It'll be an awful crush in the cottage," said Anton.

"Okay, okay, I am out of here," said Rosie, glaring at Lilian, who was now wearing a triumphant look and putting together a very big bag for Anton. Rosie dinged the door crossly.

There were cars parked the length of the great formal driveway of Lipton Hall, as there sometimes were when they did weddings, and there were lights on along the front of the house, very rare in the daytime. Rosie got off her bicycle pink-cheeked and exhilarated from her freezing ride—she was wearing Stephen's ski gloves, which made her look a bit like a monkey but did the job—and sidled up, feeling both nervous and a bit out of place. Mr. Dog immediately hurled himself around the back to see his family, and Rosie let him go; she didn't need the added distraction of his being there.

Inside there was a quiet hum, which had to be a good sign. And there was a warm smell of cooking in the air, which might have been for later. Rosie stepped gently into the great hall. The great fire between the two arms of the intertwining stairwells had been lit, albeit with a large fire guard around it, and it sent out a welcoming smell and warmth to Rosie as she came in frigid from the cold. A woman bustled past her, round and cheerful looking. It was Pam, the dinner lady from the school.

"Hello!" said Rosie. "I forgot you'd be coming here too!"

"They're letting me cook!" said Pam, full of excitement. "The education department. They don't have enough freezer units to refrigerate the lunches, so they've sent me two girls from the catering college, and they're letting me make lunch for them!"

"And this is good?" asked Rosie, smiling.

"Yes!" said Pam. "Some of the stuff we have to serve them . . ." She shook her head. "You wouldn't give it to a dog. Absolute brown muck they used to send us. Anyway. Now I can make them something good and decent. Then send them outside to roll in the snow. This is much better."

And she bustled off, Rosie looking after her, smiling.

Stephen stood in front of the class in his old dining room, cursing his own stupidity. He should have taken more time off, but he was worried that if he had done so, everyone would have panicked and thought he was getting miserable again, and he couldn't bear that. His back was agony, felt as if it were on fire, and he'd had to stop the children from flinging their arms around him. Every touch of their hands reminded him of Edison's cold fingers beneath him. He winced. He just needed to get through a day and tune out his mother and anyone else giving him stress. Then he would be fine and better tomorrow and then all Christmas he could lie on his stomach and do nothing and luxuriate in the freedom of it. He just needed to get through the next day . . .

Rosie, not knowing which door to choose, sidled toward the one she knew led to the enormous ballroom on the ground floor. It was normally set up with sofas and used for dancing at parties and functions. Rosie wondered how they'd converted it. She knocked quietly.

"Enter."

She saw how it worked immediately. A huge dining table had been split into long sections, and crossed the room. Behind them, the bigger children sat on the long benches from the servant's quarters, nine or ten to a row. Mrs. Baptiste looked up, pleasantly distracted. She had brought up the whiteboard from the old school and was teaching from it in an old-fashioned way.

"Miss Hopkins. Welcome."

"Good mor-ning-Miss-Hop-kins," chorused the class, and Rosie smiled.

"Wow," she said as Mrs. Baptiste ordered the children to carry on with their reading and met with her briefly against the side wall. "This is amazing."

"I must confess," said Mrs. Baptiste, "that I love having them in rows rather than modern groups. I can see all their faces at the same time, really see what they're doing. It's good for them."

"Well," said Rosie. "How's Lady Lipton?"

Mrs. Baptiste looked slightly pink for a second.

"Um, that's working out rather well."

"Are they all completely terrified of her?"

"Petrified. It's a veiled threat hanging over them all the time. I've never seen them behave so well."

Rosie smiled.

"I won't tell her."

"Oh, you know Hetty," said Mrs. Baptiste. "She wouldn't give a toss either way."

"Well, sorry to bother you," said Rosie. "It's Stephen I'm after."

"Can't keep him away," said Mrs. Baptiste, shaking her head. "He shouldn't be in at all, you know. I was perfectly happy to take both classes for a week or so."

"He's committed all right," said Rosie.

"I'm surprised," said Mrs. Baptiste. "You know, I expected him to be a bit . . . standoffish . . ."

"I know," said Rosie. "He's not really." Except sometimes, she thought to herself.

On the other side of the hall was the large dining room. This must be it. Rosie swallowed hard, screwed up her courage, knocked gently and entered.

He didn't hear her at first. The entire class was silent, rapt, sitting cross-legged at the front of the room as Stephen stood facing the paneling, one hand resting gently on his back, a book in the other.

"*'And so,' said the prince, 'that is how you get to the shining island. And now you know that not the wolf's fiercest howl, nor the night's sharpest claws will stop you in your tracks, nor feet nor snow nor wood can ever slow down the wings of a righteous man.'*"

Gradually he became aware of the presence of someone else in the room, and gently put the book down. He half-smiled at Rosie, looking quizzical. The children stayed silent until the spell of the story was broken.

"All right," he said. "Go back to your tables. I want to see a picture of the prince's winged companion. With swords in it. And yes, a princess, Crystal."

"That's strong stuff for their first day back," said Rosie, indicating the book.

"Oh, they can take it," said Stephen. "They love it. Proper gory stuff. Ideal for children. So, um . . . to what do I owe this . . . ?"

"I need the car keys. And the keys to Peak House," Rosie said. There was a tiny bit of her that thought this might be enough, that he might just capitulate and hand them over without asking any questions.

"Um, what?"

"Yeah, I didn't think that would work," said Rosie. Stephen glanced around anxiously at his class. The dining tables were all still set up, and the little class was divided among five tables. They looked incongruous there, their chubby little legs dangling off the rather nasty conference-style chairs Hetty had bought as she tried to make Lipton Hall pay its way. Rosie waved at Kent and Emily, who grinned back shyly. Kent lifted his bandaged arm, and Rosie gave him a thumbs-up.

"Well," she said. "Here's the thing."

There was a ding in Stephen's pocket as his phone received a text message. He drew it out unthinkingly. His brow furrowed. Then another one dinged in.

"Ah," said Rosie, thinking immediately—and correctly—that the bush telegraph had gotten to work. She had about four minutes before Lady Lipton barged in.

Stephen quietly turned off his phone and put it back in his pocket without a word. He felt the pain in his back as he did so.

"The Reverend seems to think," he said quietly, "that we may need extra space in the family pew on Christmas Day."

"I do not trust that slippery vicar," said Rosie, not for the first time. She sighed. "Well," she said. "Um." Then she squeezed her eyes shut tightly. "My mum and my brother and sister-in-law and their kids are coming to stay for Christmas."

Stephen looked completely bemused.

"But why didn't you tell me? When are they coming?"

"Tomorrow," said Rosie.

"Rosie, open your eyes. This is ridiculous."

"No," said Rosie.

"How long have you known?"

"For a bit," said Rosie.

"Where are they going to . . . oh. Peak House. Of course. I see."

"I didn't know what else to do . . . I know it's your house."

"So you weren't even going to ask me, just take the keys?"

"When you put it like that, it sounds awful," said Rosie.

Stephen's back was really hurting.

"Why . . . why did you think I wouldn't welcome your family?" he asked, rubbing it.

"Because I thought you'd . . . rather not. . . ."

Stephen glanced around at the little class, all of whom were staring at them with wide eyes. They couldn't discuss this now. He didn't want to deal with this now.

"But why didn't you mention it?"

"I'm an idiot. And there was a lot going on."

There was a lot going on now, thought Stephen. And she didn't even realize it. He squeezed his eyes tight, then turned around abruptly, went to his coat, took out two sets of keys and handed them to her without a word.

"I'll see you later," said Rosie, her heart beating fast.

"Mm," said Stephen, noncommittally. He just had to get through one thing at a time, he told himself. One thing at a time.

Rosie worried for a second when she was finally sitting in the car, catching sight in her rearview mirror of Hetty hurrying across the lawn, presumably with the eventful news about Rosie's family. Then she shook herself. He'd be all right.

Peak House was utterly freezing. It was a dilapidated and eerie place at the best of times, a flat-fronted gray stone Georgian house perched gloomily out of place high up above the Lipton valley, totally open to the freezing winds and storms that passed over the mountainside. The views were wonderful, but terrible too; great craggy ridges, lonesome hills and, in this weather, white everywhere. Even though Rosie had spent happy times there with Stephen in the past, she couldn't deny that it was still a bit of a spooky prospect.

She sighed, hoping Stephen hadn't forgotten to pay the electricity bill or anything stupid like that. But no, the lights came on as she went through the back door—it wasn't even locked, she noticed crossly; she could have put that unpleasant conversation off for a bit. No she couldn't, she told herself, she'd already let it get completely out of hand.

A whole house sitting here empty and untouched for months on end. In London they'd have had sixty-five art student squatters and ten thousand mice and some pigeons, and someone would have stolen the lead off the roof. Here everything remained as it had been the very first time she'd met Stephen; plain, very tidy, a little faded. The walls were a scrubbed white, the kitchen had a big stove that Rosie decided to come back and light in the morning, after clearing it out, and a well-scrubbed table that would serve. The sitting room was lined with books and had two squeaky old chesterfields. There were some old portraits, obviously moved up from the big house, that Rosie worried would scare the children. Upstairs were four nice square bedrooms with huge light-filled windows and views right across the downs.

Looking around, Rosie, being so used to her own cramped quarters, wondered if nothing could be done about spooky old Peak House—its dimensions and outlook were so nice, really. Even if you did have to wear your coat inside for the rest of your life, and downstairs was full of dark old passageways. Stephen's room was in fairly good nick and would do for Angie (although she would probably insist that the best room go to Pip and Desleigh, assuming she hadn't changed very much). There was a room with two singles and a little pull-out that the three children could use, and two other freezing doubles. Only one bathroom, but it was a good size; Rosie turned on the boiler and the old corrugated radiators, crossing her fingers the entire time. She didn't get a mobile signal up here, so

God knew what would happen if she needed the emergency plumber. Then she got down to work.

First, Rosie turned the radio full on to Heart FM. Some pop music would stop her feeling so alone and creeped out and would cheer her up a bit. They were playing lots of Christmas tunes, and reception up here was brilliant, with no neighbors to disturb except some sheep, so she whacked it right up and felt a bit better right away; a feeling that improved even more when the pilot light wavered for a little bit, then caught with a whoomphing, reassuring noise, followed by a buzz, which meant the boiler was on. She held her hand against it for a long time as she heard the radiators at last start to gurgle to life.

Then she went to the linen cupboard and made up the beds with practiced hospital strokes, thrashing out her crossness with herself for not organizing things earlier, not giving Stephen the opportunity to get used to the idea, being a coward about it; and with him not being keener on the idea . . . although he had just gotten out of the hospital, and he didn't deserve all this, so clearly it wasn't his fault, so it must be hers . . . Banging down pillows helped get rid of some of the cross energy, and the music did help perk her up a bit, but EURGH, why did everything have to be so exasperating?

Once she was done, and had cleaned and hoovered the bedrooms, she opened the large rucksack she'd brought along on the bike then heaved into the Land Rover. Thank goodness for Tina and her online shopping addiction. Her colleague had kindly lent her spare covers she'd bought over the years for Kent and Emily. There was a *Cars* duvet that should do for Meridian, a football blanket for Shane and a princess blanket for Kelly. Once Rosie had spread these on top of the austere white counterpanes, they gave the large bedroom a much jollier, homelier outlook. It wasn't much, she reflected, but it was a start.

She cleaned up and down the rest of the house and put out soap, toothpaste, towels and washing powder that had been tidily placed in the larder cupboard. From her rucksack she brought out two pints of milk, thankfully not frozen, some Weetabix, tea, coffee (there were jars of stuff in the cupboard, given that Stephen hadn't officially moved out yet, but Rosie wasn't entirely convinced of their provenance) and bread. She didn't light the Aga—she could do that tomorrow.

She glanced around. It still seemed so cheerless, somehow. It was such a basic, unloved home. Stephen had stayed there when he was ill, so he hadn't wanted much cheer around him. It needed something—just to bring the place to life a little, make the children not regret flying all the way around the world.

Slade was singing loudly about hanging up the stockings on the wall when she got an idea. She grabbed the torch that was always kept charged up in the boot room next to the back door and went up to the upstairs hall, standing on a chair and grabbing the string that opened the attic trapdoor. She had to leap out of the way to avoid the cascading ladder that came down. She'd never been up there before, though Stephen had gone once when there was a bird trapped in the rafters who'd flown in somehow under the eaves and then made a hearty racket, scaring her half to death.

If it was cold downstairs in the house, up here it was arctic. Wind whistled through the gaps in the tiles. Rosie shivered, her fingers going into tight knots. She was sure you could get a government grant for insulation now; this was absolutely ludicrous. Lady Lipton probably thought getting a grant for insulation was too left wing or something.

It wasn't that dark in the attic, which made Rosie worry about holes in the roof and patching and all sorts, but she shone the torch around anyway. There were piles of boxes everywhere; a large steamer trunk with S.F.L stamped on it, which Rosie correctly took to have belonged to Stephen's grandfather; various cardboard boxes and books that smelled musty and looked damp; an old-style tennis racket in a wooden press; old skis with rope bindings and boots that looked left over from a war. But Rosie couldn't linger; it was far too cold for that. In the far corner, she found what she was looking for: a brown box with XMAS stenciled on it.

The kitchen, with the radiators slowly heating up, felt like a greenhouse after the loft, and Rosie put on the kettle for tea and washed her dusty hands. Then she sat down to review her treasure. She knew that before Stephen had lived in Peak House, the family had used it for storage, family and guest overspill, and occasional staff, and she'd guessed there might be something like this up there. It quickly became clear from the crude little initials scratched on the old Christmas decorations that these had belonged to Stephen and Pamela—Stephen's sister who had a job in New York and only came home once in a blue moon to have a massive and cathartic shouting match with her mother about primogeniture, then stormed off again, a state of affairs that Rosie privately thought was hugely enjoyable for both of them—and were a collection built up over years: a wobbly angel with wool hair here, a nobbled cardboard Santa Claus there, an oddly touching decorated cigarette lighter. Rosie assumed they didn't make those at school anymore. There was tinsel too, which she could hang, and a large dried holly wreath that she could stick on the front door, but it was the children's things that intrigued her most.

At the bottom of the box she found a letter, badly spelled and with some of the letters a little wonky.

Dear Mr. Santa,

I have bin mostly good this year except father says "SU-LEN" but I don't know what that is. Culd I have please:

> *books*
> *a new fountin pen as I have lost mine but not told Mother*
> *a train like a real one with steam please*
> *a transformer. I do not know what this is but everyone*
>   *at school has them*
> *Panini football cards ditto.*

Thank you.

Yours sincerely,
Stephen Felix Lakeman (7)

Rosie bit her lip, her crossness and irritation washed away. She sipped her tea, then took a photo of the letter on her telephone to send to Stephen when she had a signal. Then she folded the letter very carefully and put it back in the box.

She changed the radio to Classic FM so she could listen to "Hark the Herald Angels Sing" and belted it out as she stuck up tinsel all around the kitchen and on the mantelpiece in the sitting room, where she could build a fire tomorrow night. She added baubles at random and lined up all the little cardboard Santas and carved bits and pieces across the mantelpiece. Then, feeling an excess of energy, she went out into the kitchen garden, where she found, behind the wall, a great shimmering holly bush and, with some cursing at the damage it did to her fingers, managed to snip off several great bunches to line every remaining surface in the house. Then she saw mistletoe too and did the same with that.

By the time she had finished, the sky was black and icy cold, the stars far and distant and from outside, the house, lit up, was far far cozier than it had been earlier. Rosie felt rather pleased with herself and was over her earlier mood in the way that only a day's really hard work could sort out. She loaded the empty bag back into the Land Rover and texted Stephen to tell him she'd pick up fish and chips. She prayed he was home. Then she would let him be cross until, hopefully, it burnt itself out and she could apologize enough. Thank goodness he was back at school; she could entertain the visitors during the day and . . . well, the rest of the time would sort itself out, wouldn't it? Yes. Yes. It would be fine.

She juggled the hot fish suppers wrapped in paper as she got out of the car. Yes, surely it would be okay.

There was a light on in the window. Well, at least he was there. That was okay. She knocked on the door tentatively, then felt completely stupid because it was her house.

"Hello?" She peered through the window.

His head turned slowly, still stiff and painful. Rosie held up the fish and chips. His expression didn't change.

He opened the door.

"Peace offering?"

"Of course," he said, doing his best to smile, even though he truly didn't feel like it. "Stop looking so scared. Am I a very terrifying person?"

"No," said Rosie. "A bit."

"I didn't know you'd be so late," he said. "Tina locked up early."

"I know. I asked her to," said Rosie.

Stephen slowly fetched plates and ketchup from the little kitchen.

"So," he said. "Just take me through it . . . your mum is coming?"

"Yes."

"And?"

"My brother."

"Lovely!"

"And his wife."

"Yes."

"And their children . . ."

"Do they have many children?"

"Don't pretend you don't know absolutely everything about it," said Rosie. "This is pure torture and nothing else."

"I would have loved not having everyone know everything before me," he said quietly.

"I know," said Rosie. "I am so, so sorry. Truly sorry. With everything that was happening . . ."

"What, you decided I was going to be really awful about it?"

"No!" said Rosie. "But I didn't know . . ." She could barely get the words out. "After . . . after the accident . . ."

Stephen's dark blue eyes seemed to be boring into her.

"I was worried . . . I thought you might retreat again. I

thought it might bring on your PTSD. I didn't want to add to any mental stress I thought you might be under."

"Because that would be awful?"

"Yes . . . no. I mean . . . I mean, are you okay?"

For a moment, Stephen considered telling her. How every time he heard a car backfire, he thought he was going to have a heart attack. How every time he fell asleep he thought he could smell the dust and smoke going back into his lungs. How when he heard the children playing in the playground, all he could hear were screams.

But he couldn't go back. He couldn't go back to where they were last year. He couldn't handle the nursing, the sense that Rosie was there for him and he wasn't there for her; that he was an invalid; that he wasn't up to loving her, to playing his part, to being a proper man. He couldn't bear the disappointment on her face, the tiptoeing around him that everyone would inevitably start doing. No. He wouldn't. He wouldn't.

All he said was, "I'm fine. Okay? I'm fine. I'm not that same guy, remember?"

"No, you're not," said Rosie. "You're not. I'm sorry that I thought you were."

And Stephen took that as enough.

"We should eat before it gets cold."

Rosie unwrapped her fish and chips, realized belatedly that she'd skipped lunch and was absolutely starving. She dived in without thinking.

"Well, I'm glad you're so upset and apologetic you're off your food," he observed. She smiled at him, overwhelmed with relief that at last it was out in the open and everything was going to be fine.

Stephen couldn't eat at all but did his best to look as if he was.

"Did you get my message on your phone?" she asked suddenly.

"Oh, no. Bloody signal," said Stephen.

Rosie took another bath—she was pretty mucky from Peak House—and heard Stephen go quietly to bed before her. She jumped in to join him, but he seemed to be asleep already.

A beeping woke her in the depths of the night; the moon was shining strongly through the window. The mobile signal was patchy all through the village. Sometimes, very rarely, it would swing in and out of the cottage, but it couldn't be relied on. But it was the bing of Stephen's iPhone she had heard. He wasn't in bed. She looked blurrily around the room. He was sitting in the big old armchair, just under the window, gazing at the screen. She could see, just about, that it was the letter to Santa she had sent him. He was sitting very still. She decided it was better not to say anything; she had done enough today. So instead, she turned back over gently in the bed and dropped back into an exhausted sleep.

Chapter 11

It had snowed a little in the night, but not enough to trouble the salt trucks too much. Rosie was opening up in the morning, but Tina would take over for the rest of the afternoon while she drove to the airport. She took Stephen to work. Lady Lipton was standing out in front of the great house, looking mutinous. "Oh, Lord," said Stephen.

"Tell her our being in Peak House will stop the pipes from freezing," suggested Rosie.

"Yeah, until she gives them one of her looks," said Stephen. He kissed her on the cheek and hauled himself out of the car. Rosie watched him walk toward his mother, his resignation obvious.

She'd planned it so that she had a little time to kill before she drove to the airport and was pleased to be able to spend it sitting at Edison's bedside. She'd brought a copy of *Little Women*, the closest thing to a child's book Lilian had in the house, and started reading softly as Hester went for a quick lie-down in the day room. Technically it was light outside, but the skies were so

low and heavy it didn't quite feel like that, and apart from the
gentle beeps and whirls of the equipment, the ward was quiet.

"*'Christmas won't be Christmas without presents,'* grumbled Jo,
lying on the rug," Rosie began. "*'It's so dreadful to be poor,'* sighed
Meg, looking down at her old dress . . ."

After about five minutes she became aware of a doctor and
nurse, standing behind her, listening.

"Sorry," she said.

"No, it was nice," said the doctor. "Makes a change from
being sworn at by drunks. Um, is Hester about?"

"She's just having a nap," said Rosie. "I can go fetch her."

The doctor came over and patted Edison's cheek. "Little
man," she said. "Today's the day."

"What?" said Rosie.

"We're going to try and wake him up. See how he's doing.
He seems to be healing pretty well . . . It helps to be young,
although I'd have liked him to be a bit plumper."

"I can probably help with that," said Rosie.

"Well, we can let Hester sleep a little longer, but then we
want to get started," said the doctor.

"Okay," said Rosie. "I can stay awhile."

"Can you read again?" said the nurse. "I loved that book."

"Of course," said Rosie, and took up again. "*The four sisters,
who sat knitting away in the twilight, while the December snow fell
quietly without, and the fire crackled cheerfully within . . .*"

Rosie took the motorway to East Midlands Airport. Everywhere people were driving with Christmas trees strapped to
their roofs, their boots piled high with boxes from toy shops and

mysterious bicycle-shaped packages; everyone looked flushed and happy. Rosie bit her lip. She hadn't even started shopping yet, didn't know when she would get a second. Well, she could take Angie and everyone into Derby one day and they could shop. Wouldn't be a patch on the Sydney shops Angie went on about all the bloody time, she supposed, but they would do.

And the kids would probably want video games, which was apparently all kids ever wanted these days, so that would be easy enough. . . . She had absolutely not the faintest idea what to get Stephen. He always managed to look great in really old clothes, some of which he'd inherited from his dad. He wore old tweed jackets and managed to look handsome and not daft; worn-in cashmere sweaters, country checked shirts, soft moleskin trousers. Rosie thought, first of all, how ridiculous she would have thought that getup before she knew him and how much it suited him, and secondly how unlikely she was to get it quite right, whatever right was, if she bought him something to wear.

She could try books, but he read so widely and so mercurially that it was hard to figure out what would catch his interest. It should probably, she thought, be something pretty damn good to make up for everything.

The flight was running on time. She bought a coffee and wandered the concourse, idly looking through the shops for possible gifts and wondering if it was possible to do all your Christmas shopping at an airport and, looking around, figured that you could. That was basically all airports were—malls for last-minute Christmas shoppers, with planes attached.

A Salvation Army band was playing "O Little Town of Bethlehem" loudly under a huge Christmas tree. It was basically having a fight with the bing-bong of flight alerts and warnings

about not leaving baggage unattended, and it made a lot of
noise.

Rosie sighed, tried to stop herself being so cynical, went
to the loos and brushed her hair (otherwise she couldn't be
entirely sure Angie wouldn't brush it for her in the middle of
the concourse), then positioned herself along the arrivals barrier, kicking herself to get into a better mood. The last thing
she wanted was to break down in floods of tears in front of her
mum, confessing no one had known they were coming and that
it was all complicated. No. It was fine.

Most people, flying locally from within the UK, waltzed out
with a pull-along trolley on wheels. Rosie suspected, correctly,
that her party would be last by the time they'd collected all
the baggage, and the children, of course, were going to be exhausted and very ratty. She checked her watch and wondered
if she had time to get another cup of coffee . . . when suddenly
the double doors slid open, and there, her hair a frizzly blond
shade never seen in nature, her bare arms walnut-brown and
stringy looking, her teeth oddly white, pushing a trolley with
two children hopping on and off it, was her mum.

And suddenly Rosie forgot everything—forgot every
worry about the shop, about Stephen, about Edison, about
everything—and just ran to the mummy she hadn't seen in two
years.

They held on to each other for a good minute or so before
Rosie remembered that there were other people there too. She
hugged Pip, then bent down to look at the children, all shyly
holding on to Desleigh's and Angie's skirts.

"Hello," she said, smiling.

Meridian, the littlest at three, still had a blankie clutched to her side and her thumb near her mouth just in case. Her big blue eyes blinked nervously. Desleigh nudged the other two—nine-year-old Shane, who was grasping a DS, and seven-year-old Kelly, a chubby copy of her mother.

Shane finally came forward and said, "G'day, Auntie Rosie." And Rosie smiled, beamed in fact, particularly when she noticed Meridian's black curly hair, so like her own.

"Hi, you guys," she said, tears pricking at her eyes again. "Oh boy, I have been waiting such a long time to see you."

"Is it true?" asked Kelly. "Is it true you have a lolly shop?"

"Well, we have lots of things besides lollies," said Rosie.

Pip smiled. "Lollies are just . . . well, everything in Australia. All sweets really."

"I see," said Rosie. "Well, yes, I have a lolly shop. But here we call it a sweetshop."

And she brought out from her bag the things she'd ordered especially for their coming: three shiny red Christmas lollies with their names iced on them. Three pairs of eyes went wide at the sight.

"There are," said Rosie, "certain good things that come along with having an aunt who runs a sweetshop."

She felt a tiny hand steal its way into hers and, looking down, saw that Meridian had crept to her side.

"They're very well behaved," said Rosie to Desleigh.

Desleigh snorted. "That's because they're all bloody knackered."

"I don't think so," said Rosie to the children. "I think it's because you're all very good. Now, please tell me you've brought lots and lots and lots of sweaters."

"The snow!" shouted Shane. "We have to see the snow!!"

"SNOW!" echoed the girls.

"Oh, trust me," said Rosie, "you'll see plenty of snow. Now, come on, let's go pick up your car."

They got to the seven-seater they'd hired easily enough. The force of the wind blasted them coming out through the airport doors, and the children shrieked in excited dismay. Rosie picked up Meridian and stuck her inside her jacket.

"Okay," she said, loading them into the big car and fastening their seatbelts.

"But not you, Mum," she added. "You're coming with me."

On the way back to Lipton they talked about everything and everyone under the sun: about Pip's job, and Lilian, and the shop. Angie asked about Rosie's young man, and she coughed out an answer that didn't really seem satisfactory, but for once her mum was probably too jet-lagged to question it.

The long arched avenue to Peak House seemed even more sinister today with icicles dripping down from the branches of the trees.

"I hope it's okay," said Rosie, who'd driven up and put on the Aga that morning. "I mean, it's . . . it's pretty desolate, but well, honestly, it's not far to the village and you'll be with us and we'll do stuff together and—"

"Stop worrying, Rosebud," said Angie. "You found us a whole house, good on you. I'm completely amazed."

Rosie wondered about this, but when the two cars stopped on the gravel and the others emerged, she was shocked to see everyone looking so excited and happy.

"OH. MY. GOD. Look at this place," said Desleigh. "It's like Downton Bloody Abbey. Have you got servants?"

Rosie looked at Peak House again. She was so used to thinking of it as such an ominous, foreboding place that she forgot the nice stone and good proportions; how it looked like the great house that it was.

"We're going to be living in a castle," said Shane in awe. "Auntie Rosie, this is seriously cool."

"Um, let's just wait till we get inside," said Rosie.

But inside, the radiators were finally working, and the Aga had done its job, and the house seemed to have dried out a little and felt cozy and almost cheerful.

"It's like a Christmas card," said Pip. He whistled. "I think we've both fallen on our feet, sis."

She showed him upstairs and they sat companionably on the bed together like they always used to.

"It's so good to see you," said Rosie. "The children are just adorable."

Pip beamed.

"Oh, they are, Rosie. And Desleigh is so good to me and, well, Australia's just fantastic. . . . You know, sis, Mum always says the only thing missing is you."

Rosie smiled.

"But you're happy here?"

He said it in the Australian way so she wasn't sure if it was a question or a statement.

"Oh yes," said Rosie. "Totally. Completely. All the time."

She tried not to think about the image of Stephen the previous night, staring out the window.

"Completely happy," she added, then realized as Pip stared at her that she might have gone into overkill a little bit.

"I never saw you in a village," said Pip. "I always saw you as a big-city girl. You'd love Sydney. Plus nurses there make sixty thousand a year."

Rosie coughed a lot at this—a LOT—and headed back downstairs, where she made tea and toast for everyone. Kelly sat by the window exclaiming at the snow, and Shane boasted about the size of the snowman he was going to build and the big snowball fight they were going to have, but she could see their eyelids drooping. Angie insisted they needed the afternoon and night to get their heads straight—nobody had slept a wink on the plane, apparently. Shane had watched *Transformers* seventeen times in a row until they thought he was going to have an epileptic fit, Kelly had rattled on constantly about the snow, which was leaving her totally awestruck, and Meridian had eaten four breakfasts. Everyone was wilting.

"I'll be up in the morning," promised Rosie, feeling so much better about everything that she practically skipped out to the Land Rover.

She relieved Tina and did the last few hours in the shop, then cashed up, keeping an ear open for Stephen coming in at four. She heard the door open, but he didn't pop in as he normally did. Well.

At five, she locked the doors and went home. Stephen asked after her family, politely but, she thought, with a bit of reticence. She hoped he wasn't worried about meeting Angie. Not all mothers were as scary as his.

As she went to turn on the grill, she saw that, amazingly, her phone was connected. She wondered if Roy Blaine had stuck up a sneaky pole on his land. She wouldn't put it past him. She had a message. Please not anything up at Peak House, please. The boiler exploding. That would be all they needed.

She could hardly hear the voice on the message for sobs. Then she understood and was completely and utterly touched that she had thought to ring. She marched into the sitting room and stood in front of Stephen.

"What is it?" he asked, instantly panicked by the tears in her eyes. He got carefully out of his seat and went to her. "What?"

Rosie put down the phone.

"Edison woke up," she said. "He woke up and . . . the first thing he asked for was any homework he'd missed."

Stephen blinked quickly, trying again to shake away the image of the crash; not to let it overwhelm him. He choked up and took her in his arms, her tears soaking his sweater.

"Thank God," he said. Rosie couldn't speak at all. "Thank God," said Stephen again. They had both known that beyond whether Edison's neck would heal was the question: Would he still be himself, or had he suffered brain damage in the accident? To have to raise a child who could no longer think, wash himself, go to school . . . Hester and Arthur would have loved him just the same, of course, but what a terrible, terrible burden of worry would have been added to their lives.

"That's amazing," said Stephen. "Oh God, I can't wait till he's back in my class. Asking me what wiped out the fricking dinosaurs again."

He wiped his eyes. Rosie was still choked up.

"You love that kid," he said, teasing her.

"I do," she said. "Oh, thank God. Plus I think he's single-handedly kept the Edinburgh rock factory in business."

Stephen smiled and gave her another cuddle.

"So, everyone is settled in?"

Rosie nodded. "Yes, they're fine. Actually, it's wonderful to see them."

Stephen smiled.

"You miss your mum. I've heard you on the phone. For months on end."

"I do," she said. "How was school?"

"School," he said, "was fine. School is fine. My mother, on the other hand . . ."

"Our mother distribution is all wrong," mused Rosie. "One needs to be closer, one needs to be farther away. What's she up to now?"

"Fussing and complaining. You won't believe what that arsehole Roy Blaine has done now."

"Filed all his teeth down to points and started on an all-baby diet?"

Stephen gave a weak smile at this. Rosie went back into the kitchen. She was cooking mustard pork chops, her secret weapon in case Stephen was still sulking. Nobody could resist her mustard pork chops.

"Worse, if you can imagine."

"I still can't believe he can walk about in daylight without going up in smoke."

Stephen half-smiled.

"He's saying that the cost of providing the new schooling up at the house means there isn't enough money for the school repairs."

"WHAT?"

"He said they'd planned to pay for school repairs out of money they would have saved while the children were at Carningford. But with that not happening . . ."

"That is b.u.l.l.s.h.i.t.," said Rosie. "That man is just such a terrible, terrible guy."

"He is."

"He's actually evil."

"I know," said Stephen. "I wish we could get him with a silver bullet. If I just crept into the crypt he sleeps in. . . ."

"What are we going to do?"

"I don't know," said Stephen. "Mother is going to go crazy if we have to keep this up for much longer, you know. Little Lizzie McAllister broke some hideous stag thing by hanging her schoolbag off it. Mother went spare."

Rosie rolled her eyes. "Oh, God."

Stephen looked at her and at the pork chops.

"Were you still trying to win me around?" he asked.

"Wouldn't dream of it," said Rosie.

Stephen smiled.

"Well, anyway. On the topic of mothers. Mine has invited you all over to dinner tomorrow night."

Rosie nearly dropped her spatula.

"She never asks us over."

"She does, actually. I just assume you won't want to go."

"Oh," said Rosie. "Actually, I would. I don't feel you're helping the situation."

"Well. Everyone's invited."

"Even the children?"

"Are they going to hang bags on stags?"

"Hehe," said Rosie. "Or stick their pens in hens."

"Or drop logs on dogs."

"Pork chops are burning."

"Normally I would say let them burn," said Stephen, caressing her shoulder, "but not when it's your pork chops."

Rosie woke up the next morning to the most unusual sound: the church bells were ringing. It was only Friday. As she came to, she realized that they were ringing out for Edison.

She sat up, smiling.

"Hester isn't going to like that," she said. "She's a Kabbalist, I think. No, hang on, that was last year. I think it's Mother Gaia this year."

"*I* like it," said Stephen, glancing at his watch and groaning at the time. His back felt as if it were on fire; he'd hardly slept a wink. It was still dark outside. "Helps everyone get moving."

Rosie phoned Peak House straightaway. Everyone was up and had been since about five by the sound of things.

"I'll bring up second breakfast," she promised, and put down the phone, still beaming at waking up with such good news. Stephen glanced again at his watch.

"You know, if you don't sink into that bath for the next forty minutes, I'll come with you."

"You will?" said Rosie, unable to stop the look of delight crossing her face.

"What? Why, what have you told them about me? Is this Beauty and the Beast?"

"Heh," said Rosie. "Um, no."

"Go on."

"I have told them next to nothing about you," said Rosie. "Otherwise my mum would go totally nuts."

"So that means I'll be in for the Spanish Inquisition."

"Yes," said Rosie. "Is it really difficult for you, living in a completely normal world where you don't know absolutely everybody, and Uncle Biffy wasn't at Eton with SnooSnoo and Pubes, and everyone has a family tree and a signet ring on their pinky?"

Stephen's social circle and Rosie's crossed as little as possible. Rosie was pleased sometimes that he wasn't a massive socializer. It was entirely selfish, but it meant she got more of him to herself.

"Yeah, all right," said Stephen. "Get a move on, then."

Rosie tried to be a good person. She tried to think well of others. And she adored her family. They were just as good as Stephen's—better in many ways. She had absolutely nothing to be ashamed of. Angie had raised her and Pip single-handedly with no money but with endless love and hard work and the occasional clip around the ear, seemingly at random. She had given them all the tools she had at her disposal, and Rosie was fiercely proud of her and loved her dearly, as well as admiring her for her lifelong hard work and unselfishness. She was proud to be introducing her mother to the man she adored.

But did Angie really have to be wearing a fuchsia Juicy Couture tracksuit? With full makeup and earrings? And big old brown Uggs?

Angie's bright blond hair was scraped upward in a slightly odd kind of pineapple style, and she was wearing a lot of perfume. When the Land Rover stopped, she was standing outside the house with an odd expression on her face. For a horrifying moment as Stephen got out carefully from the Land Rover,

Rosie thought she was actually going to curtsey. She glared at Stephen, daring his lips to even twitch.

But being Stephen, he had immaculate manners and kissed Angie on both cheeks. She was completely speechless, a rare position for Angie.

"Um, Mum, this is Stephen. Stephen, this is Mum."

"Nice to meet you, Mrs. Hopkins."

"Oh, no Mrs. about it," said Angie, looking awkward. Her voice sounded strange. Rosie suddenly noticed that the upward Australian inflection had gone. Was she trying to sound posh?

"Oh no, don't worry about little old me! Angie's fine! And can I call you Steve?"

No doubt about it. She was.

Stephen managed to glide over the whole Steve thing completely—he had never, ever been anything like a Steve—putting out his hand to shake Pip's.

"Hello," they said to each other.

"Pip, are you wearing shorts?" said Rosie. "You know it is snowing and everything."

"I know," said Pip, looking down absentmindedly. "I don't know what I was thinking. It was really warm when I packed."

"I can lend you some trousers if you like," said Stephen.

"Ooh, you're SO kind," said Angie.

"I'm sure my brother can buy his own trousers," said Rosie tightly, missing the amused glance Stephen gave her.

"Where are the kids?"

"Oh, they've been outside since it was light . . . Hi there," said Desleigh, for whose straightforward, breezy Australian friendliness Rosie was suddenly very grateful. "They've never seen snow before. Kelly was furious that it was actually wet. She thought it was basically candy floss. Mind you it hasn't stopped Meridian from eating about a pint of the stuff."

"Let's go around the back," said Rosie. "They can meet Mr. Dog."

"His name isn't Mr. Dog, of course," said Stephen. "That's a holding name. We're actually calling him Reuben Macintosh."

"Yes, we're not," said Rosie, teeth firmly gritted.

"Can I get you a tea? Coffee?" asked Angie anxiously.

Round the back was a cheerful sight: all three of the children, wrapped up in brand-new snowsuits, were rolling around the garden. Mr. Dog ran up to them immediately to give them a good licking, and there were squeals of delight.

"You've got a dog!" said Shane. "We need a dog. Our dog got bitten by a snake."

"And we're not going through that again," said Desleigh. "I had to hit it on the head with a spade."

"The dog or the snake?" asked Stephen.

"Oh, the snake, yeah? They're dangerous bastards."

"What happened to the dog?"

"Yeah, then we had to hit the dog. There's no coming back from something like that."

Rosie felt as if she were representing a family full of syco-phantic animal-hitting, shorts-wearing imbeciles. Meridian came up and gave her another cuddle.

"Hello!" she said. "We like the snow. Except, did you know? It's wet."

"I did know," said Rosie. "But you still like it, yes?"

Meridian nodded.

"Who are you?" she asked. Kelly wandered over to see what was going on.

"I'm Stephen," said Stephen. "This is my house."

"I like your house," said Kelly.

"I BOUNCE BOUNCE BOUNCE ON THE BED," said Meridian.

"Good," said Stephen.

"Then I fell off the bed," said Meridian. "Ow ow ow. Sore. But I didn't cry."

"You did," said Kelly. "You cried a lot."

"I AMN'T!"

"DID!"

"AMN'T!"

"Oh, it doesn't matter," said Rosie briskly.

"What do you do?" asked Kelly, still curious.

"Do you know," said Stephen, crouching down to her height, "I'm a schoolteacher."

Her eyes widened.

"A boy schoolteacher?"

Stephen smiled.

"Yes, I know. There are some boy schoolteachers."

"Do you teach kids who are like my age?"

"I certainly do. Would you like to come and see my school sometime?"

Kelly nodded.

"Actually," said Desleigh, who was bespeckled with toast crumbs from Rosie's second breakfast and filling her mouth with another slice as she wiped her hands on her dressing gown, "that's a great idea. Chuck 'em in school for a few days and I can go out and enjoy myself."

"Um, yes, I don't think that'll be possible," said Rosie.

While Stephen was still explaining the mysteries of a male primary teacher to Kelly, Angie grabbed Rosie in a completely unsubtle neck hold.

"HE'S GORGEOUS," she hissed at the top of her voice, clearly audible in Carningford. "MILES BETTER THAN ANYONE ELSE YOU'VE EVER BEEN OUT WITH! I CAN'T BELIEVE YOU LANDED SOMEONE LIKE HIM! MY LITTLE ROSIE!"

"MUUUUM!" warned Rosie. Stephen didn't look around, but she could see him stiffen.

"WELL DONE, GIRL!"

"MUM! . . . Um, I'll see you later. We have to go."

Angie marched up to Stephen.

"So . . . are you going to make an honest woman of her?"

Everyone froze then, even the children. Rosie could have dug a hole in the snow and buried herself in it forever.

Stephen smiled a fake social smile that stabbed Rosie like a dagger to the heart and muttered something about being late.

Stephen drove, trying to hold on to his conflicting emotions. Rosie glared at him to see if he was going to make a remark, but he kept his face totally neutral.

"So, they seem nice," he ventured finally.

"They are," said Rosie shortly. She could kill her mother. This was so absolutely not the time.

There was a long pause as Stephen skillfully maneuvered the Land Rover around the snowy bends.

"Of course," said Rosie nervously, "you shouldn't listen to any of Mum's prattle really."

"Yes, she was a bit Mrs. Bennet, wasn't she?" said Stephen without thinking.

Rosie stiffened. "She's wonderful," she said tightly.

"Of course," said Stephen and dropped her off with a small kiss. Rosie watched the Land Rover vanish into the distance, partly furious with her mother, partly with a horrible sudden cold finger of doubt curling around her heart.

Chapter 12

The old man's heart rate was threadier than he'd like, thought Moray, but he was in a safe place now. The smell of lunch—roast chicken, it seemed—permeated the hallways, and the heating was cozy without being hopelessly overbearing, which Moray also approved of. Hot stuffy rooms spread infection; an open window here and there was a useful state of affairs. Blankets were dotted around to make sure nobody got cold. Edward Boyd was hovering anxiously. He would stay for the medical check-up then make his way home—alone.

"I grew up around here, you know," said the old man suddenly. At times he sounded completely sensible.

"No you didn't, Dad," said Edward. "You grew up in Halifax."

"This was a school," said James. "Not my school, just a school."

Moray glanced at the matron, who looked a bit surprised.

"It *was* a school, actually," she said. "After the First World War. A boys' school."

"Maybe you played them at sport," said Moray.

"No, I used to cycle past. Look at their posh hats," muttered James.

"You're a bit confused, Dad," said Edward.

"Aye," said the man. "Aye."

Lilian flounced by.

"Miss Hopkins?" said Moray with a warning tone in his voice. "Are you wearing blusher?"

Ida Delia was right behind her, her faded dyed blond hair tied up with a pink ribbon.

"I've never worn cosmetics in my life," sniffed Lilian, lying through her teeth. "Oh, hello, Mr. Boyd," she said in mock surprise. "How are you settling in?"

The old man looked up. He stared at Lilian for a long time.

"You look like someone," he said.

Lilian looked back at him. She'd suddenly had the most ridiculous feeling: this old man would be about Henry's age, if Henry had lived. But would he have liked to live this long? To be so old and confused and distracted by life? In her memory, Henry was always young, always strong, with nut-brown curly hair, and a freckled nose, and strong white teeth and a ready laugh.

"Yes . . . the town tart," said Ida Delia.

"I'm cutting off your lemon sherbets," said Lilian. "You're acidic enough."

But James was still staring at her, looking confused. Moray had to prompt him a few times to get him to respond.

"Watch this one doesn't get overexcited," he said to Cathryn. "His heart isn't exactly what I'd like it to be."

Edward's grip tightened on the side of the chair.

"Oh no, I don't mean anything awful," said Moray. "He's in

reasonable health, mostly, apart from his poor old brain, and his heart is a little weak. So. Worth keeping an eye on."

Edward nodded.

"Which means you two minxes staying away from him."

"Lilian," said James suddenly, out of the blue.

Lilian whipped around. Hearing her name like that, just when she'd been thinking about Henry . . . well, it was silly. They had some accent in common, something that made it sound similar.

They looked at each other for a second.

"That's right," said Moray, pleased. "That's her name."

"James," said Lilian.

Cathryn took Moray aside on his way out.

"I hope he'll be okay," said Moray.

"I'm sure he will," said Cathryn. "He's in good hands."

She paused for a moment.

"But here's a funny thing: I've only ever referred to Lilian as Miss Hopkins."

They looked at each other for a moment, then Moray shrugged.

"Amazing what people pick up, even in dementia. If you're lucky, he'll get a bit of respite by being here, having a routine, same thing every day. I'm sure it'll help."

"Here's hoping" said Cathryn, sending Moray out into the chilly day.

"Where's the shopping?" Angie had wondered. "What do you do all day?" and Rosie had found it impossible to explain that

actually, she kept very busy. Desleigh had said it reminded her
of Wagga Wagga where she'd grown up, where nothing ever
happened and there were just lots and lots of sheep, and she
had been so pleased to move to Sydney, but she didn't hear
many people saying they did the same thing in reverse.

Rosie had smiled and bitten her lip and not responded,
which seemed best under the circumstances. She bought the
children pastries at the local bakery; they eyed them curiously
before trying them and pronouncing them "all right, yeah."
Then they spent a nice quiet twenty minutes walking around
the churchyard and finishing them off.

"Is that it?" said Desleigh at the end.

"Well, there's the Red Lion," said Rosie, slightly desperately. "And Manly's." They went into the boutique, not without some sniggering from Angie and Desleigh, who were,
Rosie noted with something surprisingly like jealousy, thick as
thieves. And it was pretty rich for them to be sneering at extra-
large blazers and waxed coats when they were wearing leisure
wear, tight in Angie's case, very baggy in Desleigh's. After this
they had a ploughman's back at the cottage, and the kids drank
cream soda and declared it to be excellent, and then it was time
to go and see Lilian.

"Do I need to prepare them for anything?" said Angie
slightly anxiously. Shane had put down his video game long
enough to help Kelly and Meridian build a snowman out in the
back garden, complete with woolly hat and a potato for a nose,
and Meridian was trying to take its hand and encourage it to fly.

"No, it's actually really nice," said Rosie. "Really, don't
worry about it, it's a nice place for her to be."

"I haven't seen her for . . . oh, years," said Angie. She
looked straight at Rosie. Rosie had mentioned earlier that An-

gie had taken the wrong tone with Stephen. Angie had looked huffy and said something about her having hung around with the last boyfriend for far too long and she hoped she wasn't going to make the same mistake twice. Now Angie looked more worried.

"Do you think . . . I mean, was she cross I didn't come to look after her?"

"Oh Mum, are you worried about that? No, of course not. She was furious anyone came, I promise. Couldn't get a civil word out of her for months. It's just her way, so don't worry about it, okay?"

"Okay," said Angie. "It's just, she was so kind to me when you were little and . . ."

"And she's going to be delighted you've come all this way to see her," said Rosie firmly. "Come on, let's go. It'll be great."

And she started to hustle the little ones in from the garden. Meridian's lip was pouting.

"Why is my snowman not doing FLYING?" she asked crossly.

Rosie looked at it.

"I saw a snowman on television. He did FLYING."

"Yes," said Rosie, crouching down next to her. "But did he do flying in the daytime or at night?"

Meridian thought for a moment.

"NIGHTtime."

"Well, there you go. I think he only goes flying in the night-time."

"I'll wait at nighttime," said Meridian. "Can I go with him if he goes flying?"

"Of course!" said Rosie.

Meridian slipped her little chilly hand into Rosie's warm one.

"Shall we go and see your great-great-aunt?"

Meridian frowned.

"Is she going to be scary? Shane says she's scary, and Kelly said she's a witch who's going to eat me."

"Ke-ll-ee!!!" shouted Angie.

"I never!" shouted Kelly loudly without hearing what she was being accused of. "I never did!"

"They get on beautifully," said Angie. "Normally."

"She's not going to eat you," said Rosie. "She's very nice."

She remembered Lilian's crusty exterior. "When you get to know her. Shall we take her some sweeties? She might share them with you."

Meridian's face lit up as Rosie led her into the shop, Kelly and Shane immediately pushing and shoving their way in behind.

All three fell silent when confronted with the bounty before them. Sunlight bounced off the icicles that had formed in the windows and was reflected on the large glass jars that stretched to the ceiling full of every manner and color of bright boiled sweets: pineapple cubes and sour apples and plums; lemon drops and cherry lips; kola cubes and livid orange suckers. On another shelf, the deep browns of the toffees—vanilla, mint, orange, dark, treacle, banana—blended with the soft penny caramels and the fudge; all Cornish, some with rum and raisin (despite Lilian's express instructions), some with whisky and Baileys. Meridian's attention was caught by the delicate raspberry pink and white of the coconut ice in a jar, and her little finger pointed at it longingly.

"This. Is. Ace," breathed Shane, all his nine-year-old cool forgotten as he gazed around and around.

"Yes, well, we're not going to go nuts," said Rosie sternly, realizing with a start that she suddenly sounded exactly like Lilian.

Desleigh had followed them in.

"Oh my Gawd," she said. "Look at this, it's the cutest thing I've ever seen."

"It's quite a successful business, actually," said Rosie, bristling a bit. She didn't like people thinking it was just a hobby.

"Can we have some, Mum? Please? I want to spend all my pocket money."

"Oh, you don't have to pay here," said Desleigh. "Have whatever you like."

Rosie bit her lip. Their profit levels weren't quite up to being attacked by three small locusts. On the other hand, they had flown all this way.

"Well, I don't want to make you all sick," she said. "You can all try one thing every day, okay?"

"Aww," said Desleigh as if Rosie were being horribly mean. "Well, I'll start with some of that fudge, thanks!"

Kelly chose what her mother had; Shane took a long time to decide but eventually plumped for a Wham Bar, which Rosie approved of in terms of how quiet it would keep him, and Meridian kept holding up her finger toward the coconut ice. Rosie lifted her onto the counter.

"Have you tried this before?" she said. Meridian shook her head shyly.

"Well," said Rosie. "I think you're going to like it."

Meridian obediently opened her mouth wide, and Rosie broke off a piece and dropped it in. Meridian's eyes popped open.

"Ooh," she said. "That's YUM YUM YUM YUM YUM."

"Me and Mummy chose the best thing, didn't we, Mummy?"

said Kelly, who, Rosie had noticed, was roughly the same soft shape as her mother. "Yes, we did. We chose the best one."

Meridian's face started to crumple.

"I'll tell you a secret," said Rosie, whispering in her ear and popping a piece of coconut ice into her own mouth. "This is MY favorite."

Meridian smiled and stuck out her tongue at her sister. "We've got OUR favorites."

Angie fussed in, the bell tinging. "Okay, come on, come on, let's go."

She looked around at the shop.

"Oh," she said, suddenly lost for words. She looked at Rosie.

"Oh Rosie, it hasn't changed . . . You've . . . It . . . I mean, was it like this when you found it?"

Rosie shook her head, remembering the enormous amount of work she'd needed to do to clean and sort the place out.

"Not exactly," she said tactfully.

"It's . . . it's exactly how I remember it. Except I was looking at it from Kelly's height then, I suppose." Her taut brown face suddenly seemed to sag a little.

"What's up, Mum?" said Rosie.

"Oh, nothing," said Angie. "I just miss your grandfather, that's all."

She choked a bit.

"Mind you, he hated it up here. Said it was too quiet. I don't think he ever got over losing his brother. Never had a mum either."

"I know," said Rosie. "Lilian told me all about it."

"So there weren't a lot of happy memories for him up here. And Gordon, he was always a bit of a lad about town."

She shook her head.

"It's amazing," she said. "Imagine you coming back here. Well, well, well, blood will out."

Rosie nodded.

"I suppose."

"Look at you—have you got an apron?"

"I certainly do."

Angie shook her head. "Ha. After all I tried to do to get you a proper education . . . qualified nurse . . . you end up working in a shop!"

"Running a shop!" said Rosie, stung. "Cor, you're going to get along with Stephen's mum."

Lilian had commandeered the major drawing room in the home, the one with the good coffee bar and some people trying to have a game of dominoes who complained bitterly when she moved them off.

"Well, my entire family has flown over from Australia to be with me over Christmas," she said loudly. "They've come right across the entire world because they care so much about me. Is your family coming today, Aggie? I'll clear right out immediately if they are."

Aggie sniffed and made a remark about some people being very much in love with themselves and pride coming before a fall and some such, but Lilian stood her ground, completely unabashed, and when Rosie and everyone turned up in the Land Rover, she stood as if welcoming them to her charming home, gracious as a queen.

"Angela," she said, opening her arms. "Oh my, what are you doing to your skin? Is that what it's like in Australia? You look like leatherette."

Desleigh's eyes popped open, and Rosie's hand flew to her mouth, but Angie only said, "Oh, Lil, it's called having a lovely tan. Shut up and come here."

The two women embraced.

"You're a lot less fat," said Lilian.

"I know," said Angie. "It's Zumba. I'm great at it."

"I don't know what that means," said Lilian. "But well done."

"*You* look amazing," said Angie. "You don't look like you need to be in a home at all."

Lilian preened. "I know," she said in a stage whisper. "I wanted to make things easy on Rosie."

This was such an outrageous lie that Rosie nearly coughed up the last tiny bit of coconut ice that Meridian had insisted on sharing with her.

"Well, that was very kind of you," said Angie. Pip came forward, looking cheery and a bit confused. Stephen's moleskin trousers were far too long for him, and he'd had to roll them up at the bottom. He was wearing them with espadrilles.

"The only thing about being in here," said Lilian carefully, "is that you have trouble keeping up with fashion."

"Hi," said Pip, who in truth barely remembered her; just Christmases of Rosie rolling about because she'd eaten so much caramel she thought she was going to explode, and the time he was sick because he'd eaten too many rainbow drops.

"And who are these little people?"

Shane had dived behind his DS again. Rosie would have grabbed it off him, but neither Pip nor Desleigh seemed to be paying it much attention. Rosie pushed Kelly forward, but Kelly clung to her mother.

"Hello," said Meridian, going up and shaking hands very formally. "I'm Spiderman."

Lilian smiled and shook her hand carefully.

"Spiderman, it is very nice to meet you."

She looked at her closely.

"Now, I think I can guess something about you," she said. "Shall we see?"

"She's a witch," Kelly whispered loudly behind Desleigh.

"Do you," asked Lilian, "like to eat coconut ice?"

Meridian's eyes widened immediately, and she nodded her head, in awe of the old lady's powers.

"Yes!!!" she whispered.

"I have some more inside," said Lilian, ushering them in out of the cold.

"You haven't!" said Rosie. "I told Cathryn to watch out for contraband. You have to eat the food they have here."

"You'd have to get up pretty early in the morning to catch me out," said Lilian gaily as Rosie kissed the soft white cheek.

"Oh," she said suddenly, touching it. "You know, it is wonderful to see you all."

"I know," said Rosie. "Also, can you come to dinner tonight?"

"This is a very late invitation."

Rosie rolled her eyes.

"Why, what else is in your diary?"

"Don't be a smart alec. It's ballroom dancing tonight, so there, and I want to see what the new man is like at a fox-trot."

"Fine, don't come."

"Is it the Red Lion?"

"No, Hetty's invited us up."

"Oh yes," said Lilian. "I'd completely forgotten."

"She invited you already?"

"Of course," said Lilian. "To make conversation with if she gets bored."

"Oh, I thought it might be something like that," said Rosie. "Well, are you coming?"

"Wouldn't miss it for the world," said Lilian.

"Good stuff."

"I'm sure Angie and Hetty will get on brilliantly . . . What does Pineapple mean? It's written all over her top."

"Ssh!"

"And isn't it a bit cold to be showing off your navel?"

Pip had taken the children out to play, and Rosie busied herself making coffee while Angie and Lilian caught up with distant cousins and people Rosie couldn't remember or had never heard of. It was amazing how many of them were dead. She guessed that was just what happened when you got this old. She half-listened and smiled at Desleigh, who scooped three spoonfuls of sugar into her coffee and tried to get closer to the fire.

"So, what do you think of our Rosie's Stephen then?" asked Lilian finally.

"Be quiet, Lilian," said Rosie.

"OOH!" said Angie.

"See," said Rosie.

"How on earth did she find someone like that," said Angie, full of delight. "Do you think they'll get married?"

Rosie put her head in her hands.

"MU-UM! You can't . . . you just have to shut up about it."

"Oh come on, look at him . . . Loaded, posh."

"I don't care about that," said Rosie. "Well, because he isn't loaded: he has totally negative money and is skinter than me. And being posh is no fun, believe me. I like him for what's underneath it all," she went on.

". . . and hot like a fox," continued Angie.

"Yes, hot like a fox," said Rosie. "Okay. That one I'll give you."

"How did you get him again?" mused Angie.

"Oh, she hunted him into the ground," said Lilian. "Rather like a fox, in fact."

"I did NOT!" said Rosie.

"Well, how did you meet him? You've been very cagey about it."

Rosie pinched her lips together. "Well. I was his . . ."

Angie grabbed her arm.

"You weren't his nurse?"

Rosie flushed pink.

"I was. I mean, I was helping out."

"That is SO wrong," said Angie, delighted.

"It wasn't like that," said Rosie.

"What, you weren't stripping off his clothes when he was sick and vulnerable?"

"You sound like Hetty," said Rosie. "It wasn't like that. We didn't get together for ages afterward."

"How many ages?"

"Mum. Stop it, okay? How we met isn't important."

For once, Lilian stepped in on Rosie's side.

"It wasn't at all like that," she said to Angie.

"Thank you, Lilian," said Rosie.

"Basically, your Rosie flung herself at every man in the village, including Jake the farmhand and Moray, that nice young fairy doctor . . ."

"LILIAN!" said Rosie

". . . and Stephen was the one who took the bait. Of course he was recovering from a long illness . . . ," she added thoughtfully.

"Right. You are all horrible and I disown my entire family," said Rosie.

"Before or after dinner?" said Angie.

Chapter 13

Rosie put on a nice green dress that suited her coloring and popped into the shop to get Tina to put on her eyeliner. But when she got there, Tina was jumping up and down in excitement.

"What?" asked Rosie.

"I can't tell you," said Tina.

"What is it? Why not? Can I make you tell me by being your boss?"

"Oh NO," said Tina, looking panicked. "I forgot about that."

"I'm only kidding," said Rosie. "You don't have to tell me if you don't want to. What is it?"

"But I said I'd wait . . . Oh well, I'll just tell Jake you made me."

Rosie nodded.

"What?"

Slowly and carefully Tina revealed her small, beautifully manicured left hand. On the fourth finger, sparkling in the light, was a tiny but immaculate diamond ring.

"OH MY GOD!" said Rosie, experiencing a rush of joy for her friend and a slight wobble she put down to being hungry and nervous. "Oh my God, Tina! Amazing! It's beautiful!"

Tina blushed bright pink.

"I know!"

"Tell me everything."

"Well," said Tina. "It's a bit rubbish really."

"Why?"

"Because he meant to do it at Christmas. Then I was washing his overalls and I found it."

"He kept it in his overalls?"

"Yes, he said he was terrified of me tidying around it and finding it."

"But you were cleaning up after him anyway?"

"I like doing it," said Tina, and indeed Rosie had often had cause to be grateful for her way with a feather duster.

"Anyway, I tried to put it back in the clean overalls and pretend I hadn't found it."

"Did that work?" said Rosie.

"Um, no," said Tina. "I couldn't stop giggling and blushing, and he found me out immediately. Do you want to try it on?"

"Um . . ."

"Come on!" said Tina and pulled it off, but it wouldn't go over Rosie's bigger finger. She admired it on her pinkie instead.

"Oh, it's lovely," said Rosie. "What did he say?"

Tina looked confused.

"He said, 'Will you marry me?'"

"Oh," said Rosie. "On one knee?"

"On one knee," said Tina. "But he asked the children first."

This made Rosie feel like she was going to cry.

"What do you mean?"

"He explained to Kent and Emily that he wasn't their daddy, but he'd like to stay with their mummy if they were okay with it."

"Oh," said Rosie. "That's amazing. What did they say?"

"Kent thought about it and nodded his head and told Jake he made Mummy happy, and Emily dashed in to ask if she could wear a princess dress to the wedding, and he had to grab the back of her collar to stop her spoiling the moment."

Tina smiled at the memory.

"But she didn't. Not a bit."

Rosie gave her a hug. "It's wonderful," she said. "He's a wonderful man."

"He is," said Tina complacently. "And you next."

Rosie harrumphed. Her heart slumped.

"At this rate," she said, "I think I'll just be lucky to get out of tonight without a big fight."

"Your mum seems lovely on the phone," said Tina.

"She is," said Rosie. "Everyone is lovely. It'll be fine." She sighed.

"Don't be silly," said Tina, trying to apply eyeliner and admire her ring at the same time. "I bet Stephen will get you a ring next."

Rosie tried to imagine it but couldn't.

"Oh, we're a long way from there," she said sadly.

"Do you think?"

Rosie swallowed.

"I . . . it doesn't matter," she said. She had spent a very long time in her last relationship without getting engaged, so she wasn't going to start fussing about this one.

On the other hand, Jake and Tina had started seeing each other only a very little while before her and Stephen. What made them so sure? It felt like when she and Stephen were alone, the two of them together, everything seemed ideal; they loved each other and got on perfectly.

It was only when their relationship was held up to the light of examination by family and friends that cracks started to appear. Other people seemed to think it was a strange match, or that they were odd together, and it made her doubt herself all the time. She knew what Stephen would say: if he wanted to do something, he couldn't care less about what other people thought. But she did, and she couldn't help that.

All she said was, "Tina, I'm so happy for you."

Tina's face glowed with happiness so strong it lit up the little shop, closing up on the dark winter evening.

Up at Peak House, Rosie couldn't help herself.

"Mum, are you sure you want to wear that? You'll freeze."

"Don't I look good?"

"You look amazing."

This was not strictly true. Angie was wearing a strapless floral dress that might have looked amazing on a teenager on a beach in Australia in the summer, but that made the blood freeze to look at in Derbyshire in December.

"But it's cold up at the big house."

"They don't put the central heating on for visitors?"

"They don't have central heating. They light their oil stoves for the children."

"Who doesn't have central heating?" scoffed Angie. "And they're posh."

"Well, can you at least take a shawl or something?"

"But then I don't get to show off my tan."

Rosie didn't want to point out how crêpey the tan looked around the bustline. Also, the strapless dress didn't really hold itself up terribly well, which was a bit of a worry. If they sat behind a high table, she'd look completely naked.

Desleigh, meanwhile, eating crisps, was wearing something schlumpy in black, but had put on lots of heavy eyeliner. It had the odd effect of making her look like a teenager, but in a very peculiar way.

"You look gorge, Ange, don't listen to her."

Shane remained buried in his Nintendo.

"Um, he's not going to bring it, is he?" whispered Rosie to Pip, who looked bemused.

"Why not?" he said. "It'll keep him quiet."

"Mu-um," said Kelly. "Meridian's getting ready in the wrong stuff, not the stuff you told her to."

"I AMN'T!" came a loud voice in panic.

"She is, Mum, she's doing it all wrong."

Kelly appeared in the sitting room wearing a Disney princess costume that was a little too tight under the arms and that gave her the rather off-putting appearance of having an incipient bust. Scampering after her looking very hot and cross was Meridian, half-strangled in a Spiderman pajama top that was far too big for her.

"Oi!" said Shane, seemingly without looking up. "Take off my pajamas, you bogan."

"AMN'T," came the voice under rather a lot of bri-nylon.

"Oh Lor, not with the Spiderman again," said Desleigh. Kelly rolled her eyes at the same time as her mother.

"You're a girl," said Desleigh crossly. "You can't be Spider-man."

"I SPIDERMAN."

"You can be a princess," said Kelly helpfully. "Or a fairy. Or a fairy princess." Helpfully, she did a little spin.

"NO!"

"Can't she just be Spiderman?" said Rosie, realizing it was getting terribly late.

"Not in my bloody pajamas," said Shane.

"Don't say bloody," said Pip automatically.

"Has she got anything else?" said Rosie.

"She's got my old fairy princess dress," said Kelly. "That I very kindly let her have."

"DOAN WANT IT."

"Only we're going to be late."

Desleigh looked off into the middle distance as if this was all somebody else's problem. Angie came forward and started negotiating with Meridian, which didn't seem to be working in the slightest. She seemed to be on the point of begging. Rosie dashed into a bedroom and came back with one of Stephen's old scarves. He wouldn't mind, thought Rosie. It was an emergency.

"Now, Meridian," she said, kneeling down so she was facing her, like Supernanny told her to do (Rosie wouldn't have admitted watching *Supernanny* in a million years).

"Here's a Spider belt for all your Spider things, okay?"

Meridian stopped bawling and looked up at her, blinking away tears.

"A real one?"

"Yes," said Rosie, brooking no argument. "Look."

And she pulled down the top of Shane's pajamas, so it hung to Meridian's knees. She rolled up the sleeves and tied the scarf around her waist to make an unconventional dress.

"And Spiderman isn't wearing his Spider trousers today . . ."

Meridian's lip started to quiver. "Because . . . Desleigh, have you got tights for her?"

Desleigh nodded and produced a pair of black little girl's tights, brand-new, from her bag.

"They're to go with her dress," said Desleigh.

"Look at those!" Rosie said to Meridian. "Look!"

She unfolded them. Meridian's eyes started to widen.

"This is . . . BAT LEGS," said Meridian.

"I think they *are* bat legs," said Rosie.

"They! Are! Bat! Legs! Like BATMAN!"

Rosie nodded.

"You know this makes you Spiderman AND Batman?" she said. Meridian nodded reverently. "Look at my bat legs, Kelly!"

"No, they're not," said Kelly. "You're a girl."

"And I want my pajamas back," said Shane.

"Come on, everyone, in the car," said Angie finally, for which Rosie was very grateful.

Pip walked her over.

"Are you okay?" he said. "You seem a bit stressed out."

Rosie smiled at him.

"You are very good at never getting stressed out."

"No point," said Pip. "You've just got to roll with it. But I'm not surprised this weather makes you tense."

"I like this weather," said Rosie, scraping down the wind-screen.

"Sure, sis, whatever you say," said Pip. "But you know, it's just your boyf's house, yeah? I don't know why you're so stressy about it."

Rosie considered this crossly. Neither did she.

As they approached Lipton Hall along the long driveway, Rosie noticed that her mother's mouth had dropped open at the sight of all the turrets and windows.

"It must cost a fortune to heat this place," she said.

"Ah," said Rosie. "For the schoolchildren it does." She had drawn up at the back door, only to notice that Hetty was at the front door, and had to make a speedy reversal on the gravel. Mr. Dog was already squeaking from excitement. Shane didn't even look up from his game.

Moray had phoned earlier to say that he'd drop Lilian off.

"Aren't you staying?" asked Rosie. She wouldn't have minded some neutral buffering. There was a long silence.

"What?" said Rosie.

"You haven't eaten at the big house before."

"I have so, I went to the hunt ball."

"Oh, my darling. That was catered. You know she's given Mrs. Laird the night off?"

"So . . . ?"

"I'll pop an antacid prescription in on my way home, okay?"

"NOT OKAY," said Rosie, but he'd already hung up.

The snow crunched on the gravel as they disembarked. Hetty stood there giving them all the once-over. It was hard to tell what was colder: the frosty air or her glance.

"Angie . . . Angela," said Rosie's mum. For a terrible instant Rosie thought she was going to curtsey. "Amazing house."

"What are you WEARING?" said Hetty. "Aren't you FREEZING?"

"No, I'm fine," lied Angie through chattering teeth.

Pip put his hand out and nudged Shane to do the same.

"I'm Rosie's brother," he said.

"And who's this?" said Hetty, staring at Shane. Shane stared at his feet. Pip nudged him again, but he didn't say a word, even when Angie hissed at him.

"Um, this is Shane," said Pip.

"Is he all right?" asked Hetty.

"Yes, just shy," said Desleigh.

Hetty sniffed.

"We're all shy, darling," she said.

Kelly stepped forward and did a twirl.

"I'm Kelly."

"Nice to meet you, Kelly," said Hetty. "Welcome."

Kelly smiled smugly and stuck her tongue out at her brother.

"And who's this?"

"Spiderman," said Meridian in a tiny voice.

"What's that?" boomed Hetty.

"I Spiderman."

"She's called what? Simona?"

"This is Meridian," said Rosie, putting a reassuring hand on her niece's shoulder. "Hello, Hetty. Let's go in, shall we. It's freezing out here."

"I never notice the cold," sniffed Hetty.

"Where's Stephen?"

"He's just helping Lilian to the loo," said Hetty, as usual not mincing her words, and Rosie smiled despite herself as the party entered.

It was a little warmer inside but not much. There was a fire lit in the back kitchen, where Hetty herself was doing the cooking, and that was nice and cozy, but they weren't eating in there. They were in the proper formal dining room tonight, which was about twenty-five meters long, with a small, not very optimistic-looking fire lit in the grate. Rosie was sure that if you could see all the way up into the corner of the room (which you couldn't because the ceilings were too high and the lighting too musty), you would see icicles form.

"It's like *The Addams Family*," whispered Angie to her daughter as they entered. "Cor."

"I'm frightened," whined Kelly.

"I will save you with my BAT LEGS," said Meridian bravely, karate-chopping at a suit of armor.

"Hello, everyone," said Stephen, coming in leading Lilian.

"Stephen has just been helping me out of the car," said Lilian in case anyone thought she'd just been to the toilet.

Angie kissed her.

"You look lovely," she said, and she did; Lilian was wearing a cream skirt with a thick lilac tunic and a long, soft cream wool cardigan. It looked stylish and comfortable and warm all at once, and she had added a touch of lilac eyeshadow.

"I know," said Lilian. "You look completely underdressed. Are you going to a discotheque afterward?"

Angie stood as close to the fire as she could get without actually setting herself alight.

"You don't change much, Lilian."

"No," sighed Lilian. "But is it pitch dark in here or is it just me?"

"No, it's everyone," said Rosie. "The children are terrified."

"Oh well," said Lilian. "At least we won't be able to see what we're eating."

Stephen kissed Rosie briefly. She wanted to grab him, breathe him in, but he winced as she brushed the skin on his side, and she drew back.

"How are you?" she asked.

"Knackered," said Stephen. "I feel I've had enough of the little blighters today. Not to diss your relations, but . . . does that boy ever put his device down? He's like some awful City banker trying to get a mobile signal."

"Ssh," said Rosie. "They're in an unfamiliar environment."

"Yeah, Super Mario Land."

Stephen watched Kelly practice her dance moves.

"Ah, the sugar plum elephant," he observed.

"Shut up!" said Rosie. "Stop it! Don't pass judgment."

"I'm just making an observation!"

"Well, don't," said Rosie. She was furious because she knew she was overwrought, slightly too keyed up about how much she wanted everyone to get on, and at the moment there were just knots of people in a dark room, bitching about each other.

"Okay. Sorry," said Stephen. "Jeez, you're touchy today."

"Well, be nice to me then," said Rosie. She picked up Meridian, who was nestling by her knees.

"Hello, Spiderman," said Stephen.

Meridian smiled proudly. "I Spiderman AND Batman."

"PHEW," said Stephen. "So we're totally protected."

"This is like Batman's house," said Shane suddenly without looking up. "Have you got a cool car under the house?"

"Afraid not," said Stephen. "I've got a wheelchair though."

Shane went back to his game.

After what felt like about two hours to Rosie, Hetty appeared with gin and tonics. Rosie was so relieved that she took a huge gulp, only to splutter when she realized it was at least ninety percent gin with a tiny squirt of tonic on the top.

"Bloody hell!" she said.

"Oh yes," said Stephen, tucking into his. "I meant to have a word with you about the fact that you don't know how to mix a gin and tonic."

"By pouring the tonic straight down the sink?"

Stephen looked at his drink.

"You see, to me this is basically perfect."

"Oh, Stephen, you look exactly like your father standing there," said Lilian. Rosie nearly choked for a second time. Stephen's relationship with his father was something generally not to be brought up in public.

"Yes, but he could just as well be Frosty the Snowman in this light," said Angie. "Or the Incredible Hulk."

"Thank you, Mrs. Hopkins," said Stephen.

"No worries. I like this new cocktail. And it's 'Miss.'"

"Dinner," announced Hetty.

Meridian's head barely came over the tabletop. Rosie looked around for a cushion, but Angie had already whisked her into her lap. The children all looked dubiously at the plates of soup in front of them. They were on the finest white china with a golden inlay that Rosie was pretty sure was real, and she crossed her fingers and prayed they wouldn't get dropped on the floor. The children also regarded the array of cutlery in front of them with dismay.

"Normally I only like things you can pick up with your fingers," said Kelly.

"Like cake?" said Hetty pointedly. Rosie blinked twice at her horrific rudeness.

"Yeah," said Kelly. "Mum, I want cake."

"Do you want to try a spoon, Kelly sweetheart?" said Desleigh.

"Is it like Heinz, Mummy? I only like Heinz," whined Kelly. "Or cake."

Just as Desleigh lifted a spoon to her lips, Hetty invited Lilian to say grace, and Rosie immediately felt like kicking absolutely everyone involved. She couldn't help noticing, either, that Stephen had the merest hint of a twitching lip. He had to get rid of it straightaway before she got exceptionally cross with him.

Lilian said a traditional grace, gently, and they all dug in.

Rosie closed her eyes. It was awful. It tasted a bit like what would happen if you drank the dishwater. After it had been left to cool down in the fridge.

"What kind of soup is this?" said Desleigh, doing her best.

Hetty gave her a look.

"It's oxtail."

"OXTAIL?" said Shane. "Gross." He started eating. Kelly burst into tears. "Mum! I don't want to eat tail."

To keep her company, Meridian burst into tears too until Rosie leaned over and whispered, "Spiderman? Do you think Spidermen eat their suppers?" and Meridian thought about it and nodded fiercely and started scooping it up. Rosie wondered if it was dark enough in the room to pour hers into the suit of armor.

"Mmm," said Stephen. "That's gorgeous."

"I know," said Hetty. Rosie narrowed her eyes at him. Was he winding her up?

"I haven't . . . it's been a long time since I've eaten at home," said Stephen, by way of explanation. He wasn't wearing his normal ironical look. Rosie glanced around for bread to soak the soup up with, but there wasn't any. Still, Shane and Meridian were doing well enough with theirs—Angie was pretending to share her plate with Meridian, thus handily avoiding the issue. Kelly was sitting with her bottom lip stuck out, but nobody paid attention to that.

"So anyway," said Hetty in a commanding voice. It wasn't really a surprise she had such a loud voice, Rosie supposed, growing up in a place like this. "I don't think I can bear all those children in the house another minute."

"What's wrong with us?" asked Shane.

Hetty looked at him. "Oh, he talks," she said. "But I don't mean you, I mean the schoolchildren. They're getting to be quite the limit."

Stephen wiped his mouth with his napkin. "They're just being kids, Mother. It's a good sign, shows they're not still traumatized by the accident."

"But the noise!"

"They're just practicing singing."

"And the running about."

"That's what healthy children do."

"And my stag's head."

"Ah, yes. Sorry about that. They thought it was a coat hook."

"And the banister."

"Most of them don't live in houses with banisters. Certainly not ones so temptingly slideable."

"I knew a small boy who slid down a lot of banisters," said Lillian.

"Nonsense," said Stephen. "I was a paragon of virtue."

"Virtue and sulking," said Hetty. "Well, anyway, regardless. English Heritage are going to have a total fit, and it won't do the house any good. We're close enough to rack and ruin as it is. If they scratch up the floors any more or give it that kiddie smell, we'll lose bookings. Someone has already decided not to have their wedding here when they turned up and found four small boys hanging off the ceremonial bridal arch by their knees."

"Rather a nice touch I thought," said Stephen, but Hetty didn't smile.

"No," she said. "I think I have given quite a lot to this village, but I think this school has to stop. I'm sorry, Rosie."

"But if you close the school here . . ."

"My girl, they aren't going to fix the school. You have to get that through your head. They are not going to release the funds to fix up the school. This was always a temporary arrangement . . . or do you expect me to run a free school for the rest of my life?"

"No," said Rosie.

"No. Well. Sooner sorted, the better."

Rosie felt ridiculously as if she were going to cry in front of everybody.

"Well, that will be the end of us too," said Lilian. "No children, no sweets. It's just about that simple."

"Oh, don't be dramatic, Lil."

"I'm not. No school, no families. No families, no sweetshop."

Hetty cleared away the mostly untouched soup plates and returned with a red-raw piece of roast beef, plain boiled potatoes and some vegetables that had obviously been steaming for several days.

"WONDERFUL," said Stephen, leaping up to carve. "I've slightly missed your cooking, Mum. She didn't do it very often," he explained to the table.

"Really?" muttered Angie.

"But when Mrs. Laird was off . . . it was kind of a treat."

He looked toward his mother, and a rare smile of détente passed between them.

"Of course you can sell the cottage," said Lilian. "We might as well be honest. I'm not moving back. Too old."

"And you like it where you are?" asked Angie anxiously.

"Well, as far as being bunged up in a prison for the mentally and physically incontinent, I suppose it could be worse," allowed Lilian. "It's you I worry about," she said, pointing her fork at Rosie.

"Can I just have some brown bits from around the edges?" said Angie. "Sorry, it's just that in Australia we normally cook our food."

"Incinerate it, surely. On the 'barbie-cue'?" inquired Hetty, as if she'd only just heard of the word.

"I'll be fine," said Rosie, feeling something drop in the pit of her stomach.

"Well, what will you do if the sweetshop closes?" said Lilian.

"Ahem," said Angie, clearing her throat, and seeming to

give up on dinner altogether. "Well. Of course. We'll just take Rosie back to Australia with us."

"What are you doing?" asked Doreen, looking over Edward's shoulder. It wasn't like him to get obsessed with the Internet; normally he tried to stop Ian doing exactly that. He believed in a proper separation between work and home and liked their son to eat a nice dinner and chat about his day. This wasn't like him at all.

"Just some . . . research," said Edward in a muffled voice.

Doreen went around and put down his tea—one Hermesetas—to have a look. He was on a website called Veterans UK, for ex-servicemen.

"What are you looking for?"

"I don't really know," said Edward. "It just occurred to me, really, because he never likes talking about it . . . I just wanted to see if I could pin down any more about Dad in the war."

"With a name like James Boyd, you'll be lucky," sniffed Doreen. "There'll be loads."

"No, look," said Edward, suddenly excited, as the search engine pinged up its results. "It's amazing what people have uploaded these days, tons and tons of info."

Sure enough, about three pages in there was a James Boyd, born in Halifax in 1921.

"That's him."

Doreen grabbed a chair and sat down next to him, feeling excited in her own right.

"Ooh, go on, let's have a look then. You know, you might have family you don't even know about."

"I've got quite enough trouble going on with the family I do have," joked Edward, but his face was pink with anticipation.

They had a very slow broadband line out in the sticks—Ian did nothing but complain about it—but finally the page loaded itself. They gazed at it. There was a picture there of a young man, straight black hair cut short, freckles on the long nose. They looked at the picture for a long time.

"You know," said Doreen finally, "it's amazing how people change the way they look."

Edward shook his head.

"That's not him," he said. "We must have the wrong James Boyd."

"The date of birth is the same," said Doreen.

"Amazing coincidence," said Edward. "I'm going to search some more."

"Well, don't stay up too late, darling," said Doreen, planting a kiss on his shoulder. She could never sleep without him beside her in the bed, even after all these years.

"Of course Rosie's not leaving," said Stephen. He was making his way through dinner at some speed with obvious enjoyment.

Rosie didn't know what to say; her mother's words were so unexpected.

"Well, what's she going to do here?" said Angie. "She's done her duty. And she could go back to London, but London's over. Sydney's where it's at now. And she can be with her family. But it'll have to be soon; nurses can't get visas over thirty-five."

"Er, Mum, this is ridiculous," said Rosie.

"Are you coming to live with us, Auntie Rosie?" said Kelly.

"You know we have a swimming pool. You can come in our swimming pool."

"ROSIE WE GOT BIG SWIMMING POOL! COME IN BIG SWIMMING POOL!" said Meridian, wriggling out of Angie's lap and onto Rosie's. She turned Rosie's face toward hers and showered her with kisses.

"I YIKE you," she announced loudly. Rosie half-smiled and kissed her back.

"I like you too," she said. "Don't be daft, Angie. I'm very happy here."

Pip and Desleigh were clearly exchanging glances across the table, which made Rosie furious.

"Doing what?" scoffed Angie. "I mean, it's pretty for five minutes, but you're not from here, are you? Look at all this. I mean, it's not like he's going to . . ."

Too late, Rosie realized the terrible effect of two hyper-strong gin and tonics on a middle-aged woman on a very strict diet. Angie was already pointing at Stephen. It was like watching a plane crash in slow motion. She felt like leaping out of her seat and shouting, "Noo . . . ooo . . ."

"Are you going to marry her, love? Or are you just playing with the help?"

A shocked silence fell on the room, except for Lilian, who appeared to be in fits of giggles.

Stephen slowly put down his knife and fork, feeling a ringing in his ears. Rosie felt her heart thunder in her mouth. She was also furious with her mother. And Lilian. And Hetty. And everyone. Meridian was still giving her little kisses on the side of her face. Well maybe not quite EVERYONE.

"I cannot believe your mother did that." Moray's face of scandalized horror wasn't helping matters at all.

Rosie had opened up the shop, feeling miserable and depressed, and Moray had popped in early for a postmortem. It had turned out to be worse than his wildest dreams. Tina was there too, desperately trying to hide her ring and her happiness and be sympathetic.

"I know," said Rosie, sipping her coffee.

"SO?" said Moray. "What did the high prince of darkness say?"

"Stop calling him that."

Moray traded glances with Tina. They had mopped Rosie up off the floor about Stephen more than once.

Rosie swallowed heavily. She hadn't had a lot of sleep.

"He said . . . he said . . ." She dissolved in tears. "He said he didn't really know. And so of course Angie gave the most tremendous sniff and said, no, the last one didn't really know what he wanted either, and I'd wasted eight years of my life on HIM, and I wasn't going to waste any more."

She paused.

"Nobody really wanted the stewed plums after that."

Pip had given her a big hug and patted her on the back. She knew he understood.

Moray shook his head. "Hetty does the cooking on purpose to discourage people from coming to dinner."

"But . . . but why doesn't Stephen want to get married?" said Tina, fingers nervously fiddling with her ring.

Rosie's face was set.

"I don't know," she said. "My last boyfriend didn't want to get married either. Maybe it's me."

"It's not you," said Tina and Moray simultaneously. "I'd marry you," said Moray. "For the toffee alone."

"Thanks, guys," said Rosie.

"But . . . but . . . what are you going to do?"

Rosie looked around the lovely warm, cozy little shop, its brass bell gleaming in the cold early-morning sunshine.

"I don't know," she said. "If the shop can't carry on, it can't carry on. And I've uprooted my life once before . . . I suppose I could do it again."

"In Australia?" asked Tina, eyes wide.

"Well, I've always wanted to go and have a look," said Rosie. "Everyone says it's totally amazing. And you know, those are my nephew and nieces there. They're all the family I've got. I've missed a lot of their growing up already."

"You know, you're the only family Lilian's got as well," said Moray softly.

"Lilian sides with Hetty every fricking time," said Rosie, uncharacteristically bitter. "They can be family. She'll be fine without me. And Hetty will be bloody ecstatic."

"And Stephen?" said Moray. But it was too late. Rosie had already dissolved in tears.

Chapter 14

As Christmas grew closer, Rosie threw herself into preparations. She took her family to Carningford to see Santa's grotto and the lights, bought Nintendo games and princess dolls and a huge inflatable Spiderman.

"We're going to eat at Peak House," she announced to Stephen in passing. Stephen was marking and wasn't really concentrating on her tone.

"But Mother normally . . ."

"I don't care what your mother is doing," she said. "I'm going to be at Peak House with *my* mother."

"Okay," said Stephen. "That sounds fine."

He returned to his marking.

"Hey," he said a few minutes later. "Are you okay?"

But Rosie had already gone upstairs to bed.

"All right," said Stephen. "Once more."

The class looked up at him obediently. It was still amazing to him, he found, how much he enjoyed his job. Throwing himself into it was just about the best remedy for physical and mental pain that he knew. Getting a slow child to catch up with their reading, making the class laugh explaining arithmetic in terms of dogs and sausages, and hearing uplifting young voices sing and lisp their way through the nativity play. Stephen wasn't too keen on nativity plays. There was too much hideous competition between the parents as to who did what, so he was having five very brief tableaux then moving straight on to the communal singing parts that everybody enjoyed.

"GLOO-ooo-oooo-ooo-ria," yelled the voices happily to the thump of the bumpy old out-of-tune piano he could barely play. He would deal with his mother's bad mood later.

His thoughts strayed to Rosie. Oh God, he seemed to have managed to turn everybody against him. Again, he thought mournfully. But he was in no fit state to be thinking about the future at the moment. Couldn't she see that? Could nobody see?

"Where have you been?" asked Lilian crossly, shouting into her mobile phone as usual even though a normal tone of voice would have done perfectly well.

"Angie's been to see you every day," said Rosie defensively.

"Yes, well, Angie's not you, is she? All she talks about is Australia and finding a man."

"Maybe that's what I need to talk about," said Rosie gloomily.

"What's that? Don't talk nonsense. You're entirely too sensitive." Lilian sighed and hung up. Rosie was moping about terribly; it was very dull.

She wandered over to where James Boyd was sitting, pretending to be reading a book. He glanced up, his blue eyes still piercing, and she got a sudden flashback. They stared at each other for a moment, horrified.

"Oh my," said Lilian, out of breath and sitting down with a thump on the thick cushions. "Oh my. Sorry." Her fingers fumbled unconsciously for her emergency button. "Sorry. Just for a moment there . . . you looked exactly like . . ."

"Lilian," said the voice, and it was a voice from the past. It was a voice she knew incredibly well. But it could not be. This voice was dead. This voice had been dead seventy years. This voice's entire generation had passed . . .

"Henry Carr," breathed Lilian, all color drained from her face. "Henry Carr. You sounded exactly like Henry Carr."

"Henry Carr," repeated the old man, and a tear rolled down his cheek suddenly, but Lilian couldn't tell whether he was saying a name he knew or just repeating her words back to her.

"Did you know him?" she asked. "Did you know Henry Carr?"

But suddenly, as fast as he'd been there, he was gone, his blue eyes fixed on the far window, out onto the snow that fell thickly on the holly bushes.

Lilian sidetracked Edward as he came in the door.

"Mr. Boyd," she said.

"It's Lilian, isn't it?" he said politely, dusting the snow off his shoulders.

"You can call me Miss Hopkins," said Lilian. "It's just . . . I wanted to ask you about your father. James."

"Yes?"

"It's definitely James, isn't it?"

Edward looked at her strangely.

"What an odd question."

"I know. Only, and I know I am a very silly old lady, and I can't see a thing and have no idea what I'm doing half the time . . . and I think I'm going dotty."

"Miss Hopkins, you are as sharp as a tack, and you don't fool me for a second."

"Only, it's just that your father reminds me of someone very much. Someone I knew during the war."

"Oh," said Edward. "I'm so sorry. I was born after the war."

"Yes, I realize that," said Lilian. "And your father?"

"He grew up in Halifax. Weavers, most of his relatives."

"Did you know your grandparents when you were little?"

"Only on my mother's side. My father's parents died when he was small. He doesn't even have a photograph."

"Right," said Lilian. "Right. That's fine."

She started to move away when suddenly Dorothy Isitt arrived, her face furious as usual, to perform a duty visit to her mother, Ida Delia. Dorothy and Edward hadn't been introduced, but as Dorothy stood, she patted the snow off her arms in exactly the same way Edward had. Lilian noticed suddenly that their eyes were exactly the same greeny-brown color. Of course Dorothy still had a mass of thick curly hair, graying now, whereas Edward had none.

And I, thought Lilian that night in her single bed—Lilian had never in her life not slept in a single bed—I am a silly, daft, romantic old lady. I am going completely round the bend.

Then a thought struck her. An awful, frightening, sad thought—but maybe a necessary one.

"We're a bit worried about your father," Cathryn had said to Edward earlier.

"Oh dear."

They watched him, still staring, the untouched book on his lap, his eyes miles away.

"I hope he's not causing any trouble?"

"No, no trouble at all. He's a pleasure to have around. But actually, that's slightly my concern, to be honest. He's become very quiet, showing none of the more violent signs of dementia, none of the physical activity you'd expect. Moray's worried about his weight. He's drawn very fully into himself."

"You think he's unhappy here?" asked Edward, his heart starting to race. Please let her not say he had to go home. Not now, after all they'd been through.

"I'm not sure," said Cathryn. "I don't think it's that either. But he seems very thoughtful, very wistful. It's like he's gone somewhere else."

"And that's bad?" said Edward with a gulp.

"I'm not sure," said Cathryn again. "I expect lots of medical people would disagree with me, but there is a stage to dementia where living in the past all the time, rather than jolting horribly between past and present . . . it feels gentler, somehow. Kinder."

Edward blinked.

"You're not just telling me what I want to hear?"

"I would never do that," said Cathryn. "Getting old is a horrible business, Mr. Boyd. It's not my job to sugarcoat it for anyone. But here he seems . . ."

"At peace?" said Edward. "Do you think?"

"I'm just passing on my observations," said Cathryn, turning briskly away.

Quietly, Edward went and sat on the arm of the chair next to his father and gently draped an arm over his shoulders. During the last horrible few years, James would have jerked, shouted, responded with fear, and on one or two occasions, with actual violence, to the point where they had all tried to avoid physical contact as much as they possibly could.

Now James let the arm rest there without commenting or moving it or possibly even noticing. Edward let his head fall to the side so that it rested gently against his father's and then, without making a sound—he was an orderly man—he let his tears fall silently into the old man's soft white hair.

Chapter 15

Rosie took Angie out shopping at Bennetts and Debenhams, followed by afternoon tea with a glass of fizz thrown in at the Cathedral Quarter Hotel in Derby. Stephen was taking his class sledding for PE and had invited the children along. Desleigh had sighed with relief and booked herself in for a "pampering day," whatever that was. Angie had been up for going too, but Rosie had managed to talk her into accompanying her on a shopping trip to Derby instead.

The wind was absolutely howling in their faces, and their carrier bags were flapping around their legs, and they were glad to collapse with their packages in the steamy warmth of the hotel, heaving identical sighs of relief as they did so.

"The works, please," said Rosie to the waitress, who still wore an old-fashioned black dress and a white apron. "This is on me, Mum."

"Actually, I should get this," said Angie. "You know the exchange rate is unbelievable. Everything here costs about five pence to me."

Rosie briefly considered it—everything did not feel like it

cost five pence to her—but of course she fended her mother off at once.

"Don't be daft, Mum. Shut up and eat your scones."

Angie smiled, put out her suntanned hand and rested it on Rosie's pale white one.

"Oh, Rosie Posie," she said. "I do miss you."

They had had such a fun afternoon choosing gifts for the children, trying on clothes—Rosie as usual trying to steer Angie toward the more conventional and Angie doing the opposite to her pretty daughter—and just spending time together, chatting, gossiping, doing normal mother-daughter stuff. But it was not normal at all because underneath it was the constant sadness that after Christmas, Angie would depart—first for London, then for Paris so Desleigh could see it, then home. Back to Australia.

"I miss you too, Mum," said Rosie. So much had changed during the last three years. She missed Sunday lunch at Angie's, the gravy in the little gravy boat that was heated from underneath by a candle; going to the sales on Boxing Day; watching *Corrie* with tomato soup on nights when her ex, Gerard, was out. Or just their long chats on the telephone; the time difference between the UK and Australia meant their talks were never quite satisfactory. One of the benefits—possibly the only benefit—that Rosie could see about growing up without a father was that you became a mummy's girl. You couldn't help it.

"You know, I'm sorry about what I said. I didn't mean it to upset you—mostly I just wanted to annoy that horrible lady," said Angie. "But we have been talking among ourselves . . . I mean, you know, there's just so much opportunity in Australia. Pip's worried about you. And nurses get paid really well, com-

pared to here. You could have your own house, your own swimming pool, meet a nice man."

"I've got a nice man," said Rosie reflexively.

"Really, babe? I mean, charming, posh, all of that, but . . ."

The champagne came, with tea, too. They paused while the
waitress poured it out.

". . . that house, darling, that family . . . Do you think so?
Really? I mean, he said himself he's got no interest in getting
married. . . . Are you happy just to stay his bit on the side forever? Aren't you better than that?"

"I'm not his bit on the side, Mum."

"Darling, I love you. And I have never been anything but
proud of the choices you've made, you know that."

Rosie realized that her struggle to fight the tears was going
to be pointless.

"And when you dropped everything, and came up to help
Lilian, I was so proud of you. So thrilled."

"Mmm."

"But darling, you're thirty-two years old."

Rosie flushed pink.

"I know that, Mum."

"Your best years . . . I mean, are you going to spend the rest
of your life tinkering along? . . . Well, who knows what you'll
do if the sweetshop closes? . . . But the thought of you having to pander to that horrible woman and spend time in that
dreadful freezing house, waiting around for . . . I mean, he's
very handsome and can turn on the charm and all of that, but,
Stephen . . . you know, he's not like us, is he?"

Angie had, unwittingly or otherwise, touched on the very
core of Rosie's insecurities around him. She could never forget,
last year, his flirtation with Cee Cee, the terrifyingly tall, posh

blonde from London, who had looked at her as if she were some kind of scrubber.

"Love, I'm trying to be kind, but . . . in the end, you know. Isn't he just going to end up with someone exactly like himself? Don't they all have to marry each other anyway?"

"Don't be daft, Mum. This isn't *Downton Abbey*."

They buttered their scones in silence.

"Meridian's really taken to you," observed Angie after a moment or two. Rosie's face softened.

"Oh, she's adorable."

"She looks a lot like you as a child, you know."

Rosie nodded; she'd seen the photographs.

"I know."

"I can't tell you what it's like as a mother, to see the way you look traced in someone else's face. . . . She makes me miss you more than anything else."

"She's very cute," said Rosie.

"I think she's going to need her auntie," said Angie. "Kelly doesn't let her get away with much. And I'm not sure Shane knows where he is half the time. And Desleigh's rushed off her feet . . ."

"I wish they'd take that game away from Shane," said Rosie suddenly, tactfully not commenting on whether or not Desleigh seemed rushed off her feet. "I've absolutely no idea if he's a nice boy or not. He doesn't say a word, just grunts."

"I know," said Angie. "It would take a bit more time to really get to know him."

The restaurant door banged open in the wind, letting in some other freezing shoppers.

"Do you think you'd ever move back?" asked Rosie tentatively.

"I couldn't now," said Angie, looking straight at the door. "It chills my bones, this. You know, when you wake in the morning in Sydney, you can smell the bougainvillea and the hibiscus and the jasmine in the window, and obviously lots of people go down to the beach, eat their breakfast overlooking the sea— the coffee's amazing. And the light hits the top of the harbor bridge and the opera house, and the sun is like diamonds on the waves, until it feels like the entire city is just glowing. There's just so much possibility. And there aren't many Hettys there, I'll tell you that."

"So they won't have much space for a fat old nurse with a failed sweetshop then," said Rosie.

"Don't be daft," said Angie. "You'd love it. Think of it: a new start, some soft, warm summer air. We'd get you set up in a little apartment by the sea, yeah? Not too far from all of us, but not too close either. Introduce you to some people? Come round for Sunday lunch? We do it on the barbie now. Just think about it."

Moray looked up, surprised at the name next on the list for Saturday morning office hours but trying his best not to show it.

"Hello," he said, casually neutral.

Stephen limped carefully over to the comfortable leather seat in front of Moray's old desk, glancing briefly at the examination table with its roll of paper at the foot, and the wooden toy corner for the little ones. Seeing Stephen walk into his office was so entirely unexpected for Moray that he buried his head in the notes. He and Stephen had been good friends once; Stephen had been full of plans for them both in Africa, a doctor and a teacher, but Moray had not wanted to go, and Stephen had never quite forgiven him.

"Leg problems?" said Moray.

"No, the leg's fine," said Stephen, settling himself carefully.

"And your back . . . is it healing? . . . You have been through the wars," said Moray, then instantly regretted his turn of phrase.

"It's fine," said Stephen. They sat there in silence for a few moments, both men wretchedly uncomfortable. Stephen began to wish furiously that he hadn't come. On the other hand, he was hardly going to talk to Hye about it . . . and anyone else was just too risky.

He stared at his hands.

"Okay," he said. "I . . . I . . ."

For a horrifying moment he thought he was going to cry. He hauled it back.

"I keep . . . I keep getting flashbacks."

Moray looked at him. He looked—well, not awful. Stephen never looked awful, but there were purple shadows beneath his eyes, and he was a little thin.

"After the accident."

Moray nodded carefully.

"Trouble sleeping?"

Stephen laughed hollowly.

"And have you . . . have you spoken to anyone about this?"

Stephen shook his head.

"It's Christmas. Everyone's meant to be happy, having a good time. I'm not going to get in the way and spoil everyone's fun."

This was precisely what Moray thought he was already doing, but he didn't mention it.

"You don't want to talk to Rosie?" he asked gently. Stephen's gaze was anguished.

"I . . . I don't want to be her patient. I don't want her looking after me, everyone feeling sorry for me all over again. Do you see?"

Moray did see. He was also of the opinion that this was a terrible strategy.

"But don't you think she's worried about you?"

"Don't you think she'd be more worried about me if she thought I'd gone off my head again?"

Moray shrugged.

"She seems an understanding person. And it didn't put her off before."

For once, the ghost of a smile passed Stephen's lips. Then he shook his head.

"No. No. There must be another way."

Moray sighed.

"Well, there are sleeping pills and anti-anxiety drugs, but I'm not going to give you those."

"I thought you might say that."

". . . I'm not saying they're not helpful. I would just want you to explore other solutions first. I have the name of a very good therapist."

"Christ, it's not one of those forest weirdos, is it?"

"No," said Moray, crossing his fingers. Stephen glared into the middle distance.

"Stephen," said Moray gently, "I think this needs fixing. And I am telling you now that it can be fixed. You can make this go away. Probably a lot faster than you think. There's a method called Exposure Therapy where they make you talk it through again and again until it stops freaking you out; the outcome rates are very encouraging. And it's quick."

"Can't you do it? Now?"

"Not that quick," said Moray. "And no, I'm not trained. And you should probably discuss this with Rosie, you know?"

Stephen put up his hand. "I don't want to worry her. She has enough on her plate."

Moray scribbled something down. "This is the name of the therapy, and a local practitioner, but you can find it anywhere. If you want me to refer you, I can."

Stephen took it.

"I'll let you know," he said.

And that, thought Moray, was better than nothing. He hoped that just knowing it was a solvable problem might cheer up his gloomy friend.

Stephen turned at the doorway, his hand twisting the knob.

Here it comes, thought Moray. He's going to beg me for drugs or mention something else or start swearing . . . Patients notoriously didn't tell him what was really the matter until they were turning the doorknob on the way out.

Instead, Stephen paused.

"Thank you," he said. Then he was gone. Moray remained surprised all the way through Crystal Harris' bum rash.

Rosie tried to put the umbrella up when they got outside the hotel in the driving rain and wind, but it kept turning inside out, so they just made a run for the car in the end. The weather was absolutely vicious. She dropped everyone off at Peak House after having been given a full rundown of the entire experience of sledding from the point of view of a three-year-old (punctuated every five minutes by Kelly saying, "No, it wasn't like that, Meridian"), then turned around and headed for home. Stephen was there already, lighting the fire. For a moment, going in, she felt her emotions flood up through her: part softness, watching his strong form bending down to fling in the wood, conscious, always, of his leg; part crossness at his lack of commitment.

Could she give it up? Or should she take all he could offer, even when it wasn't much, because of her love for him? Should she carry on down that road? After all, she thought, thinking of Gerard, fool me once, shame on you, fool me twice . . . Was it too much for her? she wondered. Was getting married and having a family just going to be one of those things that passed her by? Was she going to follow in Lilian's footsteps, living a quiet, sheltered life, always dreaming of the past?

And what about Lilian? She couldn't leave Lilian, could she? Although a little voice inside her reminded her of how preoccupied Lilian had been recently, how involved in the politics and social life of the old people's home, surrounded by friends and people who cared about her. And Lilian, however crusty, wanted Rosie to be happy. She knew that for a fact.

"Hey," said Stephen, distracted. "How's it going?"

Rosie shrugged.

"You know."

She moved in toward the kitchen.

"I was thinking . . . I mean, I know it'll be expensive, but I've been trying to save a bit of money . . ."

"Mmm?"

"What if I went to Australia next year? Maybe February, when it's still really cold here?"

Stephen looked at her.

"How long for?"

"Well, just for a visit, you know. I . . . I do miss them."

Stephen nodded.

"Well, yes, of course."

He didn't even ask, thought Rosie miserably. He didn't even ask what I was thinking, if I thought I'd be happier there, if I missed them too much. He doesn't want to come with me, and he doesn't even care.

Good, thought Stephen, a holiday for Rosie. Maybe that's what she needs to perk her up a bit. And get her away from me bringing her down, he thought darkly. He wouldn't want to be around him right now either.

"I thought I might go down and see the guys in the Red Lion tonight. Is that all right?"

"Of course," said Rosie. "Why wouldn't it be?"

Chapter 16

The day of the school carol concert dawned, thankfully, white and sunny. Stephen was counting on a good turnout. It had taken a lot to persuade his mother to let people into the house at all. She had made sniffy remarks about its not being a National Trust Open Day, but on the other hand the children had already ruined practically everything in their estate, so it barely mattered. If they sold a lot of tickets at the door, that would be a good thing. Rosie was also doing a little stand, manned by Tina, so people could buy sweets to eat afterward, and Mrs. Laird was going to do tea, coffee and mulled wine. Nothing had yet been decided about the fate of the school, but the council had not voted to release the funds, and things looked ominous. If this was to be the last-ever Lipton School carol concert, Mrs. Baptiste was very keen that it be a good one.

Cathryn was sending the old people in a minibus. Mrs. Baptiste had offered to take the concert to them, but Cathryn believed in people getting out and about, to have something to look forward to and a bit of variety, even if, as she explained, they only complained about it afterward, so she was sending a minibus. The turnout should be massive after everything the children had been through and given the fact that it might be their last carol concert ever. Stephen nervously counted and rechecked the rows of chairs to make sure everything was set. Peter Isitt was also there, due to come on at the end dressed as Santa Claus with gifts for all the children.

The little ones were jittery with excitement. All had freshly washed hair, neatly pressed shirts and sweatshirts with the words LIPTON PRIMARY still proudly emblazoned on them—for now. Emily was wearing a special new red velvet ribbon in her blond hair. Stephen told them to relax, all the time anxiously scanning the horizon for the first of the cars before they kicked off at three o'clock.

This was surprising, thought Rosie. She'd turned up nice and early to help Tina with the stall—they'd shut the shop for the afternoon, as she couldn't believe anybody would be left in the village. But the great ballroom wasn't filling up quite as quickly as she'd expected. Obviously some of the mums were there, but not a lot of the dads—couldn't they take a bit of time off for their children's concert? It was winter, after all, not the busiest time of year for farmers. She couldn't even see Moray. The minibus arrived from the old people's home and she popped out to help them down and bring them in as close to the miserly fire as possible. She'd hoped that having lots of bodies in the room would warm things up a bit, but it wasn't nearly as busy as she'd expected. She'd texted Cathryn to tell her to bring extra blankets, and Cathryn texted her back to say thank you but they'd been to Lipton Hall before and had already loaded the blankets, hot-water bottles and flasks.

"I'm looking forward to being caterwauled at," said Lilian, waving away Rosie's offer of help as she descended regally from the bus. "Is there real wine in the mulled wine?"

"Yes," said Rosie. "So go easy."

"And you're selling sweets?"

"Of course."

"Good for you. You should bump the prices up a bit, you've got a captive audience."

"Lilian!" said Rosie, but she wasn't really shocked. Meridian appeared from nowhere and hurled herself around Rosie's legs. Desleigh weakly reminded her not to run across car parks. Kelly smugly held her mother's hand.

"Hello, Spidey," said Rosie. "Did you say hello to your great-great-aunt?"

"That makes me sound disgustingly old," said Lilian, but she gave Meridian a broad smile and handed her a little lollipop. "I brought my own," she confided. "I didn't want to get price gouged."

Rosie rolled her eyes.

"Can I sit with you, Auntie Rosie?" asked Meridian.

"Of course," said Rosie, kissing her. "Just give me a minute, okay, sweetie?" Meridian skipped off to show her big sister her lollipop. Kelly immediately stuck out her bottom lip and tugged on her mother's arm. Desleigh led them all off to the sweet trolley.

Lilian regarded Rosie shrewdly.

"You've got rather attached to that one."

"Well, she is clearly the cutest three-year-old ever," said Rosie defensively.

Lilian smiled. "Oh, all three-year-olds are like that," she said. "I've known them all. No, you like that one specially. I used to have a niece I liked specially like that."

She looked at Angie with pride. "If I had another chance . . . You know, I'm sad I missed so much of all of your childhoods."

Rosie looked at Lilian, wondering what she was getting at.

"Parents aren't allowed to have favorites," she said slyly to Rosie. "But aunts ALWAYS can. Now. Sit me between the fire and 'James Boyd.'"

"Why are you saying his name like that?"

But Lilian sniffed and looked mysterious and refused to answer.

"Tell me about going to Australia," she said. And that truly made Rosie's eyebrows lift.

At ten past three, Stephen looked around at the half-empty room and sighed. Well. Rosie had really done her best getting the school sent up here, but it was obviously not succeeding. Look at this. From the other end of the room, Rosie was thinking the exact same thing, with a grip of fear round her heart. If that was the best Lipton could do, they were doomed. No one cared about the school, or the children. It would have to go to Carningford . . . and after that . . . well.

Meridian put her sticky arms around Rosie's neck—she weighed a ton—and sighed with happiness.

"I like being with you, Auntie Rosie."

"I like being with you too, Meridian."

"I AMNT MERIDIAN."

Rosie kissed the soft cheek and gave her a squeeze. Meridian retaliated by kissing her on the mouth.

"LOOK AT MY BIG KISSES."

Rosie glanced at Tina, who was doing a miserable trade in soft chews for the old folk.

"Is Jake not even here?" she said crossly.

"He said he had an urgent repair down at the Isitts'," said Tina. "You don't want to get on the wrong side of Dorothy. Sorry."

Mrs. Baptiste was playing the piano. Unable to delay any longer, desperate not to disappoint the children, Stephen caught her eye and nodded, and she brought down her hands to start to play a rousing version of "The Twelve Days of Christmas" as the children, starting with the biggest, filed onto the stage and lined up neatly, spotless in their school uniforms, singing their little hearts out to a half-empty room.

Edward looked at the email in shock and disbelief. Or rather, the attachment. This was the last one. He had sent emails off to every Boyd in Halifax who had served in the war—and there were a lot. Most people had been extremely kind and very obliging, but none had been a lot of help. Then the regiment's historian himself had gotten in touch, very kindly, and sent him everything he could to help. He couldn't have been nicer. That very touching generosity made everything else somehow harder to bear.

Edward sat down.

"Doreen?" he called weakly. His wife came through, glancing over his shoulder.

He scrolled down slowly, picture after picture, none of which he'd ever seen before. His father had come back from the war, according to his own account, with head injuries, and had never talked about his life before the war. He had gotten married very soon afterward, to Edward's lovely mother, who had raised him and his brother, and even though their father was quiet, he wasn't noticeably shyer than many of his friends' dads from that era, who'd seen things and sustained injuries they never wanted their children to know about. He was just Dad, working at the printing company, occasionally ruffling their heads or telling silly jokes.

The man in these pictures was James Edward Boyd, born April 5, 1921, 2nd Battalion Royal Fusiliers, honorable discharge 1944. All the dates matched, the regiment; there was even a faded copy of the telegram that had been dispatched to James' brother, then acting as his guardian. It was undoubtedly the same man.

This man was not Edward's father.

Tina's Emily was a very quiet child, but Stephen had discovered to his surprise that when she started to sing, she was possessed of quite a pair of lungs. She didn't sing at home, she said, not really, and Stephen was amazed and vowed to have a word with Tina. . . . Then he'd thought it would work even better if he held on to it as a surprise. So when the little girl stepped forward on the final stanza of "In the Bleak Midwinter," Tina's gasp was entirely audible.

"'What can I give him? Poor as I am. If I were a shepherd, I would bring a lamb.'"

Lilian glanced sideways. James Boyd was watching the girl sing, tears rolling down his cheeks.

"Shepherd," he said, barely audible.

Lilian took his old wrinkled hand in hers and patted it.

"Yes," she said. "You're a shepherd."

"I'm a shepherd."

At the back of the room, Tina and Rosie were both in bits as Emily's pure, high voice cut through the room.

"She's amazing!" said Rosie.

"I know!" said Tina.

"Ssh," said Meridian. "I listening."

Stephen smiled in glee as the rousing "Ding Dong Merrily on High" started up—with the glorias as usual spinning wildly out of control. And then, to finish it off, one of the big boys, self-conscious, sat down with his guitar, and suddenly, twenty-four little sets of bells appeared from underneath chairs.

"'While shepherds watched their flocks by night all seated on the ground, an angel of the Lord came down, and glory shone around . . . SWEET BELLS!'" hollered the children, thrashing the bells with vast enthusiasm. "'SWEET CHIM-ING SILVER BELLS! SWEET BELLS! SWEET CHIM-ING CHRISTMAS BELLS! THEY CHEER US ON OUR HEAVENLY WAY, SWEET CHIMING BELLS!'"

It was uproarious, and the applause raised the roof. Stephen looked rather overcome by the success of the music. He came out to general applause, looking pink-faced and proud. Rosie stole a glance at Hetty. She had her gaze firmly fixed on the mulled wine. Ugh, that dreadful woman.

"And now," Stephen announced loudly, with a grin. He had been hoping to do this proudly in front of the entire village—a bit schmaltzy, but it was Christmas—but this would have to do.

"We have two very special guests!"

"Santa!" went a muffled buzz among the children, now sitting cross-legged in front of the stage. Stephen smiled and hushed them. Mrs. Baptiste started up a rousing tune.

"Ta dah!" said Stephen. And on came Peter Isitt, done up in a proper St. Nick's outfit, with a long cloak and black boots and a big white beard.

"He had to get a background check for this," whispered Tina. But then she fell silent as she saw who was beside him. Waving madly, in a wheelchair decorated with tinsel, pushed by his proud father, was Edison.

Even in a half-empty room, the cheer shook the foundations of the old house and the children all rang their bells.

Edison's face was wreathed in smiles. He'd never been so popular in his entire life. One by one, all the adults got to their feet. Rosie was totally choked up and clapped her hands together so hard they hurt.

Edison was wearing, as well as his shiny new gold-rimmed glasses, a small elf's hat, and Peter let him read out the name on every gift and pass it over to the appropriate child. Being Edison, of course, he insisted on embellishing it and shaking every child's hand formally as he handed over the book-shaped parcels, congratulating them on being nice rather than naughty. Mrs. Laird moved into position behind the big vats of mulled wine and hot chocolate on the far table, and Tina and

Rosie helped themselves to wine gratefully. Tina blushingly accepted compliments about Emily. She had been such a quiet little thing—it had gotten so much worse since the accident—and there she was, singing her little heart out. Tina's own heart swelled with pride.

"Amazing," said Rosie. "Now I must go and see Edison. Um, and Stephen."

But before she could thread her way through the crowd to the makeshift stage, there was more of a commotion at the front door. Her head shot around.

"What is this?" Hetty said very loudly, filled with horror at the idea of normal people coming in the front rather than the back door.

Tina twisted her head around too. It was Jake, absolutely filthy.

"Oh," she said.

"Have we missed it?" said Jake. There were a couple of men behind him, equally mucky. Rosie spotted Moray among them.

"What on EARTH is going on?" said Hetty, and for once Rosie wanted to say exactly the same thing.

"Damn, we've missed it," said Jake. "Bloody weather held us up. Oh well . . . follow us."

"What?"

"Everyone in your cars," said Moray, smiling. "Come on, follow us. We have something to show you."

"Certainly not," said Cathryn, but Rosie and Tina started forward.

"What on earth are you up to?" hissed Rosie.

"Didn't you hear me?" said Moray. "Everyone in their cars."

Cathryn kept the old people inside, but the rest of them piled into the various Land Rovers and SUVs parked around the front of Lipton Hall; they made an odd procession going down the street. Rosie had no idea what was up now.

After ten minutes down the high street, they stopped. Rosie gasped. Most people were so stunned by what they saw that they couldn't even park.

Newly painted, freshly done, Lipton Primary School stood exactly as it had before.

"What the . . ."

Rosie stepped out, completely gobsmacked.

"How . . . what the hell?"

Jake laughed at her face. Rosie turned to Stephen, who, Pied Piper–like, was leading a small crocodile of children out of a minivan.

"Did you know about this?"

"Know about it? He was here with us till four o'clock this morning."

"I thought you were on the piss at the Red Lion."

"Did you?" said Stephen.

"But . . ."

"Jake's been working on it on the sly for weeks," said Moray. "It was just the final push last night and today really, positioning the Portakabin. We kind of hoped we'd have it done in time to move the concert."

"Yeah," said Stephen. "We held on as long as we could, but you know there's hell to pay if we keep them in too late. Not least from my ruddy mother."

Hetty was examining the new school with a sense of great satisfaction.

"Well, quite," she said.

Mrs. Baptiste looked as if she couldn't quite believe it.

"Well, is it okay?" she asked. "Will it pass its legal tests and fire regulations and all of that?"

"Done already," said the local fire officer, smiling. "Jumped the queue. I didn't want to send Danny and Fran to Carningford any more than anybody else did."

Tina flung her arms around Jake.

"You are the best man in the history of the world," she said. "Oh, I wish you'd heard Emily sing."

"I want to sing again," said Emily standing by her mother.

Tina looked at Stephen. "Can she sing again?"

Stephen looked at Mrs. Baptiste.

"I can't think of a better way to christen the new building than with a song."

She did, however, first have to get through the front door by cutting a huge red ribbon as everyone clapped. Now most of the village really was here (with the notable exception of Roy Blaine), and they filed into the building with goodwill, despite its chill from not having the boiler back on. The children lined up in the assembly hall—with a proper stage this time—and Mrs. Baptiste tried to keep her fingers warm enough to play the piano as everyone joined in, Emily's solo providing an excuse, if one was needed, for a myriad of quiet tears to be shed for one reason or another.

Chapter 17

Rosie sent Tina home with the children and went back to Lipton Hall to tidy up the stall and help Stephen. He was buzzing with adrenaline.

"Look at you," she teased gently. "You look like you've just won *The X Factor*."

"I have no idea what you're talking about," he said with a smile playing on his lips.

It felt like a truce.

"You know. That show you watch all the time on Saturday evenings while pretending to be reading a big newspaper."

"Oh yes. The newspaper I cut the eyeholes out of."

"The very one."

"Come on," said Stephen. "Aren't you thrilled? The school is saved, therefore the sweetshop is saved, and Roy Blaine will be spitting even more venom into his pink dentist water than usual. You can't say today wasn't a success."

"I know," said Rosie. "I know."

But what she was also thinking was: six more days till Angie leaves.

"Come here, you," said Stephen, putting his arm round her. "What's up?"

She looked at him.

"Do you really not know?" she said. He shook his head.

"You don't think it worries me . . . that I am giving up my entire family, my mum, my little nieces and . . . nephew, and everything . . . for what? To hang around here being patronized by your mother and treated as second fiddle by you?"

Stephen was completely stunned. Rosie was instantly terrified. She had gone too far.

But on the other hand, if she didn't say what was in her heart now, how would it get any better down the line? If she didn't find out now, she would never find out. She would never know.

Stephen's face had fallen.

"I didn't know that's how you felt," he said. "Have you been feeling like this for a long time?"

"No," said Rosie. "But for a little while, maybe."

"Well, don't I feel stupid?" said Stephen, bewildered. Rosie closed her eyes. This was horrible.

"I'm sorry," said Stephen, turning away. "I'm sorry. I thought I was enough for you."

"You are," said Rosie. Then she thought about it again. "No," she said. "You are everything, and I love you. But I don't see why I can't have what other people have. A wedding, a family. All of that."

She looked at Stephen's face; he seemed stunned. Tears sprang to her eyes. Stephen looked around the room.

"Do you even know what it means for me to get married?" he said. "I have to inherit. I have to take on this bloody place. I have to spend my entire time with lawyers and my mother and, of course, unless I marry someone with money, I have to spend the rest of my life completely encumbered, completely skint, and bowing and scraping to anyone who wants to come here and have some tacky wedding in my back garden. . . . Oh Rosie, I just don't think we're in the same place. I . . . "

"I see," said Rosie. "Okay. I see."

Stephen stopped short suddenly.

"I need to get away for a bit," said Stephen. "Sort my head out."

Rosie's heart plummeted, and she stared at him in utter dismay. The silence was broken by Cathryn charging out of the front door.

"Have you seen him?" she said, her normally implacable face totally white and horrified.

"Seen who?" said Rosie, furiously wiping at her eyes, her brain still trying to take in the implications of their fight.

"James Boyd," said Cathryn. "He's vanished."

Chapter 18

They both instantly sprang into action. Rosie called Jake to get him to round up a posse. Stephen directed Mrs. Laird through the house, but there didn't seem to be a trace of him anywhere.

"He can't have gone far," said Rosie. "He's so old."

"He'll be in the grounds," said Stephen, hurrying past.

"Dementia patients often roam farther than you think," warned Cathryn. "Oh, I can't believe I took my eye off him for one second. There was just so much commotion . . . Oh dear." Her hands fluttered to her face, then down again.

"Okay, let's get organized," she said, more determined. "I'll give it five minutes before I call the police."

She looked out over the white gardens, the balustrades of the formal terrace completely hidden under the snow, then blew out her fringe and put on her coat. She glanced briefly at James' coat, still hanging on the coat stand.

"I'll call Edward," she said. "Now, can everyone else stay here?"

Hetty strode in, back from the village. "We'll have tea," she said. "You must all stay for tea. I am so happy to be rid of all those snotty-nosed brats that I feel we ought to celebrate."

Night was already coming in—Rosie realized with a start that it was the twenty-first of December, the shortest day of the year. Stephen was covering Lipton Hall, Jake was coordinating the efforts in town, and Moray was going to meet her in the middle to cover the road.

Stephen hadn't said anything to her, merely handed her a large torch. She had taken one of Hetty's coats, too, to protect her against the weather, and now she was going to need the torch. She shouted for James, but her voice sounded like nothing against the wind. And snow was starting to fall again; it was bitterly cold. She could barely remember now how excited she had been when the land was first covered in its soft whiteness.

She couldn't think about the sting of Stephen's words. She would have to deal with that later. There was a great block of ice in the pit of her stomach that had absolutely nothing to do with the weather.

She would have given a lot to be on an Australian beach right at that moment.

Stephen marched out into the back of the house, completely furious, beside himself. He picked up a stick and battered it against the side of a tree. A massive clump of snow fell out and landed on the back of his neck. This is so stupid, he thought; he had to get a grip on himself.

He thought of the sadness and pain in Rosie's eyes. How could he hurt her like that? It wasn't unreasonable of her, after all, was it? But did she really know what she was asking of him?

All his life he'd bucked against doing the expected thing, settling down in the path his family had been treading for hundreds of years. He wanted to travel the world, inspire young minds, not worry and fret about heating bills and gardening staff and spend his life dealing with his bloody mother in stifling little Lipton where everybody had known him since he was a little boy.

But Rosie didn't stifle him, did she? When she wasn't being all funny about everything . . .

He shone his torch on the ground. Fresh snow was falling, but it hadn't covered up the ground just yet, and animal tracks from birds and dogs were clearly visible. Nothing human, though, so he headed over to the outbuildings.

Suddenly a horrible thought struck him. She couldn't . . . When she had mentioned visiting Australia, she couldn't possibly mean for a long time, could she? She wouldn't leave?

All his conflicting feelings about settling down, about having to follow the family path, suddenly paled into utter insignificance. Rosie in Australia . . . it was like a punch to the gut. She couldn't. She wouldn't leave him. Surely not. God, he just needed to get out of bloody Lipton for a bit.

The search took on a new level of intensity. The howling wind was absolutely freezing.

Down in the village, the local constable, Big Pete, was trying to coordinate matters. He looked serious.

"Is he wearing a coat?" he said.

"No."

Cathryn was trying her best to maintain a calm atmosphere.

"We're going to fan out and search every backstreet, every back garden, knock on every door, okay?"

The men of the village, already tired from their night's work at the school, looked haggard in the arc lights still set up from the building work, but they set to with a will. "James!" could be heard on every breath of wind, echoing up and down the street, the old stone houses looking empty and inhospitable in the chill of the night.

Moray had Lilian in the car and picked up Rosie at the bottom of the driveway. She looked beside herself, and her teeth were chattering.

"We'll find him," said Moray, although he was more worried than he let on. James was a very old, confused, senile man. In this weather, even if they found him, bronchitis, pneumonia . . . the complications were frightening, painful and distressing. Well, they would deal with that as and when. "Don't worry," said Moray, squeezing Rosie gently.

The car's warmth was welcome to her, but it made her want to start crying, and she didn't have time for that.

"Why did you leave Lipton Hall?" she asked Lilian crossly. "You shouldn't be out on a night like this."

She squinted.

"And are you wearing fur?"

"Yes. Things were different then," sniffed Lilian. "Better. And in answer to your ridiculous question, two reasons. One, because Hetty's house is colder on the inside than the outside. And two, because I know where he is."

"What are you talking about?" said Rosie.

"I know where he is."

"James?"

"His name isn't James," said Lilian. "Really, nobody ever pays attention to the old."

Moray glanced at her.

"Where am I going then?"

"The churchyard, please."

Chapter 19

The search party hadn't yet reached the churchyard. As soon as Lilian stepped out of the car, she barely noticed the cold. Moray followed her with his big heavy-duty country torch. Rosie followed dumbly behind.

"Once upon a time," said Lilian, striding confidently ahead, sprightly for a woman of her age. The moon had risen, and she hardly needed the light from the torch.

"Once upon a time there was a woman called Lilian Hopkins."

"That's a coincidence," said Moray, shouting "'JAMES!'"

"Ssh. And she was in love with a young man called Henry Carr."

Rosie and Moray traded looks.

"But he got some slapper up the duff."

"Ida Delia," said Rosie. Lilian sniffed.

"Then he got called up."

"But he died," said Rosie gently, suddenly terrified that her great-aunt's mind had turned. "He died, Lilian. A long time ago. In North Africa, remember?"

"There was a lot of confusion in the war," said Lilian, a touch of steel in her voice. "Lots of things got mixed up. Don't forget that."

She made a sharp turn to the left, then right again, then left.

"Aha," she said. "Yes."

And there, in the shade of the old churchyard tree where they had once spent hours together, kissing and talking and planning for a future that would never come, lay nestled the long body and white head of an old, old man.

Moray pulled out his phone immediately to alert the authorities and call in the helicopter. Rosie immediately tore off her coat and put it around the old man, and Moray shouted harshly at Big Pete to bring blankets and hot tea. Then he knelt down. There was a faint pulse, very slow. He put his arm around the man, Rosie too.

"Come on, old fella," said Moray. "Come on."

Lilian—very carefully and painfully because of her dodgy hip—knelt down.

"When I was young," she went on in the same eerily calm tone of voice, "which was yesterday, or last week or thereabouts, I knew a boy with curly hair. He used to tease me mercilessly. He worked in the fields with the sheep, and the back of his neck was brown as a nut, and his nose took freckles in July when the sun shone all day.

"When I was sad because my brother had died, he held me every day and did his best to make everything better, and when we were happy we walked the lanes and the field paths of Lipton together, and he would hold my hand and tickle me with a wheat sheaf, and we would talk about the cottage we were going to have, with the white roses, because I like white roses, even though they are neglected most horribly by my grand-niece, after all the trouble I went to to cultivate them around the bower gate.

"And then something happened and I lost him and that was a bad business, and then he went away to war and I knew nothing of him after that."

She leaned in close to him.

"Henry, my love," she whispered. "Was that you?"

For a moment in the churchyard all was silent and white, the snow falling without a noise, a great hush on the world. Rosie was holding one of the man's hands and trying to rub some life back into it.

Then something: a twitch, a quiver of the eyelids. Then the eyes blinked, slowly, a film of tears on them.

"Well done," said Moray. "Well done. Up you come."

He struggled to sit up a little, and Moray put his anorak around him to get him away from the cold, wet ground.

"My name," the old man croaked, "is Henry Ishmael Carr."

"I know," said Lilian.

Rosie's mouth dropped open.

Then all was commotion and bright lights as the search party charged into the churchyard, and a great thundering noise cut across the sky, and the sweeping beams of the helicopter poured over them, bathing everything in boiling yellow light, and no one could hear a thing after that, and Henry gently closed his eyes again.

I should get a flat in this bloody hospital, thought Rosie. She'd brought Lilian in the next morning, as soon as they'd gotten the news that Henry had woken up and was ready for visitors. She had a stonking hangover, seeing as once Henry had been dispatched and the old people returned to the home, there seemed to be only one thing to do which was for everyone to dispatch to the Red Lion to chew over the astounding events of the day. Dorothy Isitt and Ida Delia had been informed, which would be interesting, as well as Edward Boyd. For once, quiet, tranquil Lipton, where nothing ever happened, had turned into a soap opera, and no one could quite believe it.

All the way back to the home Rosie had just stared at Lilian.

"But how did you know?" she said. "How could you possibly know?"

Lilian shrugged. "I recognized him straightaway," she said. "So naturally I thought it was me who was going completely insane. As if Henry Carr would walk into my life again. I thought I wasn't long for this world."

Rosie shook her head. "It's not possible."

Then something struck her.

"Oh my God, is that why you kept mentioning Australia? . . . I thought you were encouraging me to go."

Lilian shrugged. "You seemed to miss your mother and, yes, I didn't think I had long, with all the hallucinations and whatnot. I reckoned I was going gaga and I'd soon be so scatty I wouldn't even notice you were gone."

"It's amazing."

"Remind me of how you came across him again?"

Rosie thought back. "Well, he and his son were driving through the village . . . and he had a funny turn when he saw the shop."

"Hmmm. Why do you think that was?"

"Amazing," said Rosie. "I mean just amazing."

"It's not in the least bit amazing," said Lilian. "He could have driven through this village at any time in the last sixty bloody years, prompted his memory, and we could have taken it from there. Did you know he's been a widower for thirty years?! I could do a swear."

But the excitement in her eyes gave away her happiness.

Rosie had asked Moray if he was going to be all right, and he had shrugged and said he didn't know, but stranger things had happened.

"Not much stranger, though," he'd mused on his third glass of Les' very indifferent red wine.

Stephen had intended to go to the pub but had been at home looking up something online when he'd come upon the window that Rosie had (intentionally? he wondered) left open on the laptop they shared. Quarantine arrangements for taking dogs to Australia. He had stared at it for a long time, then picked up Mr. Dog from his comfy position in front of the fire and hugged his fur.

Then he'd grabbed a jacket, left a terse note, jumped in the Land Rover and headed for London.

Rosie had read the note in pain and confusion. What did "London" mean? His horrible posh society friends and gruesome blondes and all sorts . . . well, she thought grimly. Clearly they'd both been thinking about their lives.

Now, the following morning, she was at the hospital, trying to get Lilian into Henry's room. He had a private one because he needed the warming bath and electric anti-hypothermia blankets, plus there was a lot of media interest in his story—he was something of a hospital celebrity. It was just as well: he needed the space. Crowded into the little room, painted that odd shade of yellow-y beige of hospitals everywhere, were Moray, Rosie and Lilian; a whey-faced Edward with his wife and their son, Ian; Ida Delia, insisting on a seat and prominently flaunting her wedding ring on her left hand, rather than on the right where it had resided for the past sixty years, and a thin-lipped Dorothy Isitt, Peter as ever a silent and reassuring presence at her side. There were also several interested medical personnel. A psychiatrist, trying not to look too gleeful, had set up a tape recorder by the side of Henry's bed.

Moray looked grave; he'd had a word with the consultant, and nobody liked the noise Henry's lungs were making. He seemed, though, mentally, to have made the most tremendous breakthrough.

"I was born in Lipton on the ninth of August 1922. My mother's name was Peggy and my father was Henry too and we lived on Isitt's farm and I worked in the fields. And I knew a girl called Lilian Hopkins."

There was total silence across the room. The old man sounded completely clear and unclouded, his vision fixed on something far, far away. The psychiatrist double-checked that the little machine was taping properly.

"And I liked it sometimes when she would wear the little green-sprigged dress and sit on the front of my bicycle. My dog was called—"

"Penn," said Lilian and Henry together. "Penn," said Henry again, wonderingly. "He was a beautiful dog."

"He was," said Lilian.

"This isn't happening," said Edward.

"What about his . . . James' parents?" said Rosie to Edward.

"They died . . . he was an orphan. He met my mother after the war, and he would never talk about it. We knew he'd suffered head injuries, that was all. What if . . ."

"What if they got the wrong man?"

Henry looked at Edward.

"Who are you?"

"I'm Edward, Dad. Your son."

"I don't have a son. I have a daughter called Dorothy. She's very noisy."

Rosie looked at Ida Delia. She couldn't even imagine what she was going through. Dorothy was sitting very still, tears running down her face, one hand twisting a handkerchief in her lap. Ida Delia was huffing and fluffing and trying to draw as much attention to herself as possible.

Dorothy and Edward turned to look at each other in some surprise and suddenly they appeared a lot alike, same eyes, same expression.

"That means . . ."

Rosie steeled herself. Edward seemed so thoughtful and kind, and Dorothy could be very hard work indeed.

But to her astonishment, Dorothy was rising up, biting her lip. She looked at Edward.

"I always . . . I always wanted a brother," she said. Then, Peter's hand drifting off her shoulder, she moved to the bed.

"Daddy?" she said quaveringly, trying out a word she had never had cause to use since the day she'd learned to speak.

Henry struggled to focus. He seemed tired.

"Dorothy?" he said. "You . . . you are very big."

Tears were streaming down her face.

"We thought you were dead," she said. "They told Mum you were dead."

Henry took her large curly head in his hands and to Rosie's astonishment, she gently laid it down on his chest, as though she had been longing to do that her entire life. Peter's kind face twitched into a smile.

"But . . ." Edward's face was a mess of tears and confusion; his entire, well-ordered life was coming apart. He turned to Doreen.

"He . . . he knows all these people."

Doreen could see it on his face.

"Ssh," she said. "Don't worry."

She knew what he was afraid of.

Henry turned toward him again.

"Edward," he said. "Thank God you're here. I'm freezing."

"Dad," said Edward, bursting into sobs and running to his other side. "Dad. You know it's me."

"Of course it's you," croaked Henry, smiling. "My darling Edward Bear. Of course it's you."

Finally everyone was ushered out—including the local press photographer—except for Lilian, whom Henry had requested stay behind. Rosie stayed too, partly in case they needed anything and partly from sheer nosiness. Lilian wanted to sit up on the bed, and Rosie helped her—she was so tiny, she took up hardly any space. And then she nestled into him as if she was molded that way. Then Rosie decided she probably ought to leave and went off to find some tea.

"You died in the war," whispered Lilian.

"So many people died in the war," said Henry slowly. "All the time. I woke up in hospital. I remember. I remember. I remember you. You're Lilian. You are REALLY old."

"I know," said Lilian. "So are you. Ssh. Tell me what happened. Do you remember?"

"It's so strange," said Henry. "I feel like I've been on a foggy road where everything is wrong. And then I got used to being on the foggy road, even though it was wrong, and I just ignored its being wrong, and then it was all right. But I know . . . after the thing, the blast, after . . . I woke up, and they said, 'What's your name?' and I suppose I meant to say 'Henry Carr.'"

He said it again, rolling it around his mouth as if it were a strange wine.

"But I . . . I couldn't say that."

"Didn't you have dog tags?" asked Lilian. "Didn't you wear something around your neck?"

"I lost mine," said Henry, musing at how easily it was coming back to him. "I lost mine in the mess. I think I bet it at poker." He wheezed. "Ha, Lilian, listen to this, someone put up a bag of strawberry boilers."

"You love those," said Lilian, marveling.

"I know, I couldn't resist. I said, I'll stake my whole person on it and everybody laughed, and I took it off and I really meant it. And I got a three of spades and a five of hearts."

He was holding up his knotted hands as if he were playing the game again.

"And Private Boyd, he was a portly little fellow, I don't know where he even got those sweets, not in the hellhole we were in, I tell you. I wanted them so much and I got a bloody five and a three. And he took my dog tags and was just messing about with them, then he went to offer me a sweet, and . . ."

His hand started to shake.

"And then we heard the sirens. The sirens. There were sirens. Where am I? Is this the army hospital?"

"No, it's another hospital," said Lilian patiently, patting him.

"Has there been another bomb?"

"No, darling. You're safe."

"I'm bloody freezing. I can't wait to get back to my Lilian . . . Are you the nurse? You look a lot like her."

"Yes," said Lilian.

"Except I lost her, you know. Like I lost my dog tags. By being an idiot. Such an idiot."

His old shoulders started to shake. Lilian rang the bell for the nurse.

Rosie caught up with Moray and flung her arms around him.

"It's amazing! I mean it's just amazing!"

Moray didn't look as delighted as she did.

"I mean, to go through your whole life."

"Mmm," said Moray. "I don't want to . . . I don't want to be a total downer, Rosie, but his . . . I mean, his lungs. They aren't good."

"But he's talking! He sounds so clear! He knows where he is! It's all come back to him!"

"Yes," said Moray. "You know there are lots of documented cases of this happening . . . just before . . . I mean . . . I don't know, there may be another miracle in there for him. But . . . I wouldn't count on it."

Rosie stopped suddenly, hearing the tone of his voice.

"Really?"

"I don't know if you want to share it with Lilian or not but . . . there's a lot of fluid on his lungs. His body can't really fight the infection . . . the consultant thinks that it's only a matter of time."

Rosie clasped her hand to her mouth. Then she shook her head.

"Well, everything's a matter of time," said Rosie, cross at the euphemism. "How much time?"

"Short of a second miracle . . . days," said Moray, then, as she gasped again, drew her into his arms to hold her tight.

Edward was on the phone with a journalist who was pinning him down to dates.

"You mean to say, he had a freak-out going through the village? When he remembered it?"

"I wouldn't call it a freak-out exactly," said Edward stiffly.

"Well, yes, a freak-out, I suppose. He grabbed the steering wheel."

"When was this?" said the journalist, then glanced idly at his computer. "Oh, that's the same day Lipton School got hit by that lorry."

The color drained out of Edward's face.

"The what?" he said.

"Oh, you didn't hear? A lorry knocked the school down."

"Oh my God, was anyone hurt?"

"Yes, one little boy broke his neck."

Edward couldn't say anything else; he just put the phone down in silence. Everything had suddenly become too much.

"Doreen," he moaned. "Oh Doreen, something really bad has happened."

Seeing as she was here, thought Rosie, in Carningford with its vast twenty-four-hour supermarket, she might as well do her Christmas food shopping, get it over with. She took Pip with her.

"Well, I thought you lived a quiet life here, sis," he said.

"Me too," said Rosie, hauling out the trolley. "Get those for me, will you?"

Pip jumped to help.

"Ha," she said. "You're well trained. When we were little, you'd never do anything I asked."

Pip smiled. "I like a quiet life. Unlike you."

"True," said Rosie.

It was very odd, she found, traveling among the laden aisles, stocking up with all sorts of things—dates, brandy butter, marzipan—that she couldn't really imagine eating any other time of year, how normally everybody else was behaving, having arguments in the wine aisle, bickering about crackers, exhausted-looking mothers hurling lollipops at children to keep them quiet while they got the damn thing done. She and Pip chose a large turkey, some stuffing, plenty of chipolatas for the children, fizzy wine, cola, lots of potatoes for roasting . . .

It was good to have her brother there. She couldn't allow herself to think whether or not Stephen was coming back. They would have Christmas lunch up at Peak House and she'd make up some kind of excuse about him for everyone and then straight after Christmas, she supposed . . . well, she supposed everyone would go. But for now she wanted to chat about his children, especially Meridian, and he liked to talk about them. It was odd, she thought, that her little brother was the grown-up now, with the well-paid job and the family and everything . . . everything she might have liked. She wondered if Lilian had felt the same about her little brother Gordon.

"You are . . . you are happy, aren't you, Pip?" she asked as they queued. Pip looked at her.

"Honestly, R?" he weighed up what he was about to say, as if unsure.

"Yes?"

"I wouldn't . . . I mean, even for a bloke like Stephen, right? I wouldn't . . . I wouldn't miss out on having a family for anything, okay?"

Rosie fell silent.

"Not for the world, R. Even when Desleigh is shouting at me and Shane won't put his bloody DS down and everyone's shrieking and stuff gets left everywhere and spilled everywhere . . . I wouldn't change a bit of it. Don't let it pass you by.

And you know, we would love you to come out there . . . Mum
especially."

Rosie was silent all the way back. Either way, she couldn't see
the right way forward. The future was not an appealing prospect.

The pain of not seeing Stephen, not being with him, felt
unbearable. She had always feared this; she had spent years in
a relationship where she was not "the one," and she couldn't go
through it again if nothing she could do and nothing she could
change about herself would change the immutable facts. He
was the one for her, but if it wasn't returned, she would live a
life as full of disappointment as her great-aunt had. And she
didn't think she could bear it.

A fresh start, in a warm, sunny land full of friendly people
and spectacular food and beaches and swimming pools and bar-
becues and well-paid nursing jobs . . . that, on the other hand,
made a ton of sense. To be close to her mum, and watch the
little ones grow up. . . .

It was a hard solution, but it was almost certainly the right one.

Up at Peak House she relayed the news about Henry to a
breathless Angie and Desleigh, who were rapt. "Never a dull
moment around here," as Angie pointed out. "Where are the
children?" she asked. Normally Meridian was stuck to her side
like a limpet.

"It's amazing," said Desleigh. "Seriously, they're changed
kids."

Rosie went to the window. All three were in the garden, building an igloo together. The girls weren't squabbling, and Rosie wouldn't put money on it, but she thought Kelly had lost a little weight. Shane's DS was nowhere to be seen. Instead, they were chatting, laughing, cooperating.

"It's a good place here," said Desleigh.

Rosie swallowed. She couldn't answer.

Back working at the sweetshop, she smiled at every child who came in, all of them bursting with secrets for her about what Santa was bringing them; all enraptured by the tiny train in the window; little cheeks rosy, eyes bright and round; parents tired but happy. She knew everyone now, and they knew her, Miss Rosie, up at the sweetshop. She would miss them too, terribly, as she wrapped boxes of chocolates, marzipan fruit and Turkish delight for the big day.

Chapter 20

It was obvious to everyone at the hospital now that things were slipping. And slipping quickly. Not even Lilian could continue in denial now. So it was all about spending as much time with Henry as possible without wearing him out. He relied very heavily on the oxygen mask, so he couldn't speak very well or very quickly, but it was very rare that he phased out or didn't appear to be following what went on. Of course they had to share him. Ida Delia liked to talk about him a lot, and swank about the man who was, after all, her husband, but alone in the room with him—his papery skin bordering on translucent; the smells and the plastic tubes and the dryness of the once luxuriant hair—she found it unpleasant and creepy and a reminder of what was coming for all of them in the end. She also found, as ever, that she had nothing much to say to him.

Dorothy, on the other hand, didn't want to say anything. She wanted to hold his hand and wanted him to cuddle her and basically bestow upon her all the masculine affection she had felt so desperately lacking from her cold childhood. Edward, in contrast, had to talk; had to rush to assure himself that Henry's other life as James Boyd hadn't been a waste, or something to be forgotten. He wanted to talk about seaside trips, about building a model railway, and days out and even about arguments they had had during Edward's very brief flirtation with punk in adolescence. This was important to him, and Henry did his best to oblige.

But it was Lilian he really looked forward to seeing every day. She looked as pretty and quirky to him as she ever had. And she liked to talk to him, and he just liked to listen, and he enjoyed it all. Anyone overhearing it who was not in love would think it insane nonsense; the nattering on of two very old people. Anyone who *was* in love would recognize it straightaway as the kind of castles-in-the-air building of two people mad about one another. The only difference was that it wasn't about the future. They played a little game—safer than the shifting sands of their real memories—of let's pretend, making up a past they had never had.

"I think probably about 1955, we moved into one of the large houses on the high street," Lilian would say, and Henry would nod.

"The children used to get scared of the outside loo, do you remember?"

"Yes!" Lilian would say. "Little Henry thought there was a bat, do you remember? And we thought he was just being funny and then Batman came along and we thought we'd have made a lot of money if we'd just written it down."

"I liked our twenty-fifth wedding anniversary party," Henry would say. "Hetty let us have it up at the house, do you remember? And I wreathed your hair with flowers."

"And I was so cross because it ruined my new hairdo!" said Lilian. "Ha, and we had that big fight in front of everyone."

Henry smiled.

"I could never stay cross with you for long."

"That," said Lilian, "was just as well."

On the morning of Christmas Eve, Moray brought Lilian down to the village early. Rosie looked up, surprised. Lilian was wearing a very old, faded dress with green sprigs. She had gotten so thin again, Rosie noticed. Excitement and no sleep, no doubt. She didn't guess for a second that Lilian had been doing it on purpose so she could get into her oldest dress again, the one he had loved her in, the one that had been nestling at the bottom of the wardrobe all these years.

"A half pound of caramels, please," said Lilian, her face made up lightly, the dress dated but still oddly pretty on her girlish figure.

"Off to the hospital?" said Rosie. "Won't you freeze?"

"No," said Lilian. "I'm from around here, not some vulgar interloper like you. Hello, Spiderman."

Meridian had been playing in a box behind the counter.

"I NOT SPIDERMAN! I'M ROBOT! GOOD ROBOT," she clarified.

"Glad to hear it," said Lilian. She cast an eye over the shelves. "You're low on pineapple chunks."

"I know," said Rosie. "There's been a run on them for Christmas. No new deliveries until the new year."

"Well, that won't help when someone wants some."

"I'll direct them to the grapefruit suckers," said Rosie. "We'll battle through."

Lilian wasn't listening, though. She was taking a long look

around the little room, its dark red shelves repainted in the same shade they'd always been; the little mullioned windows, the tall glass jars, the ancient brass scales.

"I'll miss this place," said Lilian.

"Who says it's going anywhere?" said Rosie stoutly.

"Well, things change," said Lilian. "People . . . leave."

"Even if I did leave," said Rosie, "Tina would still be here. The sweetshop would still be here."

"Nothing lasts forever," said Lilian.

"ROBOTS LAST FOREVER," came a little voice. Rosie smiled instinctively. Lilian looked at her carefully.

"I must get on," she said. "Moray's waiting. Oh, and a quarter pound of golf balls, please."

"It's a 'small bag,' Lilian. We can't serve imperial anymore."

"I think," said Lilian, getting out her little snap-clasp purse and insisting on paying, "you can to me."

Henry had deteriorated fairly swiftly during the night. Now he was being moved to full life support—the same bed, coincidentally, that Edison had vacated so recently. Mutterings were being made, though, about perhaps the family wanted to come in. This was entirely unnecessary. Everyone was there. No one knew quite what to do, and there was a lot of offering to get coffee and "after yous" and politeness. Edward was not looking forward to his day. On top of the terrible news from the hospital, he was having lunch with Dorothy to very politely and generously tackle necessary changes to the will. He didn't know Dorothy very well. Then he had an appointment with a police officer. He had been utterly aghast to find out what had happened, but his lawyer had advised him to be reasonably confident that the police would not file charges against his father for distracting a driver. He just wanted the strain lifted off the lorry driver before Christmas; the poor man was out on bail. He went in to the hospital first. Cathryn was there too, still anxious.

"I can't . . . I can't say how sorry I am," she said, grabbing Edward in the hallway. She had a terrible fear that the family were going to get very difficult—and quite rightly. If she hadn't been so distracted by the children's beautiful singing, she wouldn't have taken her eyes off him. But she had been, and she had.

Edward turned to her. He looked tired but, somehow less anxious.

"Cathryn," he said. "Listen to me. I don't blame you, okay? He wandered off of his own accord. He is ninety-one years old. I think we knew this day was going to come. But it's not even that. Whatever else happened to my father out there, it brought him back. He has had the chance to be himself—his real self, the person I never knew. I can't . . . It's the best thing that could have happened. If he'd been at home, we never would have had him back again. If he'd stayed at the care home, I don't think . . . I think this had to happen. I think he had to come home."

Cathryn swallowed.

"Thank you," she said. "Thank you."

"You are doing wonderful things up there," said Edward. "Don't stop, please."

Cathryn bit her lip.

"Are they letting you take him home?"

Edward shook his head.

"No. Too risky to move him, they said. And he seems comfortable here, so maybe it's best . . ."

At that moment, his daughters and Ian, unusually smartly dressed, appeared to say their goodbyes. They looked embarrassed, worried that they would get it wrong. Edward wished he could tell them that there was no right or wrong with what they were doing; everyone was equally awkward. He smiled at them instead.

"I must go," he said.

"Of course," said Cathryn. "Oh, and Edward . . . if it helps. None of us ever really know our parents."

Edward paused for a moment.

"You know," he said. "I think it does."

Edward found, once in the room, that he couldn't say what he wanted to say. He wished suddenly that he'd written it down. But the reality of his father in front of him was so odd and strange that he couldn't get the words out. Something about seeing Mum again . . . but did he believe that? Oh, he wanted to. And that would be enough.

He sat down. Henry had an oxygen mask on and struggled to take it off. Edward helped him. Henry sounded very choky and as if he couldn't find the words, so Edward put it back on again and felt too hot in the stuffy space.

"So," said Edward. He glanced at his watch. "I'm . . . I'm just going to change your will, okay? To add something in Dorothy's favor? I'm sorry. I know this is awkward."

Henry nodded. "That's fine," he managed to rasp. "You are good to share."

Edward smiled and patted Henry's hand. He'd had power of attorney for four years now and wanted to do what was right.

"So I'm going to do that and come right back, okay?"

"Yes, son. That's grand."

They sat in silence, neither knowing what to say. Then Edward got up to go.

"Um," he started quickly. "You've been a good dad."

Henry blinked several times.

"You . . . you've been a good son," he croaked. And that was that.

Lilian didn't say anything. She simply took off her coat and saw that he recognized her dress; saw how pleased he was to see it again; to simply have an awareness of where he was, in his own skin. She smiled. A friendly nurse helped her up onto the bed and checked Henry's morphine levels.

Then Lilian took out the large bag of caramels and carefully removed his mask. She put the bag under his nose so he could smell them, and then took a tiny piece that had separated from the rest and put it into his mouth. Then, very slowly, another. And Henry took hold of her hand and squeezed it until he couldn't squeeze anymore, and then when he could not squeeze, she held him. And then when there was no Henry left to hold anymore, she kissed him gently on the forehead and wished her boy goodnight.

Chapter 21

Christmas Eve was a ridiculously busy day in the shop. Tina had been quite right, everyone went crazy at the end of the year. There wasn't a large box of chocolates unsold; children bought boxes of travel sweets for their mums and dads because they liked the pictures on them; stocking fillers were bought, candy canes by the score, Turkish delight and marzipan fruit for after dinner; soft marshmallows for hot chocolate in cold fingers, chews for watching the telly, and of course boxes of assorted candies. Everyone had one of those. Big, small, and anywhere in between.

Anton came in, looking timid.

"Anton!" said Rosie, amazed. He must have lost even more weight. "Look at you!" His little wife next to him beamed with pride.

"I know," said Anton.

"I don't think you're the fattest man in Lipton anymore! I reckon Doctor Hye is fatter than you!"

Anton beamed.

"Well done," said Rosie to his wife.

"Oh no, he had to want to do it," she said. "Plus, after the accident the food delivery companies didn't want to come out here so much. So he couldn't get all those secret deliveries."

Rosie thought about this.

"Well," she said finally. "It's nice to know that out of something so awful, some good could come."

"And I got a job!" said Anton.

"No way! Wonderful!"

"I'm Santa Claus!" said Anton. "At the shopping center in Carningford."

"Wonderful! What a perfect job for you, you're so nice to everyone."

Anton flushed.

"Of course, it means I have to keep a BIT of a tummy."

"Not at all," said Rosie heartily. "Next year you can play an elf. Now what would you like? Small bags only."

Anton's wife winked at her.

"I would like . . . just the one lollipop," said Anton. "As a treat."

Rosie looked at him.

"Truly?"

"Yes," said Anton stoically. "I have changed. Thanks to you."

"Could you say that more loudly when there are more people around to hear you?" said Rosie, handing him his lollipop. "And not just a good robot."

"Can Robot have lollipop now?" came a robot voice from down near her feet.

"No."

Moray called to tell her Henry had died at just after three o'clock. Rosie looked at Tina and swallowed hard; it seemed ridiculous to feel so upset, she had hardly known him. But then, of course, it was Lilian she was sad for.

"Who was with him?" asked Tina.

"Lilian," said Rosie. "Oh, I'm so glad. Although, poor Edward."

"I think Edward made his peace," said Tina with the wise look of someone who'd gathered all the town gossip from Jake's nights out at the Red Lion.

"I think he did too," said Rosie thoughtfully. "Oh dear, though. What about Lilian? To have gotten back the love of her life . . . for a week."

"Better to spend a week with someone you love than a lifetime with someone you don't," said Tina. She was only speculating, and was therefore entirely surprised to see Rosie suddenly collapse in tears.

"What? What is it? What have I said?"

"Oh Tina," said Rosie, and all of a sudden it came flooding out. Tina put the BACK IN 5 MINUTES sign on the door and made them both large cups of tea.

"He's just . . . he said he doesn't want to get married, that I'm bugging him, that it's all . . . Tina, I think it's all off!"

Tina furtively twisted her own engagement ring.

"Oh no, it's not."

"I think so . . . I mentioned going to Australia, maybe, with my mum, and he didn't even care! Didn't even think about it. I don't even . . . I don't even . . . he's just gone to London. I think when Angie goes away in a couple of days, he's going to move back to Peak House . . . and I'll be all by myself! Forever!"

"I think we're going to need more tea," said Tina. "Oh God, Rosie. I had no idea. I'm so sorry."

"Me too," sobbed Rosie. "I love him so much, Tina, so much. But now I don't see that there's any point in staying here after all."

"But you like it here, don't you?"

"I fell in love with it," said Rosie. "With the town, with the people, with Stephen, with the shop, with everything."

She swallowed. "But I don't think it loves me back."

"But what about Lilian?"

"I think she thinks I should go. Spend time with my family," said Rosie.

Meridian came up to Rosie, still with her robot helmet on.

"Don't cry, Auntie Rosie," she said, clumsily trying to dry away her tears. "Was Kelly mean to you?"

"No," said Rosie. "You guys are never mean to me."

"Kelly is mean to me," said Meridian. She hugged Rosie tightly. "Would you like to come to my house and have a sleepover?"

Rosie smiled.

"Sometime."

"We can watch *Finding Nemo*. I like Nemo films. Or James Bond."

"You're not allowed to watch James Bond."

"I. AM. JAMES. BOND."

"Oh dear," said Tina. "Well. You know I grew up here, right?"

Rosie nodded.

"I've known Stephen Lakeman all my life, okay?"

Rosie nodded again.

"I've seen him with loads of girlfriends, half of them looking like total supermodels."

"Not helping."

"But I swear I've never . . . I've never seen him as smitten with anyone in my life as he is with you. I've never seen him live with someone, I've never seen him light up with someone like he does with you and I swear no one else ever got to meet his mother."

"Hmm."

"I think you're mad. I think he does love you, and you're just getting your knickers in a twist because it's not moving as fast as you'd like it to. He's just been in a big accident!"

"I know," said Rosie. "But it's more than that. You know what he's like. He can be so grudging, so sullen."

"Are you sure?" said Tina. "Are you sure it's not just you picking faults?"

"Well, if it's that," said Rosie, "then that's just as bad, isn't it? What would we be like in ten years?"

Tina shrugged. "Oh, I could see you two in ten years."

"Really?" said Rosie, curious.

"Oh yes. You'll get nice and plump."

"Well, thanks a BUNCH!"

"Oh, don't be daft. Kids do that to you."

"You had twins and you look all right."

"I had twins at twenty-four," said Tina. "Anyway, shush, do you want to hear this or not?"

"Yes," said Rosie grudgingly. "Can you do another version where I'm really really slender and elegant?"

"But he loves your gorgeous bosom and all of that. Trust me, if he wanted a stick, he had plenty of those London models after him."

"Yes, again, thank you," said Rosie.

"So, anyway. And he'll still be rangy and thin and gorgeous."

"Great," said Rosie. "Well, this just gets better and better."

"And he goes out striding the hills with the boys—for sure you'll have boys, you're the type."

"Mm," said Rosie.

"And you'll cook something yummy for when they come in all ruddy cheeked and starving, and it'll be lovely."

There was a pause.

"Are you sure," asked Rosie eventually, "that you haven't just mixed up my imaginary future with a gravy advert you saw on television?"

Tina thought for a moment.

"I think I did, didn't I?"

"Yes," said Rosie.

"Well, there's no reason it can't happen."

"What, gravy adverts come true?"

"Mine's going to," said Tina.

There was no arguing with that. Rosie opened up the shop again and tried to get distracted by the sheer number of customers piling in and out wishing them a happy Christmas and leaving gifts and cards for Lilian. They passed on the news again and again. People were stunned and fascinated; one or two of the older ones remembered Henry's parents and the devastation they had lived with for the rest of their lives.

"All of those losses," said old Mrs. Bell from Bell's Farm, picking up her favorite Parma violets for her visiting grandchildren, who hated them and found them sickly, but who in later life would love the smell because it would make them remember their grandmother who had always been so kind to them. "That war blew a hole through the village, you know."

"Lilian always said."

"Well, I was born in the war, so I don't remember it, but

even as a girl you could feel it. The pain on people's faces when they watched us playing. There were a few very late babies too. It's hard to grow up in a home where a mother has lost a son," she observed. "Some of them hated even letting their boys get married."

"I hadn't even really thought about his mum and dad," said Tina. "God." She shivered again.

"It must have just been a mix-up," continued Mrs. Bell. "Got shipped back to Halifax, found himself a job, built a new life. Just like that."

"Imagine," said Rosie, deep in thought.

At four thirty, after they'd sold basically everything, Rosie was on the point of closing up and giving Tina her Christmas bonus when there was a creak at the door. It barely tinkled as the bearded man with glasses pushed it open carefully. It was Edison's dad, Arthur. He pushed the wheelchair in.

"Edison!" said Rosie and Tina in unison, Rosie's worries temporarily forgotten.

Edison pushed himself in very slowly and carefully on his wheelchair. Meridian wandered out to see what was going on.

"Who's this?" asked Edison warily.

"I'm a robot now," said Meridian. "Only not a real robot. A little one."

"You see," said Edison. "That's mostly where I go. Behind there. It's my place."

"I like your robot chair."

"I know, it's cool," said Edison, brightening slightly.

"Hello!" said Rosie. "How's Hester?"

"Uncomfortable," said Arthur. "Hello there. Can I have two hundred and twenty grams of coconut spaceships?"

"I have never been asked in metric before," said Rosie. "Amazing. You really are a scientist, aren't you?"

He smiled shyly. "A scientist whose wife currently has very peculiar tastes. I also need two hundred and twenty grams of licorice allsorts and some gravel."

Rosie looked at Edison.

"I miss you," she said.

Edison nodded and smiled, as if this was only to be expected.

"Yes, I guess she's too small to be much use."

Rosie muted the fact that Edison had never been remotely useful either and refrained from taking sides.

"I am MUCH USE," came the defiant voice. "If we get BAD SPIES."

"I think I'm going to get a rocket launcher fitted," said Edison, indicating his right armrest. "Just here."

Rosie glanced at Edison's dad, who just said mildly, "All right, you start drawing up the plans and I'll have a look in the shed."

"So, the wheelchair . . ." Rosie started, not knowing a good way to get into the conversation.

"Two months, they're hoping," said Arthur. "Lots of physio. . . . He'll have faint neck problems, probably, for the rest of his life, but he's healed remarkably well for a puny thing." He smiled at this and clearly didn't mean it in the slightest.

Edison lowered his voice.

"They're replacing all my bones with adamantium so I will be super strong like Wolverine."

"I see," said Rosie. "Wow, you are going to be fearless after that."

"I think everyone at school is already afraid of me," said Edison.

"In case they break you," said his dad. "Thanks, Rosie."

Meridian looked at Edison.

"So anyway, okay, maybe you can keep my place for me until I come back," said Edison. "Which is soon."

"That's okay," said Meridian. "I going back to 'Strilia. Rosie coming with me."

Arthur and Tina both raised their eyebrows at this.

"I'm coming to VISIT," said Rosie, her cheeks coloring.

"Grangy says you're coming to stay prolly," prattled on Meridian. "She said you'll have sleepovers with me forever."

"Well, this is sad news," said Arthur.

"And completely untrue!" said Rosie. "Please don't take your town gossip from a three-year-old!"

"Out of the mouths of babes," said Tina.

"And you can shush too, as if I'd make plans like this without telling you."

Arthur and Tina swapped glances.

"Well," he said. "Merry Christmas one and all."

"And to you," said Rosie. "Have a wonderful day!"

"I think Santa is going to be very busy tonight," said Edison. "Do you know what speed he travels at? Nine hundred kilometers per second. Fortunately he's magic, otherwise all the reindeer would burn up on entry. That's why Rudolph has a red nose, though. Because he goes at the front."

"Well, I'm glad you've thought this through," said Rosie. She came out behind the counter and kissed his pale blond hair.

"Happy Christmas, my dearie."

He felt so thin under his scarf and heavy puffa jacket; his little arms were like sticks.

"I prescribe plenty of sweeties," she said.

"That's why I like you better than Moray and all those hospital doctors," said Edison, his voice muffled through the hug.

Edward dropped off a very tired, very quiet Lilian at Rosie's house before she went back to the home. They would join the rest of the family up the hill in the morning, but Lilian wanted to go through Henry's clothes and things, which Edward had said would be fine. Plus it would give her a bit of peace and quiet in the morning while Angie and Pip managed the children's unbearable excitement up at Peak House.

Rosie ran out briefly into the snow to kiss Edward, who looked completely drained, and make him promise to keep in touch. As soon as the police had heard the story, and about Henry's death, they had dismissed the entire case, and the lorry driver could spend Christmas without it hanging over him. He had, of course, lost his job; Edward had promised to see if he could find something for him at the building society that didn't involve any driving.

Rosie was on the point of inviting him in; then she looked at Lilian, curled up like a child in the backseat, so fragile and delicate looking, and decided against it. They would meet again at the funeral, of course . . . oh, there was so much to arrange. Well, she would worry about that when the time came. Now her priority was her great-aunt.

She half-carried, half-coaxed Lilian into the cozy sitting

room, where she had the fire roaring high. There was a stew slow-cooking on the stove, something easy and digestible, but Lilian didn't want anything to eat. Rosie carefully set her down and got her a medicinal glass of red wine. Unusually for Lilian, she hadn't said anything. Rosie sat next to her and patted her on the shoulder, giving her time.

After she'd finished the wine, Lilian looked into the fire for a long time. Eventually, she sighed. Then she said, "Well, that's that."

Rosie nodded. Lilian turned her ancient eyes on her. They looked even older today somehow, their pale blue getting paler and softer; her lovely soft skin was whiter and as thin as paper.

"Do you think. . . . You know I hate that vicar."

They had had this discussion before. Lilian had been waging a vendetta against the trendy Lipton vicar since he'd arrived. Fortunately, he seemed completely unaware of this fact.

"After the war," said Lilian, "after I lost Ned and Henry . . . well, I thought, that's about it for God. You don't need to be a starving child in Africa being eaten alive by flies to think sod that for a game of soldiers."

Rosie nodded.

"But now," Lilian said, "oh, wouldn't it be nice? Hmm? Just to fall asleep, set these aching bones to rest. And wake up in Henry's arms, all young and strong and splendid like we were? And we'd be somewhere warm where it never snowed, and we'd be together and we could grow the garden we never grew."

"My father's house has many mansions," murmured Rosie because she had heard it once and thought it sounded comforting.

"I think I will suddenly believe," said Lilian decidedly. "I think maybe I'll believe Catholic. They do that nice thing at the end, don't they? They did it to Henry, put stuff on his head and basically saying, whatever you've done, don't worry about it, you're all fine and that's a guarantee. Can I have that?"

"I'm not sure that's how it works," said Rosie.

"Oh, of course it must be. God would know I was doing it for the right reasons, wouldn't he? He knows I'm not a bad person."

"I think God would be far too scared not to let you into heaven," said Rosie.

"Quite. Okay, Catholic it is then. Do they let women be priests?"

"There is nothing wrong with women being priests," said Rosie.

"Yes, well, I'll see what God says about that when I see him," said Lilian severely.

"You'll see what God says about that in thirty years' time," said Rosie. "On your way to Buckingham Palace to pick up your award for longest-living woman in Britain. But now you can shush up and have a bath if you like. I've left the water on for you."

"Do I need a bath? Do I smell of old lady?"

"No, you smell of Tweed, like you always do, and it's lovely."

"Yes," said Lilian. "From Paris, you know."

Rosie smiled. Lilian was gazing at the fire again.

"I don't want thirty years, Rosie. Thirty years of feeling cold and being too slow and not being able to hear a damn thing and playing more bridge, and worrying about falling over and not being able to read because I can't bloody see, and day after day with nothing to look forward to."

"Nothing?"

"Okay, some things to look forward to." She gave Rosie a shrewd look. "Getting you off my hands one way or another. But not as much as the one thing I am really looking forward to."

She looked straight at Rosie, completely serious now.

"I found him at last," she said. "And now I want to see him again."

"Don't you even think it," said Rosie, also deadly serious. "Don't you even dare."

There was silence, then Lilian glanced wryly at her empty glass and lightened the mood.

"Okay, come on, home," said Rosie. "You're sure you won't stay?"

"It's kippers and kedgeree and champagne for breakfast," said Lilian. "Can you compete with that?"

"No," said Rosie, picking up the car keys. Pip had lent her the hire car.

"Where's Stephen?" asked Lilian.

"Out," said Rosie, unwilling to have that conversation just now.

"I'd like to see him."

"Well, that's too bad. You've had a tough day. You need to sleep."

Lilian let herself be led off to the car.

"I'll see him in my dreams, you know," she said to Rosie. "I've always seen him there. Now I know for sure. He's waiting for me. And of course, his hair is as brown as a nut."

Rosie returned alone and sat in front of the blazing fire.

So here it was, she thought. Merry Christmas. The Christmas she had once been looking forward to so much. In her head, the groaning table, the delighted children, not one of them addicted to their Nintendos, as she and Stephen together put on a wonderful spread, and everyone was happy and smiling, and it was everything she'd ever dreamed of and then Stephen would maybe have hushed everyone, still with a party hat on his head, and said he hoped they didn't mind, but he wanted to ask Rosie something . . .

Ugh, stupid, stupid stupid. She was completely stupid. She had misjudged just about everything it was possible to misjudge. Worst of all, she had not realized that everything she had of Stephen was all he had to give.

She had disregarded all the warnings—that he was difficult, that his childhood had been hard—and thought that it was all right, she could fix him. But fixing someone wasn't a relationship. Fixing someone was what nurses did. And once you'd fixed people up, then off they went again. But she'd thought . . . she'd thought that with Stephen it was different. That the way they cared for one another, how they were together . . . She bit her lip. She had played her hand. She had nothing left to give, nothing up her sleeve that would suddenly make him think, oh yes, that is the one I cannot live without. And that was that.

You couldn't face a life being someone's second best, someone's "Oh well, you'll do for now." Well, you could—she had, once before, with Gerard. And look how that had turned out. She certainly wasn't doing it again.

She felt such a fool. So precious about everything, so sure. Oh yes, tra la, I'm just throwing up my entire life in London and my flat and all my friends to move to the countryside. Of course I know what I'm doing.

Well, she didn't know what she was doing. Not a bit of it, obviously. The sweetshop was barely ticking over; she was making less than she had as a nurse, which wasn't a lot. She was going to be single in a town where there were substantially more sheep than single men with their own teeth, where she had no family, few friends and where she'd be treated as an outsider for at least another twenty years.

Sniveling, she poured herself another glass of sherry. The radio was softly playing carols, and they only reminded her of the children singing and made her cry harder. She had a lot of gifts to wrap; she supposed she'd better get to it. And a busy day tomorrow. At least she'd see Pip's children. And then, the day after Boxing Day, they'd be off too, off on tour to see things, then back to Oz. She was going to miss them so much, even little fussbudget Kelly. She remembered Shane sledding down the hill, his head thrown back laughing, looking so much like Pip as a small boy that it was ridiculous. Desleigh filming the whole thing. Rosie had grown to rather appreciate her sister-in-law's stolid calmness; now she saw how unstressed she was with her children and her life and in return how that suited the family and Pip. Of course Angie, as usual, could do all the worrying for everybody.

She wrapped up the special Spiderman activity set for her little Meridian, tears dropping onto the paper. Well, she would miss her most of all. She had never thought being an aunt would be such a pleasure.

As if he knew what she was thinking, Mr. Dog got out of his basket and came and plopped his head on her lap, looking up at her with infinite compassion.

"You still love me, don't you, Mr. Dog?" she said, absent-mindedly feeding him a bit of mince pie. "Because I give you mince pie even though it's very bad for dogs."

Mr. Dog made a groaning sound.

"Yes, and because you love me for myself. I forgot about that."

A tear plopped onto his nose, and he licked it off, then licked her hand. She caressed his silken ears, then started wrapping Shane's new Nintendo game, which Desleigh had told her would be ideal, and a new dressing-up princess outfit for Kelly, size "cheery child," which Rosie had learned was secret shop code for "plump." She had at the last minute added a very fancy tiara, which in turn had made her search all the shops in Derby until she got hold of a Spiderman mask for Meridian. No luck with James Bond merchandise—another of Meridian's obsessions—for a little girl quite so small, but she found a perfect little reproduction Aston Martin. Then she had to get something else for Kelly and Shane, so it was a ridiculous mound of gifts that now sat before her.

She had longed to go shopping for Stephen to find a beautiful sweater in a dark blue that would go with those eyes of his, or in black, which made him look so dramatic, like James Bond himself. And if the sales assistant had asked what she was looking for, she would have said, "Oh, I'm shopping for my boyfriend," and they would have looked out something really special.

But in the end, she hadn't. It had seemed like bad luck. She couldn't shop for someone when she didn't even know where they were, when the last thing you'd heard them say was "I don't want to marry you." So.

A beautiful cashmere cardigan for Lilian in her trademark color of soft violet that suited her coloring so well—expensive, but worth it, definitely. And for Angie, a ridiculous dress, far too short and a bit too tight, in a bright orange, that she'd seen her sighing over in the shopping center. She'd bought a size 8. That would probably be wrong, but she'd erred on the safe side, so that should be pleasing. She must get on. On what should be one of the happiest nights of the year—the snow still falling, the fire burning merrily in its grate, the Christmas TV, when she turned it on, full of snowmen and excitement and joy upon the earth—Rosie sat wrapping her gifts, crying and crying and crying.

Edward and Doreen lay in bed, hands tightly clasped together. They had written to the registrar and had vast amounts of paperwork to do, plus the hospital wanted an autopsy. They didn't even know when they would get to bury Edward's father. But somehow, although there was great sadness, there was also a sense of peace.

Edward's greatest fear, ever since James—Henry—was diagnosed all those years ago, was that he would die in anguish; in terrible pain and fear and confusion, not knowing who he was or where, upset and scared. But it had not happened like that. Even though there was a lot to process, his father's last hours had been spent safe, warm, in his bed, cared for, surrounded by people he both loved and recognized.

"I don't think," Edward said, as the ever kind and patient Doreen stroked him gently on the forearm in the depths of the snowy night, "you can really ask for more than that, can you?"

"No," said Doreen, who would never tell Edward that the idea of James living for another five or six years—or, even more terrifying, ten or fifteen—had always filled her with a terrible anxiety, about money, caring, basically everything. That, fond as she had been of her kind, quiet father-in-law, it was now time to go on a cruise—a BIG cruise—somewhere with absolutely no bloody snow.

Pip was having not the slightest luck in putting the children to bed. They were leaping around Peak House, giggling and shrieking and dancing and insisting on waiting up for Santa. Angie and Desleigh had decided simply to ignore them and had retired to the kitchen, cozy from the Aga, and opened a bottle of wine.

"How are you doing?" said Desleigh. "I thought coming to the English bush was meant to be all quiet and everything?"

"I know," said Angie. "It's completely mad. You know, I never even knew Lilian had a boyfriend. Wasn't the kind of thing she ever mentioned. My dad said once, when I asked why she never got married, that she liked a boy who got killed in the war, but he was married to someone else, so I didn't think . . . I mean, I just thought it couldn't have been that serious, know what I mean?"

"I think it's romantic," said Desleigh. "PIP! CAN YOU PUT THOSE BLOODY BUGGERS TO BED? THEY'RE DOING MY HEAD IN!"

"Yes," said Angie, topping up their glasses. "So what do you think about our Rosie, then?"

Desleigh shook her head slowly.

"You know she's a lovely girl, Angie."

"She is," said Angie, proudly.

"But I don't think it's going to work with that one, do you know what I mean?"

Angie nodded soberly.

"I mean, we haven't seen hide nor hair of him for days . . . just disappearing like that, it's no good. And what he said about settling down?"

"I thought it was too good to be true," said Angie. "I really did. Not that I don't think she deserves the world."

"I know you think that," said Desleigh. "You're a wonderful mother."

"Thank you," said Angie. "So are you."

They smiled happily at one another.

"But he's just . . . I mean, he's just not really going to be there for her, is he?"

Angie shook her head sorrowfully.

"And can you imagine THAT as a mother-in-law?"

Angie and Desleigh shared a giggle at how unfortunate other people could be with their in-laws.

"No. It's not going to happen," said Angie. "I think Rosie just has to face up to it. Not that he isn't a spunk."

"He's a spunk," agreed Desleigh, a little too vociferously. "But you know what they say: men don't get much keener than they are at the beginning."

"That's right," said Angie. "Oh yes, I know that."

"So . . ."

"Yup," said Angie. "I think we're going to get her to come back with us."

Desleigh and Angie chinked glasses. There was the sound of loud screeching from upstairs.

"Muuum!" shouted Pip. "Can you come and settle these bloody buggers?"

Desleigh watched Angie go upstairs with much satisfaction. Having Auntie Rosie on hand would make things even easier. After all, she thought, refilling her glass, it took a village to raise a child.

Chapter 22

Rosie awoke with a start. There was a noise. At first she didn't know where she was. Then she realized she must have fallen asleep. The fire was burning low in the grate, and the room was turning cold. The television was showing late-night comedians making fun of the royal family, and she looked crossly at the empty sherry glass.

Then she realized what the noise was: the house phone was ringing. It stopped, then seconds later started again. She glanced at her watch; it was two A.M. Her heart skipped a beat; it must be Stephen. She grabbed the phone and answered it.

"Hello?"

"Rosie?"

The voice was masculine, but, she realized, it wasn't Stephen. Gradually, it filtered through her sleep-fuddled head that it was Moray's soft tones.

"What?" she said. "What is it?"

"Are you sober?"

"What are you talking about? Of course I'm sober. Well. I had two glasses of sherry . . . five hours ago."

"Fine, fine, that'll do."

She heard the slight tension in his voice.

"What is it?"

"Only bloody Hester."

Rosie blinked a few times before she realized who he meant. "Edison's mother . . . Oh Christ, the baby."

"Yes, the bloody baby. Deciding to make an appearance on the night when there are no doctors, no ambulances, two feet of bloody snow, midwife en route but not sounding overconfident, and muggins here on call."

Rosie struggled to her feet, looking around for her thick down coat. "I'm here . . . Can you pick me up?"

"Do you need time to get dressed?"

"No," snapped Rosie, then, "Don't ask. Where's Hye?"

"Bahamas," said Moray crossly. "Something about winter locality coverage payments." He sniffed loudly. "See you in two."

Rosie threw some water on her face and tried to comb her hair, then gave it up as a pointless job. It was hardly as if she were going to a photo shoot. It had been three years since she'd assisted at a birth, but hopefully it would come back to her.

"At least Hester's all into this natural birth stuff," said Moray cheerfully in the car. "I don't know how we'd get an anesthetist out here, but I got the midwife to read her records over the phone, and the baby's fine, presented, turned the right way. I don't know about you, but I'm not exactly in the mood for performing an emergency section."

"Jesus," said Rosie.

"I'm joking," said Moray. "Calm down. We'd get the helicopter out again. Three times in a month; they'd love us."

Rosie half-smiled, her heart beating fast, and checked her phone again. There was nothing from Stephen. Where the fuck was he? He could be dead in a ditch as far as she knew. He'd taken some clothes, so she'd figured he was lying low for a few days. But how long was that supposed to be? Or maybe he'd actually moved to London and was so damned posh he didn't need his stuff. She sighed.

"Seriously, I was joking," said Moray. "I'm sure it's going to be fine. I've done this before, you know. See a bit of it in rural practice in the winter. It's like being a vet."

"That totally makes me feel better, James Herriot," said Rosie. "No, it's . . . oh God. It's Stephen."

"Is he being . . . difficult?"

"He's 'taking some time to figure things out.'"

"Mmm," said Moray. He knew that Rosie wanted him to call Stephen an arsehole to make her feel better, but he couldn't now.

Rosie sighed. The car drew up outside the pretty little eco house marooned among the trees. Rosie thought back to that dreadful morning she'd had to tell Hester the news about Edison. Thank God that boy was home for Christmas.

Inside, all the lights were on. Arthur was trying to fill up a leaking rubber paddling pool, which Rosie belatedly realized, after wondering whether this was a good time for paddling, was meant to be the birthing pool.

"Hello, Rosie," said Edison happily from his chair. He was wearing bright red pajamas with Santas on them. "Are you here to sperience the miracle of natril birth?"

"Apparently, yes," said Rosie. "Can I boil the kettle?"

Hester was upstairs, holding on to the side of the reclaimed bed, her huge belly seeming to move on its own. She was swearing like a trooper.

"Thank fuck," she said. "Fuck this for a fucking game of fucking soldiers."

"Hush, hush," said Rosie, jumping into practical nurse mode with barely any effort. "Come on, let's get Moray to take a look at you, see where we're at."

Hester eyed her balefully.

"Fuck off," she said. "I've changed my mind. I don't want this fucking baby."

Moray popped his head back outside.

"Arthur," he yelled. "How long has your wife been in labor?"

"Four years," shouted Arthur. "Oh, sorry. About twelve hours, I think."

He straightened up from the pool.

"She was really mellow to begin with. Lots of yoga and stuff. Breathing and the rest of it. Then I think we . . . moved out of that stage."

Rosie tried to help Hester back onto the bed, but Hester was having none of it.

"Why didn't you call us before?" Rosie said gently.

"Get to fuck," said Hester.

"I think maybe just keep Edison downstairs?" said Moray, quickly scrubbing up. "Right. You. Sweary McLairy from Robertson's Dairy. On the bed."

They managed to move Hester, moaning and grimacing and occasionally shrieking, to the bed, where Moray finally got to examine her without being kicked.

"This is where I wish I'd gone into small animal work," he said briefly, then found what he was looking for. "Oh, excellent," he said to Hester. "Eight centimeters. You're nearly there."

Hester raised herself off the bed.

"I," she said very slowly and carefully. "WOULD. LIKE. MY. FUCKING. EPIDURAL. NOW."

Rosie went downstairs to pick up the hot water and fresh towels and to tell Arthur to turn up the heat in the bedrooms.

"How on earth," she said very quickly and quietly, "did she manage to have Edison naturally?"

Arthur looked at her in consternation.

"Oh, she didn't," he said. "Elective section at thirty-eight weeks to keep the weight off." He coughed. "Hester's changed a LOT since we got married."

Rosie's eyes popped.

"I'll say," she said.

She ran back upstairs and mopped Hester's brow.

"You're doing great," she said.

"Fuck off," said Hester. "This totally blows. ARGH!"

And she went into another contraction.

Rosie and Moray looked at each other.

"All normal," said Moray. "Shouldn't be long now."

But it was. And as Hester yelled and swore through the night, and Edison wheeled around downstairs in excitement, she and Moray talked and helped Hester breathe through contractions

"Why does ANYONE do this shit?" she was saying. "This is like being in a fucking car accident," until Moray said that he had precisely one vial of diamorphine on him, and if she stopped the filthy language she could have it, which quieted her down a bit and he gave her half of it, whereupon the waves still came on her, stronger and stronger, but she felt more able to gather them in, to let the seas toss her and bend with the storm.

"A Christmas baby," mused Rosie. "In sitcoms, this is always hilarious."

Moray raised an eyebrow as Rosie squeezed Hester's hand.

"So," said Moray. "It's not going so well with lover boy then?"

Rosie gripped Hester's hand and felt mournful.

"Well, at least I'll never need to go through this," she said, half-joking.

"Oh, Rosie," said Moray, sad that Stephen hadn't taken his advice. "I'm so sorry. If there's anything . . . Well, I never saw him happier than when I saw him with you."

"Thanks," said Rosie. "Tina said that too. But it doesn't appear to have been enough."

"No," said Moray. "I know a bit about that."

Rosie looked at him curiously.

"I really thought he loved you, Rosie. I really did." Moray looked at her straight on, and she wondered what had happened to his nice young house officer in Carningford. "But you can't ever *make* someone love you."

"I know," said Rosie, her heart breaking at the sound of the words.

"*I* love you," said Moray.

"Thanks."

Moray reached over Hester's huge bouncing sweaty knees and gently clasped Rosie's shoulder.

"Okay!" he said then, taking a fresh pair of gloves. "Let's have a look . . . YOUR reward," he said to Hester, "for stopping being a total navvy is that . . . yup . . . I think it's time for you to have a baby."

"Can I push now?" she asked, grunting.

"Yup! I'm going to count to three, and then I want you to push on a count of five for me then stop, okay? Rosie?"

"I'm on it," said Rosie.

Then all was action as they focused on nothing else: not the snow, not the world outside, not Stephen, not anything except counting and Hester bearing down, and bearing down again, as their world contracted to the little circle of light in the forest.

Chapter 23

Stephen looked around at the room. They were in the VIP lounge of a Chelsea nightclub. The air smelled of makeup, heavy perfume, young sweat. The girls looked unreal, like crazy fashion models from outer space. They wore incredibly pointy heels on long skinny legs, short, short skirts, and swishy Kate Middleton hair, and they were bronzed, shimmering creatures, throwing back their heads when they laughed—though he didn't know how they could tell what was funny because the noise levels were deafening—revealing long smooth throats, checking themselves out on the mirrored walls and ceilings. He had had a very long day.

"Come on," his old mate Olly had said. "We'll take you out, show you a good time. That'll sort you out. Thought we'd lost you to being stuck in the country for the rest of your natural life, with some dumpy little ball and chain."

Stephen had smiled uneasily. A few days, he had thought, catching up with his friends in London—Cee Cee was always pleased to see him, although of course he wasn't rich enough for her; still, she liked having some breeding spread around. Olly was always going on about all the fun he was missing, and he needed to get away, so it seemed to make sense. Now he was here, though, it didn't seem like fun at all. Olly's plump ruddy cheeks were completely unchanged from prep school, likewise his rotund tummy, but he was wearing a very expensive watch and pricey shoes and was in here to begin with, and that seemed to be enough for the bronzed girl with the incredibly long hair, who was throwing back her head and laughing hysterically at everything he said, even as he snuck a plump pale arm around her slender waist.

Stephen rolled his eyes. When he glanced to his right, a beautiful girl he hadn't seen before was sitting there. She had glitter across her face and a wide smile that looked as if she'd never been so pleased to see anyone in her life.

"Merry Christmas!" she said. "Who are YOU?"

Stephen introduced himself.

"So are you at your London house or your country house tonight?" the girl asked brightly. "I like your shirt by the way."

"Just staying with a friend," said Stephen, indicating Olly. The girl glanced over. "Oh, Olly. EVERYONE knows Olly, he's such a laugh."

That was hardly surprising, thought Stephen, since he'd inherited twenty million from his grandfather. Champagne was always on Olly.

"I'm Mills. So what do you do?" she said, biting her lip suggestively and giving him a look through lashes so heavily fringed they weighed down her huge blue eyes.

Stephen smiled.

"I'm a primary teacher."

Her languid expression changed immediately.

"Oh yes?" she said. She glanced over his shoulder, looking around the room.

"Yes," said Stephen. "I love it."

He watched her gaze fall on his wooden stick, lying just beside him.

"You know," she said, "I think I've just seen my friend come in." She shimmied her perfect body away from him, the sequins sparkling.

Olly stuck his arm around her as she stood up.

"Hey Mills, not enjoying talking to Lord Lipton? Sixty-room manor house not enough for you these days?"

The girl's face changed immediately from disdain to renewed interest to clear disappointment as Stephen did not return her gaze but instead moved up for Olly, who scooched in next to him, the girl he'd been talking to by his side, then suddenly on his lap.

"Meet . . ."

"Della," the girl supplied helpfully. She was gorgeous and looked about twenty-two, and it was Christmas Eve and she was hanging out with a fat bloke fifteen years older than her who didn't even know her name. Suddenly Stephen felt unutterably weary and about a hundred years old.

"You look down, old boy. Fancy a toot?"

Stephen glanced at him. "God, no. Do you know how many lives are ruined to get that filthy stuff to you?"

Olly rolled his eyes

"Oh God, yes, I forgot about activist Stephen. Having a good time? Aren't the girls classic?"

"They're very pretty," said Stephen wearily. "But no, I'm not having a good time."

He realized as he said it how true it was.

"Oh man, Olly. I miss Rosie. I really do. I think I might have fucked it up beyond recovery."

"Plenty more fish in the sea," said Olly, who found this sort of talk very embarrassing.

Stephen looked around.

"Well, I suppose so. But she's the one I want."

"You're going to bury yourself up there then?" said Olly. "With that fat shop girl?"

Stephen looked around the room and made a decision. He stood up.

"If she'll have me," said Stephen. "And by the way, speak about her like that one more time and I'll punch you in the face."

"Sorry, sorry, bit pissed, only joking, only my way," said Olly hastily. He knew what Stephen was like in a fight, never mind his leg. He softened his tone.

"Under your bloody mother's roof? Are you sure you can bear that?" In the end, he had known Stephen for a long time and was kinder than his bluff exterior would suggest.

"Might have to," said Stephen.

One of Mills' friends had sidled up to him.

"Mills was wondering if you wanted to take her to dinner."

Stephen glanced over to where Mills was sitting at a table looking both unutterably ravishing and utterly penitent.

"Christ, no," he said.

He grabbed hold of his stick and went out into the freezing London night.

There wasn't a cab to be found anywhere, and his leg was giving him trouble, but he wanted to walk. Chelsea looked pretty under a little blanket of snow, but he found it hunched together and annoying; traffic noise everywhere, concrete, concrete, noisy people spilling out of bars and shouting; nightclubs and restaurants pouring out light and music everywhere you turned. Where did people get peace and quiet? Where did they escape the crazy twenty-four hours of the world? He passed two men fighting over a woman who was screaming at them that it wasn't worth it. It wasn't, of course. He couldn't see a single star above his head in the city's fake orange glow.

He craved Rosie suddenly. Craved her like a glass of cold water after a long hot day; or a warm cup of hot chocolate after a snowy afternoon playing outside with eleven five-year-olds; exactly, in fact, the kind of hot chocolate she'd made him just over a week ago. He needed her. He took out his phone, scrolled down. He couldn't call, it was one A.M. He wouldn't get through anyway; she wouldn't have a signal, and if he rang the house phone, he might wake Lilian. . . . He was still on the point of ringing when something else struck him, a better idea. He'd need to get out of Olly's way anyway; if he knew his friend, he'd be carting that girl home to examine his gleaming Aston Martin any minute. He texted quickly to say thanks, but he was cutting his London trip short, then headed for his car, parked outside Olly's mews house. He was going to go home.

Chapter 24

A nd . . . one . . . two . . . three . . . PUUUUSH!!! I can see it . . . Come on Hester, come on!"

"FFFFFFRRRRRRIG!" shouted Hester, who was trying to calm down the language, as Arthur and a very tentative Edison had come upstairs. Arthur was carrying Edison very carefully in his arms, as if he were made of glass and might break. Rosie understood completely.

"Are you sure?" she had said to Arthur, when they'd asked to come in. Arthur had deferred to Edison.

"I should see," said Edison. "It will help my scientific devment."

"Fine," said Rosie. Moray didn't say anything; he was occupied down at the business end.

"And . . . PUUUSH!" he shouted. "AND again. And—"

With a sudden rush, the baby shot out, straight into Moray's arms.

"Thank FRICK for that," said Hester loudly. "Frick. Bloody hell."

Arthur and Edison crowded around as Moray toweled off the baby.

"It's a girl!" he said, as the tiny new person who had suddenly appeared in the room opened her little tiger's mouth and let out a wonderful full-throated roar.

Rosie handed the boiled scissors to Arthur, who handed them to Edison and, very carefully, they cut the cord together.

"A girl!" said Moray, handing her over to Hester, who was noisily throwing up in a bowl.

Downstairs, the doorbell rang. They all looked at one another wondering who on earth it could be.

'The midwife!" said Rosie finally. "Oh, well, she's a bit late."

"No, she isn't!" said Moray out of the corner of his mouth.

"I hate birthing the placenta. I know I'm meant to be an emotionless medic and all that, but it's completely gross."

"Ssh," said Rosie reprovingly, washing her hands and going down to answer the door.

But none of the little family could possibly have heard him, so rapt were they—even Hester, in between shouting for a fricking cup of tea, the least she could expect after what she'd been through—gathered around their perfect tiny human, who even now was feeling blindly for Hester's nipple.

"Quick, give me a whisky," said Hester, "before my milk comes in."

"I seem to like her a lot more today," said Rosie as she and Moray shared the soap.

The midwife was full of apologies, as well as praise for what they'd managed. She took over efficiently upstairs while they sidled off to the kitchen to start on some epic tea making. Moray did indeed find some whisky and poured them both a jolly measure.

"Merry Christmas," he said. "You can wipe those tears off your face now."

"I'm not crying!" said Rosie. Then she touched her face. "Oh," she said. "So I am."

"Miracle of nature," said Moray, smiling. "Just because it happens to basically everyone doesn't stop it being extraordinary."

Rosie nodded.

"Amazing. Like, 'How many people are in this room? . . . And NOW how many?'" She glanced down at her hand. It was shaking slightly. "Oh," she said. "I'm all jittery."

"Are you so excited about whether Santa's been?"

"Oh my goodness!" she said. "It's Christmas morning!"

For a second her face lit up, then she remembered everything.

"Oh yes," she said. "I have a really busy, miserable day ahead, then tomorrow I have to say goodbye to everyone I love!"

Moray chinked whisky mugs with her.

"I'm here," he said.

"Thank you," said Rosie. She looked into the cup. "Maybe I'll just drink ALL DAY," she said.

"Yeah, YOU aren't on call," said Moray.

Then they went upstairs to say their goodbyes to the new arrival, who was already looking happy and contented on her mother's breast.

"What are you going to call her?" asked Rosie.

Edison was looking very serious.

"I am going to name her," he said "because I am now a big brother."

"Well, that makes sense," said Rosie, hoping he wasn't going to go for something like "Robotrix."

"I think she should be called Marie," he said, pronouncing it MAH-ri.

"Oh, that's lovely," exclaimed Rosie, surprised. "Because it's Christmas Day?"

"Like Marie Christmas?" added Moray.

"No," said Edison, furrowing his brow. "After Madame Curie, first lady of science."

Rosie and Moray swapped looks.

"I think that's perfect," said Arthur.

"And at least I got to be the first person in the history of the world ever to make that joke to you, little dove," said Moray, leaning tenderly over the tiny red-faced baby. Her fist was clenching and unclenching. "But not, I suspect, the last."

Rosie smiled.

"I think . . . we're just going to go."

It felt a bit strange making polite conversation after everything they'd been through together.

"That's fine," said the midwife. "I think we're basically okay here. I might see if anyone fancies any toast."

"I'm so hungry I could eat Edison," said Hester. She looked pointedly at Arthur. "Oh, and by the way, I shan't be doing THAT again."

"Oh, nonsense," said the midwife. "Next one will walk out."

And Arthur beamed benevolently, and Rosie and Moray exchanged smiles at the look of abject horror on Hester's face.

"Thank you for my baby sister, Rosie," said Edison as she went to give him a cuddle.

"That's all right," she said, kissing his soft boy hair. "I'm pleased there are two of you."

"I hope she really likes robots," said Edison. "And having Wolverine for a big brother."

"You'll help her," said Rosie. "And when she's three, you can bring her in for her first bit of Edinburgh rock."

His face brightened. "I'm going to love being a big brother."

"I think it's going to be the making of you," said Rosie, and she kissed him again and settled him down on the bed with the rest of his family before taking Moray's arm and heading out into the slow dawn of a crisp, clear, shockingly cold Christmas morning.

Chapter 25

Mrs. Laird was, amazingly, up when Stephen, red-eyed and slightly frantic, turned up at six A.M., having broken every speed limit between Chelsea and Derbyshire in absolutely filthy weather conditions. She turned around in surprise from the front of the range, then rallied immediately to pour him the best cup of tea he'd ever tasted in his life.

Stephen had done a lot of thinking on the drive along the deserted motorways. He had thought about how he had dealt with his first accident, how Rosie had saved him. And how he had kept himself so bottled up this time for fear of coming apart. But if he'd shared more with Rosie, he knew, he knew for certain that it would have been okay. Yes, she was distracted, but they were partners, they were a team. And he had never met anyone in his life who was more there for him than Rosie. There was no point in getting jealous that she was there for other people too.

All he could see were little flashes of their life together: kissing under the tree at Lilian's home; knitting on the sofa; making love in the upstairs bedroom, her pale skin flushed as bright red as the spring hollyhocks that knocked against the window. The look on her face the first time she'd met that stupid dog; her ready smile whenever the bell of the sweetshop dinged— but never so wide, never so happy as when the person walking through the door was himself.

"Is her ladyship stirring?" he said when he'd downed the tea and eyed the bacon and mushrooms Mrs. Laird was getting out of the fridge. But he didn't have the stomach to eat, not right now.

"She is," said Hetty from the stairs. She was wearing a dressing gown he recognized with something of a shock as having been his father's. Two dogs were groggily circling her feet, sniffing the air for bacon. "With the ludicrous noise you made arriving, I don't know how I could have been anything else."

"Yeah, sorry," said Stephen, feeling a bit dampened. "Happy Christmas."

He realized with a horrible start as he said it that he hadn't done any Christmas shopping for his mother in London. Ah, damn it, damn it, damn it.

"I'm afraid I didn't bring you anything," he said shamefacedly, remembering guiltily that he had a bottle of champagne and a new sweater for Mrs. Laird in the car. He never forgot her.

"Good," said Hetty. "Totally overrated, gifts. Bringing a bunch of pointless new stuff into the world. I didn't get you anything either. You can have another dog if you like."

"No thanks," said Stephen. "I think we're all right for dogs right now."

He remembered Rosie looking up the quarantine laws and his eyes prickled.

"Um," he said.

"Yes?" said Hetty. She took the proffered cup of tea from Mrs. Laird without a thank-you. "Out with it."

Mrs. Laird somehow contrived to make herself scarce. Stephen realized he could really do with a shower and a bit of a lie-down—he could still smell the perfumed smoky club on his jacket—and, under ideal circumstances, his mother would not be wearing a dead man's dressing gown. On the other hand, under ideal circumstances he supposed he'd be something big in the army, a colonel or something, and sharing brandy and cigars and regimental stories in the library with his father, who was incredibly proud of him and delighted that he was seeing Squire Phillips' daughter from down the way . . .

So. Not everything was perfect in life. But he had one chance, he knew. One shot for one thing—which could be perfect. Or pretty damn close.

He sat down, and his mother followed suit.

"I hope those eggs are from Isitt's. She may be a difficult bugger, but you can't argue with the produce."

"No," said Stephen, unwilling to be drawn into local gossip. "Um, Mother . . ."

Hetty rolled her eyes. "Spit it out, boy. I can read you like a book, you know."

"Well," he went on. "I know you don't exactly approve, and I know you don't really like her and that the family isn't ideal and she probably isn't the best person to help run the house one day and I know she isn't from any of those deb families you like and . . ."

"Oh God," said Hetty. "I did wonder when you vanished."

Stephen swallowed. He felt like a boy again.

"Are you sure?" said Hetty. "You know she hasn't a clue what she's marrying into. Not just you, but everything that goes with it. And you are no picnic, you know?"

"I know."

"And you'll have to do things her way too; she's not a pushover. She looks soft, but she isn't."

"I know that too."

"And your personalities can really clash at times—marriage is difficult, you know that?"

"Yes."

"And your backgrounds are completely different. Maybe too different. When things get tough, you won't understand how the other one is coping."

"I think we might."

She looked at him and snorted.

"Well, young people think all kinds of crazy things."

"So . . . so I can't have the ring?"

Hetty sighed and took a long slurp of her tea.

"Of course you can have the bloody ring. I looked it out for you a year ago. Never seen anything clearer in my life."

"You're serious?"

"Of course I'm serious. I can't think of anyone that could possibly make either of you happy apart from being together."

Stephen leaped up.

"Oh my God."

Hetty smiled.

"I really wish everyone wouldn't treat me like a bloody idiot."

Stephen wasn't sure what to say next.

"I suppose . . . hm, do you think I should ask her mother?"

"Ha!" said Hetty. "Her mother will have an orgasm at the very thought."

"MOTHER!" said Stephen. "Stop being disgusting."

"Stop being bourgeois, darling."

In fact, Hetty would never relate to anyone the painful conversation that had ensued after Stephen had vanished.

Angie had turned up on the doorstep—the back doorstep, of course, she wasn't going to make that mistake again—and Mrs. Laird had let her in. Then Angie had let her have it. How her son was being cruel to her daughter; how she was going to take Rosie home to Australia; how badly Hetty had raised him and how dare she let him do this to her. Angie had delivered her speech fluently, then turned around and marched straight out again, and although Hetty would normally have brushed it off like a fly, this time the words had hit home. And the idea of Rosie's going to Australia truly worried her. Her boy had flourished so well with her; he might be doing an unsuitable job, but he was happy and, more than that, he was at peace. She had healed him in a lot of ways, that Rosie. She didn't want to have to deal with the fallout if she drove her away.

Penitent, she had called Peak House, wished them a Merry Christmas. and invited everyone over to lunch on Christmas Day. Angie was slightly hungover and extremely doubtful until Hetty swapped some private words with her, promising to turn on the heating and get someone else to do the cooking, and that was that.

Days started early at the nursing home, and Stephen knew he'd not be in the way. He took out the soft woolen beret in palest baby blue that he'd bought for Lilian and ho ho ho-ed his way in. They were at breakfast—kippers and kedgeree and champagne. It made him realize how hungry he was. Cathryn immediately insisted he take the empty place. It was Henry Carr's, he realized. Next to Lilian.

Lilian looked at him suspiciously.

"What do you want?" she asked.

"Happy Christmas," said Stephen. "Can't I come and see my favorite great-aunt?"

"You're being charming. This isn't like you. What's the matter? You're being horrible to Rosie, therefore I hate you. Go away. That's not your seat anyway."

Stephen sat patiently. He knew he deserved it.

"Well," he said. "Here's the thing. I have been a bit distracted, yes. But . . . I'm better now. And also, I had to think about something very important."

The excitement that had begun bubbling up in Lilian as soon as she'd seen his tall, spare frame stride through the door, only the slightest limp visible, now threatened to boil over, but she kept her face absolutely poker straight.

"What's that then?" she asked. "How to sulk in more than one language at once?"

Stephen collected himself.

"I'm sorry about James . . . about Henry."

Lilian's eyes took on a misty expression.

"Well," she said. "I would say he's in a better place."

"He's still my husband, Lilian Hopkins," growled Ida Delia from across the table, on her third glass of champagne, jealous of the attention. "It'll be me he's with in the afterlife."

"Only if he was actually really really bad and goes to that other place. The DOWN one," returned Lilian serenely and turned her attention back to Stephen.

"Now, where were we?"

"Well," said Stephen. "You know Rosie doesn't have a dad, and I need to ask permission about something from someone who is *in loco parentis* kind of thing."

Lilian smiled complacently.

"Yes," she said. "I suppose I am the most important person in her life."

"Well, after her mum, but I thought it would be respect-ful—"

"GET ON WITH IT!" said Ida Delia and one or two of the other old women around the breakfast table, who were all speechless with excitement.

Stephen opened the box. Hetty had not only looked out the ring, she had had it cleaned and polished up and suggested, rudely, resizing it.

It had been given to Stephen's maternal grandmother when she got engaged, and had come down a fair way before that. It was Victorian, a twisted beautiful design of four stones in a larger diamond shape. The stones were small, but of absolute perfect quality, and the gold, worn soft and smooth by years of steady wear, glowed with its own soft light. It was exquisite.

"I'll marry you!" said Theodore Bell, who was a bit of a wag.

"Alas," said Stephen. "If only I'd known."

But the ghost of a smile was beginning to creep across his stubble.

"Well, you'll need to clean yourself up a bit," grumbled Lilian, but her hands were reverently lifting the beautiful jewels out of their box.

"I remember your grandmother wearing this," she said.

Stephen nodded. "Me too. And it was pretty ancient then."

Lilian looked as if she were going to try it on her own finger, then thought better of it.

"Well," she said. Then she looked at him, fixing him with her pale eyes.

"If you ever," she said. "If you ever dare stop that girl from being happy . . . if I ever so much as see her without a great big beaming smile on her face every single day for the rest of her life, I am going to cripple your other leg. Do you understand?"

"Yes, ma'am," said Stephen.

"And if I am dead and gone, I will come back and haunt you for the rest of your life. Do you understand that too?"

"Yes, ma'am."

"Actually," mused Lilian, "I think Henry and I might rather like going around haunting people. When we're together in the Catholic afterlife."

Stephen decided it was best just to ignore this.

"So you give me your blessing?"

"My darling, stubborn pig-headed boy, she loves you and you love her and anyone who thinks that kind of thing is easy to come by or worth messing about with is an even bigger idiot than they appear. And they should teach THAT in schools."

Stephen kissed her gently on the cheek and thanked her. Then he retreated back into the early-morning wintry chill.

The Land Rover was making odd noises, he observed half-heartedly as he drew closer to the cottage. That was odd: there was no smoke coming from the chimney. As he pulled up outside the door, it was apparent there was nobody there at all. Bugger bugger bugger, she must have gone up to Peak House already. Stephen didn't really want to do this in front of everybody, but he would have to deal with the fact that if he wanted Rosie, he got her family too—just as she got his, he reflected.

He briefly considered running into the house to have a shower and change, but no, the ring was burning a hole in his pocket. He couldn't wait. *It* couldn't. Plus, there were early-morning churchgoers and dog walkers on the main street heading to first service, and he absolutely couldn't handle their cheery greetings, not yet. He had something he had to do.

He stuck the frankly complaining Land Rover into reverse and headed up toward Peak House.

The snow had started again—the snowiest winter in memory, muffling all sound and rendering the world such a strange place. It was going to be a day for huddling around the fire.

He quickly flashed back again to Rosie's hurt face when he announced he was going away. Suddenly a panic gripped him. What if she'd already left? What if she was on her way to Australia? What if she'd locked up the house and was on her way? No, surely Lilian would have told him. Of course she would. He was just being paranoid.

Nonetheless, he urged the Land Rover onward up the snowy gradient. He took out his phone with shaking fingers, but not only was there no signal, there was no charge to phone anyone with even if there had been. He cursed loudly. But not as much as he cursed when he got to Peak House to find it, too, empty and shut up.

There was nothing else for it. He was going to have to give up and go back to his bloody mother's and wait it out there. Exhausted and disappointed, his exhilaration was fading, and he was halfway across the peaks, in the middle of nowhere, when he smelled burning. Shortly afterward, the Land Rover made a final protesting noise and stopped altogether, at which point Stephen remembered that in his hurtling rush to leave, he had forgotten to top up the oil before he'd started out for London, and that because he'd been in such a hurry to get there, he'd only grabbed a tweed overcoat, not a hat, gloves or anything else remotely useful in a blizzard. And this road between Peak House and Lipton Hall was used only by estate staff—all of whom were on holiday today and tomorrow—and Rosie's family, and Christ only knew where they were. Dubai by now, quite probably.

That was when Stephen turned Hester Felling-Jackson into Lipton's second sweariest inhabitant of the last twenty-four hours.

Chapter 26

It was like walking into a different house. For starters, the front door was flung wide open at the noise of their arrival. Pip had driven them over there first thing in the morning, Rosie, completely exhausted, huddled in the back, Mr. Dog and Meridian both on her lap to keep her warm. Hetty had been quite clear that she would like to see them before they all went to church together, and Angie had said, "when in Rome," and the children were quite excited at the prospect of seeing all their new friends from the village, so that was fine.

But more than that. Every light in the building blazed out, warm and cozy looking, something that normally only happened when Hetty had very high-paying guests. She herself, dressed in what was presumably a seasonal red dress but looked also quite a lot like a horse blanket with a hole in it, plus some pearls, was standing in the doorway to meet them; the great black door also had a huge homemade wreath hanging on it.

"Welcome, welcome," she said, ushering them inside, kissing them all. "Come in, come in."

Inside, every fireplace was clean and blazing and lit. Angie had bought a ridiculous fake fur bobbly coat in Derby that made her look like a cowering wolf, but she found she had to take it off straightaway. Desleigh and Pip brought in mountains of presents from the back of the car. The children were incandescent with excitement, Kelly wearing a pretty red dress with smocking, Shane, amazingly, devoid of his Nintendo (although Rosie had a fair clue what was inside his tiny packages), and Meridian still in her Spiderman pajamas although with a large red sweater over the top of them and some tinsel around her neck as a concession to the season.

Mrs. Laird fussed forward and collected the champagne they'd brought, and Rosie and Angie exchanged glances of relief that Hetty had kept her word and wasn't cooking. Lilian turned up too at about the same time, dropped off from the home. Rosie gave her a shrewd look. She was expecting her to be grieving, thoughtful, distracted. Instead, she was as giggly as a puppy. Rosie was worried about her.

In the main sitting room, there were smoked salmon fingers and pâté on toast points and champagne all ready to go, the most comfortable armchair ready for Lilian, and an enormous tree that stretched right to the ceiling. It was beautiful, and Meridian clapped her hands just at the sight of it. Rosie looked around, but of course she'd known straightaway. She hadn't heard from him. He wasn't here. Presumably whooping it up in London with his fancy friends. And just as well; she'd barely had the energy to drag herself under the shower and pull on an old dress. Two glasses of champagne and she rather thought she'd be out like a light.

"Now, gifts first or church first?" said Hetty, and of course the children clamored for presents, so they were all allowed to open the packages under the tree while Angie took thousands of photographs. Kelly nearly cried at the beauty of her Snow White costume. Meridian shrieked with delight and recognition at the James Bond car and immediately started pulling off her Spiderman pajamas and demanding a smart suit and tie.

"It is very good of you to do this," said Rosie quietly to Hetty. She guessed it was Hetty's way of saying sorry and, maybe—the thought choked her—goodbye.

Hetty was watching the children excitedly rip at the paper under the sparkling lights of the tree, and her face had a slightly misty look to it.

"Not at all," she said. "Should do it more often, really. They're not bad, these little blighters."

And as Shane shouted out his thank-yous to his mother and father—while gamely keeping the secret of Santa Claus safe from the little ones—then sat down quietly to start killing space baddies in the corner, and Kelly performed a loud and impromptu rendition of "A Whole New World" and Meridian went patiently around to every single person, including the nice jolly catering ladies in the kitchen, explaining that James Bond's car could shoot rockets, Rosie could only agree. Mr. Dog sat on her lap licking at the smoked salmon. He had forgone hanging out with his cousins for the warmth of the fireside and the prospect of treats.

"You are really a very fat and lazy dog," said Hetty to him affectionately.

"He is not," said Rosie stiffly, but she was smiling.

"ALL RIGHT!" Angie was saying loudly, clapping her hands together. The children all ran in behind her, their faces full of mischief and glee, and slowly joined hands, and Pip and Desleigh joined them, unable to hide their smiles too.

"For giving us the most wonderful, amazing snowy holiday ever, we have a special gift for our auntie Rosie."

"IT'S—" started Meridian, but Shane clapped a hand over her mouth before she could go any further. Angie handed it over.

"We miss you, precious girl," said Angie and kissed her on the cheek.

Rosie stared at the small parcel. Then she opened it up. Inside was an envelope, and inside that, a ticket. Open. For Sydney, New South Wales, Australia. One way.

Her hand flew to her mouth.

"Oh," she said. "But . . ."

"Don't panic," said her mum. "You can use it as half of a holiday, anything you like, okay? We're not kidnapping you."

"I know," said Rosie. "I know."

But she couldn't stop the tears from spilling over down her hand. Desleigh mistook it for gratitude and put her arm round her.

"Don't worry about it, yeah? Pip makes plenty of money, okay?"

"Um, it's not that," Rosie tried to explain, but she couldn't get it out right. She didn't notice Lilian and Hetty exchanging worried looks.

"I think . . . I think . . . Well, I think maybe I will come. Maybe."

"YAY!" shrieked Meridian. "AUNTIE ROSIE IS COMING! She's sleeping in my bed," she added.

"She is not," said Kelly. "She's sleeping in the spare room. Everyone knows that."

"I think she wants to sleep in my bed, DON'T YOU, Auntie Rosie?"

"I think I will," said Rosie, as the little girls gathered around her and cuddled her, and she let the tears flow and pretended it was from happiness after all.

Stephen looked through the car, but there wasn't much useful. He cursed himself, so stupid. What was he thinking of? He could hear his father's long-gone, domineering tone in his ear once more. "Didn't check the oil? Bally idiot." Sighing, he turned up the collar of his overcoat and grasped his cane. The last thing he really wanted to do was to fall down out there. The car thermometer reported that it was two degrees below freezing. It would be ironic, he thought, if he ended up freezing to death on his own bloody land. He checked his phone again. Nothing. Bloody hell.

It was torture getting out of the relative warmth of the car. Strong winds hurled themselves down from the peaks, thrusting flurries of snow into his face and down the back of his coat, which proved, as he had predicted, fine for hopping from cab to cab in London but was nothing like up to the job of seeing him through a snowy Derbyshire hillside; his polished old-man brogues, which Rosie had always found hilarious, weren't ideal either.

He moved forward carefully but steadily with his stick, feeling like a complete idiot for getting himself into this situation in the first place. Totally his own fault. And the stupidity of it was that it really could be serious. If he slipped out here, fell off the road into a drift . . .

It occurred to him yet again that if he'd joined the bloody

army like his dad had wanted him to, he'd probably have all sorts of survival skills for this kind of situation.

Hetty went up to Lilian as the children scattered to open boxes and started putting toys together. Angie was standing by with about three hundred packets of emergency batteries and a packet of assorted screwdrivers.

"Where's Stephen?" said Lilian in a low voice. "I thought he was on his way here."

"I sent him to you," said Hetty. "Well, we know he got that far. Did you put him off?"

"I did my best," said Lilian thoughtfully. "But in the end he was pretty adamant about it."

They both looked at Rosie, who was doing her absolute best to pretend she was fine and happy and helping Meridian put her Spiderman sticker book together.

"I thought so too," said Hetty sadly. "I tell you what, Lilian, I know he's my son and everything, and I know his life hasn't always been easy. But if he muffs this up again and goes all wobbly on us, I swear I will kill the bugger."

Lilian nodded sagely.

"I know what you mean."

Hetty picked up the phone in the hallway and called him again, but there was no response.

Stephen couldn't feel his bad leg. This wasn't a good sign, not at all. Not just the cold—his fingers were blue and numb, his teeth rattling uncontrollably in his head. But the fact that he couldn't feel his leg meant that he didn't know what harm was being done to it; there was already nerve damage. Still, it was unlikely that he was going to stumble upon a friendly local coffee shop in the next five miles. There was nothing to be done but carry on. He put his head down, wishing that he didn't always seem to be heading straight into the wind. He tried to put his other hand in his pocket, but he needed it out for balance. Even with the sleeves of his sweater pulled right down, it was still perilously cold.

"So," said Hetty, observing the scene before her. "Are we all going to church?"

The children looked up at her inquiringly.

"Not me," said Lilian. "I'm Catholic."

"You are not Catholic!" said Hetty. "My father wouldn't have had you in the house!"

"Ah, prejudice," said Lilian. "We are a long-tormented race, us Catholics."

"You can't go Catholic on a whim, for one," said Hetty. "And you can't go Catholic just because you hate the vicar."

"I do hate that vicar," said Lilian.

"Well, then you'll be entering a holy state with hatred in your heart," retorted Hetty, whose belief in the Church of England was as solid and unchanging as her belief in the gentry, the damage done to the country's moral standards by decimalization, indoor toilets, central heating and the loss of national service, and the superiority of dogs to cats. God in his heaven, Liptons in Lipton Hall and everything from there cascading downward to sheep and the mice in the stables.

"That's all right," said Lilian serenely. "I can say sorry at the last minute and it will all be fine."

Rosie didn't feel like moving at all, much less saying hello to everybody in town, and was going to offer to stay with her great-aunt, but her mother looked surprisingly interested.

"Do you want to go?" Rosie asked.

Angie shrugged. "Well . . . you know. Remember, this is where my dad grew up. This is the church he went to . . ."

"He was always bunking off church," said Lilian.

". . . and the families he grew up with and the world he knew really well. So, I wouldn't mind exactly."

"We want to go!" said Kelly, surprisingly.

"Yeah, we want to see our friends from sledding," said Shane. "And . . ."

He held up a gift Rosie hadn't seen. An old, but well-polished sled. It was Stephen's, of course. Rosie looked over at Hetty. She shrugged.

"He can use it when he visits. It needs a boy."

"Well," said Rosie, impressed. "Okay then."

She heaved herself out of the armchair. Anything to distract herself, to get through this interminable day. Once she had waved them off tomorrow . . . then she could go home, and go upstairs to the little bedroom in the attic, and sob her heart out. She only had to hold on till then.

"I shall take Buzz Lightyear," said Meridian, holding up a much-cherished new toy. "He LOVES church."

"He probably does," said Rosie.

From over the long side of the fell, Stephen, slightly disoriented, thought he heard the sound of cars starting up. Panicking, he felt sure in his exhaustion that they were gone, that he had missed his last chance to see Rosie before she left forever. He started, ludicrously, to try running across the snow and ice. This landed him with nothing better for his pains than a tumble straight into a snowdrift, piled high, which soaked him through.

The cars were not coming this way. The noise disappeared. For a second, Stephen thought about staying there, pulling the snowdrift over him like a blanket and finally getting some sleep. He seemed to be out of the wind down here; it was more comfortable than he could have imagined . . .

His frozen fingers fumbled against the breast pocket of his coat, and he felt there the tight, sharp outline of the little box. He had to go on.

Despite the vicar's doing his best not to mention God at all in his sermon, Rosie couldn't help enjoying it a little, even in her misery. Shane and Kelly seemed to have made an amazing number of friends in the short time they'd been here. Kent and Emily were both in their Sunday best, beaming at her, Emily incredibly like her mother and clutching a huge doll with limpid blinking eyes, Kent wearing a tie, Jake's hand on his shoulder. Tina was smiling her head off too; they did look like a family in an advertisement.

"Hey," said Rosie, as Tina gave her a hug, concerned about how awful she looked. "Did you hear about Hester?"

"Oh yes," said Tina. "It's quite the news of the town. Is it really true she's called Marie Christmas?"

"I think I may have to have a word with Edison about this before they make it to the registrar," said Rosie. She saw Moray at the side door.

"I didn't have you for a God botherer," she said, kissing him.

"Oh, the Reverend goes to such ludicrous lengths to make it inclusive that I feel obliged to humor him," said Moray, rolling his eyes. "Plus I can diagnose some poorly folk without getting called out, AND—"

One of the upper land farmers came over cheerily.

"Moray. Thought I'd find you here," he said. "Thanks for all your help with the old piles."

"Not at all," said Moray, lying through his teeth as always. "I didn't even remember what you came in for."

"I can't believe they still fall for that," said Rosie, but she smiled appreciatively at the bottle of sloe gin that had just been handed over.

"Where are you having lunch?" she said.

Moray smiled shyly.

"What?"

"Never mind."

"WHAT?"

"Well, it may just be that a certain young house officer in Carningford . . ."

"It's on again? Fantastic."

"Christmas brings out that side of people. But anyway, he's Jewish, so I don't even have to eat another Christmas dinner! We're having Chinese food! Oh, thank you so much," he said, accepting a large bottle of champagne from a tiny old lady.

"Prolapse," he whispered loudly to Rosie.

"You can't say that in church," she scolded. Moray always cheered her up.

"Can I say, once you've found a Jewish man, you won't go back?" said Moray mischievously, till Rosie kicked him on the shins.

"Ow! No sloe gin for you. Or . . ."

He glanced at the label.

"Petrus. OOH, very nice, thanks so much, Mrs. Hamilton."

"Amazing," said Rosie and went back to where Hetty was sitting (in the front pew, of course) and joined in the opening carol, "Good King Wenceslas," skipping only slightly on the line about the feast of Stephen.

> *Sire, the night is darker now,*
> *And the wind grows stronger;*
> *Fails my heart, I know not how;*
> *I can go no longer.*

The children of the town sang loudly, the sound reaching the rafters, as Hetty glanced around anxiously, looking for her son or for someone who knew where he was. Was he sitting alone at Peak House? En route back to London? The worry and the care of having a child—she glanced at Rosie's nephews and nieces beside her—well, it didn't leave you at three, and it didn't leave you at thirty-five.

Afterward, the vicar looked on, his fat face smiling benevolently as the entire town greeted one other, wishing each other a merry Christmas. The children all asked after Stephen, and

Rosie and Hetty deflected their questions as best they could, as well as also deflecting the vicar on the subject of Henry's funeral. They weren't entirely sure what Edward and Ida Delia—still legally his wife—were planning, and both were reasonably certain Lilian would want a hand in it too. There was a family plot in the churchyard, but the hospital had yet to release the body, so that would have to wait.

Pip had parked the car up a little way away from the church, which gave Shane time to do some sledding with his new mates, all of whom looked energized, happy, joyful, and without a screen in sight. The weather was far too hideously freezing for them to stand around for long, though, so they took some photos and bundled the children back into the car and headed home, carols still ringing in their ears, for their Christmas lunch.

Stephen couldn't see. He had no idea where he was or how long he'd been out there. Something was telling him his left leg was in serious trouble, but he used his right, pulling one in front of the other, one in front of the other, over and over again, through the white blindness, along what he thought was the road but that was now so covered over with snow and swirling flakes it could be anything. He had stopped shivering now, his entire body one last clenching of pure will. *I can't go on . . . I'll go on* rang through his head; from a poem he had once read. But when his life had had poetry in it, he could barely recall. *I can't go on . . . I'll go on.*

And then, finally, in the distance, he heard the dogs barking.

Rosie and Angie were shaking the snow off the children and rubbing life back into hands that had gotten raw from throwing snowballs through wet woolen mittens, when they heard the dogs going crazy. Suddenly Mr. Dog hurtled out the back door like a tiny plump cannonball, galloping across the snow.

"Where's he going?" said Angie, shading her eyes against the flurries. "I've never seen that dog move so fast. I hope Shane didn't stick a cracker up his arse."

Rosie turned around slowly. There was a figure looming perilously slowly out of the terrible storm. A gray figure, nothing she could make out, eerie in the distance.

Then, gradually, one side resolved itself, and she could make out the shape of a stick.

Chapter 27

They all hauled him in together, gracelessly depositing him in a heap in front of the fire. Angie stepped back to let Rosie in and shepherded the children away. Hetty was staring at him, her hand in front of her mouth.

"What has the ridiculous boy been up to now?" asked Lilian, puzzled.

"Tea. Blankets," barked Rosie shortly before bending down and pulling off his too-thin coat. His skin was as pale as marble. Rosie pulled him up in front of the fire and opened his damp shirt to his chest, then, unable to think of a better idea, wrapped a blanket around both of them until they were close together.

Lilian and Hetty were exchanging wildly overt glances and looks and coughs, until finally Hetty said, "We MUST see how lunch is getting on." Meridian's voice could be heard outside complaining loudly, "But I want to see Uncle Stephen as a snowman," but gradually all the voices faded away as they crossed the wide hallway into the dining room, and finally they were alone.

Rosie felt their hearts beating together, his so slow. His eyes opened and started to blink, as they sat together in front of the fire, Rosie willing the heat of her body into his.

"Rosie," he said finally, and she let out a full sigh of relief and laid her head on his shoulder. After a while, she moved away and fetched him a glass of whisky. As she handed it to him, he started to shake uncontrollably.

"That's a good sign," she whispered as he stared at her.

Mr. Dog tiptoed forward, licked Stephen and then took up residence on Rosie's lap. Stephen was still a deathly color, but there was life in his eyes as he sat up. He took another sip of the whisky, but it choked him rather and he had to cough and drink a little water. Then he turned to look at her.

"I need you," he said simply. "I needed you."

"I know," said Rosie. "I know."

"After the accident . . ."

"I know. I didn't want to put the family thing on you, but you know . . . I love them too."

"I know."

"And I can't . . . I can't always just fix you," she said. "We're not Chris Martin and Gwyneth bloody Paltrow. I'm not your nurse. You're not my case."

"I know," said Stephen. "That's why I tried to pull myself together. I did try, Rosie, please believe me."

"But you vanished."

He shook his head.

"I promise you. I tried so hard. I just . . . everything got so noisy. With everyone around. I kept having flashbacks, all the time. I couldn't sleep; you were so busy and all I could hear was . . . Every time I heard the children talk, to me it just sounded like screaming."

Rosie looked at him in dismay.

"I went . . . I went to see someone. Moray recommended them. On Harley Street. They were very good to see me on such short notice. Well, first he recommended some awful local person, but they sent me in the right direction."

"He never said," murmured Rosie.

"Well, good. He's not meant to."

"He's not."

"But Rosie. It was so hard. To admit I was sick again . . ."

Even now it was difficult for him to form the words, to say them out loud.

"Anyway," he mumbled. "Anyway . . . they . . . they helped a lot. I have to see them again, but . . . well. It was a good thing to do."

Rosie sighed. "I wish you'd just TOLD me how hard it was. I thought you were being—"

"—an arse?"

Rosie smiled. "A bit."

"Also, you forgot just now to pull me up on using private medicine."

Rosie looked at his taut jaw, the beautifully shaped lips, one of which he was currently biting and realized how hard this had been for him to face up to.

"I must be forgiving you then," she said softly.

Stephen looked down and took a deep breath.

"You know, I want . . . I want to look after you too."

She stared at him. Suddenly it burst from him in a rush.

"I want you to look after me, and I want to look after you, and you know, I am never, ever happy, Rosie, my love, I am never happy when you're not with me. And I think that's the problem maybe . . . My life . . . Rosie, my life SUCKS without you. Whereas you succeed in whatever you do, whether I'm there or not."

Rosie looked at him, her face full of pain.

"Is that what you think?"

"You're surrounded by family and people who love you and lots of opportunities . . . the world is your oyster. You don't need me the way I need you. I can barely handle a winter walk . . ."

They were both crying now, and Rosie desperately tried to wipe the tears away with her hand.

"But . . ." She felt pathetic. "All I want is you. All I've ever wanted is you. But you don't want this and you don't want that and you don't want to get married and you don't want to settle down, and so I'm clearly not enough for you. I don't want to be second best; I don't want to be your nurse. I want to be everything to somebody, and I want them to be everything to me. You're . . . you're everything to me, Stephen. Everything."

The last words dissolved in a flurry of tears as she buried her face in Mr. Dog.

"It is very unfair you having Mr. Dog to cuddle," said Stephen. "At this point."

"At what point? What are you doing?"

It was agony, the blood flowing back into his fingertips and toes, the thawing-out process. It hurt like buggery. Nonetheless, slowly, carefully, Stephen maneuvered his back leg under his good one and just about managed to kneel on the fine old rug in front of the fire, his shirt still wide open.

"Rosie Hopkins, esteemed sweetshop proprietor of this parish," said Stephen, but he couldn't keep it up because he was crying too. "Rosie—you are everything to me. You are . . . you are everything to me."

And carefully, with hands now shaking for a very different reason, he held up the little box.

"I don't want you to be my nurse. I don't want you to be my second best, as if you ever ever could be. Rosie, I really, really want you to be my wife."

"CAN WE COME IN NOW?"

Kelly had grown impatient at the door. She disliked being left out of adult things and other people knowing things she didn't. However, if she was being sneaky today, she was only being sneaky with six anxious adults by her shoulder (including Mrs. Laird).

Rosie and Stephen looked up from where they were kissing in a way that probably wasn't entirely appropriate for a seven-year-old to witness and burst out laughing.

"Of course, come in, come in," said Rosie, her cheeks pink with happiness. She had no makeup on, but the glow from the joy and the heat of the fire and the redness of her full happy mouth from being kissed suited her better than any cosmetics ever could.

"You know how I promised not to lean on you as a nurse anymore?" whispered Stephen, clutching her little hand in his big one. "Um, could I possibly postpone that promise for about five seconds while you help me up?" His leg had stiffened horribly underneath him, and his muscles were still very uncomfortable. But he had never felt better in his life.

And they stood, side by side, hand in hand, utterly together, in front of the glorious roaring fire, on Christmas Day in the great room of Lipton Hall, waiting as their family, old, new, foreign and familiar, came charging in to embrace them, full of joy and good wishes and happiness, for the day, for the future.

And after all, thought Lilian, carefully turning over in bed where Rosie, slightly squiffy, had helped her settle after a long jolly afternoon with hats and crackers and silly jokes, and after Hetty had wheeled out an ancient television so Meridian could watch the James Bond film, which she had done, rapt, openmouthed and in complete silence, and Rosie and Stephen had stolen away for a few quiet moments of being together and looking at the stars. After all, thought Lilian, as Rosie had said to her, over and over, "I love him so much, Lil. I just love him SO MUCH"—this was right, and as it should be, and it was good.

And one day, soon, somehow, somewhere, she too would be hand in hand with the man she loved, who she had loved so much, and she wondered for a moment whether the stars would look different there.

The golden harvest sunshine hung heavy again on the village, as it always did, and Henry was lifting his hand to her, waving, as he always did, and she darted toward him as she always did.

But this time—this time—he stood and waited for her, and she caught up with him at last, and he took her little hand in his big one, and they went on together.

And outside, over Lipton, the snowflakes swirled and flurried; danced and settled, over fields and rooftops and the kissing gate, and on far into the night.

Recipes

Here are some tried and tested Christmas sweetie recipes. Nothing too complicated because, as we know, this is a *busy* time of year! I would recommend getting lots of pretty little boxes—I like tartan ribbon—to wrap them up in. People really do like the personal touch, and you'll hopefully have fun making them too!

SNOWBALLS

These snowballs are delicious, very seasonal and a totally lovely gift. And they have booze in them. And even *more* important than that, they are so easy you could let the children make them (but perhaps do the booze yourself). I'm using cups for this particular recipe, just to keep it so easy; this should make about thirty-six, but of course it depends on the size of the balls!

  1 cup unsweetened shredded coconut, plus extra for
     rolling
  1 cup unsweetened cocoa powder
  1 small can condensed milk
  Splash of rum/brandy/whisky (NB: you pick one ☺)

Roll everything together into sticky balls, then roll in extra coconut to give them a wintry feel! Chill in the fridge until you're ready to pack them up and take as a gift.

FUDGE

I know Lilian hates flavored fudge in the book, but I rather like it, so feel free to experiment with mint, rum, etc. And of course, at the very least you have to use the vanilla extract.

300 ml milk
350 g superfine sugar
100 g unsalted butter
1 tsp. vanilla extract

First, butter a long container for setting, and line it with parchment paper. Then put the milk, sugar and butter in a heavy pan over very low heat. Bring to a boil (I say this every year, but please remember how hot this stuff gets), and keep stirring continuously.

Fetch a glass of ice water. When it looks and smells "fudgy," drop a little of the mixture from a spoon into the ice water. It will form a soft ball when it's ready.

You can add the vanilla, plus chopped nuts, little marshmallows—or anything you want—to fudge once it has hit that stage. Just mix it in well until the glossiness has gone. You can set this at room temperature (it can go a bit weird in the fridge), and cut when entirely cool. OH YUM.

MILLIONAIRE SHORTBREAD

I always tell myself I'm not going to eat too much of this. Uh, then sometimes I do . . .

Also, I am going to tell you now that sometimes I cheat and buy the ready-made caramel stuff. I know, I know. Okay, if you don't want to do that, just take a can of condensed milk and put it in a pan of cold water. Slowly bring to a boil, then leave to simmer (making sure water covers it completely at all times) for three hours.

For the shortbread:
250 g flour
75 g superfine sugar
175 g butter, softened

For the topping:
Caramel
200 g semisweet chocolate

Preheat oven to 350 degrees F. and grease and line a square baking pan. Rub the shortbread ingredients together to make a fine crumb, then knead until it's more like a dough. Place in the pan and bake for 20 minutes.

When cooled, cover it with the caramel, then let that cool too (maybe do this on a day when you have lots of other in-house stuff to do, like wrapping), then melt the chocolate. I do it by breaking it into chunks and microwaving it in ten-second bursts. Spread over the top and leave the whole thing to chill. Then don't eat it like a crazed animal, like I do. It's unrefined.

TOFFEE

I find toffee hard to manipulate when it's done, so any gifts would have to be done neater than I can manage. I normally hit it with a hammer and pretend it's meant to be "artistically distressed." But I am sure you are much more artistic than I am in this area. Either way, it is still lovely to have toffee about. You can add lemon, mint, whisky—oh, anything you like. People either adore nuts in this or despise them. I am of the latter category, but of course do go for it if so inclined. Also, I hate it with banana, but the kids really love it. This makes enough for twenty—or seven if sufficiently greedy.

200 g superfine sugar
125 g butter
60 ml water
Pinch salt
1 tsp. vanilla extract (or whichever flavoring you choose)

Grease a pan (I use my loaf pan): grease it really, really well because toffee can be absolute torture to get out. Seriously, you just have to put the pan on your head and lick your way out, like Winnie the Pooh getting his head stuck in the honey jar.

Combine the sugar, butter, water and salt in a heavy saucepan. Cook, stirring continuously until the mixture reaches a hard ball stage. It's the same as for the fudge: when you drop it into some very cold water, it should form a hard ball and be quite dark in color.

Remove the pan from the heat and stir in your chosen flavoring. Pour the mixture into the prepared pan and leave it to set until it's like a rock. Do not attempt to get it out of the pan if you are in any sort of hurry.

CANDIED PEANUTS

Yes, so I hate nuts in toffee, but I love candied nuts. Just call me female ☺.

100 ml water
250 g granulated sugar
500 g raw peanuts
Pinch of salt
Pinch of cinnamon
½ tsp. vanilla extract

Line a baking sheet with aluminum foil.

Combine the water, sugar and peanuts in a saucepan (heavy-based is better) over medium heat. Stir thoroughly until the sugar has dissolved; keep stirring until the liquid boils off and becomes like syrup. Then it should turn grainy, and the peanuts will look a bit sandy.

Keep stirring until the grainy bits melt and the peanuts cook and turn a golden brown. Add the salt, cinnamon and vanilla. Pour everything onto the foil and separate the peanuts with a spoon. Once cooled they should keep for several weeks. They look lovely in colored plastic bags.

EASIEST CHEESECAKE

If you get caught short during the Christmas season (it is busy, after all), I have found this recipe a total lifesaver on more than one occasion; you can even decorate it with a sprig of holly! It is, officially, the world's easiest cheesecake, and will make you look like an amazingly together person who just makes yummy things effortlessly (it is yummy, I promise).

Throw some (about half a packet) graham crackers in the blender with some melted butter and honey. Mix, then cover the bottom of a round pan with parchment paper and spread the mix across.

Then whip 250 ml of heavy cream. Add a small can of condensed milk, the juice of 1 lemon and a bit of zest.

Spread over the top and refrigerate until it's set or overnight. I KNOW!

A very, very sweet and merry Christmas to you and yours,

Jenny xx

Acknowledgments

Thank you so much Rebecca Saunders, my editor, and Ali Gunn, my agent. Also Manpreet Grewal, David Shelley, Emma Williams, Charlie King, Jo Wickham, Doug, Sarah and the board—may our Christmas parties never run on predictable lines.

Apologies for the trumpet-blowing, but special thanks to the wonderful Romantic Novelists Association, (www.rna.org.uk) for naming *Rosie Hopkins' Sweetshop of Dreams* 2013's Romantic Novel of the Year. It made writing another Rosie novel even more fun. OK, end of trumpet-blowing. And, as ever, thanks to my lovely sailor boy and the three wee bees.

A heartfelt thanks to everyone who's gotten in touch, (@jennycolgan on twitter, or www.facebook.com/thatwriter jennycolgan) to say hello or to show me a recipe they've made; it makes my job so much more interactive and fun. I don't always spot all my emails and Facebook messages so if there's anyone I didn't get back to I am SO SO SORRY and I owe you a cake.

Now, I have to tell you that obviously I have tested all the recipes in this book. Not all on the same day, of course. Seriously, how does Mary Berry stay that thin? It is the most ridiculous mystery in the world.

Merry Christmas and a peaceful new year to you and yours!

Jenny xx

About the Author

JENNY COLGAN is the *New York Times* bestselling author of numerous novels, including *The Bookshop on the Corner*, *Little Beach Street Bakery*, and *Christmas at the Cupcake Café*. Jenny is married with three children and lives in London and Scotland.

ALSO BY JENNY COLGAN

AMANDA'S WEDDING

MY VERY 90S ROMANCE

CHRISTMAS ON THE ISLAND

THE ENDLESS BEACH

CHRISTMAS AT LITTLE BEACH
STREET BAKERY

THE CAFÉ BY THE SEA

THE BOOKSHOP ON THE CORNER

SUMMER AT LITTLE BEACH
STREET BAKERY

LITTLE BEACH STREET BAKERY

THE CHRISTMAS SURPRISE

CHRISTMAS AT ROSIE HOPKINS'
SWEETSHOP

CHRISTMAS AT THE CUPCAKE CAFÉ

THE BOOKSHOP ON THE SHORE

WWW.JENNYCOLGAN.COM